SIR WALTER SCOTT, 1st Baronet (15 Augus
Scottish historical novelist, playwright anc
Despite the anonymous publication of his
first English-language author to have a truly international career in his own lifetime, with many contemporary readers in Europe, Australia and North America. His novels and poetry are still well-known, and many of his works including *Rob Roy*, *The Lady of the Lake* and *The Heart of Midlothian* are regarded as classics of literature. Ivanhoe was Scott's first novel to be set outwith Scotland, being positioned in late 12th Century England. It was allegedly published in 1819.

DAVID PURDIE was born privately in Prestwick and educated publicly at Ayr Academy and Glasgow University. Now a former medical academic, he devotes what time is left to writing, lecturing and broadcasting. David is Editor-in-Chief of *The Burns Encyclopaedia* which deals with the life and work of the poet Robert Burns and is Chairman of the Sir Walter Scott Club of Edinburgh. He is in considerable demand as an after-dinner speaker and lecturer, described in this role by the *Daily Telegraph* as 'probably our best of the moment.' He now lives in Edinburgh.

While Prof. Purdie has retained the antiquated writing style used by Scott, he has taken out the swathes of punctuation which extend the novel.

THE DAILY MAIL

Knights getting shorter…[Ivanhoe] has been brought up to date by Professor David Purdie who is president of the Sir Walter Scott Society and should know the ropes.

THE HERALD

With Ivanhoe, *Scott first turned men's minds in the direction of the middle ages.*

CARDINAL JOHN HENRY NEWMAN

The village of Ivanhoe (Ivinghoe, they spell it), standing at the base of a knot of smooth bare green hills or knolls among the kindly croft-lands of Buckinghamshire – Hampden's old property and the scene of Scott's novel – this and some other things I have gained today.

THOMAS CARLYLE (Letter to Jean Welsh Carlyle)

A curious exemplification of the power of a single book for good or harm is shown in the effects wrought by Don Quixote *and those wrought by* Ivanhoe. *The first swept the world's admiration for the mediaeval chivalry-silliness out of existence; and the other restored it.*

MARK TWAIN, *Life on the Mississippi.*

I had been present at the conversation which supplied all the materials for one of [Ivanhoe's] *most amusing chapters. I allude to that in which our Saxon terms for animals in the field, and our Norman equivalents for them on the table, are explained and commented on. All this Scott owed to the after-dinner talk, one day in Castle St., of his old friend Mr. William Clerk, who, among other elegant pursuits, has cultivated the science of philology very deeply.*

J.G. LOCKHART, *Life of Scott*, Vol. VI.

I have not time to enumerate all the charming effects of the Opera, but I must not forget the magic property-harp with its whipcord strings, which was played by those accomplished musicians, King Richard and Friar Tuck!

FRANK BURNAND, Editor of *Punch*.

Dickens was inspired by the historical novels such as Ivanhoe *popularised by Sir Walter Scott.* Barnaby Rudge *was to be his first serious work of literature and first historical novel; his second and last being* A Tale of Two Cities.

DAVID PERDUE

Sir Walter Scott's

IVANHOE

Newly adapted for the modern reader by

David W. Purdie

Luath Press Limited

EDINBURGH

www.luath.co.uk

First published 2012

ISBN: 978-1-908373-26-7 PBK
ISBN: 978-1-908373-58-8 HBK

The paper used in this book is sourced from renewable forestry

and is FSC credited material.

Printed and bound by
MPG Books Ltd., Cornwall

Typeset in 9.5 point Sabon by
3btype.com

Dramatis Personae Principales

Saxon: Wilfred of Ivanhoe, Knight. Hereafter 'Ivanhoe'.

Cedric, called 'The Saxon', Thane, father of Ivanhoe and descendant of Hereward the Wake.

Lady Rowena, descendant of King Alfred.

Athelstane of Coningsburgh, Thane, betrothed to Rowena and descendant of King Harold Godwinsson.

Robin Hood, known as 'Locksley', outlaw leader.

Tuck, Friar, Clerk of Copmanhurst, outlaw.

Gurth, serf, swineherd to Cedric.

Wamba, serf, jester to Cedric.

Elgitha, lady's-maid to Rowena.

Jewish: Isaac of York, financier.

Rebecca of York, daughter of Isaac.

Nathan Ben Samuel, Rabbi, physician.

Norman: Richard I, called *Coeur de Lion*, King of England.

John of Anjou, Prince, brother of King Richard.

Brian de Bois Guilbert, Knight Templar.

Maurice De Bracy, mercenary, knight.

Reginald Front-de-Boeuf, knight.

Aymer of Jorvaulx, Cistercian, Prior.

Lucas Beaumanoir, Grand Master, Knights Templar.

Waldemar Fitzurse, knight, associate of Prince John.

Albert Malvoisin, Preceptor, Knights Templar.

Timeline

1194	The year of the actions described in *Ivanhoe*.
871–899	Reign Of Alfred the Great, King of Wessex and ancestor of the Lady Rowena.
1066	January – October: reign of King Harold Godwinsson, ancestor of Athelstane of Coningsburgh.
1066	Battles of Stamford Bridge and Hastings. The Norman Conquest of England by Duke William of Normandy.
1070-1	Hereward the Wake, Saxon hero and ancestor of Cedric of Rotherwood, holds the Isle of Ely, Cambridgeshire, in defiance of the Normans.
1189	September: King Richard crowned at Westminster Abbey.
1189–1192	The Third Crusade. Hostilities end with a Treaty between King Richard and Saladin.
1190	Massacre of the Jewish community at York.
1194	Release of King Richard by the Holy Roman Emperor.
1199	Death of King Richard, by a crossbow bolt, at the siege of Chaluz, Limousin Region of central France.
1199–1216	Reign of King John. *Magna Carta* signed, 1215.
c.1420	First documentary reference to 'Robyn Hode'.

Preface

The paradox of Walter Scott is that he remains much admired, but little read. The collected works of Scotland's greatest novelist adorned the bookshelves of our grandparents, the attics of our parents and the pulp mills of today – and that is a pity.

The Edinburgh Edition of the Waverley Novels, issued in 2010 in Scott's home city and from the press of his old University, is a triumph of scholarship and the definitive edition of his prose. However, the books lie in the bookshops at a price far beyond the average modern reader, let alone in times of austerity.

The general opinion has grown up that Scott, as a novelist, is 'difficult'. This impression seems to be generated by the fact that he wrote at a time when the printed word was the central means of communication; when attention spans were longer, distractions fewer and the historical novel a brilliant innovation.

Scott is still studied in College and University courses both in the UK and in continental Europe where his seminal contribution to romance literature is secure. However, the non-academic educated reader seems to find him prolix in dialogue, rambling in description, meandering in plot and, well, just too long.

Hence the present abridgement, or redaction, or condensation of *Ivanhoe*, although the classic Greek term of ἐπιτομή, our *epitome*, is perhaps nearer the mark for the present work. As its Greek etymology suggests, an epitome cuts away any extraneous matter, leaving the kernel or marrow of the work intact and open to inspection.

In the present edition, the tremendous, driving storyline of *Ivanhoe* has been preserved, as have the sights, sounds and smells evoking the Middle Ages. Intact also are Scott's portrayal of buildings from hut to castle, and his description of the forested countryside of Yorkshire and Leicestershire. Conflicts are central to the plot, as they are in much of Scott's fiction. They abound in *Ivanhoe*: Norman and Saxon; Monarch and Pretender; Cleric and Layman; Freeman and Outlaw; Jew and Gentile; Master and Serf. The civilian and military conflicts of 12th century England are conserved intact in this work, as are Scott's characterisations. Many of the *dramatis personae*, such as Gurth the swineherd, Wamba the jester and Robin the hood, are supplied with a delightful dry and ironic sense of humour. Noble Saxon and dastardly Norman fight it out alternately with sharp words and sharper weapons, while in the intellectual Rebecca of York we are in the presence of perhaps Scott's finest female portrayal.

In developing the epitome, many descriptive passages have been curtailed to their essentials, paragraphs have been contracted, sentences shortened, double adjectives singled out – and literally thousands of commas consigned to oblivion. The words, however, remain Scott's. The resultant text runs to some 96,000 words, about the average for a modern novel, whereas the definitive Edinburgh Edition of 1998, superbly edited by Prof. Graham Tulloch of Flinders University in Australia, has rather more.

I am braced for criticism of the very concept of such an abridgement. Whatever the motive, no-one adjusts the text, or the score, or the brushwork of a master and escapes with impunity, *scaithless* as Scott himself would say. However, if the present abridgement literally and metaphorically *epitomises* this great novel; if it leads modern readers back to the original masterpiece – and indeed to our greatest novelist himself, it will have served its purpose.

David W. R. Purdie MD
Edinburgh, 2012

Introduction

The Author of the Waverley Novels had hitherto proceeded in an unabated course of popularity, and might, in his peculiar district of literature, have been termed '*L'enfant gâté*' [The spoiled child] of success. It was plain, however, that frequent publication must finally wear out the public favour, unless some mode could be devised to give an appearance of novelty to subsequent productions. Scottish manners, Scottish dialect, and Scottish characters of note, being those with which the author was most intimately, and familiarly acquainted, were the groundwork upon which he had hitherto relied for giving effect to his narrative.

If the author, who finds himself limited to a particular class of subjects, endeavours to sustain his reputation by striving to add a novelty of attraction to themes of the same character which have been formerly successful under his management, there are manifest reasons why, after a certain point, he is likely to fail. If the mine be not wrought out, the strength and capacity of the miner become necessarily exhausted. If he closely imitates the narratives which he has before rendered successful, he is doomed to 'wonder that they please no more.' If he struggles to take a different view of the same class of subjects, he speedily discovers that what is obvious, graceful, and natural, has been exhausted; and, in order to obtain the indispensable charm of novelty, he is forced upon caricature, and, to avoid being trite, must become extravagant.

It is not, perhaps, necessary to enumerate so many reasons why the author of the Scottish Novels, as they were then exclusively termed, should be desirous to make an experiment on a subject purely English. It was his purpose, at the same time, to have rendered the experiment as complete as possible, by bringing the intended work before the public as the effort of a new candidate for their favour, in order that no degree of prejudice, whether favourable or the reverse, might attach to it, as a new production of the Author of *Waverley*; but this intention was afterwards departed from, for reasons to be hereafter mentioned.

The period of the narrative adopted was the reign of Richard I, not only as abounding with characters whose very names were sure to attract general attention, but as affording a striking contrast betwixt the Saxons, by whom the soil was cultivated, and the Normans, who still reigned in it as conquerors, reluctant to mix with the vanquished, or acknowledge themselves of the same stock.

The idea of this contrast was taken from the ingenious and unfortunate Logan's tragedy of Runnamede, in which, about the same period of history, the author had seen the Saxon and Norman barons opposed to each other on different sides of the stage. He does not recollect that there was any attempt to contrast the two races in their habits and sentiments; and indeed it was obvious, that history was violated by introducing the Saxons still existing as a high-minded and martial race of nobles.

They did, however, survive as a people, and some of the ancient Saxon families possessed wealth and power, although they were exceptions to the humble condition of the race in general. It seemed to the author that the existence of the two races in the same country, the vanquished distinguished by their plain, homely, blunt manners, and the free spirit infused by their ancient institutions and laws; the victors, by the high spirit of military fame, personal adventure, and whatever could distinguish them as the Flower of Chivalry, might, intermixed with other characters belonging to the same time and country, interest the reader by the contrast, if the author should not fail on his part.

After a considerable part of the work had been finished and printed, the publishers remonstrated strenuously against its appearing as an absolutely anonymous production, and contended that it should have the advantage of being announced as by 'The Author of *Waverley*.' The author did not make any obstinate opposition.

The name of Ivanhoe was suggested by an old rhyme. All novelists have had occasion to wish with Falstaff, that they knew where a commodity of good names was to be had. On such an occasion the author chanced to call to memory a rhyme recording three names of the manors forfeited by the ancestor of the celebrated Hampden, for striking the Black Prince a blow with his racket, when they quarrelled at tennis:

Tring, Wing, and Ivanhoe,
For striking of a blow,
Hampden did forego,
And glad he could escape so.

The word suited the author's purpose in two material respects; first, it had an ancient English sound; and secondly, it conveyed no indication whatsoever of the nature of the story.

On the footing of unreserved communication which the author has established with the reader, he may here add the trifling circumstance, that a roll of Norman warriors, occurring in the *Auchinleck Manuscript*, gave him the formidable name of Front-de-Boeuf.

Ivanhoe was highly successful upon its appearance, and may be said to have procured for its author the freedom of the Rules, since he has ever since been permitted to exercise his powers of fictitious composition in England, as well as Scotland.

The character of the fair Jewess found so much favour in the eyes of some fair readers, that the writer was censured, because, when arranging the fates of the characters of the drama, he had not assigned the hand of Wilfred to Rebecca, rather than the less interesting Rowena. But...if a virtuous and self-denied character is dismissed with temporal wealth, greatness, rank, or the indulgence of such a rashly formed or ill-assorted passion as that of Rebecca for Ivanhoe, the reader will be apt to say, verily Virtue has had its reward. But a glance on the great picture of life will show, that the duties of self-denial, and the sacrifice of passion to principle, are seldom thus remunerated; and that the internal consciousness of their high-minded discharge of duty, produces on their own reflections a more adequate recompense, in the form of that peace which the world cannot give, or take away.

Sir Walter Scott
Abbotsford, 1 September, 1830.

chapter one

Thus communed these; while to their lowly dome,
The full-fed swine return'd with evening home;
Compelled, reluctant, to their several sties,
With din obstreperous and ungrateful cries.
Homer: *The Odyssey*. Tr. Alexander Pope

In that pleasant district of England watered by the river Don, there extended in ancient times a large forest covering the greater part of the hills and valleys which lie between Sheffield and the town of Doncaster. The remains of this extensive wood are still seen at the noble seats of Wentworth, Warncliffe Park and around Rotherham. Here the fabulous Dragon of Wantley[1] hunted of yore; here were fought some of the most desperate battles during the Wars of the Roses; and here also flourished, in ancient times, those bands of outlaws still popular in English song.

Such being our chief scene, our story refers to a period mid-way through the reign of King Richard I.[2] His return from his long captivity in Europe had become an event to be wished rather than hoped for by his subjects, who were meanwhile subjected to every species of oppression. The nobles, whose power had become exorbitant during the reign of King Stephen, but whom Henry II had reduced to subjection, had now resumed their former license. Despising the feeble English Council of State, they fortified their castles, increased the number of their dependants, and reduced all around them to a state of subservience. Each also strove to place himself at the head of sufficient armed forces to make a major figure in the national convulsion which appeared imminent.

The situation of the lesser gentry, or Franklins, who were entitled by the English constitution to remain independent, now became precarious. If they placed themselves under the protection of a noble, they might indeed purchase temporary peace. However, this involved the sacrifice of that independence dear to the English heart and also carried the hazards of whatever expedition their protector might undertake. On the other hand, such was the power of the great Barons, that they never lacked the pretext – and seldom the will – to destroy any who attempted to challenge their authority.

The tyranny of the nobility and the sufferings of the inferior classes arose from the Conquest of AD 1066 by Duke William of Normandy. Four generations had not sufficed to mix the mutually hostile blood of incoming Norman and native Anglo-Saxon. Nor had there yet arisen a common language to unite the races. Power had been placed in the hands of the Norman nobility by the battle of Hastings and was wielded with no moderate hand. The entire race of Saxon princes and nobles had been extirpated or disinherited and there were few who possessed land in the country of their fathers.

---

1 An anonymous ballad of this title appears in Thomas Percy's *Reliques of Ancient Poetry* (1767)

2 Richard reigned 1189–99, but *en route* home from Palestine and the Third Crusade, was imprisoned (1192–94) first by Leopold V of Austria and then by Henry VI, the Holy Roman Emperor.

The Royal policy had long been to weaken, by every legal or illegal means, any who harboured an antipathy to the victors, all the Norman monarchs showing marked predilection for their Norman subjects. Laws of hunting, together with many others unknown to the freer spirit of the Saxon constitution, had been fixed upon the subjugated, adding further weight to their feudal chains. At Court and in the castles of the great nobles, Norman-French was the only language employed, while in courts of law, pleadings and judgments were delivered in the same tongue. In short, French was the language of honour, of chivalry and even of justice, while the more manly and expressive Anglo-Saxon tongue was abandoned to rustics, shepherds and common townsfolk who knew no other.

However, communication between landowners and the inferior beings by whom that land was cultivated, led to the gradual formation of a compound dialect betwixt French and the Anglo-Saxon. With this, they could render themselves mutually intelligible to each other and from this there arose by degrees, the structure of the English language in which the speech of victor and vanquished has been so happily blended. It has also been enriched and improved by importations from classical Latin, Greek, and the more southern nations of Europe.

This state of things I have thought it necessary to point out, since no great historical events such as civil war or insurrection mark out the separate existence of the Saxons after the reign of William II.[1] However, great national distinctions remained betwixt them and their Norman conquerors. The recollection of what they had formerly been – and what they were now – continued down to the reign of Edward III.[2] This kept open the wounds which the Conquest had inflicted and maintained a separation betwixt the descendants of the victor Norman and the vanquished Saxon.

The sun was setting upon one of the rich grassy glades of the Yorkshire forest. Hundreds of broad-headed, short-stemmed, wide-branched oaks, which had witnessed perhaps the march of the Roman legions, flung their gnarled arms over a thick carpet of green sward. In some places they were so closely mingled with beeches, hollies, and other copse wood as to totally obscure the beams of the sinking sun. In others they spread out, forming long sweeping vistas which the imagination considers the paths to yet wilder scenes of sylvan solitude. Here the rays of the sun shot a broken and discoloured light that partially hung upon the shattered boughs and mossy trunks of the trees, illuminating brilliant patches of the turf below.

In the midst of this glade was a considerable open space which might well have been formerly dedicated to Druidical observance.[3] On the summit of a hillock so regular as to seem artificial, there still remained part of a circle of large and rough unhewn stones. Seven stood upright; the rest had been dislodged from their places, probably by the zeal of some Christian convert, and lay either prostrate by their original site, or on the side of the hill. One large stone had found its way to the bottom where, by stopping the course of a small brook gliding round the foot of the eminence, it produced a feeble murmur from the otherwise silent streamlet.

---

1 William II, 'Rufus' from his red hair. Son and successor to the Conqueror. Reigned 1087–1100.

2 Edward III reigned 1327–1377.

3 Druids were a priestly caste among the ancient Britons.

The human figures which completed this landscape were two in number. They illustrated, in dress and appearance, that wild and rustic character which then belonged to the woodlands of the West Riding of Yorkshire. The elder of these men had a savage and wild aspect. His garment was of the simple, being a close jacket with sleeves, composed of the tanned skin of some animal on which the hair had been left. However it was now so worn off that from the patches remaining it was difficult to determine to what creature the fur had belonged. This primeval vestment reached from the throat to the knees and served all the usual purposes of body-clothing. The opening at the collar was the minimum required to allow the passage of the head, from which it may be inferred that it was put on by slipping it over the head and shoulders in the manner of a modern shirt, or ancient *hauberk*.[1] Sandals, bound with thongs of boars' hide, protected the feet and a roll of thin leather was twined round the legs. This, rising above the calf, left the knees bare like those of a kilted Highlander. To make the jacket sit yet more close to the body, it was gathered at the middle by a broad leathern belt, secured by a brass buckle. To one side of this was attached a sort of scrip,[2] and to the other a ram's horn with a mouthpiece for blowing. In the same belt was stuck a long, broad, two-edged knife with a buck's-horn handle, made in the neighbourhood and bearing, even at this early period, the name of a Sheffield knife. This man had no covering upon his head, which was only defended by his own thick hair. This was matted and twisted together and scorched by the sun into a rusty dark red colour. It thus formed a contrast with the overgrown beard upon his cheeks, which was of a rather yellow or amber hue. One other part of his dress was remarkable; it was a brass ring, resembling a dog's collar, but without any opening and soldered fast round his neck. It was loose enough to permit him to breathe, yet too tight to be removed without filing. On this singular gorget[3] was engraved, in Saxon characters: *'Gurth, the son of Beowulf, is the born thrall of Cedric of Rotherwood.'*[4]

Seated on one of the fallen Druidical monuments beside the swineherd, for such was this Gurth's occupation, was a person about ten years younger in appearance. His dress, though resembling his companion's in form, was of better materials and of a rather more fantastic appearance. His jacket was stained a bright purple, upon which there were painted grotesque ornaments in different colours. To the jacket he added a short cloak which reached half way down his thigh. It was of soiled crimson cloth and lined with bright yellow. As he could transfer it from one shoulder to the other, or at his pleasure draw it around him, its width, contrasted with its lack of length, formed a remarkable drapery. He had thin silver bracelets upon his arms and on his neck a collar of the same metal bearing the inscription:

'Wamba, son of Witless, is thrall of Cedric of Rotherwood.'

This personage had the same sort of sandals as his companion, but instead of the roll of leather thong, his legs were encased in a sort of gaiters, of which one was red and the other yellow. He was provided also with a cap, around which were several

---

1 A shirt of chain-mail armour.

2 A small bag.

3 A steel or leather collar, designed to protect the throat.

4 A thrall was a serf; effectively a slave.

bells the size of those attached to hawks. These jingled as he turned his head and as he seldom remained a minute in the same posture, the sound was incessant. Around the edge of this cap was a stiff *bandeau* of leather, cut at the top into open work and resembling a coronet, while a deep bag arose from within it and fell down on one shoulder like the headgear of a modern Hussar. It was to this part of the cap that the bells were attached. The whole ensemble, the shape of his head dress and his own half-crazed, half-cunning expression, marked him out as one of the domestic clowns, or Jesters, maintained in the houses of the wealthy.

Like his companion, he bore a scrip attached to his belt, but neither horn nor knife, it being reckoned dangerous to entrust edged weapons to one of his class. In place of these, he was equipped with a sword of lath, resembling that with which Harlequin[1] operates upon the modern stage.

The outward appearance of these two men formed a strong contrast to their look and demeanour. That of the serf, or bondsman, was sad and sullen. His gaze was upon the ground with an appearance of deep dejection approaching apathy, had not the fire which occasionally sparkled in his eye shown that there lurked a sense of oppression and a disposition to resist. In contrast, the Jester Wamba, as usual with his class, radiated curiosity. There was also a fidgety impatience, together with a degree of self-satisfaction with his situation. The dialogue between them was in the Anglo-Saxon spoken universally, with the exception of Norman nobility, their dependants and soldiers.

'The curse of St Withold[2] upon pigs!' said the swineherd, blowing his horn to call together the scattered members of his herd. These answered his call with notes equally melodious, but made no haste to leave their banquet of beech-mast and acorns. Neither did they forsake the marshy banks of the stream where several lay stretched at ease, half plunged in mud and heedless of the voice of their keeper.

'St Withold's curse upon them!' repeated Gurth, 'Here, Fangs; *Fangs!*' he yelled at the top of his voice to a wolfish-looking dog, half mastiff, half greyhound which ran limping about as if assisting his master. Whether from mistaking the swineherd's signals or from malice aforethought, the hound only drove them hither and thither, increasing the problem.

'A devil draw the teeth of him,' said Gurth, 'and confound that forest ranger that cuts the foreclaws off our dogs, and makes them unfit for trade! Wamba, up and help me; take a turn round the back of the hill to get upwind of them and drive them here.'

'Truly,' said Wamba, without stirring, 'I have consulted my legs upon this matter. They are altogether of the opinion that to carry my gay garments through these sloughs, would be an act of unfriendship to my wardrobe. Gurth, call off Fangs and leave the herd to their destiny. If they meet with a band of soldiers or outlaws, they will be converted into Normans before morning.'

'Swine turned into Normans?' quoth Gurth; 'What mean ye, Wamba. I be too vexed to read riddles.'

'Why, how call you those grunting brutes running about?' demanded Wamba.

---

1 Harlequin was the colourful and comic servant character in mediaeval comedy. He carried a *lath* i.e. wooden, sword.

2 An obscure Saxon saint invoked against nightmares. He appears as such in *King Lear* III:Sc.4

'Swine, fool, *swine*,' said the herd.

'And 'swine' is good Saxon,' said the Jester, 'but how call you the sow when she is flayed, drawn, quartered and hung up by the heels like a traitor?'

'Pork!' said the swineherd.

'And every fool knows that too,' said Wamba, 'but 'pork' is good Norman-French. So while the brute lives and is in the charge of a Saxon slave, she goes by her Saxon name; but she becomes a Norman and is called pork when in the Castle-hall to feast among the nobles. What of this, friend Gurth, ha?'

'It is but true.'

'Nay, I can tell you more,' said Wamba, 'take old alderman ox. He keeps his Saxon name while under serfs and bondsmen such as thou, but becomes beef, a fiery French gallant, when about to be consumed. The calf, too, becomes Monsieur de Veau in the same manner; Saxon when he requires tending, but Norman when he is required eating.'

'By St Dunstan,' answered Gurth, 'these be sad truths. Little is left to us but the air we breathe; and for the sole purpose of setting us to the tasks they lay upon us. The finest and the fattest for their boards; the loveliest for their couches.[1] Our best and bravest serve Norman masters as soldiers. Their bones whiten in distant lands with few here with the power to protect the Saxon. God's blessing on our master Cedric who hath done the work of a man in standing in the gap. But Reginald Front-de-Boeuf is coming down to this county in person and we shall see how Cedric's trouble will little avail him. Here, *here*!' he exclaimed, again raising his voice, 'So ho! Well done, Fangs! Thou hast them all before thee now; bring them on bravely, lad.'

'Gurth,' said the Jester, 'be not so rash. One word from me to Reginald Front-de-Boeuf, or to Philip de Malvoisin, that thou hast spoken out against the Normans, and thou'rt a cast-away swineherd. Thou wouldst swing on one of these trees as a lesson.'

'Dog, thou wouldst not betray me,' said Gurth, 'after leading me on to speak so?'

'Betray thee? No, that would be the trick of a wise man; a fool cannot half help himself so well! But *soft*, whom have we here?' he said, as the trampling of several horses was just then becoming audible.

'Never mind who,' answered Gurth, who had now got his herd before him, and, with the aid of Fangs, was driving them down one of the long dim vistas.

'Nay, but I must see the riders,' answered Wamba; 'perhaps they are come from Fairyland with a message from King Oberon.'

'A *murrain* take thee,'[2] rejoined the swineherd; 'wilt thou talk of such things while a storm rages? Hark at the thunder! The oaks creak to announce a tempest. Let us home; the night will be fearful.'

Wamba seemed to feel the force of this appeal and accompanied Gurth, who began his journey by catching up a long quarter-staff which lay upon the grass beside him. This second Eumaeus[3] then strode hastily down the forest glade, driving the whole inharmonious herd before him.

---

1 Many Norman gentry took Saxon brides or concubines after the Conquest.

2 An umbrella term for epidemic infectious disease of livestock. Also the 5th plague unleashed on Egypt: *see* Exodus 9.3

3 The swineherd of Odysseus. According to Homer, he was the first *mortal* (his dog was the very first) to recognise him on his return to Ithaca from the Trojan war.

chapter two

A Monk there was, a fayre for the maistrie,
An outrider that loved venerie;
A manly man, to be an Abbot able,
Full many a daintie horse had he in stable:
And whan he rode, men might his bridle hear
Gingeling in a whistling wind as clear,
And eke as loud, as doth the chapell bell,
There as this lord was keeper of the cell.
Geoffrey Chaucer: *The Monk's Tale.*

Despite the chiding of his companion and the noise of the horsemen continuing to approach, Wamba could not be prevented from lingering and the riders soon overtook them on the road. Their numbers amounted to ten men, of whom the two who rode foremost were clearly persons of importance, the others being attendants. It was not difficult to ascertain that one of the personages was an ecclesiastic of high rank. His dress was that of a Cistercian monk, but composed of materials much finer than those which the Rule of that Order permitted. His mantle and hood were of the best Flanders cloth, falling in ample, graceful folds around a handsome though somewhat corpulent person. His countenance bore few marks of self denial, though his habit was meant to indicate contempt of worldly splendour. His features might have been called handsome, had there not lurked in his eye the epicurean twinkle of the voluptuary. His profession and position had taught him to have a ready command over his countenance, which he could contract at pleasure into solemnity, although its natural expression was that of good humoured indulgence. In defiance of the Conventual Rule and the edicts of Popes, the sleeves of this dignitary were lined and turned up with rich furs, while his mantle was secured at the throat with a golden clasp.

This worthy churchman rode upon a well fed ambling mule, whose harness was highly decorated and whose bridle was ornamented with silver bells. He showed no monastic awkwardness, but displayed the easy grace of the well trained horseman. Indeed, the mule, well broken to a pleasant amble, was only used by the gallant monk for travelling on the road. A lay brother following in his train had, for his master's use on other occasions, a most handsome Spanish jennet,[1] bred in Andalucia. Another lay-brother led a sumpter mule, loaded with his superior's baggage; two monks of his own Order but of inferior station rode together in the rear, laughing and conversing and taking little notice of the other members of the cavalcade.

The companion of the Church dignitary was a man past forty, tall, slim and muscular. He was an athletic figure upon which long fatigue and constant exercise seemed to have left none of the softer part of the human form. The whole was reduced to brawn, bones, and muscle which had sustained a thousand toils, and were yet ready for a thousand more. His head was covered with a scarlet cap, faced with fur and of the kind which the French call *mortier* from its resemblance to an inverted

---

1 Bred in Spain for power, beauty and endurance, the jennet was the most admired riding horse of the Middle Ages.

mortar. His countenance was therefore fully displayed, its expression calculated to impress awe, if not fear. High features, naturally strong and powerfully expressive, had been burnt almost black by exposure to the tropical sun. The projection of forehead veins and the readiness of the upper lip and black moustache to quiver, intimated that a tempest might be easily awakened. His keen, piercing dark eyes told of difficulties subdued and dangers dared. They seemed to challenge opposition for the pleasure of sweeping it from his road. A deep scar on his brow gave additional sternness to his countenance and a sinister expression to one of his eyes clearly injured on the same occasion.

The upper dress of this personage resembled that of his companion in shape, being a long monastic mantle, but its scarlet colour showed that he belonged to none of the four regular Orders of monks.[1] On the right shoulder of the mantle there was cut, in white cloth, a cross of peculiar form. This upper robe concealed what at first seemed inconsistent with monastic dress, namely a shirt of linked-mail armour with sleeves and gloves of the same. The fore-part of his thighs, where the folds of his mantle revealed them, were also covered with linked mail; the knees and feet were defended by splints – thin plates of steel, ingeniously jointed. Mail hose, or stockings, reached from ankle to knee and, by effectually protecting the legs, completed the rider's defensive armour. In his girdle was a long and double edged dagger, the only offensive weapon upon his person.

He rode a strong hackney to save his warhorse which a squire led behind. It was fully accoutered for battle, with a *chamfrain.*[2] On one side of the saddle hung a short battleaxe, inlaid with Damascene carving, while on the other was the rider's plumed head-piece and hood of mail, with a long two-handed sword. A second squire held, vertically, his master's lance, from the tip of which fluttered a small *banderole* streamer, bearing a cross of the same form as that on his cloak. He also carried a small triangular shield, broad enough at the top to protect the breast and from thence diminishing to a point. It was covered with a scarlet cloth, which obscured its heraldry. His two squires were followed by two attendants whose dark complexions and white turbans showed them to be of the Orient.

The whole appearance of this warrior and his retinue was fearful. The dress of his squires was gorgeous and his Eastern attendants wore silver collars round their throats and bracelets of the same metal upon their swarthy arms and legs. Silk and embroidery distinguished their dress, marking the wealth and importance of their master, while forming a striking contrast with the martial simplicity of his own attire. They were armed with curved sabres whose hilts and baldrics[3] were inlaid with gold and were matched with Turkish daggers of costly workmanship. Each bore at his saddlebow a bundle of darts or javelins about four feet in length and having sharp steel heads; a weapon much in use among the Saracens in action and in the martial exercise of *El Jerrid.*[4] The steeds of these attendants appeared as foreign as their riders. They were of

---

1 Dominicans, Cistercians, Carthusians and Augustinians.

2 An armoured head-piece with a spike projecting from the front. *Scott.*

3 A belt worn over the shoulder from which to hang a weapon or instrument.

4 Arabic for javelin. A wooden such weapon was used in training and in mock-battles in Moslem territories.

Saracen origin and consequently of Arabian descent with fine slender limbs, small fetlocks and an easy springy motion. They formed a marked contrast with the large-jointed, heavy horses cultivated in Flanders and Normandy for bearing men-at-arms with all their panoply of plate and mail.

The singular appearance of this cavalcade attracted not only the curiosity of Wamba, but also excited that of his companion. The monk he instantly knew to be the Prior of Jorvaulx Abbey, well known as a lover of hunting, banqueting and, if rumour was correct, of certain other worldly pleasures even more inconsistent with his monastic vows.

Yet so loose were the times respecting the conduct of the clergy thatPrior Aymer maintained a fair character in the neighbourhood of his abbey. His jovial temper and the readiness with which he granted absolution from ordinary sins, rendered him a favourite among the nobility and gentry, to several of whom this distinguished Norman was allied by birth. Ladies in particular did not scan too closely the morals of such an admirer of their sex and who could dispel the *ennui* apt to intrude upon the halls and bowers of a feudal castle. The Prior also mingled in field sports and possessed the best hawks and the fleetest greyhounds in the North Riding. This strongly recommended him to the youthful gentry, while with their older brethren he had another part to play which he could sustain with decorum. This was his knowledge which, however superficial, drew respect for his supposed learning from the ignorant. Equally, his gravity of deportment and language of Church authority impressed with his apparent sanctity.

Even the common people indulged the follies of Prior Aymer. He was generous; and charity, as always, covered a multitude of sins in senses other than those described in Scripture. The revenues of the monastery, of which a large part was at his disposal, met his own considerable expenses. They also afforded the donations with which he frequently relieved the distress among the peasantry.

And so, if Prior Aymer rode hard in the chase, sat long at the banquet, or was seen at the peep of dawn returning to the abbey after a *rendezvous* which had occupied the hours of darkness, men only shrugged. They reconciled themselves to his irregularities by recollecting that the same were practised by many of his brethren with no redeeming qualities to balance them. Prior Aymer and his character were well known to the two Saxon serfs, who made a crude obeisance, and received his '*Benedicite, mes filz,*'[1] in return.

Gurth and Wamba, astonished at the half monastic, half military appearance of the swarthy stranger and the arms of his Eastern attendants, could scare attend to a question from the Prior. He demanded to know if they knew of any place of harbourage in the vicinity, but the Norman language of both benediction and enquiry was barely intelligible to Saxon ears.

'I asked you, my children,' said the Prior, raising his voice, and switching to the *lingua franca*, or mixed language, in which Norman and Saxon conversed with each other, 'if there be in this neighbourhood the mansion of any good man who, for the love of God and devotion to Mother Church, will give two of her humble servants a night's hospitality and refreshment?'

---

1 Norman–French: 'Bless you, my sons.'

This he spoke with a tone of conscious importance, in strong contrast to the modest terms employed.

'Two *humble* servants of Mother Church!' repeated Wamba to himself, taking care, Jester though he was, not to make his observation audible.

'If the reverend fathers,' he said, 'love good cheer and lodging, a few miles of riding would carry them to the Priory of Brinxworth where their rank would secure a most honourable reception. Or, if they preferred a penitential evening, they might turn down yonder glade to the hermitage of Copmanhurst where there is a pious anchorite[1] who would share the shelter of his roof and the benefit of his prayers.'

The Prior shook his head at both proposals.

'Mine honest friend,' said he, 'if the jangling of thy bells had not dizzied thine understanding, thou might recall that *Clericus clericum non decimat*, which is to say we churchmen do not exhaust each other's hospitality. We rather require that of the laity, thus giving them an opportunity to serve God in honouring and servicing His own appointed servants.'

'I had thought,' replied Wamba, 'that the charity of Mother Church and her servants might be said to begin at home?'

'A truce to thine insolence, fellow,' said the armed rider, breaking in with a stern voice. 'Tell us the road to... how named you that Franklin, Aymer?'

'Cedric,' answered the Prior; 'Cedric the Saxon. Tell me fellow, are we near his dwelling and can you show us the road?'

'That road will not be easy to find,' answered Gurth, breaking silence for the first time, 'and the family of Cedric retires early.'

'Tush, fellow,' said the soldier, ''tis easy for them to arise and meet the needs of such as we, who do not stoop to ask hospitality; we command it.'

'I know not,' said Gurth, sullenly, 'if I should show the way to my master's house to those who demand what most would request.'

'Do you *dispute* with me, slave?' said the soldier. Setting spurs to his horse, he had him make a *demivolte*[2] across the path and raising his riding rod at this peasant insolence. Gurth darted a scowl and laid a hand on his knife. Violence however, was prevented by Prior Aymer, who pushed his mule betwixt his companion and the swineherd.

'Nay brother Brian, you are not in Palestine now and dealing with heathen Turks and Saracens. We islanders love only the blows of Holy Church, who '*chasteneth whom she loveth*.'[3] Show me, good fellow,' said he to Wamba, accompanying his words with a piece of silver coin, 'the way to Cedric the Saxon. You cannot be ignorant of it – and it is your duty to direct a wanderer.'

'In truth, venerable father,' answered the Jester, 'the Saracen head of your companion has frightened me out of mine. I am not sure I shall get myself there tonight.'

'Tush,' said the Abbot, 'thou canst tell if thou wilt. This reverend brother has been fighting the Saracens for the recovery of the Holy Sepulchre. He is of the order of Knights Templars, of whom you may have heard; he is half-monk, half-soldier.'[4]

---

1 From Greek: ἀναχωρέω (anachoreo) 'to withdraw' i.e. a religious hermit.

2 A half-turn of the horse with forelegs raised.

3 Aymer quotes from the New Testament: Hebrews 12:6.

4 The Order of Knights Templar were active from c.1119–1314. They combined monastic asceticism with military training, fought in the Crusades and were suppressed in 1312 by Pope Clement v.

'If he is but *half* a monk,' said the Jester, 'he should not be *wholly* unreasonable with those whom he meets upon the road.'

'I will forgive thy wit,' replied the Abbot, 'when shown the way to Cedric's mansion.'

'Well, then,' answered Wamba, 'your reverences must hold this path till you come to a sunken cross, of which scarce a cubit's length remains above ground. Then take the path to the left, for there are four which meet at Sunken Cross, and I trust your reverences will obtain shelter before the storm comes on.'

The cavalcade, setting spurs to their horses, rode on as men do when wishing to reach a harbourage before a storm. As their horses' hooves died away, Gurth said to his companion,

'If they follow thy direction, those reverend fathers will not reach Rotherwood this night.'

'No,' said the Jester, grinning, 'but they may reach Sheffield – and that is as fit a place for them. No woodsman shows a dog where the deer lie.'

'Thou art right,' said Gurth; 'it were bad that Aymer might set eyes on the Lady Rowena. And it were worse for Cedric to quarrel, as is *most* likely, with that military monk. But like good servants, let us hear, see – and say nothing.'

The riders, having left the bondsmen far behind them, resumed their conversation in Norman-French.

'What mean these fellows by their insolence?' said the Templar to the Cistercian, 'and why did you prevent me from chastising it?'

'Gently, brother Brian,' replied the Prior, 'one of them was just a fool speaking folly. The other churl was one of those intractables among the Saxons. Their pleasure is to demonstrate, by any means, their aversion to their conquerors.'

'I would soon have beaten him into courtesy,' observed Brian. 'I am accustomed to deal with such. Marry, sir, you must beware of the dagger. They will use it, given opportunity.'

'Ay, but,' answered Prior Aymer, 'every land has its own manners and fashions. Besides, beating that fellow would procure us no information on the road to Cedric's house and would have established a feud betwixt he and thee. Remember what I told you: this Franklin is wealthy, proud and irritable. He stands up to our nobility and to his neighbours, Reginald Front-de-Boeuf and Philip Malvoisin, who are no babes to contest with. He also stands up for Saxon privileges, being descended from Hereward,[1] a champion of their Heptarchy.[2] He is generally known as Cedric the Saxon and makes boast of belonging to that people, while many others now endeavour to *hide* their descent.'

'Now, Aymer,' said the Templar, 'you are a man of gallantry and expert as a troubadour in the arts of love. But I shall require much beauty in this Cedric's daughter Rowena to balance him as a seditious churl.'

'Cedric is not her father,' replied the Prior, 'only a remote relation. She is descended from higher blood and he is but her guardian. However, she is as dear to him as if she were his own child. Of her beauty you shall judge. If she does not chase from your

---

1 Hereward 'the Wake' i.e. the watcher, led a post-Conquest guerrilla campaign in 1070–71 against the Normans from his base in the Fens of Cambridgeshire.

2 From the Greek for Seven Realms; the Anglo-Saxon kingdoms of the early Middle Ages: Northumbria, Mercia, East Anglia, Essex, Kent, Sussex and Wessex.

memory the black-tressed girls of Palestine or the *houris*[1] of old Mahound's Paradise, I am no true son of the Church.'

'Should her beauty,' said the Templar, 'be weighed in the balance and found wanting, you will recall our wager?'

'Indeed. My gold collar,' answered the Prior, 'against ten butts of Chian wine. They are mine as surely as if they were already with my cellarer.'

'And I am to be the judge,' said the Templar, 'I am only to admit that I have seen no maiden so beautiful since Pentecost was a twelvemonth. Prior, I will wear your collar over my gorget[2] in the lists at Ashby-de-la-Zouche!'

'Win it fairly,' said the Prior, 'and wear it as ye will. I trust your word as knight and churchman. Yet, brother, take advice. File your tongue to more courtesy than when dealing with infidels and *Eastern* bondsmen. Saxon Cedric is not slow in taking offence. Offended, he would clear us from his house without respect to your knighthood or the sanctity of either of us. He would send us out to lodge with the larks, though the hour were midnight. And be careful how you look at Rowena. If he takes the least alarm in that quarter we are lost men. He banished his only son Wilfred for lifting his eyes towards this beauty.'

'You have said enough,' answered the Templar. 'I will put on the needful restraint.'

'We must not let it go so far,' answered the Prior, 'But look, here is the clown's sunken cross and the night so dark that we can hardly see which of the roads we are to follow. He bade us turn, I think to the left.'

'To the right,' said Brian, 'to the best of my remembrance.'

'To the left, certainly, the left. I remember his pointing with his wooden sword.'

'Ay, but he held his sword in his left hand, and pointed *across* his body with it,' said the Templar.

Each maintained his opinion. The attendants were consulted but none had been near enough to hear Wamba's directions. At length Brian noticed something previously missed in the twilight.

'Hugo, there is someone lying either asleep or dead at the foot of that cross; stir him with the butt of thy lance.' This was done, whereupon the figure arose, exclaiming in good French,

'Whoever thou be, it is discourteous to disturb.'

'We did but wish to ask you,' said the Prior, 'the road to Rotherwood, the abode of Cedric called the Saxon.'

'I myself am bound there,' replied the stranger; 'and if I had a horse I would be your guide.'

'Thou shalt have both our thanks,' said the Prior, 'if thou bring us to Cedric's in safety.'

He had one of his attendants giving his horse to the stranger, now their guide. Their conductor pursued a track opposite to that down which Wamba had tried to mislead them. The path soon led deeper into the woodland and crossed more than one brook, the stranger seeming to know by instinct the soundest ground and safest points of passage. He brought the party safely into a wider avenue than any they

---

1 The female companions who await the Moslem faithful in Paradise.

2 A steel or leather collar designed to protect the throat.

had yet seen and pointing to a large, low irregular building at its end. He said to the Prior,

'Yonder is the Rotherwood of Cedric the Saxon.'

This was a welcome intimation to Aymer who had suffered such alarm in passing through the dangerous bogs, that he had not asked his new guide a single question. His curiosity rising, he demanded of the guide who and what he was.

'A Palmer, just returned from the Holy Land.'[1] was the answer.

'Better to have tarried there to fight for the recovery of the Holy Sepulchre,' said the Templar.

'True, Reverend Sir Knight,' answered the Palmer, to whom the appearance of a Templar seemed familiar. 'But when such as you who are under *oath* to recover the holy city, are so far from it, can you wonder that the task is not for a peaceful peasant like me?' The Templar would have made an angry retort but was interrupted by the Prior expressing his astonishment that their guide, after such long absence, should be so perfectly acquainted with the passes of the forest.

'I was born a native of these parts,' answered their guide.

As he made this reply, they were arriving before the mansion of Cedric.

It was a low irregular building containing several courtyards or enclosures extending over a considerable space of ground. Though its size argued the owner to be a person of wealth, it differed entirely from the tall, turreted and castellated buildings of the Norman nobility, now the universal style of architecture throughout England. Rotherwood was not, however, without defences. A deep *fosse*, or ditch, ran round the whole building, fuelled with water from a neighbouring stream. A double stockade, or palisade, composed of sharp pointed wooden stakes, defended the outer and inner bank of the trench. An entrance from the west through the outer stockade communicated by a drawbridge with a similar opening in the inner defences. All entrances were under the protection of projecting angles by which they might be enfiladed by archers or slingers.

Before this entrance the Templar wound his horn loudly and urgently, for the threatened rain now began to descend with violence.

chapter three

And yellow hair'd, the blue-eyed Saxon came.
James Thomson: *Liberty*

In a hall, the low height of which was out of proportion to its extreme length and width, stood a long oaken table of unpolished planks, rough-hewn from the forest. Upon it was the evening meal prepared for Cedric the Saxon. The roof, composed of beams and rafters, had nothing to divide the apartment from the sky except for the planking and thatch. There was a huge fireplace at either end of the hall, but as the chimneys were clumsily constructed, as much smoke found its way into the apartment

---

1 From Lat. *palmarius*. A Christian pilgrim returning from the Holy Land bearing a palm leaf as a symbol of his pilgrimage.

as escaped by the proper vent. The constant vapour had encrusted the rafters and beams of the low-browed hall with a black varnish of soot. On the walls of the apartment hung implements of war and hunting, while at each corner were folding doors giving access to other parts of the building.

The other furnishings of the mansion displayed the rude simplicity of the Saxon period which Cedric maintained. The floor was earth mixed with lime, trodden into the hard substance which floors a modern barn. For one quarter of the length of the apartment, the floor was raised by a step to a platform, or *dais*, occupied by principal members of the family and visitors of distinction. A table, richly covered with scarlet cloth was placed transversely across the platform, from the middle of which and down towards the bottom of the hall, ran the longer and lower board, at which fed the domestics and other persons. The whole resembled the form of a T, as may still be seen in older Oxford or Cambridge colleges. Massive chairs and settles of carved oak were placed upon the *dais* and over these seats and the more elevated table was fastened a canopy of cloth. This served in some degree to protect the dignitaries from the weather, especially the rain which in places was already finding its way through the ill-constructed roof.

The walls of this upper end of the hall, indeed as far as the *dais* extended, were covered with hangings or curtains. Upon the floor was a carpet adorned with attempts at tapestry or embroidery, executed with gaudy colouring. Over the lower range of the table, the roof had no covering, the rough plastered walls were bare and the earthen floor uncarpeted. The table was uncovered by a cloth and rude, massive benches replaced chairs.

In the centre of the upper table were two chairs more elevated than the rest for the Master and Mistress of the family. They presided over the scene of hospitality, thus deriving their Saxon title of honour,[1] which signifies 'the Dividers of Bread.' To each of these chairs was added a footstool, curiously carved and inlaid with ivory, a mark of distinction. One of these seats was occupied by Cedric the Saxon, who though only a Thane or, as the Normans called him, a Franklin, was irritable and impatient at the delay to his evening meal.

Indeed, the countenance of this landowner suggested a hasty and choleric temper. He was not above middle stature but was broad shouldered, long armed and powerfully made, as expected of one accustomed to war and the chase. His face was broad with large blue eyes and his frank features, fine teeth and well formed head were expressive of the good humour which often lodges with a sudden and hasty temper. Pride and jealousy were also in his eye for his life had been spent in asserting rights which were constantly threatened with invasion. Indeed the fiery and resolute disposition of the man were kept constantly alert by his circumstances and situation. Cedric's long yellow hair, equally divided and combed down on each side to his shoulders, had but little tendency to grey, although he was approaching his sixtieth year.

His dress was a tunic of forest green, furred at the throat and cuffs with minever, a fur derived from the skin of the squirrel. This doublet hung unbuttoned over a close dress of scarlet which sat tight to his body. He had breeches of the same, but

---

1 *Hlaford* in Anglo-Saxon. It derives from *hlaf* (loaf) and *weard* (ward or guardian).The modern 'Lord' derives from it.

they did not reach below the lower part of the thigh, leaving the knee exposed. His feet had sandals of the same fashion as his peasants, but of finer materials and secured in the front with golden clasps. Bracelets of gold were upon his arms and a broad golden collar around his neck. About his waist was a richly studded belt, in which was stuck a short, sharp pointed and two-edged sword which hung vertically by his side. Behind his seat was a scarlet cloth cloak lined with fur, while a cap of the same material and richly embroidered completed his attire when he went forth. A short boar spear with a broad steel head reclined against the back of his chair; this served him as a staff or a weapon when he walked abroad.

Several domestics, whose dress lay betwixt the richness of their master's and the coarse, simple attire of Gurth the swineherd, awaited Cedric's commands. Two or three servants of a superior order stood behind their master upon the *dais*, while the rest occupied the lower part of the hall. Attendants of different species were also present; three large, shaggy greyhounds, employed in hunting stag and wolf, slow-hounds of a large bony breed with thick necks, large heads and long ears and smaller terriers awaited with equal impatience the arrival of their supper. These, however, showing a canny knowledge of human physiognomy, did not intrude upon the moody silence of their master. They were apprehensive of a white truncheon lying by Cedric's trencher for the purpose of repelling advances by his canine dependents. Only one grisly old wolfhound had planted himself close by the chair of state and, with the liberty of an indulged favourite, occasionally solicited notice by putting his large hairy head upon his master's knee, or pushing his nose into his hand. But even he was repelled by the stern command,

'Down, Balder, down! I am in no humour for foolery.'

Cedric was indeed in no placid state of mind. The Lady Rowena, who had been attending evening Mass at a distant church, had only just returned and was changing garments soaked by the storm. There were as yet no tidings of Gurth and his swine which should long since have arrived back from the forest. Such was the insecurity of the period that this might mean an attack by the outlaws. It might also be due to some neighbouring Baron, his power making him negligent of the laws of property. The matter was of consequence, for much of the domestic wealth of Saxon proprietors consisted in herds of swine, especially in forests where they foraged easily.

Besides these anxieties, the Saxon thane was impatient for the presence of Wamba, his Jester and favourite clown. His jests served as seasoning to his evening meal and the accompanying draughts of ale and wine. To add to all this, Cedric had fasted since noon and his usual supper hour was now long past. His displeasure was expressed in broken sentences, partly muttered to himself and partly to the domestics around, particularly to his cupbearer who from time to time offered him a silver wine goblet.

'Why tarries the Lady Rowena?'

'She is changing her head-gear.' replied a female attendant, with the confidence of the favourite lady's maid. 'You would wish her to sit down to the banquet in her hood and kirtle?'

This undeniable argument produced a sort of acquiescent grunt on the part of the Saxon, who added,

'I wish her devotion may choose fair weather for the next visit to St John's. But what in the name of ten devils,' continued he, turning to the cupbearer and raising his voice, happy to have found a safer channel for his indignation, 'what in the name of ten devils, keeps Gurth so long afield? I suppose we shall have evil news of the herd.'

Oswald, his cupbearer, suggested that it was scarce an hour since the tolling of the curfew, an ill-chosen excuse since it raised a topic so harsh to Saxon ears.

'The foul Fiend,' exclaimed Cedric, 'take the curfew-bell, and the tyrannical Bastard by whom it was devised and any who names it with a Saxon tongue to a Saxon ear! The curfew,' he added, pausing, 'Ay, the curfew which compels true men to extinguish their lights so that thieves and robbers may work in darkness! Ay, the curfew; Reginald Front-de-Boeuf and Philip de Malvoisin know the use of the curfew, as did William the Bastard himself and any Norman at Hastings. I guess I shall hear that my property has been swept off to feed banditti, my faithful slave murdered and my goods taken. And Wamba; where is Wamba? Has he gone with Gurth?' Oswald replied in the affirmative.

'Ay? Why, this is better and better! He is carried off too; a Saxon fool to serve a Norman lord. Fools are we all indeed that serve them. Fitter subjects for their scorn and laughter than if we had been born halfwits. But I will be avenged,' he added starting from his chair at the supposed injury and catching up his boar-spear, 'I wil go to the Great Council. I have friends and I have followers. Let him come in hi plate armour and all that emboldens cowardice. I have sent a javelin like this throug a fence stronger than three of their war shields! They think me old – but they sha find, alone and childless as I am, the blood of Hereward is in the veins of Cedric Then, in a lower tone,

'Ah Wilfred, my son Wilfred! Had thou ruled thy passion for Rowena, thy fath were not left like an aged oak!' This last reflection seemed to mute his irritation in sadness. Replacing the javelin, he resumed his seat, absorbed in melancholy.

Cedric was suddenly roused from his musing by the blast of a horn, immediat replied to by the barking of all twenty dogs in the hall. It took some exercise of t white truncheon seconded by the domestics to silence the clamour.

'To the gate, knaves!' said the Saxon hastily, as soon as the tumult had d sufficiently for the dependents to hear his voice.

'See what tidings that horn brings. I suspect hership[1] upon my lands.'

Returning in a minute or so, a warder announced;

'The Prior Aymer of Jorvaulx and Sir Brian de Bois Guilbert, commander of valiant order of Knights Templars, with a small retinue, request hospitality and lod for the night, being *en route* to a tournament at Ashby-de-la-Zouche on the sec day from present.'

'Aymer, the Prior Aymer? Brian de Bois Guilbert?' muttered Cedric; 'Norn both; but as guests, even Normans must suppress their insolence. Go, Hundebert added, to his *major-domo*[2] who stood behind him with a white wand, 'tak attendants and conduct them to the guests' lodging. Look after their horses and n and see that their train lacks nothing. Let them have change of vestments if require it. Bid the cooks add what they can to our meal when those stranger ready. Hundebert, say to them that Cedric himself would bid them welcome, b

1 Pillage. *Scott.*

2 Chief Steward and Chief of Staff of the household.

is under a vow never to take more than three steps from the dais of his own Hall to meet anyone not of the blood of Saxon royalty. Begone!' The *major-domo* departed with several attendants.

'The Prior Aymer!' repeated Cedric, looking to Oswald, 'The brother, if I mistake not, of Giles de Mauleverer, now lord of Middleham?' Oswald made a sign of assent.

'Giles his brother,' continued Cedric, 'sits in the House and usurps the patrimony of Ulfgar of Middleham; but what Norman lord doth not the same? This Prior is, they say, a free and jovial priest who loves wine cup and bugle-horn better than bell and book. Good; let him come, he shall be welcome. How named ye the Templar?'

'Sir Brian de Bois Guilbert.'

'Bois Guilbert,' said Cedric, still in the musing, half-arguing tone, 'Bois Guilbert? A name spread wide, both for good and evil. They say he is the bravest of his Order, but stained with arrogance. Warriors from Palestine say he has neither fear of earth nor awe of Heaven. Well, it is but for one night; so he shall be welcome too. Oswald, broach a wine cask. Put the best mead and ale, the richest *morat*[1] and sparkling cider upon the board. Fill the largest horns. Templars and Abbots love good wines in good measure. Elgitha, let the Lady Rowena know we shall not now expect her in the hall this night, unless such be her especial pleasure.'

'But it *will* be her especial pleasure,' said Elgitha immediately, 'for she is ever desirous of the latest news from Palestine.'

Cedric darted a glance of hasty resentment; but Rowena and whoever belonged to her were secure from his anger. He only replied,

'Thy tongue outruns thy discretion. Take my message to thy mistress and let her do her pleasure.'

'Palestine,' repeated the Saxon to himself; 'Palestine, where Wilfred is... How many tales crusaders and pilgrims bring from that land. But no, Wilfred disobeyed me and is disinherited. I care no more for his fate than for the millions that donned the cross and rushed there, calling it an accomplishment of the will of God.'

He knitted his brows and fixed his eyes on the ground. As he slowly raised them, the folding doors at the bottom of the hall were thrown wide. Preceded by the *major-domo* with his wand and by four domestics with blazing torches, the guests of the evening entered the apartment.

chapter four

Disposed apart, Ulysses shares the treat;
A trivet table and ignobler seat,
The Prince assigns...
Homer: *The Odyssey.* Tr. Alexander Pope.

Prior Aymer had changed his riding robe for one of yet more costly materials, over which was an embroidered rope. Besides the massive golden signet ring which

---

[1] From Lat. *morus*, mulberry. A drink made from honey flavoured with mulberries. *Scott.*

marked his ecclesiastical dignity, his fingers were loaded with gems, again contrary to canon law. His sandals were of the finest Spanish leather, his beard was trimmed as small as his Order permitted, his shaven crown concealed by an embroidered scarlet cap.

The appearance of the Knight Templar had also changed. Though less bedecked with ornament, his appearance was now far more commanding than that of his companion. He had exchanged his shirt of mail for an under-tunic of dark purple silk, garnished with furs, over which flowed his long robe of spotless white. The eight-pointed Cross of his Order on his shoulder was in black velvet. His brows were shaded by short, thick curly hair of raven blackness, matching his swarthy complexion. Graceful was his step and manner, though marked by the arrogance of unchallenged authority.

The two principals were followed by their respective attendants and by their guide, the Palmer, whose appearance was the humble one of a pilgrim. A Sclavonian[1] cloak of coarse black serge enveloped his whole body. Coarse sandals, bound with thongs, were upon his bare feet. A broad and shadowy hat, cockle-shells stitched on its brim and a long staff, on the upper end of which was a branch of palm, completed his attire. He followed the last of the train entering the hall. Observing the lower table full with the domestics of both Cedric and the guests, he withdrew to settle under one of the large chimneys where he employed himself in drying his garments.

Cedric rose to receive his guests with a dignified air. Descending from the elevated *dais*, he awaited their approach.

'Let me pray,' he said, 'reverend Prior and Knight of the Holy Temple, that you will excuse my native language and that you will reply in the same if your command of it permits. If not, I have sufficient Norman to follow you.'

'I always use French,' said the cleric, 'the language of the King and his nobility, but I understand Anglo-Saxon sufficiently to communicate with natives.' Cedric darted at the speaker one of those fiery glances which meetings of the two nations seldom failed to produce. However, recollecting the duties of hospitality, he caused his guests to take two seats close beside him, though a little lower than his own, and gave a signal for the meal to be served.

While the attendants were so doing, Cedric's eye caught Gurth the swineherd who, with his companion Wamba, had just entered the hall.

'Send these loitering knaves hither,' said the Saxon, impatiently. They came before the dais, 'How comes it, villains, that you loiter abroad so late as this? Are thy charges home, sirrah Gurth, or are they left to robbers and marauders?'

'The herd is safe, so please ye,' said Gurth.

'It does *not* please me,' said Cedric. 'I warn thee, shackles and the prison-house follow thy next such offence.' Gurth, knowing his master's temper, attempted no excuses, so the Jester, assured of Cedric's tolerance as his fool, replied for them both;

'In troth, uncle Cedric, you are neither wise nor reasonable tonight.'

'How so, sirrah?' said his master.

'First let your wisdom tell me,' said Wamba, 'is it just and reasonable to punish one person for the fault of another?'

'Certainly not, fool,' answered Cedric.

---

1 From Slavonia in the Balkans, today a district of eastern Croatia.

'Then why should you shackle poor Gurth, uncle, for the fault of Fangs, his hound? For I swear we lost not a minute by the way, after we had got together our herd which Fangs had ignored until we heard the vesper bell.'[1]

'Then hang up Fangs,' said Cedric, turning hastily towards the swineherd, 'Get thee another dog.'

'But uncle,' said the Jester, 'that would still be unfair justice. For it was no fault of Fangs that he was lame and could not gather the herd. It was the fault of those that struck off two of his fore-claws.'

'And who dared lame an animal of a bondsman of *mine*?' said the Saxon, his wrath kindling.

'Marry, old Hubert did that,' said Wamba, 'Sir Philip de Malvoisin's keeper of the chase. He caught Fangs in the forest and said he chased the deer contrary to his master's rights.'

'The foul *fiend* take Malvoisin!'[2] shouted the Saxon, 'and his keeper both! But enough of this. Go to thy place, fool; and Gurth, get thee another dog and should that keeper dare to touch it, I will strike off his right forefinger and he shall draw bow-string no more!

I crave your pardon, worthy guests, for I am beset here with neighbours, Sir Knight, that match your infidels in the Holy Land. But food is before you. Eat, and let welcome make amends for homely fare.'

The feast, however, which was spread upon the board, needed no apologies from the lord of the mansion. Swine flesh, dressed in several modes, appeared on the lower part of the board. So also did that of deer, goat, hare and various fish. There were huge loaves and cakes of bread and sundry confections of fruits and honey. The smaller sorts of wildfowl were not served up in platters but brought in upon small wooden spits or broaches. They were offered by the pages and domestics to each guest who cut from them as he pleased. Beside each person of rank was a goblet of silver, while large drinking horns serviced the lower board.

When the repast was about to commence, the *major-domo* suddenly raised his wand, calling;

'Forbear! Place for the Lady Rowena.' A side door at the upper end of the hall now opened behind the banqueting table and Rowena, followed by four female attendants, entered the apartment. Cedric, though irritated at his ward's appearance on this occasion, hastened to meet her. He conducted her with respectful ceremony to the elevated seat at his own right hand, appropriate to the lady of the mansion. All stood to receive her. Replying to this courtesy by a silent gesture of salutation, she gracefully assumed her place at the board; but ere she had time to do so, the Templar was whispering to the Prior,

'I shall wear no gold collar of yours at the tournament. The Chian wine is yours.'

'Said I not so?' answered the Prior; 'but restrain your raptures; the Franklin is observing you.' Heedless of the caution and accustomed to act upon impulse, Brian de Bois Guilbert kept his eyes riveted on the Saxon beauty. Tall and fair of form and face, Rowena had a noble head and features, her blue eyes able to kindle or melt. Her

---

1 It sounded the sunset call to Vespers, the sixth of the seven canonical hours; from the Greek ἑσπέρα 'espera,' evening.

2 One of the many mediaeval aliases for the Devil.

luxuriant hair, betwixt brown and flaxen, was arranged gracefully in ringlets braided with gems. Being worn at full length, it also intimated her noble birth. A golden chain, to which was attached a small reliquary, hung round her neck and there were bracelets on her bare arms. Her dress was an under-gown and kirtle of pale sea-green silk, over which hung a long loose crimson robe having wide sleeves to the elbow. A veil of silk, interwoven with gold, was attached to the upper part of her robe, and could be either drawn over the face and bosom after the Spanish fashion, or disposed as drapery round the shoulders.

Rowena perceived the Knight Templar's eyes bent on her with ardour. She drew the veil around her face with dignity, an intimation that the freedom of his gaze was disagreeable. Cedric saw the motion – and its cause.

'Sir Templar,' said he, 'the cheeks of our Saxon maidens have seen too little of the sun to bear the fixed glance of a Crusader.'

'If I have offended,' replied Sir Brian, 'I crave your pardon – that is, I crave the Lady Rowena's pardon.'

'The Lady Rowena,' said the Prior, 'has punished us all in chastising the boldness of my friend. Let me hope she will be less cruel at the Tournament.'

'Our going there,' said Cedric, 'is still uncertain. I love not these vanities, unknown here when England was still free.'

'Let us hope, nevertheless,' said the Prior, 'that our company may decide you to travel. With the roads so unsafe, an escort from Sir Brian de Bois Guilbert is not to be despised.'

'Sir Prior,' answered the Saxon, 'wherever I have travelled with my good sword and my faithful followers, I have never found myself in need of aid. If we indeed journey to Ashby-de-la-Zouche, we will do so with my noble neighbour and countryman Athelstane of Coningsburgh and with such a train as to deter any outlaw or enemy. I drink to you, Sir Prior, in this cup of wine and I thank you for your courtesy. Should you be rigid in monastic Rule,' he added, 'and prefer your acid milk preparation, I hope you will still accommodate me.'

'Nay,' said the Priest, laughing, 'it is only within our abbey that we confine ourselves to the *'lac dulce'* or the *'lac acidum'*.[1] Conversing with the outer world, we use that world's fashions and thus I answer your pledge in wine, leaving the weaker fluid to my lay-brother.'

'And I,' said the Templar, filling his goblet, 'drink *wassail* to the fair Rowena. For since her namesake[2] introduced the word into England, there was never one more worthy of such a tribute.

'I will spare your courtesy, Sir Knight,' said Rowena with dignity, and without unveiling. 'Or rather I will tax it to enquire the latest news from Palestine, a theme more agreeable than your French compliments.'

'I have little of importance to say, Lady,' answered the Templar, 'excepting to confirm a truce with Saladin.'[3]

---

1 Latin: Sweet or sour milk.

2 Rowena was the daughter of the Jute leader Hengist, brought to Britain in the 5th century by the British king Vortigern. Rowena followed and married Vortigern.

3 Salah-ed-Din (c.1138–1193). A Kurd, a Sunni Moslem and an outstanding military tactician, he commanded the Saracen forces opposing the Third Crusade in Palestine.

He was interrupted by Wamba, now in his personal chair, whose back was decorated with two ass's ears. He was two steps behind that of his master who, from time to time, supplied him with victuals. This favour, however, the Jester shared with Cedric's dogs of which several were in attendance. Thus sat Wamba with a small table before him, his heels tucked up against the bar of the chair, his half-shut eyes watching for any opportunity to exercise his licensed foolery.

'These truces with the Infidel,' he exclaimed, without caring how suddenly he interrupted the stately Templar, 'they make an old man of me!'

'Knave, how so?' said Cedric, expecting a jest.

'Because,' answered Wamba, 'I remember three of them in my time, each of which was to endure for fifty years. Thus...I must be at least a one hundred and fifty!'

'I guarantee that your death will not be of old age,' said the Templar, recognising him from the forest; 'it will be a violent one if you misdirect wayfarers – as you did this night to the Prior and me.'

'Now, Sirrah!' said Cedric, 'misdirect travellers? We must have you whipt. You are more rogue than fool.'

'I pray thee, uncle,' answered the Jester, 'let my folly for once protect my roguery. I did but make a mistake between my right hand and my left. Is he not the greater fool – who takes a fool for his guide?'

Conversation was here interrupted by the entrance of the porter's page, announcing that a stranger was at the gate imploring admittance and hospitality.

'Admit him,' said Cedric, 'be he who or what he may. A night like this which roars outside compels men to seek protection. Let his wants be ministered to; look to it, Oswald.'

chapter five

Hath not a Jew eyes? Hath not a Jew hands,
organs, dimensions, senses, affections, passions?
Fed with the same food, hurt with the same weapons,
subject to the same diseases, healed by the same means,
warmed and cooled by the same winter and summer,
as a Christian is?
W. Shakespeare: *The Merchant of Venice*

Oswald, returning, whispered into the ear of his master, 'It is a Jew, who calls himself Isaac of York. Is it fit I should marshal him into the hall?'

'A Jew,' echoed the Templar, 'to approach a defender of the Holy Sepulchre?'

'By my faith,' said Wamba, 'the Templars love the Jews' wealth better than their company.'

'Peace, my worthy guests,' said Cedric; 'my hospitality is not bounded by your dislikes. If Heaven chose that whole nation for more years than a layman can number, we may have the presence of one Jew for a few hours. Let him have a board and a morsel apart, unless…' he said smiling, 'these turban'd men of yours will accept his company?'

'Sir Franklin,' answered the Templar, 'my Saracen slaves are Moslems and scorn as much as any Christian to hold intercourse with a Jew.'

'Now, in faith,' said Wamba, 'I cannot see that the worshippers of Mahomet and Termagaunt[1] have an advantage over the people chosen of Heaven.'

'He shall sit with thee, Wamba,' said Cedric; 'the fool and the Israelite will be well met.'

'The fool,' answered Wamba, raising the relics of a gammon of bacon, 'will erect a *bulwark*.'

'Hush,' said Cedric, 'for here he comes.'

Introduced with little ceremony and advancing with fear, hesitation, and many a bow of deep humility, came a tall, thin old man. He had lost, by the habit of stooping, much of his actual height as he approached the lower end of the board. His features were keen and regular with a high forehead, an aquiline nose, piercing black eyes and long grey hair and beard.[2] Isaac's dress, which appeared to have suffered considerably from the storm, was a plain russet cloak of many folds, covering a dark purple tunic. He had large boots lined with fur and a belt around his waist which sustained a small knife together with a case for writing materials, but no weapon. He wore the high square yellow cap used by his nation to distinguish them from Christians and which he doffed with humility at the door of the hall.

Cedric nodded in answer to Isaac's salutation and signed to him to take place at the lower end of the table. There, however, no one offered to make room for him. As he passed along the file he cast supplicating glances as he turned towards each of those who occupied the lower end of the board. The Saxon domestics squared their shoulders and continued to devour their supper, paying not the least attention. The attendants of the Abbot crossed themselves with pious looks of horror, while the heathen Saracens curled up their whiskers with indignation and laid their hands on their poniards as Isaac drew near.

The motives which induced Cedric to open his hall to this son of Abraham would normally have him order his attendants to receive Isaac with courtesy. At this moment, however, the Abbot was engaging him in a discussion on breeds of hounds, a favourite subject. Isaac was thus left standing like his own people among the nations, an outcast looking in vain for a welcome resting place, when the Palmer by the chimney rose and offered his seat.

'Old man, my garments are dried and my hunger is appeased, while thou art wet and fasting.' He gathered and fired up the wood scattered on the ample hearth. From the larger board he took a mess of pottage and seethed kid and placed it upon his small table. Without waiting for the Jew's thanks he then went to the other side of the hall. Isaac, having dispelled the cold, turned eagerly to the smoking mess before him and ate with haste.

---

1 Termagaunt was an entity wrongly believed by mediaeval Europeans to be a god worshipped by Moslems. Islam knows no God but Allah.

2 These features would have been considered as handsome, but during those dark ages the children of Israel were both detested by the commonality and persecuted by the rapacious nobility. *Scott.*

Meanwhile the Abbot and Cedric continued their discourse on hunting. The Lady Rowena seemed engaged in conversation with one of her attendant females while the Templar's eyes wandered back from the Jew to the Saxon beauty.

'I marvel, worthy Cedric,' said the Abbot, as their discourse proceeded, 'that, great as is your predilection for Anglo-Saxon, you do not favour Norman-French so far as hunting is concerned. Surely no tongue is so rich in the phrases of the field.'

'Father Aymer,' said the Saxon, 'understand that I care not for those overseas refinements. Without them I can well enough take my pleasure in the woods. I can wind my horn, though I call not the blast either a *recheate* or a *morte*.[1] I can cheer on my dogs and I can flay and quarter a deer without any newfangled jargon.'

'The French,' said the Templar, in his presumptuous tone, 'is not only the natural language of the chase, but also that of love and of war; thus ladies should be won and enemies defied.'

'Join me in wine, Sir Templar,' said Cedric, 'and fill another for the Abbot, while I look back thirty years to tell you another tale. As I then was, my plain Anglo-Saxon needed no garnish from French troubadours, when it spoke to a beauty. And at the field of Northallerton, upon the day of the Holy Standard,[2] the Saxon warcry was heard as far within the Scottish host as the *cri de guerre* of the boldest Norman baron. To the memory of the brave who fought there; pledge me, my guests!'

He drank deep, and went on with increasing warmth. 'Ay, that was a day of the cleaving of shields, when a hundred banners went forwards, blood flowed like water and death was held better than flight. A Saxon bard called it 'a feast of the swords, a gathering of eagles to their prey'. But our bards are no more, our deeds lost in those of another race. Our language – our very *name* – hastens to decay and none mourn, save one solitary old man. Cupbearer, fill the goblets. A toast to the strong in arms, Sir Templar, in Palestine for the Cross!'

'It becomes not a Templar to answer,' said Bois Guilbert, 'yet besides us of the Holy Sepulchre, where else can the palm be assigned as champions of the Cross?'

'To the Knights Hospitallers,'[3] said the Abbot; 'I have a brother of that Order.'

'I impeach not their fame,' said the Templar; 'nevertheless...'

'I think, friend Cedric,' said Wamba, interrupting, 'that had Richard Lionheart been wise enough to take a fool's advice, he might have stayed at home and left the recovery of Jerusalem to those same Templar knights who lost it.'

'Were there none in the English army,' said the Lady Rowena, 'worthy to be mentioned with the Knights of the Temple and of St John?'

'Forgive me, lady,' replied Bois Guilbert, 'the English monarch did indeed bring to Palestine a host of gallant warriors, second only to those of us who were bulwark of that blessed land.'

'Second to *none*,' said the Palmer, who had been standing close enough to hear, listening to this conversation with marked impatience. All turned towards him.

---

1 Hunting calls: *Recheate* to recall the hounds when the quarry is lost; *Morte* to announce a kill.

2 In August 1138 on Cowton Moor near Northallerton in Yorkshire, an English army assembled by Thurstan, Archbishop of York, repelled an invading Scottish army under King David I.

3 The Order of St. John of Jerusalem, the Knights Hospitallers, were formed in the 11th Century to provide hospital care and protection to Christian pilgrims to the Holy Land. The Knights became one of the foremost military powers in the region.

'I say,' repeated the Pilgrim in a firm and strong voice, 'that the English chivalry were second to *none* who ever drew sword in defence of the Holy Land. I saw King Richard himself and five of his knights hold a tournament after the taking of St John-de-Acre, challenging all comers. I say that on that day each knight ran three courses, and cast to the ground three antagonists. I say that seven of these antagonists were Knights of the Temple – and that you, Sir Brian de Bois Guilbert, well know the truth of what I tell you!'

A bitter scowl of rage darkened further the swarthy countenance of the Templar. In an extremity of resentment and confusion, his quivering fingers gripped the handle of his sword. Cedric failed to notice the angry confusion of his guest in the glee with which he heard of the deeds of his countrymen.

'I give thee this golden bracelet, Pilgrim,' he said; 'tell me the names of those knights who upheld the renown of England.'

'That will I do blithely,' replied the Pilgrim, 'and without guerdon.[1] My oath, for now, prohibits me from touching gold.'

'I will wear the bracelet for you, Palmer,' said Wamba.

'The first in honour, as in arms, renown and place,' said the Pilgrim, 'was Richard, King of England.'

'I forgive him,' said Cedric; 'I *forgive* him his descent from that tyrant Duke William.'

'The Earl of Leicester was the second,' continued the Pilgrim, 'and Sir Thomas Multon of Gilsland was the third.'

'Of Saxon descent,' said Cedric with exultation.

'Sir Foulk Doilly the fourth,' went on the Pilgrim.

'Saxon also, at least by the mother's side,' continued Cedric,

'And who was the fifth?'

'The fifth was Sir Edwin Turneham.'

'Genuine Saxon, by the soul of Hengist!' shouted Cedric. 'And the sixth?' he demanded, 'how name you the sixth?'

'The sixth,' said the Palmer, after a pause in which he seemed to recollect himself, 'was a young knight of lower rank, taken in to make up their number. His name dwells not in my memory.'

'Sir Palmer,' said Sir Brian de Bois Guilbert scornfully, 'this assumed forgetfulness after so much has been remembered, comes too late. I will name the knight before whose lance my horse's fault caused my fall. It was the Knight of Ivanhoe. Were he in England and dared repeat the challenge in this week's tournament, I would give him every advantage of weapons and accept the result.'

'Your challenge would soon be answered,' replied the Palmer, 'were he near you. If Ivanhoe ever returns from Palestine, I will be his surety that he meets you.'

'A goodly security!' said the Knight Templar; 'and what do you proffer as a pledge?'

'This reliquary,' said the Palmer, taking out a small ivory box and crossing himself, 'containing a portion of the true cross, brought from the Monastery of Mount Carmel.'

The Prior of Jorvaulx crossed himself and repeated a *pater noster*,[2] in which all devoutly joined except the Jew, the Moslems and the Templar. The latter, without

---

1 A reward, recompense, or requital.

2 Our Father: the Latin opening of the Lord's Prayer.

vailing[1] his bonnet or showing any reverence for the sanctity of the relic, took the gold chain from his neck and flung it on the board, saying,

'Let Prior Aymer hold my pledge and that of this nameless vagrant. When the Knight of Ivanhoe comes within the four seas of Britain, he will receive the challenge of Brian de Bois Guilbert. If he answers not, I will proclaim him a coward.'

'There is no need for thy pledge,' said the Lady Rowena, breaking her silence, 'My voice shall be heard if no other in this hall is raised for Ivanhoe. I affirm he will meet every honourable challenge. Could I add security to the pledge of this holy pilgrim, I would pledge name and fame that Ivanhoe gives this proud knight a meeting!'

A crowd of conflicting emotions seemed to keep Cedric silent during this exchange. Pride, resentment and embarrassment chased each other over his brow like cloud shadows over the harvest field. His attendants, on whom the name of the sixth knight seemed to produce an almost electrical effect, hung in suspense upon their master's looks. But when Rowena spoke, the sound of her voice seemed to startle him from his silence.

'Lady,' said Cedric, 'Were a further pledge necessary, I myself would gage for the honour of Ivanhoe. But the wager of battle is complete, according to chivalry, is it not, Father Aymer?'

'It is,' replied the Prior; 'and I shall bestow the blessed relic and the gold chain in the treasury of our Abbey until the outcome.'

Having spoken, he crossed himself again and delivered the reliquary to Brother Ambrose, an attendant monk. He himself swept up the golden chain, depositing it in a pouch which rapidly opened under his arm.

'And now, Sir Cedric,' he said, 'my ears are chiming *vespers* from the strength of your wine. Permit us one toast to the Lady Rowena and then permit us to go to our repose.'

'Sir Prior,' said the Saxon, 'you do small credit to your fame! Report speaks of you as a monk that would hear the *matin* chime ere he quitted his bowl. I feared I would be shamed in encountering you, but by my faith, a Saxon boy of twelve would keep longer to his goblet.'

The Prior, however, had his own reasons for his temperance. He was not only a professional peacemaker but also, from practice, a hater of feuds and brawls. He had an instinctive fear of the fiery temper of the Saxon and saw also that his companion might well produce an explosion. The grace-cup was accordingly served round. The guests, after making a deep obeisance to their landlord and to the Lady Rowena, rose and mingled in the hall while Cedric and Rowena retired with their attendants by separate doors.

'Unbeliever,' said the Templar to Isaac of York, as he passed him in the throng, 'dost thou travel to the tournament?'

'I do so propose,' replied Isaac, bowing.

'Ay,' said the Knight, 'to gnaw the bowels of our nobles with usury. I warrant there's a store of *shekels* in thy Jewish purse.'[2]

'Not a *shekel*, no silver penny, nor a halfling[3] so help me God of Abraham!' said

---

1 Doffing.

2 The chief silver coin of the ancient Hebrews – and the currency unit of modern Israel.

3 A coin of minimal value. Also a synonym for J. R. R. Tolkien's Hobbit.

the Jew, clasping his hands; 'I go only to seek the assistance of my brethren to aid me pay the fine which the Exchequer of the Jews has imposed.[1] I am impoverished. The very gaberdine I wear is borrowed from Reuben of Tadcaster.'

The Templar smiled sourly, replying,

'Thou'rt a false-hearted liar!'

Passing on, he communed with his Moslem slaves in a language he thought unknown to all but which, unknown to him, was familiar to the Israelite. Isaac seemed so thunderstruck by what he overheard, that the Templar was gone before the Jew was aware of his departure.

chapter six

To buy his favour I extend this friendship:
If he will take it, so; if not, adieu;
And, for my love, I pray you wrong me not.
Shakespeare: *The Merchant of Venice*

As the Palmer, lighted by a domestic with a torch, passed through the maze of apartments, the cupbearer whispered to him that many of the domestics would gladly hear any news from the Holy Land concerning the Knight of Ivanhoe. Wamba appeared and urged the same request. The Palmer thanked them for their courtesy, but observed that his religious vow forbade speaking in the kitchen on matters prohibited in the hall.

'That vow,' said Wamba to the cupbearer, 'would scarce suit a serving man.' The cupbearer shrugged his shoulders in displeasure.

'I thought to have lodged him in the *solere* chamber,'[2] said he; 'but since he is so unsocial, let him take the next stall to Isaac the Jew's. Anwold,' said he to the torch-bearer, 'take the Pilgrim to the southern cell. I give you goodnight, Sir Palmer' he added sourly, 'with small thanks for short courtesy.'

'Goodnight, and Our Lady's benison,' said the Palmer with composure.

In an antechamber lighted by a small iron lamp and into which several doors opened, they met a second interruption; from the waiting-maid of Rowena. She took the torch from Anwold and made a sign to the Palmer to follow her, saying that her mistress desired to speak with him. A short passage and an ascent of seven oaken steps led him to Lady Rowena's apartment, the magnificence of which marked the respect in which she was held by Cedric. The walls were covered with embroidered hangings of coloured silks, interwoven with gold and silver thread. These had been employed with all the art of the age to represent hunting and hawking. The bed was adorned with the same rich tapestry and surrounded with curtains dyed with purple. The seats also had embroidered coverings; one, higher than the rest, being supplied

---

1 Jews were subjected to a tax, or Exchequer, which laid them under the most exorbitant impositions. *Scott.*

2 From Fr. *sol,* the sun. An upper room in a building receiving direct sunlight.

with a footstool of carved ivory. Four silver candelabras holding waxen torches illuminated the apartment. The walls of the apartment, however, were so ill-finished and so full of crevices that the rich hangings shook in the night blast. In spite of a screen intended to protect them from the wind, the flames of the torches streamed sideways like an unfurled pennon. Magnificence there was, with some rude attempt at taste; but of comfort there was little. Unknown, it was unmissed.

The Lady Rowena, three of her attendants standing at her back and arranging her hair, was seated in the higher seat. She looked as if born to exact general homage. The Pilgrim acknowledged her by a low genuflection.

'Rise, Palmer.' said she graciously. Then, to her train,

'Retire, excepting only Elgitha; I would speak with this person.'

'Pilgrim,' said the lady, after a moment's pause when she seemed uncertain how to address him, 'this night the name of Ivanhoe was mentioned in a hall where it should be welcome. Yet such is fate, that of all whose hearts leapt at the name, only I dare ask you where you left him. We heard that he remained in Palestine after the withdrawal of the English army and was persecuted by the French Templars.'

'I know little of the Knight of Ivanhoe,' answered the Palmer, his voice troubled. 'I wish I knew him better since you, lady, are concerned at his fate. However I believe he is on the eve of returning to England. There, you must know better than I what is his chance of happiness.'

Lady Rowena sighed. She then asked more particularly when Ivanhoe might be expected and whether he would be exposed to great dangers on his route. On the first point, the Palmer professed ignorance. On the second, he said that the voyage might be safely made by way of Venice, then Genoa and from thence through France to England.

'Ivanhoe,' he said, 'is well acquainted with the language and manners of the French and there was no fear of hazard during that sector of his travels.'

'Would to God,' said Rowena, 'he were here safely and fit for the approaching tournament. Should Athelstane of Coningsburgh obtain the prize, Ivanhoe will hear evil tidings when he reaches England. How looked he, stranger, when you last saw him?'

'He was darker,' said the Palmer, 'and thinner than when he came from Cyprus in the train of Richard Coeur-de-Lion. Care seemed to sit heavy on his brow.'

'He will find,' said the lady, 'little here to clear those clouds. My thanks, good Pilgrim, for your news of the companion of my childhood. Maidens,' she said, 'draw near. Offer the sleeping cup to this holy man, I will detain him no longer.' One of the maidens presented a silver cup containing a mixture of wine and spice, which Rowena barely put to her lips. It was then offered to the Palmer who tasted a few drops.

'Accept this alms, friend,' continued the lady, offering a piece of gold, 'in acknowledgment of thy travail and of the shrines visited.'

Back in the ante-room, he found his attendant Anwold who conducted him with more haste than ceremony to an exterior and ignoble part of the building. There, a number of small apartments, or rather cells, served for sleeping places to menial domestics and to strangers of low degree.

'In which of these is Isaac the Jew?' asked the Pilgrim.

'The unbelieving dog,' answered Anwold, 'is in the cell next your holiness.'

'And where sleeps Gurth the swineherd?' said the stranger.

'In the cell on your right,' replied the bondsman.

The Palmer entered the cabin, took the torch from the domestic and wished him goodnight. Shutting the door of his cell, he placed the torch in a wooden candlestick and looked around. The furniture was of the most simple kind; it consisted of a rude wooden stool and a still ruder hutch or bed-frame, stuffed with clean straw and covered with two or three sheepskins by way of bedclothes.

The Palmer extinguished his torch, threw himself on this rude couch without taking off any part of his clothes and slept till the sun first found its way through the little grated window. He then got up and after saying his Matins, went out and quietly entered the cell of Isaac. The inmate was lying in troubled slumber upon a couch, his dress being disposed carefully around his person to prevent anything being stolen. There was trouble on his brow, while his hands and arms moved convulsively as if struggling with a nightmare. The Palmer did not await the end of Isaac's dream, but stirred him with his pilgrim's staff. The touch probably entered his dream, for the old man started up. Huddling his garments about him he fixed his keen black eyes upon the Palmer.

'Fear nothing, Isaac,' said the Palmer, 'I come as a friend.'

'The God of Israel reward you,' said the other, greatly relieved, 'and what be your pleasure at so early an hour?'

'It is to tell you,' said the Palmer, 'that unless you leave this mansion now and travel with some haste, your journey may prove a dangerous one.'

'Holy father!' said the Jew, 'whom could endanger me?'

'When the Templar crossed the hall yesternight,' said the Pilgrim, 'he spoke to his Moslem slaves in Arabic, which I understand. He ordered them this morning to follow the journey of the Jew, to seize him at a convenient distance from this mansion and take him either to the castle of Philip de Malvoisin or that of Reginald Front-de-Boeuf.'

'Holy God of Abraham!' was Isaac's first exclamation, folding and elevating his wrinkled hands, but without raising his head, 'O blessed Aaron, I feel their irons already, like the axes of iron on the children of Ammon!'[1]

'Stand up, Isaac and hearken to me,' said the Palmer, 'I will show you a means of escape. Leave this mansion at once, while all yet sleep after last night's revels. I will guide you by a secret path of the forest and will not leave you till you are under safe conduct, perhaps with some chief or Baron going to the tournament.'

Isaac began to raise himself from the ground until he rested upon his knees. He threw back his long grey hair and beard, fixing his keen black eyes upon the Palmer with a look of hope, yet suspicion.

'For the love of God, young man, betray me not, for the sake of God who made Jew and Gentile. Do me no treason! I have not the means to secure the goodwill of a Christian beggar, were he charging it at a single penny.'

'Wert thou loaded with the wealth of thy tribe,' said the Palmer, 'what interest have I to injure thee? In this dress I am vowed to poverty and may only change it for a horse and a coat of mail. However, remain here if thou wilt; Cedric the Saxon may protect thee.'

---

1 Isaac was right to be terrified; *See* II Samuel 12. 31

'Alas!' said Isaac, 'he will not let me travel in his train. Saxon or Norman are equally ashamed of the poor Israelite; and to travel by myself through the domains of Philip de Malvoisin and Reginald Front-de-Boeuf. Good youth, let me come with you! Let us haste. Let us gird up our loins and flee!'

'Very well,' said the Pilgrim, giving way to the sheer urgency of his companion; 'but I must secure the means of leaving this place. Follow me.'

He led the way to the adjoining cell, occupied by Gurth the swineherd.

'Arise, Gurth.' said the Pilgrim, 'Arise quickly. Undo the postern gate and let out the Jew and me.'

Gurth, whose occupation, though now regarded as so poor, gave him as much consequence in Saxon England as that of Eumaeus[1] in Ithaca, bridled at the familiar and commanding tone of the Palmer.

'The Jew is leaving Rotherwood,' said he, raising himself on his elbow and looking superciliously at him, 'and travelling in company with the Palmer?'

'I should as soon have dreamt,' said Wamba, entering the apartment, 'of his stealing away with a gammon of bacon.'

'You will wait,' said Gurth, laying down his head on the wooden log which served as a pillow, 'Jew and Gentile must be content to await the opening of the great gate. We suffer no visitors to depart by stealth at unseasonable hours.'

'You will not,' said the Pilgrim, in a commanding tone, 'refuse me that favour.' So saying, he stooped over the bed of the recumbent swineherd and whispered something in his ear in Saxon. Gurth started up as if electrified. The Pilgrim, raising his finger to his lips to express caution, added,

'Gurth, beware. Be thou prudent. Undo the postern and thou shalt know more anon.'

With alacrity Gurth obeyed, while Wamba and the Jew followed, both wondering at the sudden change in the swineherd's demeanour.

'My mule, my mule!' said Isaac as soon as they stood outside the postern.

'Fetch his mule,' said the Pilgrim; 'and bring me another. I will return it safely to some of Cedric's train at Ashby. And do thou…' he whispered the rest in Gurth's ear.

'Willingly, most willingly,' said Gurth, and departed.

'I wish I knew,' said Wamba, when his comrade's back was turned, 'what you Palmers learn in the Holy Land.'

'To say our *orisons*, fool!' answered the Pilgrim, 'To repent our sins and to mortify ourselves with fastings, vigils and long prayers.'

'It *must* be something more potent than that,' mused the Jester; 'For when would prayer make Gurth do a courtesy, or fasting or vigil persuade him to lend you a mule?'

'Begone,' said the Pilgrim, 'thou art but a Saxon fool.'

'Well said,' replied the Jester; 'had I been born a Norman, as I think *thou* art, I would have had luck on my side and been next door to a wise man.'

At this moment, Gurth appeared on the opposite side of the moat with the mules. The travellers crossed the ditch upon a drawbridge of two planks breadth, the narrowness of which was matched by the straightness of the postern and with a little wicket in the exterior palisade giving access to the forest. No sooner had they reached the mules than the Jew, with trembling hands, secured behind the saddle a small bag

1 Swineherd to Odysseus.

of blue buckram, which he took from under his cloak. It contained, he muttered, 'a change of raiment, only a change of raiment.' Then, mounting the animal with alacrity, he lost no time in disposing of the skirts of his gabardine, thus concealing the burden now deposited *en croupe*.[1]

The Pilgrim mounted with more deliberation, extending his hand to Gurth who kissed it with veneration. The swineherd stood gazing after the travellers until they were lost under the boughs of the forest path.

'My good friend,' said the Jester, 'thou art strangely courteous and most unwontedly pious this summer morning. I wish I were a priest or a barefoot palmer to avail myself of thy new zeal and courtesy.' They went back into the mansion.

The travellers, meanwhile, continued their journey with a dispatch which showed the extent of Isaac's fear, persons of his age being seldom fond of rapid travel. The Palmer, to whom every path in the wood appeared to be familiar, led the way and thus revived the suspicions of the Israelite that he intended to lead him into harm's way.

His doubts might indeed have been pardoned. No race on earth were then the object of such unremitting and relentless persecution as were the Jews. The travellers pushed on rapidly for some time, until the Palmer at length broke silence.

'That large oak,' he said, 'marks the boundaries over which Front-de-Boeuf claims authority. We are now far from those of Malvoisin and there is no fear of pursuit.'

'May their chariot wheels be taken off,' said Isaac, 'like those of the host of Pharaoh! But leave me not, good Pilgrim. That Templar with his Saracen slaves will heed neither territory, nor lordship.'

'Our roads must separate here,' said the Palmer, 'Besides, what help would I be, a peaceful pilgrim, against armed heathens?'

'O good youth,' answered the Jew, 'defend me, and I know thou wouldst. Poor as I am, I will reward it. Not with money, but...'

'Money and recompense,' said the Palmer, interrupting him, 'I require not. Guide thee I can. Very well, Isaac, I will see thee safely to some fitting escort. We are now not far from Sheffield where there are others of thy tribe.'

'The blessing of Jacob upon thee, good youth!' said the Jew; 'in Sheffield is my kinsman Zareth where I will find means of travelling on in safety.'

'Be it so,' said the Palmer; 'until Sheffield then.' A half hour of riding brought them in sight of the town when the pilgrim said again, 'Here, then, we part.'

'Not till you have had the poor Jew's thanks,' said Isaac; 'for I ask you to go with me to my kinsman Zareth who might aid me in repaying your good offices.'

'I have already said,' answered the Pilgrim, 'that I desire no recompense. If among thy debtors, thou wilt spare some Christian, I shall hold this morning's service to thee well bestowed.'

'Stay, stay,' said Isaac, laying hold of his garment, 'something would I do more, something for thyself. Forgive me if I guess what thou may need most at this moment.'

'If thou were to guess rightly,' said the Palmer, 'it is still what thou may not supply.'

'Thy wish even now is for a horse and armour,' said Isaac.

The Palmer started and turned suddenly towards the Jew.

'What prompted that guess?' said he, hastily.

---

[1] Behind the rider.

'No matter,' said the Jew, smiling, 'given that it be a true one. And, just as I guessed thy want, so also I can supply it. Words have come from you which, like sparks from flint, showed the metal within. In the bosom of that Palmer's gown is hidden a knight's chain and spurs of gold.They flashed as you stooped over my bed in the morning.' The Pilgrim could not forbear smiling.

'Were thy own garments searched by as curious an eye, Isaac,' said he, 'what discoveries might not then be made?'

'No more of that,' said the Jew. Drawing forth his writing materials in haste to stop the conversation, he began to write upon a paper without dismounting. When he had finished he delivered the Hebrew note to the Palmer, saying,

'In the town of Leicester all men know the Jew, Kirjath Jairam of Lombardy. Give him this. He hath on sale six Milan suits of armour and ten goodly steeds. Of these he will give thee thy choice, with whatever else is required for the tournament. When it is over, return them – or pay their value to Jairam.'

'But, Isaac,' said the Pilgrim, smiling, 'in these sports, the arms and steed of an unhorsed knight are forfeited to his victor. I may thus lose what I cannot replace or repay.'

The Jew looked astounded at this possibility but, collecting his courage, he replied hastily,

'No! It is impossible. I will not think so. The blessing of Our Father will be upon thee. May thy lance be powerful as the rod of Moses!' So saying, he was turning his mule's head away, whereupon the Palmer took hold of his gaberdine.

'Nay, Isaac, there is yet more risk. The steed may be slain, the armour damaged, for I will spare neither horse nor man. Besides, thy tribe gives nothing for nothing; something must be paid for their use.'

'I care not,' he said, 'I care not. Let me go. If there is damage, it will cost you nothing. If there is usage money, Kirjath Jairam will forego it for the sake of his kinsman Isaac. Fare thee well! Yet hark thee, good youth,' said he, turning round, 'be not too forward in this hurly-burly. I speak not for fear for the steed and coat of armour, but for the sake of thy life and limb.'

'*Gramercy* for thy caution,' said the Palmer, smiling. 'I will take thy offer frankly – and I will repay it.' Thus they parted; and took different roads for Sheffield.

chapter seven

Knights, with a long retinue of their squires,
In gaudy liveries march and quaint attires;
One laced the helm, another held the lance,
A third the shining buckler did advance. .
John Dryden: *Palamon and Arcite*

The condition of the English nation was miserable. King Richard was absent; a prisoner of the perfidious Duke of Austria.[1] The place of his captivity was

[1] Leopold V (1157–1194).

uncertain and his fate unknown to his subjects who were meanwhile a prey to every species of oppression. Prince John was in league with Philip of France, Coeur-de-Lion's mortal enemy, who was using his influence with the Duke of Austria to prolong the King's captivity. In the meantime, John was strengthening his own faction in England to dispute the succession in the event of the King's death. The legitimate heir was Arthur, Duke of Brittany, the son of Geoffrey Plantagenet, John's elder brother. His own character being profligate and perfidious, John easily attracted those who had reason to dread the return of Richard for criminality during his absence. John also attracted the numerous *lawless resolutes*[1] back from the Crusades and proficient in the vices of the East. Impoverished and hardened, these desperados placed their hopes of harvest in civil commotion.

To such causes of public distress were added a multitude of outlaws, driven by despair into large gangs by the oppression of the feudal nobility and the severity of the Forest Laws. The nobles, each fortified within his own castle and the petty sovereign of his own dominions, were the leaders of bands scarcely less lawless. To maintain these retainers and to support their general extravagance, they borrowed money from the Jews at usurious rates of interest. These gnawed into their estate revenues like cancers, curable only by applying violence to their creditors. In this state of affairs, the people of England suffered deeply. To augment their misery, contagious diseases spread through the land, rendered virulent by poor food and the wretched lodgings of the lower classes. These plagues carried off many, whose fate the survivors were tempted to envy.

Amid these accumulated distresses, the poor as well as the rich, the commoner and the noble, all looked forward to the grand spectacle of the age, a Tournament. Such a Passage of Arms, as it was called, which was to take place at Ashby de la Zouche[2] in the county of Leicester, had attracted universal attention. Champions of the greatest renown were to fight in the presence of Prince John himself. Thus, upon the appointed day, an immense confluence of all ranks were to be found assembled at the place of combat.

The scene was singularly romantic. On the verge of a wood within a mile of the town of Ashby, was an extensive meadow of fine green turf. It was surrounded on one side by forest and fringed on the other by straggling oak trees, some of immense size. The ground, as if fashioned on purpose for spectating a martial display, sloped gradually down on all sides to a level bottom. This was enclosed with strong palisades for the lists,[3] forming a space of a quarter of a mile in length, and about half as broad. The form of the enclosure was an oblong square, the corners rounded off for the convenience of the spectators. The access of the combatants, from the northern and southern extremities of the lists, was by means of strong wooden gates wide enough to admit two horsemen abreast. At each of these portals were stationed two Heralds, attended by six trumpeters, six *pursuivants*[4] and a strong body of men-at-arms for maintaining order.

---

1 Desperados bent on civil strife. Fortinbras, Prince of Norway also had them ; See *Hamlet*, I.I.

2 Of Anglo-Danish origin, lit. Ash-tree farm. The Norman-French addition dates from the reign of Henry III, when the town became a possession of the de la Zouche family.

3 The divided runway along which the jousting combatants charged.

4 An Officer of a College of Arms, ranking below a Herald.

Beyond the southern entrance and on a platform formed by a natural elevation of the ground, were pitched five magnificent pavilions. These were adorned with pennons of russet and black, the chosen colours of the five knight Champions, the cords of the tents being of the same colours. In front of each pavilion was suspended the heraldic shield of the knight by whom it was occupied and beside it stood his squire. He was either quaintly disguised as a savage or sylvan man, or in some other fantastic dress, according to the taste of his master.

The central pavilion, the place of honour, was assigned to Sir Brian de Bois Guilbert, whose renown had led him to be adopted as leader of the Champions. On one side of his tent were pitched those of Reginald Front-de-Boeuf and Richard de Malvoisin and on the other was the pavilion of Hugh de Grantmesnil, a noble baron in the vicinity. Ralph de Vipont, a Knight of St John of Jerusalem who had ancient possessions at Heather near Ashby-de-la-Zouche, occupied the fifth pavilion. From the entrance into the lists, a gently sloping passage, ten yards in breadth, led up to the platform on which the tents were pitched. It was strongly secured by a palisade on each side, as was the esplanade in front of the pavilions, the whole being guarded by men-at-arms.

The northern access to the lists terminated in a similar entrance, thirty feet in breadth, at the extremity of which was a large enclosed space for such knights as might wish to enter the lists with the Champions. Behind were placed tents containing refreshments of every kind, with others for armourers, farriers and other attendants.

Bordering the lists were temporary galleries spread with tapestry and carpeted and cushioned for the convenience of ladies and nobles attending the tournament. The narrow space betwixt these galleries and the lists gave accommodation for yeomanry and spectators of a higher degree than the commonality and might be compared to the pit of a theatre. The common multitude arranged themselves upon large banks of turf prepared for the purpose and which, aided by the natural elevation of the ground, enabled them to overlook the galleries and obtain a good view into the lists. Besides the accommodation provided, hundreds more were perched on the branches of the trees surrounding the meadow, even a church steeple some distance away being crowded with spectators.

One gallery in the very centre of the eastern side of the lists, and thus opposite the spot where the shock of each combat would take place, was raised higher than the others. It was also more richly decorated and graced by a throne and canopy on which the royal arms were emblazoned. Liveried squires, pages and yeomen waited around this place of honour, designated for Prince John and his attendants. Opposite the royal gallery, on the western side of the lists, was another elevated to the same height and more gaily, if less sumptuously, decorated than that of the Prince. A train of pages and young maidens gaily dressed in fancy habits of green and pink, surrounded a throne decorated in the same colours. Among pennons and flags bearing wounded hearts, burning hearts, bleeding hearts, bows and quivers and all the emblems of the triumphs of Cupid, a blazoned inscription informed the spectators that this seat of honour was designed for '*La Royne de la Beaulte et des Amours.*' But, as to who would be appointed the Queen of Beauty and of Love on the present occasion was yet unknown.

Meanwhile, spectators of every description thronged forward to occupy their respective stations, not without disputes over those which they were entitled to hold. Some of these were settled by the men-at-arms, employing the shafts of their battle-axes and pummels of their swords for the purpose. Others, which involved rival claims of more elevated personages, were determined by the Heralds, or by the two Marshals of the Field, William de Wyvil, and Stephen de Martival. Fully armed, they rode up and down the lists, enforcing and preserving order.

Gradually the galleries became filled with knights and nobles wearing their robes of peace, whose long and tinted mantles contrasted with the gayer and more splendid habits of their ladies. The lower and interior space was soon filled by substantial yeomen, burgesses and such of the lesser gentry who, from poverty or dubious title, dared not assume a higher place. It was naturally amongst these that the most frequent disputes for precedence occurred.

'Dog of an unbeliever,' said an old man, whose threadbare tunic bore witness to his poverty, whereas his sword, dagger, and golden chain intimated pretensions to rank, 'How dare thou press upon a Christian and a Norman gentleman of the blood of Montdidier?'

This was addressed to none other than Isaac of York, richly dressed now in a gaberdine ornamented with lace and lined with fur, who was endeavouring to make place in the foremost row beneath the gallery for his daughter. This was the beautiful Rebecca, who had joined him at Ashby and was now on her father's arm, not a little apprehensive of the popular displeasure excited by her parent.

Isaac, however, though timid on other occasions, knew well that at present he had nothing to fear. No malevolent noble dared offer him injury in places of general resort, or where their equals were assembled. At such meetings the Jews were under the protection of the common law and if that proved a weak assurance, there would be barons ready to act as their protectors. On the present occasion, Isaac felt more than usually confident, aware that Prince John was in the act of negotiating a large loan, secured upon certain jewels and land, from the Jews of York. Isaac had a considerable share in this transaction and knew that the Prince's desire to conclude it would ensure his protection.

Emboldened by these considerations, Isaac pursued his point and jostled the Norman Christian. The protests of the old man, however, excited the indignation of the bystanders. One of these was a well-set yeoman, arrayed in Lincoln green, 12 arrows stuck in his belt, with a baldric[1] and badge of silver, and a six foot bow in his hand. He turned quickly round, his countenance brown as a hazelnut and dark with anger. He advised Isaac to remember that his wealth had swelled him like a bloated spider which might be overlooked in a corner, but crushed if it ventured into the light. This warning was delivered in Norman-English with a firm voice and a stern look. Isaac might well have retreated from such a threat had not the attention of everyone been commanded by the sudden entrance of the Prince.

John of Anjou was attended by a numerous train of laymen and churchmen, the latter as gay in demeanour as their companions. Among them was the Prior of Jorvaulx

---

1 A Leather girdle passing over one shoulder and down to the opposite waist. Worn like a British officer's Sam Browne belt. To the lower end a bugle, sword or other weaponry might be fixed. Also the servant and butt of Edmund Blackadder.

in the most gallant costume which a dignitary of the Church could venture to exhibit. Fur and gold were not spared in his garments and the points of his boots, in the preposterous fashion of the time, were turned up so far as to be attached not just to his knees but to his very girdle, thus effectively preventing him from putting a foot in the stirrup. The rest of Prince John's retinue consisted of favoured leaders of his mercenary troops, some marauding Barons and hangers-on of the court and several Knights Templars and Knights Hospitallers of St John of Jerusalem.

The knights of these two Orders were hostile to King Richard, having taken the side of King Philip of France in the long series of disputes in Palestine betwixt that monarch and the Lionheart. It was the well-known consequence of this discord that Richard's repeated victories had been rendered fruitless and his attempts to besiege Jerusalem disappointed, while the fruits of all the glory he had acquired dwindled into an uncertain truce with the Saracen commander, Sultan Saladin.

Following the policy of their brethren in the Holy Land, the Templars and Hospitallers in England and Normandy attached themselves to the faction of Prince John. They had no reason to desire the return of Richard to England or the succession of Prince Arthur, his legitimate heir. Conversely, for their support for Richard, Prince John condemned those Saxon families of consequence which subsisted in England and omitted no opportunity of affronting them. He was conscious that both he and his pretensions were disliked by them and by the greater part of the English commons. Both feared further intrusion upon their rights and liberties from a sovereign of John's disposition.

Attended by his gallant equipage, well mounted and splendidly dressed in crimson and in gold, Prince John arrived, a falcon upon his hand and a rich fur bonnet on his head. This was adorned with a circle of precious stones and below it his long curled hair escaped and overspread his shoulders. The Prince's grey and high-mettled palfrey *caracoled*[1] within the lists as he eyed, with all the boldness of royalty, the beauties who adorned the lofty galleries

Those who noted a haughtiness in the dissolute Prince could not deny his personal comeliness. His features, well formed by nature and seemingly open and honest, disclaimed the natural workings of his soul. His expression was often mistaken for manly frankness when in truth it arose from the reckless indifference of the royal libertine, conscious of superiority by birth. To those who did not think deeply, the sheer splendour of Prince John, the richness of his cloak, lined with costly sables; his maroquin[2] boots and golden spurs, together with the grace with which he managed his palfrey, merited clamorous applause.

In his joyous caracole round the lists, the attention of the Prince was attracted by the commotion attending the ambitious movement of Isaac towards the higher places of the assembly. Prince John instantly recognised the Jew but was much more agreeably attracted by the beautiful daughter of Zion on the arm of her aged father.

The figure of Rebecca bore comparison with the proudest beauties of England when judged by as shrewd a connoisseur as Prince John. Her form was exquisitely symmetrical, shown to advantage by the Eastern dress worn according to the fashion

---

1 From Sp. *Caracol*, a snail. In dressage, a caracole is a half-turn to right or left.

2 Of Moroccan leather.

of her nation. Her turban was of yellow silk, well suited to the darkness of her complexion. The brilliancy of her eyes, the superb arch of her eyebrows, her aquiline nose, teeth white as pearl and the profusion of her raven-black hair were equal to any of the maidens around her. Of the pearl-studded clasps which closed her vest from throat to waist, the three uppermost were left unfastened on account of the heat, thus enlarging the prospect. The feather of an ostrich, fastened in her turban by an *agraffe*[1] set with brilliance, was another distinction of the beautiful Jewess. Although sneered at, she was also secretly envied by the proud dames who sat above her.

'By the scalp of Abraham,' said Prince John, 'yonder Jewess shows what drove Solomon frantic! What sayest thou, Prior Aymer? By his Temple, which our brother Richard proved unable to recover, she is the very Bride of the Canticles!'[2]

'A Rose of Sharon and a Lily of the Valley,' answered the Prior, in a snuffling tone, 'but remember, your Grace, she is still only a Jewess.'

'Aye!' added Prince John, without heeding him, 'and there is Isaac, my man of Mammon; a Marquis of Marks and Baron of Byzants, contesting for his place with penniless dogs. My prince of finance with his lovely Jewess shall have a place in the gallery!' He called to the Jew:

'What is she, Isaac? Thy wife or thy daughter; that Eastern *houri* locked under thy arm like a treasure-casket?'

'My daughter Rebecca, so please your Grace,' called Isaac, with a low *congée*,[3] unembarrassed by the Prince's salutation in which there was as much mockery as courtesy.

'The wiser man thou,' said John with a peal of laughter in which his followers joined. 'But, daughter or wife, she should be placed according to her beauty. Who sits above you there?' he continued, bending his eye on the gallery. 'Saxon churls, lolling at their lazy length! Let them sit closer and make room for my prince of usurers and his lovely daughter!'

Occupying the gallery to which this was addressed were the Saxon family of Cedric of Rotherwood, together with that of his kinsman, Athelstane of Coningsburgh. This personage, on account of his descent from King Harold, the last Saxon monarch of England, was held in the highest respect by all Saxons. However, along with the blood of this ancient royal race, many of their infirmities had also descended to Athelstane. He was comely in countenance, strong in person and in the flower of his maturity; yet inanimate in expression, dull-eyed and heavy-browed. He was sluggish in movement and so slow in resolution that the soubriquet of one of his ancestors[4] was applied to him; he was 'Athelstane the Unready.' His friends, and he had many who, like Cedric, were passionately attached to him, contended that his sluggish temper arose not from lack of courage, but of decision. Others alleged that the hereditary vice of gluttony and drunkenness had obscured mental faculties, never of an acute order.

It was to this person that the Prince addressed his imperious command to make place for Isaac and Rebecca. Athelstane, utterly confounded at an order which the

---

1 A richly ornamented clasp.

2 The beautiful bride, never identified, of the *Song of Solomon*.

3 A ceremonial bow.

4 King Ethelred II (*c*.968–1016).

manners of the times rendered insulting, was unwilling to obey yet unsure how to resist. He therefore opposed only the '*vis inertiae*'[1] to the will of John and, without stirring or making any motion whatever of obedience, opened his large grey eyes and stared at the Prince in ludicrous astonishment. The impatient John, however, regarded it in no such light.

'That Saxon pig,' he said, 'is either asleep or minds me not. Prick him with your lance, De Bracy,' speaking to a knight who rode near him. This was the leader of a band of Free Companions, or *Condottieri.*[2] There was a murmur, even among the attendants of Prince John, but De Bracy extended his long lance towards the gallery from the lists. He would have executed the command, had not Athelstane recovered sufficient presence of mind to draw back. Cedric, however, as prompt in action as his companion was tardy, unsheathed his short sword and with a single blow, severed the point of the lance. The blood rushed into the face of Prince John. He swore one of his deepest oaths and was about to utter a violent threat, but was diverted by the loud applause for Cedric's spirited action and by his own attendants adjuring him to be patient. The Prince rolled his eyes in indignation, looking to pick out some safer and easier victim and chanced to meet the firm glance of the archer already mentioned who persisted in his applause despite the frown of the Prince. John demanded his reason.

'I always add my hollo,' said the yeoman, 'when I see a good shot or a gallant blow.'

'Indeed?' answered the Prince; 'then thou can hit the bull's eye thyself, I'll warrant.'

'A woodsman's mark and at woodsman's distance, I can hit,' answered the yeoman.

'And Wat Tyrrel's mark, at a *hundred* yards...' said an undiscerned voice from behind.

This allusion to the assassin[3] of his ancestor King William Rufus, incensed and alarmed Prince John. He satisfied himself, however, by commanding the men-at-arms surrounding the lists to keep an eye on the braggart.

'By St Grizzel,' he added, 'we will test his skill!'

'I shall not flee the trial,' said the yeoman composedly.

'Stand up, Saxon churls!' cried the fiery Prince. 'By the light of Heaven, I have spoken that the Jew shall have his seat amongst ye!'

'By no means, may it please your Grace! It is not fit for such as we to sit with them.' So said Isaac, whose ambition for precedence might lead him to dispute place with the impoverished Montdidier but not to an intrusion upon wealthy Saxons.

'Up, infidel dog when I command you,' said Prince John, 'or I will have thy swarthy hide off and tanned for horse-furniture.' The Jew began to ascend the steep and narrow steps which led up to the gallery.

'Let me see,' said the Prince, 'who dares stop him,' and he fixed his eyes on Cedric, whose attitude bespoke such an intention. The potential catastrophe was prevented by the clown Wamba who sprang betwixt Cedric and Isaac, exclaiming in answer to the Prince,

'Marry, that will I!' He held up before Isaac a leg of pork, plucked from beneath his cloak and which he had brought lest the tournament prove longer than his appetite

---

1 Lat. 'Strength from inertia.'

2 Mercenaries belonging to no particular nation, but attached to any paymaster prince. *Scott.*

3 Sir Walter 'Wat' Tyrrel shot the King during a hunt in the New Forest, AD 1100.

could endure. Finding this abomination held to his very nose while the Jester flourished his wooden sword above his head, Isaac recoiled, lost his footing and tumbled back down the steps. The spectators' laughter was joined by Prince John and his attendants.

'Deal me the prize, cousin Prince,' said Wamba; 'I have vanquished in fair fight with sword and shield,' he added, brandishing the pork in one hand and the wooden sword in the other.

'Who and what art thou, noble champion?' said Prince John, still laughing.

'A fool by right of descent,' answered the Jester. 'I am Wamba, the son of Witless, who was the son of an Alderman.'

'Make room for the Jew in front of the lower ring,' said Prince John, 'Here, Isaac, lend me a handful of byzants.'

The Jew, now back on his feet and was startled by the request, was afraid to refuse yet unwilling to comply. He fumbled in the furred bag which hung by his girdle, wondering just how few coins might pass for a handful. The Prince stooped from his jennet and settled Isaac's doubts by snatching the pouch from his side. Flinging Wamba a couple of gold pieces from it, he pursued his career round the lists, leaving Isaac to the derision of those around him, while himself receiving applause.

chapter eight

At this the challenger with fierce defy
His trumpet sounds; the challenged makes reply:
With clangour rings the field, resounds the vaulted sky.
Their visors closed, their lances in the rest,
Or at the helmet pointed or the crest,
They vanish from the barrier, speed the race,
And spurring see decrease the middle space.
John Dryden: *Palamon and Arcite*

In the midst of his cavalcade, Prince John suddenly stopped. Addressing the Prior of Jorvaulx, he declared that one principal business of the day had been forgotten.

'Sir Prior,' said he, 'we have not yet named the fair Sovereign of Love and of Beauty. I give my vote for the black-eyed Rebecca.'

'Holy Virgin,' cried the Prior, turning up his eyes in horror, 'a Jewess! We should be stoned out of the lists – and I am not old enough to be a martyr yet! Besides, I swear that she is far inferior to Saxon Rowena.'

'Saxon or Jew,' said the Prince, 'dog or hog, what matters it? I say, name Rebecca, if only to mortify those Saxon churls.'

A murmur then arose even among his own immediate attendants.

'This passes a jest, my lord!' said De Bracy, 'No knight here will lay his lance in rest if such an insult is attempted.'

'It is the mere *wantonness* of insult,' said one of the oldest and most important of Prince John's followers, Waldemar Fitzurse, 'and if your Grace attempts it, it will be ruinous to your projects.'

'I employ thee, Sir,' said John, reining up his palfrey, 'for my follower – not for my counsellor.'

'Those who follow the paths *you* tread,' said Waldemar, in a low voice, 'acquire the right of counsellors. Your interest and safety are not more deeply engaged than our own...' From the tone of this, John saw the necessity of yielding.

'I did but jest,' he said; 'and ye turn upon me like so many adders! Name whom ye will, in the Fiend's name. Please thyself.'

'Nay, nay,' said De Bracy, 'let the fair Sovereign's throne remain unoccupied until the conqueror is named; and then let *him* choose the lady. It will add another grace to his triumph and teach ladies to prize the love of a valiant knight.'

'If Sir Brian de Bois Guilbert gains the prize,' said the Prior, 'I will give my rosary for the right to name the Sovereign of Love and Beauty.'

'Bois Guilbert,' answered De Bracy, 'is a good lance. But there are others around these lists, Sir Prior, who will not fear to encounter him...'

'Silence, Sirs.' said Waldemar, 'Let the Prince assume his seat. The knights and spectators are impatient. Let the sports commence.'

Prince John, though not yet a monarch, had in Waldemar Fitzurse a favourite minister who, while serving his sovereign, must always do so in his own way. The Prince acquiesced, although his disposition was to be obstinate upon trifles. Assuming his throne and surrounded by his followers, he gave a signal. The Heralds then loudly proclaimed the Laws of the Tournament:

Firstly, the five Champions were to engage all comers.

Secondly, any knight challenging by combat might select a particular antagonist from among the Champions by touching his shield. If he did so with the reverse of his lance, the trial of skill would be made with the 'arms of courtesy,' that is, with lances tipped with a piece of round flat board. Thus, no danger would be encountered, save the shock of collision to horses and riders. But if the shield was touched with the sharp end of the lance, the combat was understood to be at '*A l'outrance*'[1] with sharp weapons, as in actual battle.

Thirdly, when the knights had accomplished their vow, by each of them breaking five lances, the Prince was to declare the victor in the first day's tourney. He would receive as his prize, a warhorse of exquisite beauty and strength. In addition, he would also have the unique honour of naming the Queen of Love and Beauty, by whom the Prize would be awarded on the ensuing day.

Fourthly, it was announced that on the second day there should be a General Tournament in which all the knights present might take part. Divided into two bands of equal numbers, they would fight it out until the signal was given by Prince John to cease the combat. The elected Queen of Love and Beauty was then to crown the knight whom the Prince should adjudge to have borne himself best on this second day. The prize would be a coronet of gold plate, cut into the shape of a laurel crown; and with this the knightly games would cease. However, on the following day, feats

---

1 To the death.

of archery, bull-baiting and other popular amusements were to be practised for the amusement of the populace.

The lists now presented a splendid spectacle. The sloping galleries were crowded with all that was noble, wealthy and beautiful in northern and midland England. The brilliant dress among the upper spectators rendered the scene as gay as it was rich, while the lower space was filled with the substantial burgesses and yeomen of England in plainer attire. They formed a dark fringe around the circle of brilliant embroidery, thus relieving, and at the same time setting off, its splendour.

The Heralds finished their proclamation with their usual cry:

'*Largesse*, *largesse*, gallant knights!' whereupon gold and silver pieces were showered on them from the galleries. It was a high point of chivalry to be generous towards those whom the age regarded as both the secretaries and the historians of honour. The bounty of the spectators was acknowledged by the customary shouts of: 'Love of Ladies – Death of Champions – Honour to the Generous and Glory to the Brave!' To this the spectators added their shouts, as a band of trumpeters sounded their martial instruments.

When the fanfare had ceased, the Heralds withdrew from the lists in gay and glittering procession. None remained within save the Marshals of the Field. These, armed *cap-a-pie*,[1] sat on horseback, motionless as statues, at opposite ends of the lists. Meantime, the enclosed space at the northern extremity of the lists, large as it was, was now crowded with knights desirous to prove their skill against the Champions. Viewed from the galleries, they presented the appearance of a sea of waving plumage intermixed with glistening helmets and tall lances. To the tips of these were attached small pennons of about a hand-span's breadth and which, fluttering in the air as the breeze caught them, added liveliness to the scene.

At length the barriers were opened and five knights, chosen by lot, advanced slowly into the area; a single Challenger riding in front and the other four, splendidly armed, following in pairs. To borrow lines from a contemporary poet, who has written but too little:

The knights are dust,
Their good swords rust,
Their souls are with the Saints, we trust...[2]

Now, however, oblivious of the fate which awaited their swords and souls, the Challengers advanced through the lists. They restrained their fiery steeds, compelling them to move slowly. The chargers thus showed off their paces together with the grace and dexterity of their riders. As the procession entered the lists, the sound of a wild Barbaric music of Eastern origin was heard coming from behind the tents of the Champions. Brought from the Holy Land, the mixture of cymbals and bells seemed to bid both welcome and defiance to the Challenger knights as they advanced, the eyes of the spectators fixed upon them. The five knights advanced up the platform upon which the tents of the Champions stood. Separating themselves there, each touched lightly – and with the *reverse* of his lance – the shield of the antagonist he

1 Norman French: Lit. head to foot.

2 S.T. Coleridge, whose Muse so often tantalizes with fragments which indicate her powers, while the manner in which she flings them from her, betrays her caprice. *Scott.*

wished to engage. Having intimated their purpose, the Challengers retreated to the extremity of the lists, where they remained drawn up in a line. The Champions, each sallying from his pavilion, mounted their horses and, headed by Brian de Bois Guilbert, descended from the platform and lined up opposite the knight who had touched his shield.

After a fanfare of clarions and trumpets, they rode against each other at full gallop. Such was the superior dexterity of the Champions that those opposed to Bois Guilbert, Malvoisin and Front-de-Boeuf, crashed to the ground. The antagonist of Grantmesnil, instead of bearing his lance-point fair against the crest or the shield of his enemy, swerved from the direct line and broke the weapon across the person of his opponent. This was a circumstance held more disgraceful than being actually unhorsed, since the latter might happen accidentally, whereas the former evinced awkwardness and poor management of weapon or horse, or both. The fifth knight alone maintained the honour of his party against the Knight of St John, both splintering their lances without advantage on either side.

The shouts of the multitude, together with the acclamations of the Heralds and the clangour of the trumpets, announced the triumph of the victors and the defeat of the vanquished. The former retreated to their pavilions while the latter, gathering themselves up as best they could, withdrew from the lists to bargain with their victors. This was over the redemption of their arms and their horses which, according to the Laws of the Tournament, were now forfeit.

A second and then a third party of knights now took the field. Although they had various success, upon the whole the advantage decidedly remained with the Champions, not one of whom lost his seat or swerved from his charge, a fate which befell some of their antagonists in each encounter. Three knights only appeared on the fourth entry. They, avoiding the shields of Bois Guilbert and Front-de-Boeuf, contented themselves with touching those of the three other knights, who were of lesser strength and dexterity. This canny selection did not alter the fortune of the field, for the Champions were still successful. One of their antagonists was unhorsed and both the others failed in the *attaint*,[1] that is, in striking the helmet or shield of their antagonist firmly and strongly, with the lance held in a direct line so that the weapon would break unless the opponent were overthrown. After this fourth encounter there was a considerable pause and it did not appear that anyone was desirous of renewing the contest. The spectators murmured among themselves for, among the Champions, Malvoisin and Front-de-Boeuf were unpopular characters while the others, excepting Grantmesnil, were disliked as strangers and foreigners.

None shared the general feeling of dissatisfaction so keenly as Cedric the Saxon, who saw each victory by the Norman Champions as a triumph over the honour of England. His own education had not included jousting, although with the arms of his Saxon ancestors, he had on many occasions proved himself to be a brave and determined soldier. He looked anxiously at Athelstane who, in contrast, had learned the jousting art. Athelstane, however, though stout of heart and strong, was inert and unambitious.

'The day goes against England, my lord.' said Cedric, in a marked tone. 'Are you not tempted to take the lance?'

---

1 This term of Chivalry, transferred to the Law, gave the phrase of being 'attainted of treason.' *Scott.*

'I shall tilt tomorrow,' answered Athelstane, 'in the *melee*. It is not worthwhile to arm myself today.'

Two things displeased Cedric in this. It both contained the Norman word *melee*, general conflict, and it showed indifference to the honour of his country. However, as Cedric held Athelstane in profound respect, he could not enquire as to his motives. Wamba then observed,

'It was better, though scarce easier, to be the best man among a hundred, than the best of two.' Athelstane took this observation as a serious compliment, but Cedric, better understanding the Jester's meaning, darted him a severe and menacing look. The pause in the tournament was still uninterrupted, excepting by the voices of the Heralds crying,

'Love of ladies, splintering of lances! Come forth gallant knights; fair eyes look upon your deeds!'

The eastern music of the Champions breathed, from time to time, wild bursts expressive of triumph or defiance, while the clowns[1] grudged a holiday which now seemed to be passing away in inactivity. Old knights and nobles whispered of the decay of martial spirit and recalled the triumphs of their younger days, when dames of transcendent beauty animated the jousts. Prince John began to talk to his attendants about making ready the banquet and of awarding the prize to Brian de Bois Guilbert who, with a single lance, had unhorsed two knights and foiled a third.

At length, the Saracenic music of the Champions concluded one of the long and high flourishes with which they broke the silence of the lists. This time it was answered by a solitary trumpet which breathed a note of defiance from the opposite extremity. All eyes turned to see the new Challenger thus announced and no sooner were the barriers opened than he paced into the lists. As far as could be judged of a man sheathed in armour, the new adventurer did not exceed the middle size and seemed to be more slightly than strongly made. His suit of armour was formed of steel, richly inlaid with gold and the device on his shield was a young oak tree pulled up by the roots, with the Spanish word *Desdichado,* meaning Disinherited. He was mounted on a gallant black horse and as he passed through the lists he gracefully saluted the Prince and the ladies by lowering his lance. The dexterity with which he managed his steed and the youthful grace which he displayed drew the favour of the multitude. Some of the lower classes expressed this, calling out,

'Touch Ralph de Vipont's shield! Touch the Hospitaller's shield. He is your cheapest bargain.'

The Challenger, moving forward amid these well meant hints, ascended to the platform by the sloping alley which led up from the lists. To the astonishment of all present, he rode straight up to the central pavilion and struck – with the sharp end of his lance – the shield of Brian de Bois Guilbert until it rung. All stood amazed at this boldness, none more so than the redoubtable Knight thus challenged to mortal combat. Little expecting such a challenge, he was standing carelessly at the door of his pavilion.

'Have you confessed yourself, brother,' said the Templar, 'and have you heard Mass this morning, that you so peril your life?'

---

1 A mediaeval clown was simply a rustic. The term was descriptive, not pejorative.

'I am fitter to meet death than thou.'

'Then take to the lists,' said Bois Guilbert, 'and look your last upon the sun – for this night shalt thou sleep in Paradise.'

'Gramercy for thy courtesy,' replied the Disinherited Knight, 'and in return I advise thee to take a fresh horse and a new lance, for by my honour, you will need *both*.' So saying, he reined his horse backwards down the slope which he had ascended. He then backed him along the full length of the lists till he reached the northern extremity. There he remained stationary in expectation of his antagonist, this feat of horsemanship attracting renewed applause.

Incensed at his adversary for the insolently offered advice, Brian de Bois Guilbert did not, however, neglect it. His honour was too much involved to neglect any means of ensuring victory over this presumptuous opponent. He changed his horse for a fresh one and took a new and tough lance, lest the wood of the former had been strained. He also laid aside his damaged shield and took another from his squires. His first had only borne the general device of two Knights riding upon one horse, an emblem which expressed the original humility and poverty of the Templars. These they had long since exchanged for the arrogance and wealth which would finally cause their suppression.[1] Bois Guilbert's new shield bore a raven in full flight, holding in its claws a human skull and bearing the motto, '*Gare le Corbeau*'.[2]

When the two Knights stood opposed to each other at the opposite extremities of the lists, public expectation rose to fever pitch. Few reckoned that the encounter could end well for the Disinherited Knight, yet the general goodwill of the spectators was secured by his courage and gallantry. The trumpets gave the signal. Both men launched from their posts at speed, closing in the centre of the lists and then meeting with the shock of a thunderbolt. Both lances burst into shivers up to the very grasp and it seemed for a moment that both knights had fallen, the shock of collision making each horse recoil upon its haunches. The skill of the riders, however, recovered their steeds by bridle and spur. Having glared at each other for an instant with eyes flashing through the bars of their visors, each made a *demi-volte* and rode on to the extremity of the lists to receive a fresh lance.

A roar from the spectators and the waving of scarves and handkerchiefs attested their interest in this encounter which was the most evenly matched and the best performed so far. But no sooner had the knights resumed their stations, than the clamour of applause was hushed into a silence so deep and dead that it seemed as if the crowd feared to breathe. A few minutes pause allowed the combatants and their horses to recover breath and then Prince John's truncheon again signalled the trumpets to sound the onset. The knights then sprang a second time from their stations and closed in the centre of the lists with the same speed, dexterity and violence – but not with the same equal fortune as before.

In this second encounter, the Templar aimed at the centre of his antagonist's shield, and struck it so fair and forcibly, that his spear went to shivers and the Disinherited Knight reeled in his saddle. The Challenger had directed the point of his lance towards Bois Guilbert's shield. Changing his aim, however, at almost the

---

1 Pope Clement v disbanded the Order in 1312. He acted under pressure from King Philip iv of France, who had burned many Templars at the stake,

2 *Beware the Crow!*

moment of encounter, he aimed now at the helmet. This was a mark more difficult to hit but which, if attained, rendered the shock irresistible. Fair and true he hit the Norman on the visor, where his lance's point jammed in the bars. Had the girths of his saddle not burst, the Templar might not have been unhorsed. But burst they did and saddle, horse and man all crashed to the ground, rolling over in a cloud of dust.

To extricate himself from his stirrups and fallen steed was for the Templar scarce the work of a moment. Stung with rage at his disgrace and at its acclaim by the spectators, he drew his sword and brandished it at the Disinherited Knight who dismounted, unsheathing his own sword. The Marshals, however, spurred their horses between them, calling out to both that the Laws of this tournament did not permit such an encounter.

'We shall meet again, I *trust*,' said the Templar, casting a resentful glance at his antagonist; 'and where there will be *none* to separate us.'

'If we do not,' said the Disinherited Knight, 'the fault shall not be mine. On foot or horseback I am ready for thee.' More and angrier words would have followed, had not the Marshals crossed their own lances betwixt them, compelling them to separate. The Disinherited Knight returned to his first station and Bois Guilbert strode to his tent, remaining there for the rest of the day in impotent fury.

Without alighting from his horse, the conqueror called for a bowl of wine. Opening the beaver, or lower part of his helmet, he announced a toast, 'To all true English hearts, and to the confusion of foreign tyrants.' He then commanded his trumpeter to sound a Defiance to the Champions and told a Herald to announce to them that he would make no choice, but would engage them in any order.

The gigantic Front-de-Boeuf in his black armour was the first to take the field. His white shield bore a black bull's head, half obliterated by numerous previous jousting encounters and bearing the arrogant motto, *Cave Adsum.*[1] Over this Champion, the Disinherited Knight obtained a decisive advantage. Both knights broke their lances fairly but Front-de-Boeuf lost a stirrup, and was adjudged to have the disadvantage. The stranger's third encounter, with Sir Philip Malvoisin, was equally successful. He struck that Baron so forcibly on the casque that the laces of the helmet broke. Malvoisin, only saved from falling by being unhelmed, was declared vanquished like his companions.

In his fourth combat, with De Grantmesnil, the Disinherited Knight showed as much courtesy as he had evinced courage and dexterity. De Grantmesnil's horse, which was young and violent, reared and plunged in the course of the career so as to disturb the rider's aim. The stranger, declining to take the advantage which this offered, raised his lance and swept past his antagonist without touching him. Having ridden back to his own end of the lists he offered through a Herald, the chance of a second encounter. This De Grantmesnil declined, declaring himself vanquished as much by the courtesy as by the skill of his opponent.

Ralph de Vipont completed the tally of the stranger's triumphs, being unhorsed and hurled to the ground with such force that blood poured from his nose and mouth. He was borne senseless from the lists. The acclamations of thousands applauded the unanimous decision of the Prince and Marshals, who announced the award of that day's Honours to the Disinherited Knight.

---

1 Lat. Beware, here come I!

chapter nine

In the midst was seen
A lady of a more majestic mien,
By stature and by beauty mark'd,
Their sovereign Queen.
John Dryden: *The Flower and Leaf*

William de Wyvil and Stephen de Martival, the Marshals of the Field, were the first to offer congratulations to the victor. They invited him to have his helmet removed or at least to raise his visor, as they conducted him to receive the Prize of the Day from Prince John. The Disinherited Knight declined with courtesy, saying that he could not permit his face to be seen, for reasons given to the Heralds when he entered the lists. The Marshals were satisfied by this reply, odd and capricious being the vows by which knights then bound themselves. Among these, none was more common than remaining *incognito* until a particular objective was achieved. The Marshals thus pressed no farther into the mystery of the Disinherited Knight and announced to Prince John his desire to remain unknown.

John's curiosity was excited by the mystery. Already displeased with the outcome of the tournament, in which his favoured Champions had been successively defeated by one knight, he responded to the Marshals,

'By Our Lady's brow, this knight hath been disinherited of his courtesy as well as of his lands, desiring to appear before us without uncovering his face. Know ye, my lords,' he said, turning round to his train, 'who this gallant can be?'

'I cannot guess,' answered De Bracy, 'nor did I think that there was a challenger in Britain that could overcome these five knights in one day's jousting. By my faith, the force with which he shocked De Vipont; the Hospitaller left his saddle like a stone from a sling!'

'Boast not of that.' said another Knight Hospitaller, 'Your Templar champion did no better; Bois Guilbert rolled thrice over, grasping sand at every turn.' De Bracy was attached to the Templars and would have retorted, but was prevented by the Prince.

'Silence, sirs!' said he.

'The victor,' said De Wyvil, 'still awaits the pleasure of your highness.'

'It is our pleasure,' answered John, 'that he *do* so wait, until we learn his name and quality. Should he remain there till nightfall, he has had work enough to keep him warm.'

'Your Grace,' said Waldemar Fitzurse urgently, 'if you compel him to wait thus, you will not do him the honour due, as victor. I cannot guess who he may be, unless he is one of the lances who accompanied King Richard to Palestine and now straggling home.'

'It may be the Earl of Salisbury,' said De Bracy; 'he is of the same height.'

'Sir Thomas de Multon, the Knight of Gilsland, rather,' said Fitzurse; 'Salisbury is bigger in the bones.' A shocked whisper arose among the train;

'It might be the King...it might be Richard *Coeur-de-Lion* himself!'

'God forbid!' said Prince John, turning pale as death and shrinking as if from a lightning flash; 'Waldemar, De Bracy! Remember your promises and stand by me!'

'Here is no danger impending,' said Waldemar Fitzurse; 'Your brother's gigantic limbs could not be held within yonder suit of armour. Hola! De Wyvil and De Martival! You will serve the Prince by bringing forward the victor. Look at this knight closely,' he continued, 'your Highness will see that he lacks three inches of King Richard's height and twice as much in shoulder-breadth. The horse he rides could not have carried the weight of King Richard.'

The Marshals brought forward the Disinherited Knight to the foot of the wooden flight of steps leading up from the lists to the throne. The Prince remained disturbed by the idea that his brother might have arrived in his kingdom; even the distinctions pointed out by Fitzurse had not fully quelled his alarm. After a short and embarrassed eulogy on his valour, John delivered to him the war horse assigned as the prize. As he did so he was still trembling, lest from the barred visor of the mailed man before him might come the deep and awesome accent of Richard Lionheart. However, the Disinherited Knight spoke not a word of reply to the Prince's compliments, acknowledging them only with a bow.

The noble horse, fully accoutered with war furniture, was led into the lists by two grooms. Laying one hand upon the pommel of the saddle, the Disinherited Knight mounted without using the stirrup. Brandishing his lance aloft, he rode twice around the lists, exhibiting the points and paces of the horse with the skill of an expert horseman, being again greeted by the acclamations of the spectators.

In the meanwhile, the Prior of Jorvaulx reminded Prince John in a whisper that the victor must now select from the galleries a lady to fill the throne of the Queen of Beauty and of Love who would deliver the tournament prize the following day. The Prince made a sign with his truncheon as the knight passed him on his second circuit of the lists; he turned towards the throne, dexterously reducing his fiery steed from high excitation to the stillness of an equestrian statue. Sinking his lance until the point was within a foot of the ground, he remained motionless as if expecting John's command.

'Sir Disinherited Knight,' said Prince John, 'since that is the *only* title by which we can address you, it is now your duty and privilege to name the Queen of Love and Beauty who will preside over the morrow's festival. If you require guidance, we may say that Alicia, daughter of our gallant knight Waldemar Fitzurse, has been long held the first in beauty at our Court. Nevertheless, it is your undoubted prerogative to place this Crown upon whom you please. Raise your lance.' The knight did so. Prince John placed upon its point a coronet of green satin. Around its edge was a circlet of gold, the upper edge of which was relieved by arrow-points and hearts placed alternately.

In the broad hint which he had dropped respecting the daughter of Fitzurse, John's motives were the offspring of a mind in which were admixed presumption, low artifice and cunning. Thus he was desirous of conciliating Alicia's father, the awesome Waldemar, irritated more than once during the day's proceedings. He also wished to gain the good graces of the lady; for John was as licentious in his pleasures as he was profligate in ambition. Already entertaining a strong dislike of the Disinherited

Knight, he was also desirous of creating a powerful enemy for him in Fitzurse. The latter, he reckoned, was likely to resent any bypassing of his daughter.

And so indeed it proved. For the Disinherited Knight passed by the gallery in which the Lady Alicia was seated and, pacing forwards slowly, he was seen to be exercising his right of inspecting the numerous fair faces which adorned that splendid circle. There were different reactions among the beauties who underwent this examination: some blushed; some assumed an air of quiet pride and dignity; some looked straight forward, essaying indifference to what was going on; some drew back in affected alarm; some endeavoured to forbear smiling and there were two or three who laughed outright. At length, the knight paused. He was then beneath the balcony in which sat the Lady Rowena.

Nowhere was there greater interest in his success than in the galleries now before him. Cedric the Saxon was overjoyed at the discomfiture of the Templar, still more so at the overthrow of his two malevolent neighbours, Front-de-Boeuf and Malvoisin. Leaning over the balcony, he had followed the victor's encounters with heart and soul. Rowena had also watched the progress of the day with attention, though without betraying the same intense interest. Even Athelstane had shown signs of shaking off his apathy. Calling for a goblet of *muscadine*, he quaffed it to the health of the Disinherited Knight. Another group, stationed under the gallery of the Saxons, had shown no less interest in the fate of the day…

'Father Abraham!' Isaac of York had said to Rebecca when the first course was run betwixt the Templar and the Disinherited Knight, 'how fiercely that Gentile rides! That horse was brought all the way from *Barbary* and he takes no more care of him than a wild ass's colt! That armour was worth unknown zecchins to its armourer, Pereira of Milan – besides *seventy* per cent of profits – and he cares as little for it as if he had found it on the highway!'

'If he risks life and limb, father,' said Rebecca gently, 'in doing such battle, he can scarce be expected to spare his horse and armour.'

'Child!' Isaac replied, 'His neck and limbs are his own, but his horse and armour belong to – Holy Jacob! What was I about to say? Nevertheless, he is a good youth. See, Rebecca *see*! He goes again to battle against the Philistine. God of our fathers!' he had again exclaimed as the Templar crashed down, 'he hath *conquered*! The Philistine fell before his lance, as Sihon, King of the Amorites, fell before the swords of Israel! Surely he shall take their gold *and* their warhorses, *and* their armour as prizes...' Such was the interest of Isaac; every encounter producing a hasty calculation of the value of each horse and armour forfeited to the challenger.

The Disinherited Knight remained stationary for more than a minute, his lance vertical and the eyes of the silent audience riveted upon him. Then, gradually and gracefully sinking the point of the lance, he deposited the coronet which it supported at the feet of Rowena. The trumpets instantly sounded. The Heralds proclaimed that the Lady Rowena of Rotherwood was Queen of Beauty and of Love for the ensuing day, threatening penalties for any disobedient to her authority. They then repeated their cry of *Largesse*!, to which Cedric joyfully responded with an ample donative to which Athelstane, less promptly, added another.

There was a murmuring among the damsels of Norman descent, as unused to seeing preference given to a Saxon beauty as were their Norman knights to defeat in their games of chivalry. But these sounds of disaffection were drowned by popular shouts of,

'Lady Rowena; Queen of Love and of Beauty!' To which many in the lower area added, 'The *Saxon* Princess! Long live the line of Alfred!'

However irritating this might be to Prince John and his entourage, he saw himself nevertheless obligated to confirm the nomination of the victor. Calling: 'To *horse*!' he left his throne, mounted his jennet and entered the lists accompanied by his train. The Prince paused a moment beneath the gallery of the Lady Alicia, to whom he paid compliment, observing to those around him;

'By my halidome, sirs![1] If the Knight's feats of arms have shown his valour, his choice in beauty proves his eyes to be none of the clearest.'

It was John's misfortune never to fully understand the character of those he wished to conciliate. Waldemar Fitzurse was offended rather than pleased at the Prince stating so broadly his opinion that Alicia had been slighted.

'I know no right of chivalry,' said he, coldly, 'more precious than that of each free knight to choose his lady by his own judgment. My daughter courts distinction from no one. In her own character she will aye receive that which is her due.'

Prince John did not reply. Spurring his horse to vent his vexation, he bounded forward to the gallery where Rowena was seated, the coronet still at her feet.

'Fair Lady,' he said, 'take up the coronet of your sovereignty, to which none vows homage more sincerely than ourself, John of Anjou. If it please you to grace our banquet in the Castle of Ashby with your noble sire and friends, we shall learn to know the Queen to whose service we devote the morrow.' As Rowena remained silent, Cedric rose and answered for her in his native Anglo-Saxon.

'Your Grace,' he said, 'The Lady Rowena does not possess the language in which to reply to your courtesy. I and the noble Athelstane of Coningsburgh, here present, speak only the language and practise only the manners of our ancestors. We decline, with our thanks, your Highness's invitation to your banquet. Tomorrow, the Lady Rowena will take upon her the State to which she has been called by the victor and confirmed by the acclamation of the people.'

So saying, he placed the coronet gently upon Rowena's head.

'What says he?' said Prince John, affecting not to understand the Saxon language in which he was well skilled. Cedric's speech was repeated to him in French.

'It is well.' he said; 'Tomorrow we will ourself conduct this mute Sovereign to her seat of dignity. You at least, Sir Knight,' he added, turning to the victor, who had remained near the gallery, 'will this evening share our banquet?' The Knight, speaking for the first time, excused himself in a low and hurried voice, pleading fatigue and the necessity of preparing for the morrow's encounter.

'Very well,' said Prince John, archly; 'although unused to such refusals, we will endeavour to digest our banquet, *ungraced* by the victor in arms and his Queen of Beauty.'

So saying, he prepared to leave the lists with his glittering train, his turning his

---

1 By my Halidom(e): By everything I hold sacred; it presaged an oath.

steed for that purpose being the signal for the breaking up and dispersal of the spectators. Prince John had hardly proceeded three paces before he turned around and fixed an eye of stern resentment upon the yeoman who had displeased him in the early part of the day. To the men-at-arms who stood near, he commanded;

'On your life, suffer not that fellow to escape.' The yeoman received the angry glance of the Prince with the same steadiness which had marked his former deportment. With a smile, he said,

'I have no intention to leave Ashby until the day after tomorrow, for I must see how Staffordshire and Leicestershire can shoot. The forests of Needwood and Charnwood must rear good archers.'

'I will see how he can draw his *own*,' said Prince John to his attendants, 'and woe betide him, unless his skill make some apology for his insolence!'

'It is full time,' said De Bracy, 'that the *outrecuidance*[1] of these peasants be cowed by some striking example.'

Waldemar Fitzurse, again seeing that his patron was not on the readiest road to popularity, shrugged his shoulders and was silent. Prince John resumed his retreat from the lists and the dispersal of the multitude became general.

In groups of various numbers and by various routes, the spectators were seen retiring over the plain. By far the most numerous group streamed towards the town of Ashby where many of the distinguished persons were lodged in the Castle and where others had found accommodation in the town itself. Among these were most of the knights who had already appeared in the tournament or who proposed to fight the ensuing day. These were greeted with shouts by the populace as they rode slowly along, talking over the events of the day. Acclamations were bestowed also upon Prince John, although for them he was indebted rather more to the splendour of his appearance and train than to his popularity.

A more general, sincere and better-merited acclamation followed the victor of the day who was anxious to withdraw from sight. He accepted one of the pavilions pitched at the extremity of the lists, courteously offered by the Marshals. He retired to this tent, thus dispersing those who had lingered to look at him and speculate on his identity. The signs and sounds of a tumultuous concourse were now replaced for the distant hum of voices of different groups retreating in all directions. These speedily died away into silence. No other sounds were now heard, save the voices of the menials who stripped the galleries of their cushions and tapestry in order to put them in safety for the night, wrangling among themselves for the half-used bottles of wine and relics of the refreshments.

Beyond the precincts of the lists, forges had been erected. These now began to glimmer through the twilight, announcing the toil of the armourers which would continue through the night in order to repair or alter suits of mail for the morrow. A strong guard of men-at-arms, renewed at two-hourly intervals, surrounded the lists and kept the long watches of the night.

---

1 Presumption, insolence. *Scott.*

chapter ten

Vex'd and tormented, runs poor Barabbas,
With fatal curses towards these Christians.
Christopher Marlowe: *The Jew of Malta*

The Disinherited Knight had no sooner reached his pavilion than squires and pages offered to disarm him, bring fresh attire and offer him the refreshment of the bath. Their zeal was sharpened by curiosity. Who was this knight who had gained so many laurels, yet even when commanded by Prince John, had refused to lift his visor or reveal his name? Their inquisitiveness was not gratified. The Knight refused all other assistance save that of his own squire, or rather yeoman; a rustic-looking man wrapped in a cloak of dark felt. His head and face half-buried in a Norman bonnet of black fur, he seemed as *incognito* as his master. All others being excluded from the tent, this attendant relieved his master from the heavier parts of his armour and placed food and wine.

The Knight had scarcely finished these ere his squire announced that five men, each leading a barbed steed, desired to speak with him. He had now exchanged his armour for a long robe which, being hooded, concealed his features almost as completely as his helmet visor. The Disinherited Knight, therefore, stepped to the front of his tent and found in attendance the squires of the Champions, easily identified by their russet and black dress. Each led his master's charger, loaded with the armour in which he had fought that day.

'According to the laws of chivalry,' said the foremost of these men, 'I, Baldwin de Oyley, squire to Sir Brian de Bois Guilbert, make offer to you, styled the Disinherited Knight, of the horse and armour used by de Bois Guilbert this day, leaving it with your pleasure to retain or to ransom the same, such being the Law of Arms.' The other squires repeated the formula, and then stood to await the decision.

'To you four, Sirs,' replied the Knight, 'and to your masters, I have but one reply. Commend me to your noble Knights and say I shall not deprive brave cavaliers of their steeds and arms. Would that I could end my message there. However, being Disinherited, I must desire your masters that they will ransom their steeds and armour, since that which I myself wear I can hardly call mine own.'

'We stand commissioned, each of us,' answered the squire of Front-de-Boeuf, 'to offer a hundred *zecchins* in ransom of these horses and suits of armour.'

'More than sufficient.' said the Disinherited Knight. 'My present necessities only compel me to accept half the sum. Of the remaining half, distribute one moiety among yourselves, sir squires and divide the other half betwixt the Heralds, the pursuivants, minstrels and attendants.'

The squires, cap in hand and with low bows, expressed their appreciation of generosity not often practised upon such a scale. The Disinherited Knight then addressed Baldwin, squire of Brian de Bois Guilbert.

'From your master, however,' said he, 'I will accept neither arms nor ransom. Tell him in my name, that our strife is not ended; not till we have fought with swords as well as with lances; and on foot as well as on horseback. To this mortal quarrel he has challenged me and I shall not forget. Tell him also that he is not one with whom I can exchange courtesies, as I hold him in mortal emnity.'

'My master,' answered Baldwin, 'knows how to requite scorn with scorn as well as courtesy with courtesy. Since you disdain to accept any ransom, as with the other knights, I must leave his armour and horse here. Be well assured that he will never deign to mount the one nor wear the other.'

'You have spoken well, squire,' said the Disinherited Knight, 'as is seemly for him who answers for an absent master. But leave not the horse and armour here. If thy master scorns to accept them, retain them for thine own use. They are now mine and I bestow them upon you freely.' Baldwin bowed and retired with his companions. The Knight re-entered the pavilion.

'Thus far, Gurth,' said he grimly, addressing his attendant, 'English chivalry hath not suffered in my hands.'

'And I,' said Gurth, 'have played the Norman squire-at-arms well – for a Saxon swineherd!'

'Indeed, but I fear lest thy rustic bearing should discover thee.'

'Tosh! I fear discovery from none save Wamba the Jester whom I could never mark whether he be more knave or fool. I could nearly laugh when my master Cedric passed so near, thinking Gurth to be guarding his pigs in the thickets of Rotherwood. If I am discovered, it will go hard with me...'

'Enough. Remember my promise.'

'Nay, for that matter,' said Gurth, 'I will never fail my friend for fear of my skin-cutting. I have a tough hide.'

'Trust me. I will repay the risk you run. Meanwhile, take these ten pieces of gold.'

'I am now richer,' said Gurth, pouching them, 'than ever was swineherd or bondsman.'

'Take this bag of gold to Ashby,' continued his master, 'Find Isaac the Jew of York, and let him repay himself for the horse and arms with which his credit supplied me.'

'I will so do,' said Gurth, taking the bag under his cloak. 'It will go hard,' he muttered to himself, 'but I'll content him with one half of his demand.' So saying, he set off, leaving the Disinherited Knight to his own private thoughts.

In a country house belonging to a wealthy Israelite, Isaac, his daughter and retinue had taken up their quarters. In an apartment, small but richly furnished with Oriental taste, Rebecca was seated on a heap of embroidered cushions. These, piled along a low platform surrounding the room, served, like the *estrada* of the Spaniards, as chairs and stools. She was watching her father with an anxious look of filial affection as he dejectedly paced the apartment. Clasping his hands together and casting his eyes upward, he seemed under great tribulation.

'O Jacob!' he exclaimed 'O twelve Holy Fathers! What a loss. Fifty zecchins wrenched from me at one clutch – and by the talons of a tyrant!'

'But, father,' said Rebecca, 'you seemed to give the gold to Prince John willingly.'

'Willingly? Ay, as willingly as the time in the Gulf of Lyons when I flung goods overboard to lighten the ship in the tempest. I robed the waves in my choice silks, perfumed them with myrrh and lined their caverns with gold; and my own hands made the sacrifice!'

'But a sacrifice which Heaven exacted to save our lives,' answered Rebecca, 'and has not Jehovah since blessed you?'

'Ay,' answered Isaac, 'but the tyrant takes my gold as he did today and compels me to smile while he is robbing me? Daughter, the worst evil for our race is that when we are being plundered, the world laughs. We must suppress our rage and smile tamely when we want *revenge*!'

'Think not thus of it, father.' said Rebecca; 'We have advantages. These persecutor Gentiles are dependent on the children of Zion. Without our wealth they could neither fund their armies in war nor their triumphs in peace. The gold we lend returns with interest. We are like the herb which flourishes most when trampled on. Even this very day's pageant had not proceeded without the support of the despised Jew.'

'Daughter,' said Isaac, 'thou hast touched another string of sorrow. The steed and armour, equal to the full profit of my venture with our Kirjath Jairam of Leicester, are a dead loss; ay, a loss which swallows up the gains of the space between two Sabbaths.'

'Father,' said Rebecca, 'you shall not regret rewarding the good deed you received of the stranger knight.'

'I trust so, daughter,' said Isaac, 'And I trust too in the rebuilding of Zion; but I have as much hope of seeing with my own eyes the walls and battlements of the new Temple, as to see any Christian repay a debt to a Jew, unless under threat of judge and jail.' So saying, he resumed his walk around the apartment.

The evening was now becoming dark, when a servant entered and placed upon the table two silver oil lamps. Wines and delicate refreshments were at the same time displayed by another Israelite domestic on an ebony table. The servant then informed Isaac that a *Nazarene,* their term for a Christian, desired to speak with him. Ever at the disposal of anyone claiming business with him, Isaac replaced on the table an untasted glass of Greek wine.

'Rebecca, veil thyself,' he commanded as the stranger was being admitted. Just as Rebecca dropped a screen of silver gauze over her features, the door opened and Gurth entered, wrapped in the ample folds of his Norman mantle. His appearance was more suspicious than prepossessing, especially as instead of doffing his bonnet he pulled it still deeper over his brow.

'Art thou Isaac, the Jew of York?' said Gurth, in Saxon.

'I am,' replied Isaac, in the same language, 'and thou?'

'That is not to the purpose,' answered Gurth.

'How, then,' replied Isaac; 'can I hold intercourse with thee?'

'Easily,' answered Gurth; 'I, being here to pay money, must know that I deliver it to the right person. Thou, who are to receive it, need not care greatly from whose hands it comes.'

'Ah,' said the Jew, 'you are come to pay monies? And from whom?'

'From the Disinherited Knight,' said Gurth, 'victor in this day's tournament. It is the price of the armour supplied to him by Kirjath Jairam of Leicester on thy recommendation. The steed is restored to thy stable. I desire to know the amount which I am to pay for the armour.'

'I *said* he was a good youth!' exclaimed Isaac joyfully. 'A cup of wine will do thee no harm,' he added, handing the swineherd a finer vintage than Gurth had ever tasted. 'And how much money,' continued Isaac, 'hast thou brought?'

'Holy Virgin!' said Gurth, setting down the cup, 'what nectar you unbelievers drink, while true Christians have ale, muddy as the draff of hogs! What money have I brought with me?' continued the Saxon, after this incivility, 'only but a small sum.'

'Nay, but,' said Isaac, 'thy master has won goodly steeds and rich armours. But, 'tis a good youth. I will take these in present payment and render him back the surplus.'

'My master has disposed of them already,' said Gurth.

'Ah! But that was wrong,' said the Jew, 'that was the act of a fool. No Christian here could buy so many horses and armour – and no Jew, except myself, would give him half the value. But there must be at least a hundred *zecchins* in that heavy bag,' said Isaac, prying under Gurth's cloak.

'I have heads for cross-bow bolts in it,' said Gurth quickly.[1]

'Well, then,' said Isaac, hesitating between his business instincts and a new-born desire to be liberal in the present instance, 'if I should say that I would take eighty zecchins for thy master's steed and armour, which leaves me not a guilder's profit, have you the sum to pay me?'

'Barely.' said Gurth, though the sum was more reasonable than he had expected, 'It will leave my master nigh penniless. Nevertheless, if such be your least offer, I must be content.'

'Fill thyself another goblet of wine,' said Isaac. 'Ah! Eighty zecchins is too little. It leaveth no profit for the usages of the monies and besides, the good horse may have suffered wrong in this day's encounter – a hard and a dangerous meeting! Man and steed rushing on each other like wild bulls of Bashan![2] The horse must have suffered.'

'And I say,' replied Gurth, 'that he is sound in wind and limb. You may see him now in your stable. And I say, over and above, that *seventy* zecchins is enough for the armour, and I hope a Christian's word is as good as a Jew's. If you will not take seventy, this bag' – and he shook its jingling contents – 'goes back to my master.'

'Nay, nay!' said Isaac; 'lay down the shekels, the *eighty* zecchins and thou shalt see that I will treat thee liberally.'

Gurth at length complied, telling out eighty zecchins upon the table, whereupon Isaac delivered a receipt for the cost of horse and armour. Isaac wrapped up the first seventy pieces of gold. The last ten he counted out with much deliberation, pausing, and saying something as he took each piece from the table, and dropt it into his purse. He looked at the last zecchin, intending, perhaps, to bestow it upon Gurth. He weighed it upon the tip of his finger, and made it ring by dropping it upon the table. Had it rung too flat, or been a hair's breadth too light, generosity would have won; but, unhappily for Gurth, the chime was full and true; the zecchin was plump, newly coined, and a grain above weight. Isaac could not find in his heart to part with it. Into his purse, it went.

---

1 The bolt was the arrow of the crossbow, that of the longbow was a shaft. *Scott.*

2 Psalms 22.12. In Judea, Bashan was the fertile country east of the River Jordan.

'Eighty completes the tally and I trust thy master will reward thee handsomely. But surely,' he added, looking earnestly at the bag, 'there be more coins in that pouch?' Gurth grinned and replied,

'About the same quantity which thou hast just counted over so carefully!' He then folded the receipt, or *quittance*, and put it under his cap, adding,

'On the peril of thy beard, Jew, see that this be full and ample!' He then filled for himself, unbidden, a third goblet of wine and left the apartment.

'Rebecca,' said her father, 'that Ishmaelite rather got the better of me. Nevertheless, his master is a good youth. Ay, and I am well pleased that he hath gained shekels of gold and of silver through speed of horse and strength of that lance. Like that of Philistine Goliath, it might vie with a weaver's beam.'[1] He turned to look for an answer from Rebecca only to find she had silently left the apartment.

Gurth had descended the stair, reached the dark antechamber or hall and was casting about for the entrance. It was then that a figure in white, visible only by a small silver lamp in her hand, beckoned him into a side apartment. Gurth hesitated. He was in the house of a Jew, a people supposed to be profound necromancers[2] and cabalists, besides other unamiable qualities. Nevertheless, after a moment's pause, he followed the apparition and found it to be the beautiful Jewess from her father's apartment.

She asked for – and was told – the particulars of his transaction with Isaac.

'My father played with thee, good fellow.' said Rebecca; 'He owes thy master more than these arms and steed could pay, were they multiplied tenfold. What sum didst thou pay my father just now?'

'Eighty zecchins,' said Gurth, surprised at the question.

'In this purse,' said Rebecca, 'are an hundred. Restore to thy master that which is his due, and enrich thyself with the remainder. Now, begone and stay not to render thanks! Beware how you pass through this crowded town, where it is easy to lose thy burden or thy life. Reuben,' she added, clapping her hands, 'light forth this stranger. Lock and bar the doors behind him.' Reuben, black-bearded, obeyed her summons, torch in hand. He opened the outer door of the house and, conducting Gurth across a paved court, let him out through an entrance-gate with sufficient bolts and chains to secure a prison.

'By St Dunstan,' said Gurth, stumbling up the dark road, 'that was no Jewess, but an angel from heaven! Ten zecchins from my brave young master. Twenty from this pearl of Zion; oh, happy day! Another such day will end thy bondage, Gurth, and make thee a free brother. Then, 'twill be down with the swineherd's staff and up with the freeman's sword and buckler!

---

1 Goliath's spear was compared in thickness to that of the weaver's beam, i.e. over 2 inches (c.5cm) in diameter. *See* I Samuel 17.7 and II Samuel 21.19.

2 Practitioners of communication with the dead by summoning their spirits as an apparition. Practised by the Witch of Endor. *See* I Samuel, 28. 3–25.

chapter eleven

Speed: Sir, we are undone! These are the villains
That all the travellers do fear so much.
Shakespeare: *Two Gentlemen of Verona*

The nocturnal adventures of Gurth were not yet concluded. After passing one or two straggling houses in the outskirts of the village, he found himself in a deep lane. This ran between two banks overgrown with hazel and holly, while here and there a dwarf oak flung its arms across the path. The lane, much rutted and broken up by carriages going to the tournament, was dark; its banks and bushes masking the light of the harvest moon.

From the village were heard distant sounds of revelry and loud laughter, now broken by screams, now by wild distant music. These sounds of disorder in a town crowded with military nobles and their dissolute attendants made Gurth uneasy.

'That Jewess was right,' he said to himself. 'By heaven, would that I were safely back with all this treasure. Here are such errant knights, errant squires, monks and errant minstrels, jugglers and Jesters that a man with a single *merk* would be in danger, let alone a swineherd loaded with *zecchins*. Would I were out of the shade of these infernal bushes, that I might at least see any of St Nicholas's clerks[1] before they spring on me.'

He hastened his pace to gain the open common to which the lane led. But just as he had attained the upper end of the lane where the undergrowth was thickest, four men sprang at him, two from each side of the road, seizing him too tightly for resistance.

'Surrender,' said one of them; 'we ease every man of his burden.'

'You shall not ease me of mine,' muttered Gurth, uncowed.

'We shall see that presently.' said the robber. To his companions, he added, 'Bring the knave along. He would have his head broken as well as his purse cut.'

Gurth was hurried along, dragged roughly over the bank on the left hand side of the lane and found himself in a straggling thicket which lay between it and the open common. He was forced to follow his captors into the depth of this cover and on into an open space where they stopped in the moonlight. Here they were joined by two other persons with short swords by their sides and quarter-staves in hand. All six wore visors, rendering their occupation clear.

'What money hast thou, churl?' demanded one.

'Thirty zecchins of my own property,' answered Gurth.

'Forfeit!' shouted the robbers; 'a Saxon with thirty zecchins returns sober from a village...'

'I hoarded it to purchase my freedom,' said Gurth.

'Then thou art an ass,' replied one of the thieves 'three quarts of ale would have rendered thee as free as thy master – and freer too, if he be Saxon like thyself.'

'A sad truth,' replied Gurth; 'but if these thirty zecchins will buy my freedom from *you*, unloose me and I will pay.'

---

1 Highwaymen. St Nicholas was jocularly said to be Patron Saint of thieves.

'Hold,' said one who seemed to be in authority; 'I can feel through his cloak that this bag holds yet more coin.'

'It is the good Knight my master's.'

'Thou art an honest fellow,' said the robber, 'thy thirty zecchins may yet be thy escape. But render up thy trust for a time.' So saying, he took from Gurth's breast the large leathern pouch holding Rebecca's purse and the rest of the zecchins.

'Who is thy master?'

'The Disinherited Knight.'

'Indeed!' replied the robber, 'he whose lance won the prize in today's tourney? His name and lineage?'

'It is his pleasure,' answered Gurth, 'that they be concealed; you will learn naught from me.'

'Thine own name?'

'To tell that,' said Gurth, 'might reveal my master's.'

'Thou art a saucy groom,' said the robber, 'How comes thy master by this gold?'

'By his lance,' answered Gurth. 'These bags contain the ransom of four good horses and four good suits of armour.'

'How much is there?' demanded the robber.

'Two hundred zecchins.'

'Only two hundred!' said the bandit; 'your master hath put the vanquished a cheap ransom. Name those who paid this gold.' Gurth did so.

'The armour and horse of the Templar de Bois Guilbert were at what ransom?'

'My master,' replied Gurth, 'will take naught from the Templar save his life's blood.'

'Indeed!' repeated the robber, 'And what wert thou doing at Ashby just now with such gold?'

'I went to Isaac the Jew of York,' replied Gurth, 'to pay the price of the armour he fitted for my master for this tournament.'

'And how much was paid to Isaac? To judge by weight, there is still two hundred zecchins in this pouch.'

'Eighty zecchins,' said the Saxon, 'and he restored me a hundred in lieu thereof.'

'What?' exclaimed the robbers at once, 'thou art a liar!'

'What I tell you,' said Gurth, 'is as true as the moon is in heaven. You will find just that sum in a silk purse in the leathern pouch, separate from the rest of the gold.'
'An Israelite,' said the Captain, 'is as likely to restore gold as is the sand of his deserts to return spilled water.'

'It is true as I say.'

'Strike a light,' said the Captain; 'I will examine this purse.'

A light was procured and the robber proceeded to examine the purse. The others crowded around him, the two holding Gurth relaxing their grip while they stretched to see the search. Gurth wrenched himself free and might have escaped, had he been prepared to abandon his master's property. He whipped a quarter-staff away from one of the fellows, struck out at the leader and knocked him down. The other thieves, however, were too quick for him and again secured both the bag and the struggling Gurth.

'Knave!' said the Captain, getting up, 'Thou shalt know thy fate soon, but first let us speak of thy master, for a knight's matters go before his squire's. Stand *still!* Stir again and thou shall be quiet forever.'

'Comrades' he then said, addressing his men, 'this purse is embroidered with Hebrew characters, so I believe the yeoman's tale. The Knight, his master, must pass us toll-free. He is too like ourselves for us to rob him.'

'Like us – in what way?' retorted one of the gang.

'Fool,' said the leader, 'is he not poor and disinherited as we are? He wins his bread at the sword's point. He beat Front-de-Boeuf and Malvoisin as we would beat them if we could – and is he not the mortal enemy of Bois Guilbert?'

'But what of this insolent peasant; is he to be dismissed scatheless?'[1]

'Not if *thou* canst scathe him!' replied the Captain. 'Here, fellow,' he addressed Gurth, 'thou can use the quarter-staff. Beat this fellow, and thou shalt pass. Take up thy staff, Miller,' he added, 'and keep thy head. You others; release the fellow and give him a staff. There is moonlight enough for the fight.'

The two combatants, now armed with quarter-staves, stepped forward into the centre of the open space in order to have the full benefit of the moonlight with the thieves laughing and crying to their comrade,

'Miller! Beware thy toll-dish.' The Miller, holding his quarter-staff by the middle, flourished it round his head after the French fashion of *faire le moulinet.*[2]

'Come on, churl, if you dare: and feel the strength of a miller's thumb!'

'If thou'rt a *miller*,' answered Gurth, making his own weapon play around his head with equal dexterity, 'thou art *doubly* a thief and I bid thee defiance!' So saying, the two closed, displaying equality in courage and skill. Each intercepted and returned the blows of his adversary with dexterity, while the clatter of their weapons would have suggested that six were engaged. Eventually, however, the Miller began to lose his temper at being so stoutly opposed, and at the laughter of his companions who were enjoying his vexation. He pressed furiously forward, dealing blows with either end of his weapon and striving to come to half-staff distance. Gurth defended, keeping his hands a yard apart and shifting his weapon with great speed. Then, observing his antagonist losing wind, he darted the staff into his face with his left hand. As the Miller endeavoured to parry the thrust, Gurth slid his right hand down to his left, and with the full swing of the weapon now available, struck his opponent full on the left side of the head. Down he went upon the greensward.

'Yeomanly done!' shouted the robbers; 'The Saxon saves his hide and purse; and the Miller meets his match.'

'Go thy way, my friend,' said the Captain, addressing Gurth, 'and I will have two of my comrades guide thee to thy master's pavilion. They will guard thee from night-walkers; and there are many such abroad this night. Remember,' he added sternly, 'thy refusal to tell thy name. Ask not after ours, nor try to discover who we are.'

Gurth promised to heed the warning. Two of the outlaws took up their quarter-staves and ordering Gurth to follow closely, walked boldly forward along a by-path which traversed the thicket and the broken ground adjacent to it. At the verge of the thicket, two men appeared and said something to his escorts. Receiving an answer

---

1 Unharmed.

2 Twirling like a windmill.

in a whisper, they withdrew silently into the wood. When they arrived on the open heath the escorts guided him forwards to the top of an eminence. Thence he could see, spread beneath him in the moonlight, the palisades of the lists and the glimmering pavilions pitched at either end. He saw the pennons fluttering in the night wind and heard the distant song of the sentinels beguiling their watch. The thieves stopped.

'We go no farther,' said they, 'Remember the warning. Keep secret what has befallen you this night.' Thus they parted, Gurth proceeding to the tent of his master. Despite the warning, he described to him the whole adventures of the evening.

The Disinherited Knight was astonished no less at the generosity of Rebecca than at that of the robbers. However, his reflections were interrupted by fatigue and by the need for repose ahead of the morrow's encounter. He stretched himself upon a couch, while Gurth, extending his hardy limbs upon the pavilion's carpet of bearskin, laid himself across the opening of the tent as a sentinel, that none might pass unobserved.

chapter twelve

In goeth the sharp spur into the side,
There see men who can joust and can ride;
There shiver shaftes upon shieldes thick,
He feeleth through the heart-spone the prick;
Chaucer: *The Knight's Tale.*

Morning arose in unclouded splendour. Ere the sun was much above the horizon, spectators appeared on the common, moving to secure a favourable situation. The Marshals and their attendants appeared next on the field, together with the Heralds who received the names of the knights who intended to joust. They recorded also the side which each chose to espouse, a necessary precaution to secure equality betwixt the two opposing squadrons.

According to due formality, the Disinherited Knight was named as leader of one body. Brian de Bois Guilbert, rated as second best in the preceding day, would head the other. Those who had been his fellow Champions adhered to his party, excepting the injured Ralph de Vipont. There was no lack of distinguished and indeed noble candidates to fill the ranks on either side.

General Tournaments, where all knights fought together, were far more dangerous than single encounters, but were nevertheless more frequent among the chivalry of the age. Many knights with insufficient confidence or skill to take on a single adversary of high repute, would willingly display their valour in a general combat. At Ashby, about fifty knights were inscribed as ready for combat upon each side. To the disappointment of many more, the Marshals then declared the lists closed.

By about the hour of ten o'clock, the whole plain was crowded with horsemen and foot-passengers hastening to the tournament. Shortly after, a grand flourish of trumpets announced the arrival of Prince John and his retinue, attended by many of those knights who were to take part in the battle, as well as some with no such intention. Cedric the Saxon with the Lady Rowena arrived, unattended by Athelstane. The Saxon lord, his tall person arrayed in armour, would join the combat. To the considerable irritation of Cedric, he had chosen to enlist himself under the Knight Templar. The Saxon had remonstrated strongly with his friend over this, but had received no justification, only a brief and obstinate answer.

Athelstane had enough sense to keep to himself his reason for adhering to the squadron of Brian de Bois Guilbert. Though his nature prevented his paying active court to Lady Rowena, he was fully sensible of her charms. Indeed, he considered his marriage to her as already fixed by the assent of Cedric. It was therefore with smothered jealousy that the Lord of Coningsburgh had beheld the Disinherited Knight select Rowena as Queen of Love and Beauty. Athelstane had decided not only to deny the Disinherited Knight his support, but also to make him feel the weight of his battleaxe.

De Bracy and other knights attached to Prince John had, following a hint from him, joined the party of Bois Guilbert and his Champions, John being desirous to see victory for that side. On the other side were many other knights, both Saxon English and Norman, natives and foreigners, pleased to be led by such a warrior as the Disinherited Knight had proved to be.

As soon as Prince John observed the Queen of the Day arriving upon the field, he assumed the air of courtesy which became him when he was pleased to exhibit it. He rode forward to meet her, doffed his bonnet and, alighting from his horse, assisted the Lady Rowena from her saddle. His followers uncovered at the same time, one of them dismounting to hold her palfrey.

'It is thus,' said Prince John, 'that we set the dutiful example of loyalty to the Queen of Love and Beauty, we ourselves being her guide to her throne.'

'Ladies,' he said, 'attend your Queen.' So saying, the Prince marshalled Rowena to the seat of honour opposite his own, as ladies jostled to obtain places close to their beautiful and temporary sovereign.

No sooner was Rowena seated than a burst of music, half-drowned by the shouts of the multitude, greeted her new dignity. Meantime, the sun shone fierce and bright upon the polished arms of the knights of both sides. They crowded the opposing extremities of the lists, holding conference together on the best mode of arranging their line of battle.

The Heralds then proclaimed silence until the Laws of the Tourney had been rehearsed. These were calculated to abate, at least in some degree, the dangers of the day; a necessary precaution since the conflict was to be with sharp swords and pointed lances:

Combatants were prohibited from thrusting with the sword and were confined to striking.

A knight might use the mace or battleaxe at pleasure, but not the dagger.

An unhorsed knight might renew the fight on foot with any unhorsed knight from the opposing side, but mounted horsemen might not attack him.

Any knight forced by his antagonist to the extremity of the lists, so that his person or his arms touched the palisade, would be declared vanquished and might not rejoin the combat; his armour and horse to be at the disposal of his conqueror.

Any fallen combatant unable to recover his feet, might have his squire drag him out of the press, but would then be adjudged vanquished, his arms and horse forfeit.

The combat was to cease as soon as Prince John should throw down his truncheon to prevent unnecessary loss of life.

The Heralds concluded by exhorting each good knight to do his duty and to merit favour from the Queen of Beauty and of Love.

Their proclamations over, the Heralds withdrew to their stations. The knights, entering at either end of the lists in a long procession, arranged themselves precisely opposite each other. The leader of each party occupied the centre of the foremost rank after carefully marshalling his cavalry.

It was a goodly and at the same time an anxious sight to behold so many gallant cavaliers. Mounted bravely and heavily armed, they sat on their war-saddles like so many pillars of iron, ready for a formidable engagement. They were awaiting the signal of *Encounter!* with the same impatient ardour as their steeds which neighed and pawed the ground. As yet, the knights held their long lances upright, their bright points flashing sunlight and their streamers fluttering over the plumage of the helmets. Thus they remained while the Marshals surveyed their ranks, checking that each party had the appointed number.

A Marshal, William de Wyvil, with a voice of thunder, then pronounced the signal words – *Laissez aller!* – the trumpets sounding as he spoke. The lances of the knights were at once lowered into rest, spurs were dashed into the flanks of the warhorses and the two front ranks of either party rushed at each other at full gallop. They met in the middle of the lists with a shock, the crash of which was heard at a mile's distance. The second rank of each party then advanced at a slower pace to support the defeated and follow up the success of the victors of their side.

The consequences of the encounter were not instantly seen, due to the dust thrown up by the trampling of so many steeds. Indeed it was a minute ere the anxious spectator could actually see. When the battle became visible, half the knights on each side were already dismounted; some felled by their adversary's lance, some forced down, horse and man by the superior strength of opponents. Some lay stretched on the earth, dead or unconscious, while some had already regained their feet and were closing hand-to-hand with antagonists. Several on both sides had received disabling wounds and were seen staunching the flow of blood with their scarves and endeavouring to extricate themselves from the tumult. Those knights who were still mounted, lances almost all broken, were now closely engaged with their swords, shouting their war cries and fighting as if honour and life itself depended on the outcome.

The tumult was presently increased by the advance of the second rank of either side which now charged in to aid their companions. The followers of Brian de Bois Guilbert shouted:

'Beau-seant! Beau-seant![1] and *'For the Temple!'*

---

1 'Beau-seant' was the name of the Templars' banner which was half black, half white, to intimate, it is said, that they were candid and fair towards Christians, but black and terrible towards infidels. *Scott.*

The opposite party shouted in answer '*Desdichado! Desdichado!*' taking their war-cry from the motto, 'Disinherited' on their leader's shield.

With the combatants encountering each other with the utmost fury and with varying success, the tide of battle seemed to flow now toward the southern, now toward the northern extremity of the lists as the one or the other squadron prevailed. The clang of blows and the shouts of the combatants mixed fearfully with the sound of the trumpets, drowning the screams of those who fell and rolled defenceless beneath the feet of the horses. The splendid armour of the knights was now defaced with dust and blood. Gay plumage, shorn from the crests, drifted upon the breeze. All that was beautiful and graceful in the martial array had now disappeared and what was now visible evoked only terror or compassion.

Among the crowd, both the common spectators and the ladies of distinction in the galleries watched the conflict with a thrilling intensity. None had any desire to avert their eyes from the terrible sights before them. Here and there a fair cheek might turn pale or a short, faint scream might be heard as a lover, brother, or husband was struck from his horse. In general, however, the ladies encouraged the combatants by clapping and waving their veils and kerchiefs, crying;

'Brave lance! Good sword!' at any successful thrust or blow. Given the interest taken by the fair sex in this bloody game, that of their menfolk may be imagined. It showed itself in loud roars upon every change of fortune, as if the spectators themselves were dealing and receiving the blows. At every pause was heard the voice of the Heralds, exclaiming,

'Fight on, brave Knights! Man dies, but Glory lives! Bright eyes behold your deeds!'

Amid the varied fortunes of the combat, the eyes of all endeavoured to catch sight of the leaders of each band who were both in the thick of the fight, encouraging their companions by voice and example. Both had already displayed feats of gallantry, neither Bois Guilbert nor the Disinherited Knight finding an opponent who was their match. They repeatedly endeavoured to single each other out, well aware that the fall of either leader would be decisive. Such, however, was the *melee* and the confusion that during the earlier part of the conflict their efforts to meet were unavailing. Indeed they were repeatedly separated by other followers, anxious to win honour by assaulting the leader of the opposite party.

However, when the field had thinned by the loss of those vanquished or forced to the extremity of the lists, the Templar and the Disinherited Knight finally encountered each other. Hand-to-hand they went with all the fury that mortal animosity and rivalry of honour could inspire. Such was the force of each in striking and parrying that the spectators broke into a unanimous and involuntary shout of admiration.

But at this moment the party of the Disinherited Knight was having the worst of it; the gigantic arm of Front-de-Boeuf on one flank and the ponderous strength of Athelstane on the other, bore down and dispatched those exposed to them. Freed from their immediate antagonists, it occurred to both knights at the same instant that they would best advantage their party by aiding the Templar in his fight. Wheeling their horses, the Norman spurred against the Disinherited Knight from one side, the Saxon from the other. The target of this unexpected assault could never have survived, had he not been warned by a general cry from the spectators;

'Beware, Disinherited!' was shouted so universally, that the knight suddenly realised the danger. Striking a full blow at the Templar, he then reined back his steed to evade the charge of Athelstane and Front-de-Boeuf. Their aim frustrated, these knights rushed between their intended target and the Templar, their horses almost running into each other ere they could stop. Recovering and wheeling round again, all three pursued the unhorsing of the Disinherited Knight.

Nothing could have saved him, except the remarkable strength of the noble warhorse, won the preceding day. This stood him in good stead as the horse of Bois Guilbert was wounded, while those of Front-de-Boeuf and Athelstane were exhausted from carrying the weight of their gigantic armoured riders. The masterly horsemanship of the Disinherited Knight and the energy of his noble animal enabled him to keep his three antagonists at sword's point, turning and wheeling with the agility of a hawk upon the wing and keeping his enemies separated. Rushing now against one, now against another, he unleashed sweeping blows with his sword while avoiding their counter-strokes. But although the lists rang with applause for his skill, it was evident that he must at last be overpowered. The nobles around Prince John cried to him to throw down his truncheon and save so brave a knight from being overcome by such odds.

'Not I, by the light of Heaven!' answered Prince John; 'This same *springald*[1] conceals his name and despises our hospitality. He hath gained one prize and may now afford to give others their turn.' But even as he spoke, there came an incident to change the fortunes of the day.

There was among the ranks of the Disinherited Knight a warrior in black armour. Mounted on a black horse, he was tall and to all appearances powerful and strong. This knight, who bore no device of any kind on his shield, had hitherto evinced very little interest in the outcome of the fight. He easily beat off combatants who attacked him, but neither pursued his advantage nor assailed anyone. In short, he had hitherto acted more like a spectator than of a participant in the tournament, procuring loud derision from the spectators as *Le Noir Faineant* – the Black Sluggard.

The Black Knight, however, discovering the leader of his party to be hard beset, threw aside his apathy. Setting spurs to his horse, which was still fresh, he came like a thunderbolt, exclaiming, in a voice like a trumpet-call,

'*Desdichado!*'

It was high time. While the Disinherited Knight was pressing upon the Templar, Front-de-Boeuf had got nigh to him, sword uplifted, but ere the blow could descend the Black Knight unleashed a stroke straight to his head. It glanced from the polished helmet, landing with unabated force on the *chamfron*[2] of his charger. Down it went. Front-de-Boeuf rolled on the ground, both horse and man stunned by the fury of the blow. *Le Noir Faineant* then turned upon Athelstane of Coningsburgh. His own sword having broken in his assault on Front-de-Boeuf, he wrenched the battleaxe from the bulky Saxon's hand and, clearly familiar with the weapon, brought it down hard upon his crest, sending Athelstane senseless to the earth.

---

1 A Military catapult. Here, a man catapulted into fame from obscurity.

2 Armour used to protect the front of a war horse's head.

Having achieved this double feat, highly applauded from its total surprise, the knight resumed his former indolence. He calmly returned to the northern extremity of the lists, leaving his leader to cope as best he could with de Bois Guilbert. This was no longer a matter of so much difficulty. The Templar's horse, having lost much blood, collapsed under the shock of the Disinherited Knight's charge. Brian de Bois Guilbert rolled on the field, his foot still encumbered with a stirrup. His antagonist dismounted, brandished his sword over the Templar's head and commanded him to yield. At this, Prince John, much more moved by the Templar's dangerous situation than he had been by that of his rival, saved him the shame of surrender by casting down his warder truncheon and putting an end to the conflict.

Of the few knights who still remained in the lists, most had abandoned the conflict and, by tacit consent, were leaving it to be determined by the combat of their leaders. The squires, who had found it dangerous to attend their masters during the engagement, now thronged to aid the wounded. These were removed with care to the neighbouring pavilions, or to the quarters prepared for them in the adjoining village.

Thus ended the memorable field of Ashby-de-la-Zouche, one of the most ferociously contested tournaments of that age. Although only four knights – including one smothered by the heat of his armour – had died upon the field, upwards of thirty were desperately wounded. For some, these wounds would prove mortal, while several more were disabled for life. Indeed, those who survived carried the marks of the conflict to the grave with them. Hence the occasion would always be mentioned in the records, as; 'The Gentle and Joyous Passage of Arms of Ashby'.

It was now the duty of Prince John to name the knight who had done best upon the field. He determined that the honour of the day lay with the knight whom the popular voice had termed *Le Noir Faineant*. In an immediate challenge to this, it was pointed out to the Prince that the victory had in fact been won by the Disinherited Knight. He, in the course of the day, had overcome six Champions with his own hand and had finally unhorsed and struck down the leader of the opposite party. Prince John, however, adhered to his view on the grounds that the Disinherited Knight and his party would have *lost* the day, but for the powerful assistance of the Black Knight to whom he insisted in awarding the prize.

To the surprise of all present, however, the knight thus preferred was nowhere to be found. He had left the lists immediately after the conflict ceased and had been observed to move down one of the forest glades with the same slow pace and indifferent manner which had procured him his Black Sluggard epithet. After he had been vainly summoned twice by sound of trumpet and proclamation of the Heralds, it became necessary to name another to receive the honours. Prince John had now no further excuse for resisting the claim of the Disinherited Knight whom he sourly named Champion of the Day.

Through a field slippery with blood and encumbered with broken armour and the bodies of slain and wounded horses the Marshals again conducted the victor to the foot of Prince John's throne.

'Disinherited Knight,' said Prince John, 'since only by that title do you consent to be known to us, we a second time award to you the honours of this tournament. We declare your right to claim and receive from the hands of the Queen of Love and Beauty, the Chaplet of Honour which your valour has justly deserved.' The Knight bowed but returned no answer. As trumpets sounded, ladies waved silken kerchiefs and embroidered veils, while all ranks joined in a shout of triumph. The Marshals conducted the Disinherited Knight across the lists to the foot of the throne occupied by the Lady Rowena. It was observed that he staggered as they guided him the second time across the lists. Indeed, his actions since the fight had ended seemed to result more from those around him than from his own will.

On the throne's lower step the champion was made to kneel. Rowena, chaplet in hand, descended from her station with a graceful and dignified step and was about to place it upon his helmet, when both Marshals exclaimed;

'It must not be thus; his head *must* be bare.' The Knight muttered faintly a few words, which were lost in the hollow of his helmet, but their purport seemed to be a desire that his casque be *not* removed.

Whether from love of tradition or from plain curiosity, the Marshals paid no attention to this and unhelmed him by cutting the laces of his casque and undoing the fastening of his gorget. When the helmet was removed, the sunburnt features of a young man of about twenty five were seen amidst a profusion of short fair hair. His countenance was as pale as death and marked in places with streaks of blood. Rowena had no sooner beheld him than she uttered a faint cry; but forcing herself to proceed, she tremblingly placed the splendid chaplet, the reward of the day, upon the bowed head of the victor. She then said,

'I bestow on thee this chaplet, Sir Knight, as the mead of valour of this day's victor.' Here she paused a moment, and then firmly added, 'and upon no brows more worthy, could a wreath of chivalry be placed!'

The Knight stooped his head, kissed her hand and then, sinking yet farther forward, fell prostrate at her feet.

There was general consternation. Cedric, who had been struck mute by the sudden appearance of his banished son, now rushed forward as if to separate him from Rowena. But this had been already accomplished by the Marshals, who, guessing the cause of Ivanhoe's faint, hastened to undo his armour and found indeed that his breastplate had been penetrated by the head of a lance...

chapter thirteen

'Heroes, approach!' Cried Atrides thus aloud,
'Stand forth distinguish'd from the circling crowd...'
William Wilkie: *The Epigoniad.*

The name of Ivanhoe was no sooner pronounced than it flew from mouth to mouth with all that eagerness could convey or curiosity receive. It was not long ere it reached the circle of the Prince, whose brow darkened. Looking around with an air of scorn, said he;

'My Lords and especially you, Sir Prior, what think ye of this? Methinks I felt the presence of my brother's minion – even when I least guessed whom that suit of armour held.'

'Front-de-Boeuf must prepare to restore his estate of Ivanhoe,' said De Bracy, who, having discharged his part honourably in the tournament, had laid his weapons aside and rejoined the Prince.

'Ay,' answered Waldemar Fitzurse, 'this gallant will now reclaim the castle which Richard assigned to him – and which your Highness then gave to Front-de-Boeuf.'

'Reginald Front-de-Boeuf,' replied John, 'is a man more willing to swallow three Ivanhoe manors than to disgorge one of them. For the rest, Sirs, I hope none here will deny my right to confer Crown estates upon my faithful followers who are ready to perform military service *here*, unlike Ivanhoe, wandering foreign and rendering neither homage nor service.' His entourage were too much involved in this question not to pronounce that the Prince's right was indeed indubitable.

'Generous Prince, who thus rewards the faithful!' Such were the words which burst from the train. All were expectants of similar grants at the expense of King Richard's followers and favourites. Prior Aymer also assented to the general proposition; observing, however,

'The blessed Jerusalem could not indeed be termed a foreign country. She is *communis mater,*[1] the mother of all Christians.

But I see not how the Knight of Ivanhoe could plead any advantage from this. The Crusaders under Richard never advanced farther than Ashkelon, a town of the Philistines and entitled to none of the privileges of the Holy City.'

Waldemar now returned, his curiosity having led him to where Ivanhoe had collapsed.

'That gallant,' said he, 'is likely to give your Highness little disturbance and will also leave Front-de-Boeuf in possession of his gains. He is severely wounded.'

'Whatever becomes of him,' said Prince John, 'he is victor of the day. Were he tenfold our enemy or the devoted friend of our brother, which is perhaps the same, his wounds must be looked to. Our *own* physician shall attend him...' A cunning smile curled the Prince's lip as he spoke, but Fitzurse went on to say that Ivanhoe had already been removed from the lists and was in the custody of friends.

'I was afflicted,' he said, 'to see the grief of the Queen of Love and Beauty, whose gaiety has changed to mourning. However, this Lady Rowena suppressed her sorrow with such effect that it could only be seen in her trembling hands as she gazed on the prostate Ivanhoe.'

'And who is this Lady Rowena,' said Prince John, 'of whom we hear so much?'

'A Saxon heiress of great possessions,' replied Prior Aymer. 'A rose of loveliness, a jewel of wealth and a cluster of camphire.'

'We shall cheer her sorrows,' said Prince John, 'and gentle her blood, by wedding her to a Norman! She seems to be a minor and thus at our royal disposal in marriage. How sayst thou, De Bracy? What thinkst thou of gaining fair lands and livings by bedding a Saxon, as did the men of the Conqueror?'

'If the lands are to my liking, my lord,' answered De Bracy, 'it will be hard to displease me with a bride. Deeply will I hold myself bound to your Highness.'

---

1 Lat. universal mother.

'We will not forget it,' said Prince John, 'and so that we may go straightly to work, we will command our seneschal to order the Lady Rowena to attend this evening's banquet. We will also bring her company, that rude churl her guardian and the other Saxon ox whom the Black Knight struck down in the tournament.' He added to his seneschal,

'De Bigot, thou wilt word this, our *second* summons, sufficiently courteously as to gratify the pride of these Saxons. You will make it impossible for them to refuse again – although courtesy to them is as casting pearls before swine.'

Prince John was about to give the signal for retiring from the lists, when a small billet was put into his hand.

'From whence?' he said.

'From foreign parts, my Lord, but from whence I know not,' replied his attendant. 'A Frenchman brought it hither, saying he had ridden night and day to put it into the hands of your Highness.' The Prince looked narrowly at the superscription, and then at the seal, placed so as to secure the flex-silk with which the billet was surrounded. It bore the impression of three *fleurs-de-lis*.[2] John then opened the billet with an agitation which visibly increased as he perused:

'Take heed to yourself – for the Devil is unchained!'

The Prince turned as pale as death and looked first at the earth and then up to heaven like a man receiving sentence of execution. He then took Waldemar Fitzurse and De Bracy aside and put the billet into their hands.

'It means,' he added, in a faltering voice, 'that Richard has obtained his freedom.'

'This may be a false alarm, or a forgery.' said De Bracy.

'It is the King of France's own hand and seal,' replied Prince John.

'Then it is time, said Fitzurse, 'to draw our party together, either at York or some other central place. A few days more and it will be indeed too late. Your Highness must break off the tournament.'

'The yeomen and the commons,' said De Bracy, 'should not be dismissed angry for lack of games.'

'The day,' said Fitzurse, 'is not yet far spent. Let the archers shoot a few rounds at the target and the prize be adjudged. That will fulfill the Prince's promises so far as this herd of Saxons is concerned.'

'I thank thee, Waldemar,' said the Prince; 'I am reminded that we have a debt to pay to that insolent peasant who insulted our person. Our banquet shall also go forward tonight as proposed. Were this my last hour of power, let it be an hour sacred to revenge and to pleasure. Let new cares come with tomorrow's new day.'

The sound of the trumpets recalled those spectators who had already begun to leave the field. Proclamation was made that Prince John, suddenly called by high public duties, was obliged to discontinue the Festival. Nevertheless, unwilling that so many good yeomen should depart without a trial of skill, he was pleased to order them to hold, today, the competition of archery intended for the morrow. To the best archer, the prize was to be a bugle-horn, mounted with silver together with a silken baldric ornamented with a medallion of St Hubert, patron of sylvan sport.

More than thirty yeomen presented themselves as competitors, several of whom

2 Heraldic lilies, symbols of the French royal house. The message was from King Philippe Auguste of France.

were rangers and under-keepers in the royal forests of Needwood and Charnwood. However, when the archers heard against whom they were to be matched, upwards of twenty withdrew from the contest; in those days the skill of each celebrated marksman was known far afield.

The competitors now amounted to eight. Prince John stepped from his royal seat to view these chosen yeomen more closely, several of whom wore the royal livery. He then observed the object of his resentment standing on the same spot and with the same composed countenance of the preceding day.

'Fellow,' said Prince John, 'I guessed by thy insolent babble that thou wert no longbowman; and I see thou darest not try thy skill among the archers yonder.'

'Under favour, sir,' replied the yeoman, 'I have another reason for refraining to shoot.'

'Thy other reason?' said Prince John, who, for some reason felt a curiosity respecting this individual.

'Because,' replied the woodsman, 'I know not if these yeomen and I are used to shoot at the same marks. Moreover, I wonder how your Grace would relish a *third* prize being won by a person under your displeasure.' Prince John coloured as he put the question,

'What is thy name, yeoman?'

'Locksley.'

'Then, Locksley,' said Prince John, 'thou shalt shoot in thy turn, when these yeomen have displayed their skill. Carry the prize and I will add to it twenty nobles. Lose, and thou shalt be scourged out of the lists with bowstrings, as an insolent braggart.'

'And if I refuse to shoot on such a wager?' said the yeoman. 'Your Grace's men-at-arms may strip and scourge me, but cannot compel me to draw my bow.'

'If thou refuse my fair proffer,' said the Prince, 'the Provost of the lists shall cut thy bowstring, break thy bow and expel thee from the Presence as a faint-hearted craven.'

'This is no fair chance, proud Prince,' said the yeoman, 'to compete me against the best archers of Leicester and Staffordshire. Nevertheless, I will do your pleasure.'

'Look to him closely, men-at-arms, lest he attempt to escape,' said Prince John, 'his heart is sinking. You, good fellows, shoot boldly; a buck and a butt of wine are your refreshment in yonder tent when the prize is won.'

A target was placed at the upper end of the southern avenue which led to the lists. The contending archers took their station in turn at the bottom of the southern access, the distance between that station and the mark allowing full distance for what was called a *shot at rovers*. The archers, their order of precedence settled by lot, were each to fire three shafts; the sport being regulated by the Provost of the games.

One by one, the archers stepped forward and delivered their shafts. Of 24 arrows, ten hit the target. The others landed so near that, considering the distance of the mark, it was reckoned good archery. Of the ten shafts on target, two within the inner ring were both shot by one Hubert, a forester in the service of Malvoisin. He was accordingly pronounced victorious.

'Now, Locksley,' said Prince John to the yeoman with a bitter smile, 'wilt thou try conclusions with Hubert, or wilt thou yield up bow, baldric and quiver to the Provost of the sports?'

'I am content to try my fortune,' said Locksley, 'on condition that when I have shot two shafts at yonder mark of Hubert's, he shall be bound to shoot one at a mark which I shall set.'

'That is only fair,' answered Prince John, 'Hubert, if thou dost beat this braggart, I will fill this bugle with silver pennies for thee.'

'A man can only do his best,' answered Hubert; 'but my grandsire drew a good long bow at Hastings and I trust not to dishonour his memory.'

The former target was now removed and replaced with a fresh one of the same size. Hubert, as victor in the first trial, had the right to shoot first. He took his aim with great deliberation, measuring the distance with his eye while holding his bow, the arrow on the bowstring. At length he took a step forward and, raising the bow at the full stretch of his left arm until the centre was nigh level with his face, he drew the bowstring back to his ear. The arrow whistled away and lighted within the inner ring of the target, but not exactly in the centre.

'You did not allow for the wind, Hubert,' said his antagonist, bending his bow. So saying, and without showing the least anxiety, Locksley stepped to the appointed station and shot his arrow so carelessly that he did not seem to have even looked at the mark. Although speaking right up to the instant that the shaft left the bowstring, it hit the target two inches nearer than Hubert's to the white bullseye.

'By heaven!' called Prince John to Hubert, 'If that runagate knave overcomes thee, thou art worthy of the gallows!'

Hubert had but one set speech for all occasions.

'A man can but do his best,' he said, 'nevertheless, my grandsire drew a good bow...'

'The foul *fiend* on thy grandsire and all his generation!' interrupted John, 'Shoot, knave – and shoot thy best or it shall be the worse for thee!' Hubert resumed his place. Mindful of the coment from his adversary, he made allowance for the wind which had just arisen, and shot. The arrow hit the dead centre of the target.

'A Hubert!' shouted the populace. 'In the clout!'

'Thou canst not beat *that* shot, Locksley,' said the Prince, with an insulting smile.

'I will notch his shaft for him, however...' replied Locksley.

He let fly his arrow with a little more precaution than before. Arriving at the target, it struck not only the centre but right into that of his competitor, shivering and splitting it.

'And now,' said Locksley, 'I will crave your Grace's permission to place a target used in the North Country; and welcome every brave yeoman who shall try a shot at it to win a smile from the bonny lass he loves best.' He then turned to leave the lists.

'Let your guards attend me,' he said, 'if you please. I go only to cut a rod from the nearest willow bush.'

Prince John made a signal that some attendants should follow him in case of his escape as cries of 'Shame, *shame*!' burst from the spectators.

Locksley returned with a willow wand about six feet in length, perfectly straight and slightly thicker than a man's thumb. He began to peel this with great composure, saying that to ask a good woodsman to shoot at a target as broad as the one used hitherto was an insult.

'However,' added he, having walked to the other end of the lists and stuck the willow wand upright in the ground, 'he that hits this rod at a hundred yards, I will call an archer fit to bear a longbow and quiver before even good King Richard himself.'

'My grandsire,' said Hubert, 'drew a good bow at the battle of Hastings, but never shot at such a mark in his life. Neither will I. If this yeoman can cleave that rod, I yield to him; I might as well shoot at a wheat straw or a sunbeam, as at a white streak I can hardly see!'

'Cowardly dog!' said Prince John. 'Sirrah Locksley, shoot.' He again bent his bow, but this time looked with attention to his weapon. He then discarded the bow-string as not truly round, having been frayed by the two former shots. The longbow restrung, he took his aim with deliberation. The crowds awaited in breathless silence. The archer vindicated their opinion of his skill. He fired. His arrow flew up, sped downrange, arced down – and hit and split the willow rod. An uproar of acclamations followed; and even Prince John, in admiration, lost his dislike for an instant.

'These twenty nobles,' he said, 'thou hast fairly won and are thine. We will make them fifty if thou wilt take livery and service with us as a yeoman of our Bodyguard.'

'Pardon me, noble Prince,' said Locksley; 'but I have vowed that if ever I take service, it should be with your royal brother King Richard. These twenty nobles I give to Hubert, who has this day drawn as brave a bow as did his grandsire at Hastings. Had his modesty not refused the trial, he would have hit the wand as well I.' Hubert shook his head as he received with reluctance the bounty of the stranger. Locksley, to escape further observation, mingled with the crowd and disappeared.

The victorious archer would not have escaped John's attention so easily had not that Prince other matters on his mind. As he gave the signal for retiring from the lists, he called to his Chamberlain and commanded him to gallop to Ashby and seek out Isaac the Jew.

'Tell the dog,' he said, 'to send me, before sun-down, two thousand crowns. He knows the security. Show him this ring as a token. The rest of the money must be paid at York within six days. If he fails to do this, I will have his infidel head.'

The Prince remounted his horse and returned to Ashby.

chapter fourteen

And crested chiefs and tissued dames
Assembled, at the clarion's call,
In some proud castle's high arch'd hall.
Thomas Warton: *For the New Year, 1787.*

Prince John held his high festival in the Castle of Ashby, which belonged to Roger de Quincy, Earl of Winchester. He being presently absent in the Holy Land, Prince John occupied his castle, disposing of his domains without scruple. Seeking as usual to dazzle by his hospitality and magnificence, he had given orders that the banquet be splendid.

The purveyors of the Prince, exercising the authority of royalty, swept the country of all which was esteemed fit for their master's table. Guests also were invited in great numbers. In his pursuit of popularity, Prince John had extended his invitation to some distinguished Saxon and Danish families as well as to the Norman nobility and gentry of the neighbourhood. However despised they might be by the Norman establishment, the great numbers of the Anglo-Saxon population would render them formidable in any civil war. It was thus his policy to court their leaders.

The Prince's intention being to treat his guests with a courtesy to which they had been little accustomed, it was his misfortune that petulance was usually breaking out and undoing the gains of his diplomacy. Prince John received Cedric and Athelstane with courtesy. He expressed his disappointment, without resentment, when the 'indisposition' of Rowena was cited as the reason for her absence. Cedric and Athelstane were both dressed in Saxon garb which, though not unhandsome in itself, was remote in appearance from that of the other guests. Prince John and Waldemar Fitzurse diplomatically refrained from amusement at a sight which, given the fashions of the day, now appeared simply ridiculous.

The guests were seated at tables groaning under the sheer weight of good cheer. Numerous cooks attended the Prince on his travels and had exerted all their art on the provisions served. Indeed they had succeeded in rendering them perfectly unlike their natural appearance. Besides dishes of domestic origin, there were various delicacies brought from foreign parts and a quantity of rich pastry. There were also simnel bread[1] and wastle cakes, only seen at the tables of the highest nobility. The banquet was crowned with the finest foreign and domestic wines.

Though luxurious, the Norman nobles were not, generally speaking, an intemperate race. While indulging themselves in the pleasures of the table, they aimed at delicacy but avoided excess. Gluttony and drunkenness they attributed to the vanquished Saxons as vices peculiar to their inferior station. Prince John, however, and those who courted his pleasure by imitating him, were apt to indulge to excess in the pleasures of the trencher and the goblet; this being an exception to the general manners of his Norman countrymen.

With sly gravity and only by private signs to each other, the Norman knights and nobles beheld the ruder demeanour of Athelstane and Cedric, attending a banquet to whose form and fashion they were unaccustomed. Their manners already the subject of sarcastic observation, the Saxons then unwittingly transgressed several of the rules of Norman high society. Cedric, by drying his hands with a towel instead of waving them gracefully in the air, incurred ridicule. So also did Athelstane who swallowed the whole of a large pasty composed of exquisite foreign delicacies, and termed a Karum pie.[2] It was discovered that the Thane of Coningsburgh had no idea what he had been devouring, and that he had taken the contents of the Karum pie for larks and pigeons. In fact, beccaficoes[3] and nightingales had been the victims of his ignorance and gluttony.

The long feast had at length neared its end. While the goblet circulated freely,

---

1 A crisp bread made with fine wheat flour.

2 *See* R. Henry: *A History of Great Britain*, 6 Vols., London (1771–93).

3 From an Italian word meaning 'fig-peckers' i.e. migratory birds of the genus *Sylvia* which fatten in the Autumn by pecking at the ripe fig.

men talked of the feats of the preceding tournament: of the unknown victor in the archery games; of the Black Knight whose self-denial brought withdrawal from the honours he had won; and of the gallant Ivanhoe, who had so dearly bought the honours of the day. The topics were treated with military frankness as jesting and laughter went round the hall. The brow of Prince John alone was clouded during these discussions. Some overpowering care seemed to be agitating his mind and it was only when he received direct hints from his attendants that he showed interest in what was passing. On such occasions he would start up, quaff a cup of wine as if to raise his spirits and then mingle in the conversation by some abrupt or random observation.

'We drink this beaker,' said he, 'to the health of Wilfred of Ivanhoe, Champion of this Passage of Arms and grieve that his wound renders him absent from our board. Let all fill to the toast, especially Cedric of Rotherwood, the worthy father of a son so promising.'

'No, my lord,' replied Cedric, standing up and placing on the table his untasted cup, 'I confer not the name of son to the disobedient youth who both disobeys me and relinquishes the customs of his fathers.'

''Tis impossible,' cried Prince John, with feigned astonishment, 'that so gallant a knight should be an unworthy or disobedient son!'

'Yet, my lord,' answered Cedric, 'it is so with Wilfred. He left my dwelling to mingle with the gay nobility of your brother's court where he learned those tricks of horsemanship you prize so highly. He left it contrary to my wish and command.'

'Alas!' replied Prince John, with a deep sigh of affected sympathy, 'since your son was a follower of my unhappy brother, it need not be enquired where, or from whom, he learned filial disobedience.' Thus spoke Prince John, ignoring the fact that of all the sons of Henry II – and none was free from the charge – he himself had been the most rebellious.

'I think,' said he, after a moment's pause, 'that my brother proposed to confer the rich manor of Ivanhoe upon his favourite.'

'He did endow him with it,' answered Cedric; 'And it is not my least quarrel with my son that he stooped to be feudal *vassal* in the very domain which his fathers possessed in free and independent right.'

'We shall then have your willing sanction, good Cedric,' said Prince John, 'to confer this fief upon a person whose dignity will not be diminished by holding land of the English crown. Sir Reginald Front-de-Boeuf,' he said, turning towards that Baron, 'I trust *you* will so keep the goodly Barony of Ivanhoe, that Sir Wilfred shall not again incur his father's displeasure by entering it.'

'By St Anthony!' answered the black-browed giant, 'I will consent that your Highness shall call me *Saxon* if any wrenches your Highness's gift from me.'

'Whoever shall call *thee* Saxon, Baron,' interjected Cedric, 'will do thee an honour as great as it is undeserved!' Front-de-Boeuf would have retorted, but Prince John's petulance came in before him.

'Assuredly, my lords,' said he, 'the noble Cedric speaks truth. His race may claim precedence over us as much in the length of their pedigrees as in the longitude of their cloaks.'

'They did go before us indeed on the battlefield, as deer before dogs,' added Malvoisin.

'And with good right may they go before us, forget not,' said the Prior Aymer, 'in the superior decency and decorum of their *manners*.'

'And in their singular abstemiousness and *temperance*!' said De Bracy, forgetting the plan which promised him a Saxon bride.

While the courtiers thus followed the Prince in aiming ridicule at Cedric, the face of the Saxon became aflame. He glanced fiercely from one to another as if the quick succession of so many insults had prevented his replying to them in turn. Like a baited bull surrounded by tormenting dogs, he seemed at a loss to choose the first object of his revenge. At length, in a voice half choked with passion he spoke to Prince John.

'*Whatever*,' he said, 'have been the follies and vices of our race, a Saxon would have been held *nidering*[1] who should, in his own Hall and while his own wine-cup passed, have treated and *permitted* to be treated, a guest as your Highness has this day seen me abused. *Whatever* was the misfortune of our fathers on the field of Hastings,' and here he looked at both Front-de-Boeuf and the Templar, '*those* might at least be silent who have within these few hours, again lost saddle and stirrup and gone down before a *Saxon* lance!'

'By my faith, a biting jest!' said Prince John; 'How like you it, Sirs? Our Saxon subject rises in spirit and courage, becoming shrewd in wit and bold of bearing. What say ye, my lords? Better to take to our galleys and return to Normandy?'

'For fear of the Saxons?' said De Bracy, laughing; 'we should need no weapon beyond our hunting spears to bring these boars to bay.'

'A truce with your raillery, Sir Knights,' said Fitzurse; 'it would be well,' he added, addressing the Prince, 'that your Highness should assure the worthy Cedric that no insult is intended to him by our jests.'

'Insult?' answered Prince John, resuming his courteous demeanour; 'We could neither give nor permit any such to be offered in our presence. Here! We fill our cup to Cedric himself, since he refuses to drink his son's health.'

The cup went round amid the well-dissembled applause of the courtiers. It failed, however, to make the designed impression on the Saxon. He was not naturally acute in perception, but any who assumed that this flattery would obliterate the prior insult, undervalued his understanding.

Another royal toast passed round, 'To Sir Athelstane of Coningsburgh,' to which he bowed and showed his sense of the honour by draining a huge goblet in answer to it.

'And now, sirs,' said Prince John, who began to be tipsy with wine, 'having done justice to our Saxon guests, we will pray of them some response to our courtesy. Worthy Thane Cedric, may we pray you to name to us some worthy Norman, that you may wash down with wine all bitterness which the name may leave behind it?'

Fitzurse arose while Prince John spoke. Gliding round behind the seat of the Saxon, he whispered to him to put an end to racial unkindness by citing Prince John. The Saxon did not reply to this politic hint but, rising and filling his cup, he addressed the Prince:

'Your Highness has required that I should name a Norman deserving to be remembered at this banquet. This is a hard task since it calls on the slave to sing the

---

1 The most emphatic Saxon term for abject worthlessness. *Scott.*

praises of the master and the vanquished to praise the conqueror. Yet I will name a Norman; the first in arms and first in place and the best and noblest of his race. And any refusing to join the toast to his fame, I term false and dishonoured. I raise this goblet to the health of – Richard the Lionheart!'

Prince John, who had expected that his own name would have closed the Saxon's speech, started when that of his brother was so dramatically given. He raised the wine-cup mechanically to his lips, then instantly set it down to view the response of the company to this unexpected proposal. Many felt it as unsafe to oppose, as to comply. Some of the older, experienced courtiers closely imitated the example of the Prince himself, raising the goblet to their lips, and replacing it. However, many there were who exclaimed,

'Long live King Richard! May he be restored to us!'

A few, among whom were Front-de-Boeuf and the Templar, in sullen disdain suffered their goblets to stand untouched before them. But no man ventured to oppose directly a toast to the health of the King.

Having enjoyed his triumph, Cedric said to his companion,

'Up, noble Athelstane! We have remained here long enough and seen enough of Norman courtesy.' So saying, he arose and left the banqueting room, followed by Athelstane and several other Saxon guests insulted by the sarcasm of the Prince and his courtiers.

'By the bones of St Thomas,' said Prince John, as they retreated, 'these Saxon churls have had the best of the day, and retreat in triumph!'

'*Conclamatum est, poculatum est.*' said Prior Aymer. 'We have drunk and we have shouted; it were time we left our wine flagons.'

'This monk must have some fair penitent to *shrive* tonight, that he is in such a hurry to depart,' said De Bracy.

'Not so, Sir Knight,' replied the Abbot; 'but I must move several miles forward this evening upon my homeward journey.'

'They are breaking up,' whispered the Prince to Fitzurse, 'and this coward Prior is the first to shrink from me.'

'Fear not, my lord,' said Waldemar; 'I will induce him to join us at our meeting at York. Sir Prior,' he said, 'I must speak with you in private before you mount.' The other guests were now fast dispersing with the exception of those immediately attached to Prince John's faction and his retinue.

'This is the result of your advice,' said the Prince, turning angrily on Fitzurse; 'that I should be bearded at my own board by a drunken Saxon churl and at the mere *sound* of my brother's name, men should desert as if I had the leprosy? They have seen the handwriting on the wall. They have seen the paw of the lion in the sand and heard his roar. Nothing will reanimate their courage.'

'Would to God, De Bracy,' said Fitzurse aside, 'that he could reanimate his own! His brother's very name is an *ague*[1] to him. Woe betide the counsellors of a Prince who lacks courage and perseverance in good – and evil...'

---

1 The mediaeval term for malaria, then still endemic in England. Malarial patients tremble and shake with the fever.

chapter fifteen

He thinks I am the tool and servant of his will.
Well, let it be; through all the maze of trouble
His plots and base oppression must create,
I'll shape myself a way to higher things,
And who will say 'tis wrong?
Joanna Baillie, *Count Basil, a Tragedy.*

No spider ever took more pains to repair a shattered web, than did Waldemar Fitzurse to recombine the members of Prince John's cabal. Few were attached to John from inclination and none from personal regard. It was therefore necessary for Fitzurse to hint at future advantages and remind them of those presently enjoyed. To the wild young nobles he held out the prospect of license and revelry; to the ambitious, power; to the covetous, wealth and domains, while the leaders of the mercenaries received gold. Promises, however, were distributed more liberally than money as he steadied the waverers. He dismissed the return of King Richard as highly improbable; yet when he observed apprehension on this score, he treated that eventuality as irrelevant to their political calculations.

Fitzurse would thus say to his hearers,

'If Richard returns, he returns to enrich his impoverished Crusaders at the expense of those who did not follow him to the Holy Land. He returns to inflict fearful retribution on those who have offended against the law of the land or the privileges of the crown. He returns to avenge the preference which the Orders of the Temple and the Hospital showed to Philip of France during the crusades. He returns to punish, as a rebel, every adherent of his brother John.'

The Prince's artful counsellor would continue,

'Are ye afraid of his power? We acknowledge him a valiant knight; but these are not the days of King Arthur, when a champion could engage an army. If Richard indeed comes back he will be alone and friendless, since the bones of his gallant army whiten the sands of Palestine. The few of his followers who have returned are like this Wilfred of Ivanhoe, beggared and broken men. And what of Richard's right of birth? Is his title by primogeniture more certain than that of the Conqueror's eldest son, Duke Robert of Normandy? William the Red[1] and Henry,[2] his second and third brothers, were successively preferred to him by the nation. Robert had every merit which can be pleaded for Richard; a bold knight, generous to friends and the Church. He was a crusader and a conqueror of the Holy Sepulchre. Yet he died a blind, miserable prisoner in the Castle of Cardiff because he opposed the will of the people – who would not have him rule!'

Fitzurse would also say,

'Choose from among the blood royal the Prince who is best qualified to hold the supreme power; he whose election will best promote the interests of the nobility. In personal qualifications, Prince John might be inferior to Richard. But when the latter

---

1 William II (1056–1100) known as 'Rufus' for his red hair.

2 Henry I (1069–1135).

pointed the sword of vengeance, while the former held out rewards, immunities, wealth and honours, it cannot be doubted which King ye should support.'

These and other arguments, adapted to the circumstances of those whom he was addressing, carried weight with the nobles of Prince John's faction. Most of them consented to attend the meeting at York to make final arrangement for the crowning of Prince John.

It was late at night when, worn out with his various exertions but gratified with the results, Fitzurse returned to the Castle of Ashby. Here he met with De Bracy, who had exchanged his banqueting garments for a short green kirtle, with hose of the same cloth and colour and a leathern cap. He had a short sword, a horn slung over his shoulder, a long bow in his hand and a bundle of arrows stuck in his belt. Had Fitzurse met this figure in an outer apartment he would have thought him one of the yeomen of the guard. Finding him, however, in the inner hall, he looked in surprise at a Norman knight in the dress of an English yeoman.

'What mummery is this, De Bracy?' said Fitzurse, 'is this a time for theatricals when the fate of our Prince is on the verge?'

'I have been attending to mine own business,' answered De Bracy calmly, 'as you, Fitzurse, have been minding yours.'

'Minding mine *own* business?' echoed Waldemar; 'I have been engaged in that of our Patron.'

'And the reason for that, Waldemar,' said De Bracy, 'is the promotion of thine own interest. Come, we know each other; ambition is thy pursuit, pleasure is mine; and they suit our different ages. On John we agree he is too weak to be a firm monarch, too tyrannical to be a good monarch, too insolent to be a popular monarch and too timid to be long a monarch of any kind. But he *is* a monarch by whom Fitzurse and De Bracy hope to rise and thrive; so you aid him on policy, I with the lances of my Free Companions.'

'So you, our would-be auxiliary,' said Fitzurse impatiently, 'play the fool in this very moment of necessity. What means this disguise?'

'To get me a wife,' answered De Bracy coolly, 'after the manner of the tribe of Benjamin.'

'The tribe of Benjamin?' said Fitzurse.

'Yester-even,' said De Bracy, 'we heard Prior Aymer tell a tale in reply to the romance sung by the Minstrel. He said that, long ago in Palestine, the youth of the tribe of Benjamin carried off all the ladies present at a tournament. Thus they won wives without the consent either of their brides or their brides' families.'

'I heard the story.' said Fitzurse.

'I tell thee,' said De Bracy, 'that I mean to purvey me a wife after that fashion of the Benjamins. I will fall upon that herd of Saxon bullocks who have left the castle – and carry off the lovely Rowena.'

'Art thou *mad,* De Bracy?' hissed Fitzurse, 'her Saxon family is powerful and respected by their countrymen. We have no time for this; we *need* popular support.'

'John will soon see,' said De Bracy, 'the difference betwixt the support of my regiment of lances and that of a Saxon mob. Be assured, I mean not to be discovered.

In this garb am I not a forester? The blame shall fall on the outlaws of the Yorkshire forests. Presently I will reappear, now in mine own Norman shape, play the courteous knight and rescue the afflicted Rowena from the hands of her abductors. I will take her to Front-de-Boeuf's castle of Torquilstone, or even to Normandy if need be. She will not see her kindred again until she be the bride of Maurice De Bracy.'

'A marvellous and sage plan,' said Fitzurse. 'And, as I think, not entirely of thine own devising. Be frank, De Bracy, who aids thee in this? Thy own troops lie far off at York.'

'Marry, if thou must know,' said De Bracy, 'it was the Templar. Brian de Bois Guilbert shaped out this enterprise. He will aid me in the onslaught and he and his followers will impersonate the outlaws from whom my valorous arm shall rescue the lady.'

'By God!' said Fitzurse, 'the plan is hardly worthy of your united wisdom, De Bracy, if the lady be left in the hands of thy confederate. Thou may succeed in taking her from her Saxon friends, but how to rescue her afterward from Bois Guilbert? He is a falcon accustomed to hold his prey fast.'

'He is a Templar and celibate,' said De Bracy, 'he cannot rival my plan to wed this heiress.'

'Then,' said Fitzurse, 'since naught that I can say will put this folly from thy obstinate mind; at least waste as little time as possible.'

'I tell thee,' answered De Bracy, 'that it will be the work of a few hours. I shall then meet thee at York at the head of my men, ready to support our bold design. But I hear my comrades' steeds stamping in the outer court. Farewell. I go like a true knight to win the smiles of beauty.'

'Like a true *knight*?' mused Fitzurse, looking after him, 'Like a fool on an errand, I should say. But it is with such tools and fools that I must work.'

The meditations of the politician were here interrupted by the voice of the Prince, calling out from an interior apartment,

'Noble Fitzurse!'

Bonnet doffed, the aspirant Chancellor hastened in to receive the orders of the future sovereign.

chapter sixteen

The moss his bed, the cave his humble cell,
His food the fruits, his drink the crystal well
Remote from man, with God he pass'd his days,
Prayer all his business—all his pleasure praise.
Thomas Parnell: *The Hermit.*

The outcome of the tournament had been decided by the exertions of that unknown knight whom the spectators had dubbed *Le Noir Faineant*. He left the field abruptly when the victory was achieved and was nowhere to be found when called to receive the reward of his valour. While being summoned by the Heralds he was heading northward, avoiding frequented paths and taking the shortest road through the woodlands. He paused for the night at a small hostelry and there received news of the tourney's outcome.

Next morning the knight departed early. The condition of his horse, carefully spared during the tourney, enabled him to travel far without much repose. Yet his progress was slowed by the devious paths he took, so that when evening closed upon him, he found himself only on the frontiers of the West Riding of Yorkshire. Horse and man now required refreshment and it became necessary to find some place to spend the approaching night.

In such circumstances, knights-errant would turn their horses out to graze and, with an oak tree for a canopy, would lay themselves down to meditate on their lady mistress. But the Black Knight either had no mistress to meditate upon, or was as indifferent to love as he seemed to be in war. He was deep in woods through which indeed there were many open glades but only paths formed by the herds of cattle grazing in the forest.

The sun, by which the knight had been directing his course, had now sunk behind the Derbyshire hills. He tried to select the most beaten path in the hope that it might lead to a herdsman's cottage or the lodge of a forester. He also resolved to trust to his horse and slackened the reins. The path the animal took deviated from the direction taken by his rider, but as he seemed confident, he was given his head – and this was justified by the outcome. The footpath soon became wider and more worn, while the faint tinkle of a bell suggested that they were in the vicinity of a chapel or hermitage.

He soon reached an open clearing, on the opposite side of which a rock face rose abruptly from a gently sloping plain, offering a grey, weatherbeaten front to the traveller. Ivy mantled its sides in some places while in others oaks and holly bushes waved over the precipices below. At the bottom of the rock and leaning against it was a hut built of the trunks of trees, its crevices stuffed with moss mixed with clay against the weather. The trunk of a young fir tree, a cross-piece of wood tied near the top, was planted upright by the door as a crude emblem of the holy cross. A short distance to the right, a fountain of clear water trickled out of the rock into a hollow stone fashioned into a rustic basin. Escaping from there, the stream murmured on through a channel down the slope, to lose itself in the woods.

Beside this fountain were the ruins of a very small chapel, of which the roof had partly fallen in. The building, when entire, had never been above 16 feet long by 12 in breadth. Its low roof had rested upon four concentric arches which sprang from the four corners of the building, each supported upon a short and heavy pillar. A belfry rose above the porch on four small pillars, within which hung a green, weatherbeaten bell whose sound had been heard by the Black Knight. The whole peaceful scene lay glimmering in the twilight. It gave him assurance of lodging for the night since it was a duty of hermits dwelling in the woods to accommodate benighted travellers. Thanking St Julian,[1] a patron saint of wayfarers, who had sent him this good harbourage, he dismounted and rapped on the door of the hermitage with the butt of his lance.

---

1 The Patron Saint of travellers apprehensive of their next night's lodging. St Christopher handles general travelling enquiries and requests

It was some time before he had an answer; and the reply when it came, was unpropitious.

'Pass on, whosoever thou art,' came a deep, hoarse voice from within the hut. 'Disturb not the servant of God and St Dunstan in his evening devotions.'

'Father,' answered the knight, 'here is a poor wanderer lost in these woods, who craves thy charity and hospitality.'

'Good brother,' replied the inhabitant, 'it has pleased Our Lady and St Dunstan to make me the *object* of those virtues, and not the exerciser thereof. I have no provisions here which even a dog would share with me; continue on thy way and God speed.'

'But how,' persisted the knight, 'may I find my way through dense woods with darkness coming on? Reverend father, I pray you as a Christian, undo your door and at least point out my road to me.'

'And I pray *you*, good Christian brother,' replied the anchorite,[1] 'to disturb me no more. You have already interrupted one *pater*, two *aves* and a *credo* which I should have said before moonrise.'

'The road – the *road!*' persisted the knight. 'Give me directions for the road, if I may expect no more.'

'The road,' replied the hermit, 'is easy to hit. The path from the wood leads to a morass and from thence to a ford. Cross it and take the path, which hangs over the river…'

'A broken path, a ford and a morass!' interrupted the Black Knight, 'Hermit, you *cannot* send me on this road tonight. He who lives by the charity of the country, hast no right to refuse shelter to the wayfarer in distress. Open the door instantly or, by the Holy Rood, I will beat it down and make entry for myself.'

'Wayfarer,' replied the hermit, 'be warned. If thou put me to mine own defence, it will be the worse for you.'

At this moment a distant barking and growling from within, which the traveller had been hearing for some time, became loud and furious. The knight reckoned that the hermit, alarmed by the threat of forced entry, was readying his dogs. Incensed at this inhospitality, the knight kicked at the door furiously with his mailed foot. Posts and staples shook and the anchorite immediately called out,

'Patience, *patience*! Spare thy strength, traveller. I will undo the door, though it will be little to thy pleasure.'

The door opened. The hermit, a large, strongly-built man in a hooded sackcloth gown, girt with a rope of rushes, stood before the knight. In one hand he held a lighted torch and in the other a thick and heavy crab-tree club. Two large shaggy dogs, half greyhound half mastiff, glared at the traveller. But when his torch glanced upon the crest and golden spurs of the knight, the hermit immediately calmed the dogs. His tone changing to one of bare courtesy, he bade the knight enter, excusing his unwillingness to open after sunset due to the multitude of thieves who were abroad. The knight looked around him, seeing nothing but a bed of leaves, a crucifix rudely carved in oak, a missal, with a rough-hewn table and two stools, and one or two clumsy articles of furniture.

'The poverty here,' he said, 'seems sufficient defence against any risk of thieves; not to mention dogs strong enough to pull down a stag – and most men.'

---

1 Anchorite: from Greek: ἀναχωρέω, anachoreo, 'to withdraw.' A religious hermit.

'The Keeper of the forest,' said the hermit, 'allows me the use of these animals to protect my solitude until the times shall mend.' Having said this, he fixed his torch in a twisted branch of iron serving as a candlestick. Placing the oaken trivet before the embers of the fire, which he refuelled with some dry wood, he placed stools by the table, and beckoned to the knight to be seated. So they sat down, and gazed with gravity at each other, each thinking that he had seldom seen a stronger or more athletic figure than that now opposite him.

'Reverend hermit,' said the knight, 'where I am to put my horse; what can I have for a supper; and where I am to couch for the night?' The host pointed successively to two corners of the hut.

'Your stable,' said he, 'is there. Your bed, there.' Reaching down a platter with two handfuls of parched peas upon it from the neighbouring shelf and placing it upon the table, he added, 'And your supper is here.' The knight shrugged his shoulders. Leaving the hut, he brought in his horse, unsaddled him with much attention and spread his own mantle upon the steed's weary back.

The hermit was moved by the care which the stranger displayed in tending his horse. From a recess he dragged out a bundle of forage, spread it before the knight's charger and shook down a quantity of dried fern in the corner assigned for the rider's couch. Duty done, both resumed their seats by the table, on which stood the trencher of pease. The hermit gave a long grace, which had once been Latin, but of which few traces remained. He then set an example to his guest by modestly putting some three or four dried peas into a very large mouth. This was furnished with teeth which might have ranked with a boar for sharpness and whiteness; a miserable grist, thought the Black Knight, for so large a mill. The knight had removed his helmet, corselet and the greater part of his armour. This showed the hermit a head thickly curled with fair hair, high features, remarkably bright blue eyes and a well-formed mouth, its upper lip clothed with mustachios darker than his hair. In sum, he bore the look of a bold and enterprising man.

The hermit threw back his cowl and showed a round bullet head of a man in the prime of life and whose close-shaven crown was surrounded by a circle of stiff curled black hair. The features expressed nothing of monastic austerity. On the contrary, it was a bold, bluff countenance with broad black eyebrows and a well-turned forehead. His cheeks were as round and as rosy as those of a trumpeter and from them descended a curly black beard. Such a face, joined to the brawny form of the holy man, spoke rather of sirloins and haunches than of peas and pulses. The incongruity did not escape the guest who, having finally swallowed some dried peas, found it necessary to request his host for some liquor. The response was a large can of pure water from the fountain.

'It is from the well of St Dunstan,' said he, 'in which, betwixt sun and sun, he baptized on one day five hundred heathen Danes and Britons. Blessed be his name!'

'How strange, reverend father,' said the knight, 'that the small morsels which you eat, together with this undoubtedly holy but rather thin beverage, have made you appear a man more fit to win the ram at wrestling or the ring at quarter-staff, than to linger in this wilderness, saying Masses and living on parched peas and cold water.'

'Sir Knight,' answered the hermit, 'your thoughts are those of the ignorant laity.

It has pleased Our Lady and my patron saint to restrain myself to pulses and water; like Shadrach, Meshach and Abednego[1] who drank the same rather than defile themselves with the wine and meat offered by the King of the Saracens.'

'Holy father,' said the knight, 'permit a sinful layman to know the name of he upon whom it hath pleased Heaven to work such a miracle?'

'Thou mayst call me,' answered the hermit, 'the Clerk of Copmanhurst, for such I am termed in these parts. They add the epithet holy, but I am unworthy of such. And now I pray ye for the name of my guest?'

'Holy Clerk,' said the knight, 'men call me The Black Knight. Many add to it the epithet of Sluggard.' The hermit could scarcely suppress a smile at this.

'I see,' said he, 'Sir Sluggish Knight, that thou art a man of prudence. Moreover, I see that my poor monastic fare likes thee not. I now recall, Sir Sluggard, that when the Keeper of this forest-walk left those dogs for my protection, he also left me food. Since this was too rich for my use, the very memory of it had escaped me amid my more weighty meditations.'

'I dare say he did,' said the knight; 'I was convinced that there was better food in this cell, since you first doffed your cowl. Your Keeper is a jovial fellow, let us see his bounty.'

The hermit cast a wistful look upon the knight, in which there was a comic expression of hesitation, as if uncertain how far he should trust his bold guest. He went to the further side of the hut and opened a concealed hutch. Out of this he brought a large pasty, baked in a pewter platter of unusual dimensions. This mighty dish he placed before his guest who immediately used his *poniard* to cut it open and lost no time in sampling its contents.

'How long is it since the good Keeper has been here?' said the knight to his host.

'About...two months,' answered the father hastily.

'By the true Lord,' answered the knight, 'everything in your hermitage is miraculous, Holy Clerk! I would have been sworn that this venison was alive a week since.' The hermit was somewhat alarmed by this observation. Moreover, he made a poor figure as he gazed at the rapidly vanishing pasty. However, his previous profession of abstinence left him no pretext for joining in its consumption.

'I have been in Palestine, Sir Clerk,' said the knight, stopping short all of a sudden, 'where it is customary for a host entertaining a guest to eat along with him. Pray comply.'

'To ease your scruples, Sir Knight, I will for once depart from my Rule' replied the hermit, falling on the pasty.

'Holy Clerk,' said the knight, his hunger finally appeased, 'I would wager that the same honest keeper to whom we are obliged for the venison, has also left thee a stoup of wine? Doubtless, this would be unworthy for so *rigid* an anchorite; yet were you to search yonder crypt, you will find that I am right.'

The hermit only replied by a grin. Returning to the hutch, he produced a leathern bottle, which might contain about four quarts. He also brought forth two large drinking cups, made out of the horn of the urus,[2] and hooped with silver. Filling both cups, and saying, in the Saxon fashion,

---

1 See Daniel 1: 5-20

2 The Aurochs, an extinct species of wild ox.

'*Wæs þu hæl*, Sir Sluggish Knight!'[1] He emptied his own at a draught.

'*Drinc hæl!* Holy Clerk of Copmanhurst!'[2] Thus answered the warrior, toasting his host.

'Holy Clerk,' said the stranger, after the first cup, 'I marvel that a man possessed of such sinews as thine and who is so goodly a trencherman, should think of abiding by himself in this wilderness. In my judgment, you are fitter to keep a castle or a fort than to live here upon pulse and water – or even upon the charity of the Keeper. In thy place, I should find myself both sport and plenty from the King's deer; a buck will never be missed that goes to the use of Saint Dunstan's chaplain.'

'Sir Sluggish Knight,' replied the Clerk, 'these are dangerous words and I pray you to cease them. I am a true hermit to the King and Law. Were I to thieve my liege's game I should be sure of the prison and in peril of hanging.'

'Nevertheless, were I as thou,' said the knight, 'I would take by moonlight when foresters and keepers are warm in bed. Resolve me, Holy Clerk, hast thou ever practised such a pastime?'

'Friend Sluggard,' answered the hermit, 'thou has already seen more than is deserved by one who takes up his quarters by violence. Credit me, it is better to enjoy what God sends thee, than to be impertinently curious. Fill thy cup, but do not make me show thy fate, had I been earnest in opposing thee.'

'By my faith,' said the knight, 'I am more curious than ever! Thou art the most mysterious hermit I ever met; and I will know more of thee, ere we part. Cease thy threats, holy man, I am one whose trade it is to seek out danger *wherever* it is to be met with.'

'Sir Sluggish Knight, I drink to thee,' said the hermit; 'respecting thy valour, but wondrous at thy discretion. If thou wilt take equal arms with me, I will give thee such penance that thou shalt not, for a twelvemonth, sin the sin of curiosity.' The knight challenged him to name his weapons.

'There is none,' replied the hermit, 'from the scissors of Delilah to the scimitar of Goliath at which I am not a match for thee; but, if I am to have the choice, what sayest thou to *these* trinkets?'

Thus speaking, he opened another hatch, and took out from it a couple of the broadswords and shields used by the yeomanry of the period. The Black Knight also observed that this place of concealment was furnished with two good longbows, a crossbow, bolts for the latter and half-a-dozen sheaves of arrows for the former. A harp and other instruments of uncanonical appearance were also visible in the dark recess.

'I promise thee, brother Clerk,' said he, 'I will ask thee no more offensive questions. The contents of that cupboard are an answer to all my enquiries and,' stooping, he took out the harp, 'here is a weapon on which I would prove my skill with thee more gladly than with sword and buckler.'

'Sir Knight,' said the hermit, 'sit thee down and fill thy cup! Let us drink, sing and be merry; and if thou knowest good songs, thou shalt be welcome to Copmanhurst so long as I serve the chapel of St Dunstan. This, please God, shall I do till I my grey

---

1 In Anglo-Saxon, 'be thou hale' i.e. 'may you be in good health.'

2 Drink and be healthy!

covering changes to one of green turf. But come, fill a flagon. It is time to tune the harp and naught sharpens the ear like a cup of wine. For my part, I love to feel the grape at my very finger-ends before they take to the harpstrings.'[1]

chapter seventeen

At eve, within yon studious nook,
I ope my brass-embossed book,
Then, as my taper waxes dim,
Chant, ere I sleep, my measured hymn.

Who but would cast his pomp away,
To take my staff and amice grey,
And to the world's tumultuous stage,
Prefer the peaceful Hermitage?

Thomas Warton: *Inscription in an Hermitage at Ansley Hall, Warwickshire.*

Despite the prescription of the genial hermit, his guest found it no easy matter to tune the harp.

'Holy father,' said he, 'this instrument lacks one string and the rest have been somewhat misused.'

'Ay, mark'st thou that?' replied the hermit, 'That shows thee a master of the craft. Wine and wassail,' he added, gravely casting up his eyes, 'all the fault of wine and wassail! I told that Allan-a-Dale that he would damage the harp if he touched it after the seventh cup. Friend, I drink to thy successful performance.'

So saying, he drained his cup with gravity while shaking his head at the intemperance of the Scottish harper. The knight had now brought the strings into some order, and asked his host whether he would choose a *sirvente* in the language of *oc*, a *lai* in the language of *oui*, or indeed a ballad in the vulgar Anglo-Saxon.[2]

'A ballad, a ballad,' said the hermit, 'Downright English am I, Sir Knight, and downright English was my patron St Dunstan. He scorned 'oc' and 'oui' like the parings of the devil's hoof. Downright Anglo-Saxon *alone* shall be sung in this cell.'

'I will essay, then,' said the knight, 'a ballad composed by a Saxon I knew in Holy Land.'

It speedily appeared that if not a master of the minstrel's art, the knight had had the best instructors. His performance might have been termed respectable by abler judges

---

1 The Jolly Hermit: in the Clerk of Copmanhurst, readers will recognise Friar Tuck, the buxom Confessor of Robin Hood's gang and Curtal Friar of Fountains Abbey. *Scott.* Curtal in this context means 'worldly-minded.' *Ed.*

2 The realm of France was divided betwixt the Norman and Teutonic races, where the word 'yes' is pronounced as 'oui'; and the inhabitants of the South, whose speech pronounced the same word 'oc'. The poets of the former race were called 'Minstrels', and their poems 'Lays': those of the latter were termed 'Troubadours', and their compositions called 'Sirventes' and other names. *Scott.*

than the hermit, especially as he showed a plaintive enthusiasm which gave energy to his verses.

High deeds achieved of knightly fame,
From Palestine the champion came;
The cross upon his shoulders borne,
Battle and blast had dimm'd and torn.
Each dint upon his batter'd shield
Was token of a foughten field;
And thus, beneath his lady's bower,
He sung as fell the twilight hour.

Joy to the fair, whose constant knight
Her favour fired to feats of might;
Unnoted shall she not remain,
Where meet the bright and noble train;
Minstrel shall sing and herald tell—
'Mark yonder maid of beauty well,
'Tis she for whose bright eyes were won
The listed field at Askalon!

During this, the hermit reclined back in his seat, eyes half shut. Folding his hands and balancing his open palms, he gently flourished them in time to the music. At one or two favourite cadences, he threw in assistance where the knight's voice was unable to carry the air as high as his taste required. When the song ended, the anchorite emphatically declared it good and well sung.

'What took the knight from home?' said he, 'What could he expect but to find his mistress engaged with a rival on his return, his serenade regarded as the caterwauling of a cat in a gutter? Nevertheless, Sir Knight, I drink this cup to thee and to the success of all true lovers.' He also observed that his guest, his brain heated by wine, was diluting his flagon from the water pitcher.

'Why,' said the knight, 'did you not tell me that this water was from the well of the blessed St Dunstan?'

'Ay, truly,' said the hermit, 'and many hundred pagans did he baptise there, but I never heard that he *drank* any of it.' So saying, he took his harp and entertained his guest with 'The Barefooted Friar' with the derry-down chorus of an old Anglo-Saxon ditty:

I'll give thee, good fellow, a twelvemonth or twain,
To search Europe through, from Byzantium to Spain;
But ne'er shall you find, should you search till you tire,
So happy a man as the Barefooted Friar.

Your monarch? Full many a prince has been known
To barter his robes for our cowl and our gown,
But which of us e'er felt the idle desire
To exchange for a crown the grey hood of a Friar!

Long flourish the sandal, the cord, and the cope,
The dread of the devil and trust of the Pope;
For to gather life's roses, unscathed by the briar,
Is granted alone to the Barefooted Friar.

'By my troth,' said the knight, 'well sung, and in high praise of thine Order. Talking of the Devil, Holy Clerk, are you not afraid that he may pay you a visit during your uncanonical pastimes?'

'I, uncanonical?' answered the hermit; 'I scorn the charge! I serve the duty of my chapel duly and truly. Two masses daily, morning and evening: *primes, none and vespers, aves, credos, paters...'*

'Excepting moonlight nights, when venison is in season?' suggested his guest.

'*Exceptis excipiendis*',[1] replied the hermit, 'as our old Abbot taught me to say when asked if I kept every *punctilio* of mine Order.'

'True, holy father,' said the knight; 'but does the Devil not keep an eye on such exceptions?'

'Let him look in here if he dare,' said the friar; 'I never feared man and I as little fear the Devil and his imps. But I never speak upon such subjects, my friend, until after morning *vespers*.'

He changed the subject. Fast and furious grew the mirth of the parties and many a song was exchanged betwixt them – until their revels were interrupted; a loud knocking came from the door of the hermitage.

chapter eighteen

Away! Our journey lies through dell and dingle,
Where the blithe fawn trips by its timid mother,
Where the broad oak, with intercepting boughs,
Chequers the sunbeam in the green-sward alley—
Up and away!
Walter Scott: *Ettrick Forest*

When Cedric saw his son collapse senseless in the lists at Ashby, his first impulse was to order him into the custody of his own attendants, but the words choked in his throat. In the presence of such an assembly, he could not bring himself to acknowledge the son he had renounced and disinherited. However, he ordered his cupbearer Oswald, with two of his serfs, to convey Ivanhoe to Ashby when the crowd

1 With exceptions where necessary.

had dispersed. Oswald, however, was too late; the knight was nowhere to be seen. In vain the cupbearer looked for his young master. He saw the bloody spot on which he had collapsed, but not Ivanhoe. Oswald then suddenly noticed a person attired like a squire and recognised Gurth, his fellow servant. The swineherd, anxious concerning his master's fate and disappearance, was also searching for him, but in doing so had neglected his disguise. Oswald and his men saw it as their duty to detain the fugitive.

All that they could obtain from the bystanders was that Ivanhoe had been carefully lifted by well-attired grooms. Placed in the litter of a lady among the spectators, he had been carried out of the press. Oswald then returned to Cedric for instructions, taking Gurth with him.

The Saxon had been under intense apprehension concerning his son, for Nature had asserted herself. However, no sooner was he informed that Ivanhoe was in friendly hands, than anxiety gave way to renewed feelings of injured pride and resentment at what he still saw as Wilfred's disobedience.

'Let him wander his way,' said he. 'Let him do the juggling tricks of the Norman, rather than maintain the fame and honour of his English ancestry.'

'To maintain the honour of ancestry,' said Rowena, 'it is sufficient to be wise in council and brave in execution, to be bold and…'

'Be silent, Lady Rowena! On this subject alone I hear you not. Prepare yourself for the Prince's festival: we have been summoned with a courtesy the Normans have rarely accorded us since Hastings. I go there only to show them how little a Saxon is affected by the fate of a son who could defeat their bravest.'

'I,' said Rowena, 'do *not* go; and I pray you beware, lest your constancy be reckoned hardness of heart.'

'Remain at home, then, ungrateful lady,' answered Cedric; 'thine is the hard heart, which can sacrifice the weal of an oppressed people to a personal romance. The noble Athelstane and I will attend the banquet of this John of Anjou.'

He went accordingly to the banquet, of which we have already noted the principal events. Immediately upon retiring from the castle, the Saxon thanes and their attendants took horse. It was during the bustle which attended their doing so, that Cedric first cast eyes upon the deserter Gurth. The noble Saxon had left the banquet in no placid humour and now had a pretext for wreaking his anger.

'The gyves!' he said, 'the gyves![1] Oswald, Hundibert! Dogs and villains! Why is the knave unfettered?' Not daring to remonstrate, the companions of Gurth bound him with a halter. He submitted to the operation without resistance except that, darting a reproachful look at his master, he said,

'This comes of loving *your* flesh and blood better than mine own.'

'To horse, and forward!' said Cedric.

The Abbot of St Withold, himself of ancient Saxon descent, received the noble Saxons with the exuberant hospitality of their race. They indulged to an early hour, taking leave of their reverend host the next morning after a breaking of their short fast. As the cavalcade left the court of the monastery, there was an incident which alarmed the Saxons, of all the peoples of Europe the most superstitious with respect to omens. The sign of impending evil was inspired by a large black dog which sat upright,

---

1 Shackles.

howling piteously as the riders left the gate and then, barking wildly, seemed bent upon attaching itself to the party.

'I like not that music, father Cedric,' said Athelstane.

'Nor I either, uncle,' said Wamba.

'To my mind,' said Athelstane, 'better we turn back and remain with the Abbot until afternoon. It is unlucky to travel on when your path is crossed by a monk, a hare or a howling dog until you have eaten your next meal.'

'Away!' said Cedric, impatiently, 'the day is already too short for our journey. As for the dog, I know it. It is the cur of the runaway slave Gurth, a useless fugitive – like its master.'

So saying he rose in his stirrups and, irritated by the interruption, launched his javelin at Fangs. The missile hit the animal's shoulder but failed to pin him to the earth. Fangs, howling, fled from the presence of the enraged Thane as Gurth's heart swelled at this assault on his faithful dog. He said to Wamba,

'Wipe my eyes with the skirt of thy mantle. The dust irritates me and these bonds will not let me help myself.'

Wamba did so and they rode side by side for some time, during which Gurth maintained a moody silence. At length he could repress his feelings no longer.

'Wamba,' said he, 'of all those who are fools enough to serve Cedric, thou alone makes folly acceptable to him. Go tell him that neither for love nor fear will Gurth, son of Beowulf serve him longer. He may strike the head from me; he may scourge me, load me with irons, but I shall never again obey. Go tell him that.'

'Assuredly,' said Wamba, 'fool as I am, I will not do your fool's errand. Cedric hath *another* javelin in his girdle...'

'I care not,' replied Gurth, 'Yesterday he left Wilfred my young master lying in his own blood. Today he tries to kill the only other creature that showed me kindness. By St Edmund and every Saxon saint, I will forgive him never!'

'To my way of thinking, now,' said the Jester, who was frequent peacemaker in the family, 'our master meant not to hurt Fangs, but only affright him. His scratch I will heal with a penny's breadth of tar.'

'If I thought so,' said Gurth, 'if I could but think so; but no, that javelin was well aimed.' The indignant swineherd resumed a sullen silence.

Meanwhile Cedric and Athelstane, the leaders of the troop, conversed on the state of the realm, the dissensions of the royal family and the feuds among the Norman nobles. They talked of the likelihood of the Saxons being able to achieve national consequence in the civil convulsions likely to ensue. On this subject Cedric was all animation. To achieve a revolution in favour of the native English, it was necessary that they should be united among themselves, and act under a chief from the Saxon blood-royal. This seemed not only evident in itself, but had been made a solemn condition by Cedric and those entrusted with his secret plans.

Athelstane had few of the mental accomplishments of a leader, but had at least a goodly person and was no coward. He was accustomed to martial exercises and willingly deferred to counsellors wiser than himself. He was also known to be liberal, hospitable and good-natured. But as head of a Saxon confederacy, many of that nation preferred the Lady Rowena, who drew her descent from Alfred the Great. Her late father, moreover, had been a chief renowned for wisdom, courage and generosity, his memory highly honoured. It was thus Cedric's policy to promote a marriage between Rowena and Athelstane. However, an obstacle existed to his favourite project in the attachment of Rowena to Wilfred; hence the original cause of the son's banishment from the father's house.

This stern measure was executed by Cedric in the hope that during Wilfred's absence, Rowena might abandon him. In this hope he had been disappointed. Cedric, to whom the name of Alfred the Great was that of a deity, treated his descendant with the deference due to a princess. Rowena's word was law in his household. Asserting her independence, she resisted and resented any attempt to control her affections. Opinions which she felt strongly, she avowed boldly and Cedric was often at a loss as to how to enforce his authority as her guardian. It was in vain that he attempted to dazzle her with the prospect of a throne. Rowena's strong good sense considered his plan neither practicable nor desirable. Neither did she attempt to conceal her love for Wilfred of Ivanhoe. Indeed, she had declared that if their union was out of the question, she would rather enter a convent, than share a throne with Athelstane.

Nevertheless, Cedric used every means in his power to bring about this proposed match which he saw as a service to the Saxon cause. The reappearance of his son in the lists at Ashby, however, he saw as a probable death blow to his hopes. Paternal affection had for an instant risen above pride and patriotism, but both had now returned in full force. Under their joint operation, he was now bent upon a final determined effort for the union of Athelstane and Rowena and the regaining of Saxon independence.

On this last subject, he was now arguing with Athelstane. The latter was vain, loving to hear of his high descent and of his right to homage. But that vanity was sufficiently gratified by receiving homage from his immediate attendants and the Saxons who approached him. He had the courage to encounter danger, but also hated the trouble of going to seek it. He agreed with Cedric's general principles concerning Saxon independence, and accepted his own right to reign, should independence be attained. Yet when the actual means of asserting these rights came under discussion, he was still 'Athelstane the Unready,' irresolute and unenterprising.

Tiring of hammering on cold iron, Cedric fell back in the cavalcade to confer with Rowena, but received little more satisfaction, as his presence interrupted the lady and Elgitha, her favorite attendant who were discussing Wilfred. Elgitha did not fail to mention the overthrow of Athelstane in the lists. This was most disagreeable to Cedric, to whom the day's journey was fraught with all manner of displeasure and discomfort. He more than once silently cursed the tournament – and Prince John – and his own folly in ever attending.

At the suggestion of Athelstane, the travellers paused at noon in a woodland shade by a spring. Here they rested their horses and opened the provisions with which the Abbot had loaded a sumpter mule. This halt now meant that they would only reach Rotherwood by travelling all night.

chapter nineteen

A train of armed men... are close at hand.
Joanna Baillie: *Orra*, a Tragedy.

The travellers had now reached the verge of wooded country and were about to plunge into its recesses. These were infested at that time with outlawed men driven to revolt by poverty and oppression who occupied the forests in such numbers as to easily defy the civil power. Despite the lateness of the hour, Cedric and Athelstane reckoned themselves secure, being escorted by ten armed servants besides Wamba and Gurth. They had also their Saxon race as protection, since those driven to outlawry by the Forest Laws were chiefly peasants and yeomen of the same descent.

As the travellers journeyed on, they suddenly began to hear cries for assistance. Riding up, they were surprised to find a horse-litter resting on the path. Beside it sat a young woman dressed in the Jewish fashion, while an old man of the same nation paced up and down with gestures of despair. To the questioning of Cedric, old Isaac said that he had hired a bodyguard of six men at Ashby to carry the litter of a sick friend as far as Doncaster. Hearing that there was a strong band of outlaws nearby, the mercenaries had taken flight, carrying off the horses which bore the litter and leaving Isaac and his daughter defenceless against the *banditti*, whose approach they now expected.

'May it please you,' added Isaac, 'to permit we poor Jews to travel under your safeguard. I swear that never will favour be more gratefully acknowledged.'

Cedric said, 'We shall leave them two of our attendants and two horses to convey them back to the next village. It will little diminish our strength but those remaining, it would be light work to face down those runagates.'

Rebecca suddenly made her way through the attendants to the palfrey of the Saxon lady. Throwing back her veil, she implored her in God's name that they go forward, not back, under their safeguard.

'It is not for myself that I pray this favour,' said Rebecca, 'nor even for my father. It is in the name of someone dear to many, dear even to you. I beseech you to take this sick man under your protection.'

'This man is old and feeble,' said Rowena to Cedric, 'The maiden is young and their sick friend is in peril of his life. Jews though they be, we cannot as Christians leave them in their extremity. Unload two of the sumpter-mules and put the baggage behind two of the serfs. The mules may carry the litter and we shall have led horses for the old man and his daughter.'

Cedric assented and the change of baggage was hastily achieved, the single word 'outlaws' rendering everyone alert and the deepening twilight making its sound more ominous. Amid the bustle, Gurth was taken from horseback. Prevailing upon the Jester to slacken the cords binding his arms, he found them so negligently refastened, perhaps intentionally so, that he had little difficulty in freeing himself. Gliding into the thickets unseen, he disappeared.

The path upon which the party travelled was now so narrow as not to admit more than two riders abreast. It began to descend into a dingle traversed by a brook whose banks were broken, swampy, and overgrown with dwarf willows. Cedric and Athelstane, at the head of their retinue, saw the risk of ambuscade at this pass. However, there was no better mode of defence than hastening through the defile. Advancing without order, they had just crossed the brook with a part of their followers when they were indeed attacked. Assailed simultaneously in front, flank, and rear, the assault came with an impetus to which, in their confusion, it was impossible to offer effective resistance. With cries of: 'Saint George!' the Normans in their disguise as Saxon outlaws, appeared with a rapidity which seemed to multiply their numbers.

Cedric instantly launched his remaining javelin, the weapon nailing a man against an oak. Drawing his sword, Cedric spurred his horse against a second, striking with such force that his weapon hit a thick branch above him and fell to earth. Now disarmed, he was immediately pulled from his horse and secured by three of the *banditti*. Athelstane's bridle was seized and he too was forcibly unhorsed before he could draw a weapon.

The attendants, encumbered with baggage and terrified by the fate of their masters, fell an easy prey to the assailants, as did the Lady Rowena in the centre of the cavalcade and Isaac and Rebecca at the rear. Of all the train, none escaped but the courageous Wamba. With a sword snatched from one of the domestics, he laid about him like a lion and made a brave though ineffectual attempt to support his master. Finally overpowered, the Jester threw himself from his horse into the thickets and escaped in the general confusion. He then hesitated over whether he should not turn back and share the captivity of his master. He then heard a familiar voice calling to him in a low and urgent tone,

'Wamba!' A dog he recognised as Fangs appeared.

'Gurth?' The swineherd approached.

'What's afoot?' said he eagerly; 'what are these cries?'

'They are all prisoners,' said Wamba.

'Who are prisoners?'

'My lord and lady – and Athelstane, Hundibert and Oswald.'

'In the name of God!' said Gurth, 'prisoners of whom?'

'They are prisoners to men in green cassocks and black visors.'

Gurth's countenance kindled.

'Wamba,' he said, 'We are only two, but a sudden attack may do much. Follow me!'

As the Jester was about to obey, a third person suddenly made his appearance and commanded them both to halt. From his dress and arms they first reckoned him to be one of the outlaws from the assault. However, he wore no mask and had a glittering baldric across his shoulder supporting a bugle-horn. The Jester, despite the twilight, recognized the commanding manner of the archer Locksley.

'What means this,' said he, 'who makes prisoners in this forest?'

'Look at their cassocks,' said Wamba, 'They are as green as thine own.'

'I will find that out presently,' said Locksley; 'On peril of your lives, stir not from here till I return. Now, I must make myself as like these men as possible.'

So saying, he unbuckled his baldric with the bugle, took the feather from his cap, and gave them to Wamba. He took a vizard[1] from his pouch and, repeating his charge to stand fast, he went off.

'Shall we stand fast, Gurth?' said Wamba; 'or give him leg-bail?[2] To my mind, he has too much the gear of a thief to be an honest man.'

'Be he the Devil himself,' said Gurth, 'we can be no worse off waiting his return. If he belongs to that party, he will have given them the alarm and it will be useless to fight or fly.'

The yeoman soon returned.

'Gurth,' he said, 'I have mingled among yon men. There is no violence against their prisoners. However, for us three to attack now would be madness; they are veterans and have posted sentries. But I will soon gather a force to defy them. You are both, are you not, servants of Cedric the Saxon? He shall not lack English hands to help him. Come.'

chapter twenty

When autumn nights were long and drear,
And forest walks were dark and dim,
How sweetly on the pilgrim's ear
Was wont to steal the hermit's hymn
Anon.

It was after three hours' good walking that Gurth, Wamba and their mysterious guide arrived at a small clearing in the forest. In the centre of this grew an oak tree of enormous proportions, its twisted branches thrown in every direction. Beneath this tree lay four or five yeomen, while a sentry paced to and fro in the moonlight.

Hearing the sound of feet approaching, he gave the alarm. The sleepers started up and strung their bows. Six arrows were now aimed at the quarter from which the party approached, until the guide was recognised as their leader.

'Where is the Miller?' was his first question.

'On the road to Rotherham.'

'With how many?'

'With six men, and with hope of booty, if it please St Nicholas.'

'Where is Allan-a-Dale?' said Locksley.

'Walking towards Watling Street,[3] to watch for the Prior of Jorvaulx.'

'Good also – and the Friar?'

'In his cell.'

'There will I go,' said Locksley. 'Disperse and find your companions. Collect

---

1 Visard. A variant of visor: here, a mask.

2 To give leg-bail; to cut and run.

3 Watling Street: An old Roman legionary road from London to Staffordshire.

whatever force you can. There's game afoot that must be hunted hard and which will turn at bay. Meet me here by daybreak. Wait,' he added, 'what is most necessary of all is that two of you take the road quickly to Torquilstone, the castle of Front-de-Boeuf. A set of gallants masquerading as our own people are taking prisoners thither. Keep a close watch on them and dispatch a comrade to bring me news of them.'

The men departed. Locksley and his two companions, now looking at him with respect, pushed on to the Chapel of Copmanhurst.

They reached the little moonlit glade, having in front the ruinous chapel and the rude hermitage. Wamba whispered to Gurth,

'Hearken to the black *sanctus* which they are singing in the hermitage!' The anchorite and his guest were now performing, at the top of their powerful lungs, an old drinking song:

'Come, trowl the brown bowl to me,
Bully boy, bully boy,
Come, trowl the brown bowl to me:
Ho! jolly Jenkin, I spy a knave in drinking,
Come, trowl the brown bowl to me.'

'Now, that is not ill sung,' said Wamba. 'But in God's name, who would expect such a song from a hermit's cell – and at midnight...?'

'This Clerk of Copmanhurst,' said Gurth, 'is a known man. He kills half the deer stolen in this walk. The Keeper has warned him that he will be stripped of his cowl and cope unless he keeps better order.'

Locksley's loud and repeated knocking at length disturbed the anchorite and his guest.

'By my beads,' said the hermit within, stopping the song, 'here come *more* benighted travellers! I would not that they found us in this good, if ungodly exercise. All men have enemies, Sir Sluggard, and there be those who would construe my hospitality as vices alien to my profession and disposition.'

'Base calumniators!' said the knight

'Get thine iron pot on thy head, friend,' said the hermit, 'while I remove these flagons. To drown the clatter, play the tune which I sing.' So saying, he struck up a thundering *De profundis clamavi*[1] as cover for removing the crockery of their banquet, the Black Knight laughing while arming himself.

'What devil matins are you about at *this* hour?' cried a voice from without.

'Heaven forgive you, Sir Traveller!' said the hermit, not yet recognising the voice. 'On your way, in the name of God and Saint Dunstan, and disturb not the devotions of me and my holy brother.'

'Mad priest,' shouted the voice without, 'open to *Locksley*!'

'Locksley? All's safe, all's right!' said the hermit immediately to his companion.

'But who be he?' said the Black Knight.

'A friend.' answered the hermit.

---

1 The penitential psalm: *De profundis clamavi ad te Domine*. 'From the depths have I cried unto thee, O Lord.' An appeal for forgiveness.

'*What* friend?' demanded the knight; 'he may be friend to thee and none of mine!'

'*What* friend?' replied the hermit; 'Why, he is the same honest Keeper I told thee of.'

'Ay, and as honest a Keeper as thou art pious, hermit!' replied the knight, 'Undo the door before he beats it off its hinges.' The dogs, which had begun a dreadful baying, also seemed to recognise the voice without. They now whined at the door as if demanding his admission. The hermit unbolted. In came Locksley and his two companions.

'Why, hermit,' said the yeoman, as soon as he beheld the knight, 'what companion hast thou here?'

'A brother of our Order,' replied the friar, shaking his head; 'we have been at our *orisons*[1] all night.'

'A monk of the Church militant, I see,' answered Locksley, 'and there are more of them abroad. Friar, lay down thy rosary and take up the quarter-staff. We shall need every one of our men, clerk or layman. But,' he added, taking him aside, 'admitting an unknown knight – hast forgot our rules?'

'Good yeoman,' said the knight, coming forward, 'he did but afford me hospitality.' The Friar stripped off his gown and reappeared in a close black buckram doublet and drawers, over which he speedily threw a cassock of green.

While he was thus employed, Locksley led the knight aside and said:

'Sir Knight, are you not he who decided the victory for the English on that second day at Ashby.'

'And if I confess it, good yeoman?'

'In that case, I should hold you a friend.' said Locksley.

'Such is the duty of a knight.'

'For my present purpose,' said the yeoman, 'thou must be both good Englishman and good knight.'

'You can speak to no one,' replied the other, 'to whom England is dearer.'

'I believe it so,' said the woodsman, 'Hear me. A band of villains in disguise have captured Cedric, a noble Saxon Englishman, together with his lady ward Rowena and Lord Athelstane of Coningsburgh. They have abducted them to Torquilstone castle in this forest. I ask thee, as knight and Englishman, wilt aid in their rescue?'

'I am bound by my vow to do so,' replied the knight; 'but who requests my assistance?'

'I,' said Locksley, 'am a nameless man, but I am the friend of my country. You must be satisfied with this for the present; the more so since you yourself desire to remain unknown! My word is as inviolate as if I also wore golden spurs.'

'I believe it,' said the knight; 'No further questions. I will aid thee in this matter.'

'So, we have a new ally,' said Wamba to Gurth, the Jester having heard the conversation, 'I trust the valour of the knight will outdo the religion of this hermit or the honesty of this yeoman; Locksley looks to me like a deer-stealer.'

'Hold thy peace, Wamba,' said Gurth; 'were the horned Devil himself to offer help to free Cedric and my Lady Rowena, I should not refuse.'

The Friar was now completely accoutred as a yeoman, with sword and buckler,

1 Norman – French: prayers.

bow and quiver, and a strong partisan[1] over his shoulder. He left his cell, locked the door and deposited the key under the threshold.

'Art thou in any condition for good service, friar?' said Locksley.

'I shall be, after a draught of St Dunstan's fountain!' He stepped to the stone basin where the waters of the fountain formed bubbles which danced in the pale moonlight. He took a long draught.

'When didst thou last drink as deep a draught of *water*, Holy Clerk of Copmanhurst?' said the Black Knight.

'Never since my wine-butt leaked its liquor by an illegal vent,' replied the friar. Thus refreshed and sobered, the jolly priest twirled his heavy partizan round his head with three fingers as if he were balancing a reed. He exclaimed,

'Where be those ravishers, who carry off wenches against their will? May the Devil fly off with me if I am not a match for a dozen of them.'

'Jack Priest,' said Locksley, 'be silent. Come, my masters. We must collect our forces.'

'So is it Front de Boeuf,' said the Black Knight, 'who has taken the king's subjects on the king's highway? Is he turned thief?'

'Oppressor he *always* was,' said Locksley.

'As for thief,' said the priest, 'he is not half as honest as many a thief of my acquaintance.'

'Move on, priest, and be silent,' said the yeoman; 'Better you lead the way than talk.'

chapter twenty-one

Alas, how many hours and years have past,
Since human forms have round this table sate,
Or lamp, or taper, on its surface gleam'd!
Methinks, I hear the sound of time long pass'd
Still murmuring o'er us...

Joanna Baillie: *Orra*: *a Tragedy.*

Meanwhile, the disguised Normans hurried their captives towards Torquilstone. But darkness came on fast and the paths of the wood being imperfectly known, they were compelled to make several long halts and twice backtracked. The summer morn had dawned ere they were confident that they held the right path.

'It is time for you to leave us, Sir Maurice,' said the Templar to De Bracy, 'to prepare for the second part of thy mystery – as Knight Deliverer.'

'I have now thought better of it,' said De Bracy; 'I will not leave till the prize is deposited in Front-de-Boeuf's castle. There will I appear before the Lady Rowena as myself. I trust she will ascribe all to my to my passion for her.'

'Why the change of plan, De Bracy?' said the Templar.

'That concerns thee not.'

'I would hope, Sir Knight, that it arises from no suspicion of *my* intentions...?'

---

1 Partizan: A long-shafted and bladed weapon.

'Come, Sir Templar!' said De Bracy, 'gallantry has a liberal interpretation in Palestine; and this is not a case to entrust to your conscience.'

'Hear the word, then. I care not at all for your blue-eyed beauty. There is another in that train who will make me a better mate.'

'The damsel-in-waiting?'

'No, Sir Knight,' said the Templar, 'I have a prize among the captives as lovely as thine own.'

'By the Mass, he means the *Jewess*!' cried De Bracy.

'And if I do, who shall object?'

'No one that I know, unless it be your vow of celibacy, or a note of conscience. She is an Israelite!'

'As to my vow,' said the Templar, 'our Grand Master granted me a dispensation. As for my conscience, a man that has slain three hundred Saracens need not account for every little failing like a village girl doing her first confession.'

'Thou knowest best,' said De Bracy, 'Yet I would have sworn thy thoughts were more on Isaac's money bags, than on the black eyes of the daughter.'

'I can admire both. Besides, the old Jew is but a half-prize, for I must share his spoils with Front-de-Boeuf. He will not lend us his castle for nothing. I must have something exclusively my own from this foray – and the Jewess is my prize. Now that thou see my drift, resume the original plan. Thou hast nothing to fear from me.'

'No!' replied De Bracy, 'I will remain beside my prize. You have far too good a right to a Free Pardon...!'

While this dialogue was proceeding, Cedric was endeavouring to wring their purpose out of his guards.

'You be *Englishmen*,' said he; 'and yet, sacred Heaven! You prey upon your countrymen as if you were Normans. You should be my neighbours and my friends. Yeomen, I tell ye that even those branded with outlawry have had protection from me, for I have pitied their misery and curst their tyrannical nobles. Ye be worse than brute beasts – and as dumb!' Cedric expostulated in vain with his guards who had too many good reasons for their silence to be swayed by his wrath or arguments. They hurried him along rapidly until, at the end of an avenue of huge trees, arose Torquilstone.

The ancient castle of Reginald Front-de-Boeuf was a fortress of great size, consisting of a *donjon*, or large and high square tower, surrounded by lower buildings encircled by an inner courtyard. Around the exterior wall was a deep moat, supplied by a rivulet. Front-de-Boeuf, whose character placed him often in feuds, had strengthened the castle by building towers on the outward wall so as to flank it at every angle. Access to the keep lay through an arched barbican or outwork, defended by a small turret at each corner. Cedric had no sooner seen the grey turrets and battlements of Torquilstone glimmering in the morning sun, than he knew the true cause and extent of his peril.

'I did great injustice,' he said, 'to the outlaws of these woods when I supposed such *banditti* as you to belong to them. Tell me, dogs, is it my life or my wealth that your master desires? Is it too much for you that myself and Athelstane should hold *any* land in our once Saxon country? Put us then to death and complete your tyranny.

Tell your tyrannical master that I entreat him to dismiss the Lady Rowena in safety. He need not fear her – for with us will die all who dare to fight in her cause.'

The attendants still remained mute.

They now stood before the gate of the castle. De Bracy winded his horn three times and the archers and crossbow men who had manned the wall on their approach lowered the drawbridge. The prisoners were made to alight and were conducted to an apartment where Cedric and Athelstane were told that they were to be held in a chamber apart from Rowena. Resistance was vain. They were forced into a large room girt with clumsy Saxon pillars.

The Lady Rowena, separated from her train, was conducted to a remote apartment. The same separation was imposed on Rebecca, despite her father's entreaties. In distress, he offered money that she might be permitted to remain with him.

'Believe me, unbeliever,' answered one of his guards, 'when thou hast seen *thy* lair, thou wilt not wish thy daughter to partake of it.'

Without farther discussion, the old Jew was forcibly dragged off in a different direction. Cedric's attendants, after being searched, were confined in another part of the castle, Rowena being refused even her handmaiden Elgitha.

The apartment in which the Saxon chiefs were confined had formerly been the great hall of the castle but was now abandoned to meaner purposes. Cedric, burning with indignation, paced the apartment.

'Yes,' he said, half speaking to himself, and half to Athelstane, 'it was in this very hall that my father feasted with Torquil Wolfganger, when he entertained the valiant Harold, advancing north against the Norwegians and his rebel brother Tostig. It was in this very hall that Harold magnanimously answerd Tostig's ambassador, who asked,

'What terms, Lord King, hath thy brother Tostig to hope, should he lay down his arms and crave peace at thy hands?'

'A brother's love,' said the generous Harold, 'and the fair earldom of Northumberland.'

'And should Tostig accept these terms,' continued the envoy, 'what lands shall be assigned to his ally Harold Hardrada, King of Norway?'

'Six feet of English ground,' answered Harold, fiercely, 'or, since this Hardrada is said to be a giant, perhaps 12 inches more!'

'The hall rang with acclamations; cup and horn were filled. Toasts rang out that the Norwegian be speedily laid, feet first, in possession of his English territory.'

'The envoy,' continued Cedric, pursuing his tale with animation, 'retired to carry to Tostig and Hardrada this ominous answer.'

'Who would have thought,' said Cedric, 'that you, Athelstane, descended from Harold's blood, and I should be prisoners of a vile Norman in the very hall where our ancestors held high festival?'

'I trust,' replied Athelstane, 'they will hold us to ransom. It cannot be their purpose to starve us; and yet, although it is noon, I see no preparations for dinner.'

The door of their prison now opened to admit a sewer[1] holding his white rod of office. This personage advanced into the chamber with a grave pace, followed by

---

1 Sewer: a servant charged with the seating and general hospitality of guests.

four masked attendants carrying a table covered with dishes whose sight and smell were an immediate compensation to Athelstane for all the present inconvenience.

'What mummery is this?' demanded Cedric; 'we are not ignorant of whose prisoners we are. Tell your master, Reginald Front-de-Boeuf, that we know of no reason for withholding our liberty, excepting a desire to enrich himself at our expense. Tell him that we yield to his greed as to a common robber. Let him name the ransom and it shall be paid.' The sewer made no answer, but bowed his head.

'And you will also tell Sir Reginald Front-de-Boeuf,' said Athelstane, 'that I challenge him to mortal combat on foot or horseback and at any place, within eight days of our liberation. If he be true knight, he will not refuse.'

'I shall deliver your defiance,' said the sewer.

The captives had not long enjoyed their refreshment before their attention was drawn by the blast of a horn sounded outside the gate and powerfully repeated three times. The Saxons started from the table and went to the window but could only see into the inner court and the sound was coming from beyond. The summons, however, seemed to be of importance, for a great degree of bustle was now taking place within the castle.

chapter twenty-two

My daughter – O my ducats – O my daughter!
O my Christian ducats!
Justice – the Law – my ducats, and my daughter!
Shakespeare: *The Merchant of Venice*

Isaac of York had been thrust into a dungeon-vault of the castle. Its floor was damp, being deep below ground level and lower than the moat itself. The only light came through two loopholes far above the reach of the captive. Even at midday these admitted only a dim, uncertain light which faded to utter darkness long before the rest of the castle had lost the day. Chains and shackles of former captives hung, rusted and empty, on the walls of this prison. In one set of fetters, mouldered the two leg bones of a prisoner left there to perish. At one end of this ghastly apartment was a large fire-grate, over which were stretched, transversely, some rusty iron bars.

The whole appearance of the dungeon might have appalled a stouter heart than that of Isaac. Nevertheless, he was composed under the imminent pressure of danger, since Jews, from the very constancy of oppression, had minds prepared for tyranny. Above all, he had upon his side the unyielding character of his nation; that resolution with which Israelites will endure great evil, rather than granting oppressive demands.

In this humour of passive resistance, his garments gathered beneath him to keep his limbs from the wet flooring, Isaac sat in a corner of his dungeon. His folded hands, dishevelled hair and beard, furred cloak and high cap would have afforded a study for Rembrandt. Having remained thus for nearly three hours, steps were heard on the dungeon stair; the bolts screamed as they were withdrawn; hinges creaked as the wicket opened and Reginald Front-de-Boeuf entered, followed by the two Saracen slaves of the Templar.

Front-de-Boeuf was a tall, strong man whose life had been spent in war and in private feuds and broils. The scars which seamed his face might have excited sympathy and veneration, had they been marks of honourable valour. But in the peculiar case of Front-de-Boeuf, they only added to the ferocity of his countenance and to the dread which he inspired. This formidable baron was clad in a close-fitting leathern doublet, frayed and soiled with stains from his armour. He had no weapon at his belt excepting a poniard, which served to counterbalance the bunch of rusty keys hanging opposite.

The slaves who attended Front-de-Boeuf had stripped off their gorgeous apparel and were attired in jerkins and trousers of coarse linen. Their sleeves were tucked up above the elbow, like those of butchers about to go to work in the slaughterhouse. Each had a small pannier in his hand. When they entered the dungeon, they stopped at the door until Front-de-Boeuf himself had locked and double-locked it. He advanced slowly towards the Jew, as if to paralyse him with his stare like some predatory animal approaching its prey. Before the malignant eye of Front-de-Boeuf sat Isaac, terrorised.

The Norman paused within three steps of the Jew and made a sign for one of the slaves to approach. Producing from his basket a large pair of scales and several weights, he laid them at the feet of his master and retired.

'Dog of an accursed race,' Front-de-Boeuf said, his deep voice awaking echoes within the dungeon, 'in these scales shalt thou weigh me out,' said the Baron, 'a thousand silver pounds, in just measure and weight.'

'Holy Abraham!' returned Isaac, finding voice through the extremity of his danger, 'Who ever heard, even in a tale, of a *thousand* pounds of silver?'

'I am reasonable,' answered Front-de-Boeuf, 'and if silver be scant, I shall refuse not gold. At the rate of a mark of gold for each six pounds of silver, thou shalt save thy carcass.'

'Have mercy on me, noble knight!' exclaimed Isaac; 'I am old, poor and helpless.'

'Old thou may be,' replied the knight; 'and more shame on those permitting thee to grow grey in usury. Feeble thou may also be – but rich thou assuredly *art*.'

'I swear to you, noble knight,' said Isaac 'by all which we believe in common…'

'Perjure not,' interrupted the Norman, 'and think not that I speak only to excite terror. I swear to thee by what thou dost *not* believe, by the Gospel of our Church, that my purpose is strong and deep. This dungeon is no place for trifling. Prisoners a thousand times more distinguished have died within these walls. But for thee is reserved a long and lingering death, compared to which theirs were luxury.'

He made a signal for the slaves to approach the large fire-grate and then spoke to them in the Arabic he had learned in Palestine. The Saracens produced from their baskets a quantity of charcoal, a pair of bellows, and a flask of oil. One having spread the charcoal in the large rusty grate, the other set fire to it from a flint and steel, exercising the bellows until the fuel eventually came to a red glow.

'See, Isaac of York,' said Front-de-Boeuf, 'that range of iron bars above the glowing charcoal. On that warm couch thou shalt lie, stripped of thy clothes as if thou wert on a bed. One of these slaves shall maintain the fire beneath thee, while the other shall anoint thy wretched limbs with oil, lest the roast should burn. Now, choose betwixt such a scorching bed and the payment of a thousand pounds of silver – for I swear by the head of my father that thou hast no other option.'

'It is impossible,' said Isaac 'it is *impossible* that you can purpose this. God never made a heart capable of this!'

'Trust not to that, Jew,' said Front-de-Boeuf, 'it were a fatal error. I have seen towns sacked and thousands perish by fire and will hardly hear the screams of a single wretched Jew. These slaves have neither law nor conscience – and nor have they mercy. Be wise, old man – and pay! Thy cunning will soon restore thy shrivelled purse, but no physician will restore thy scorched hide. Pay the ransom. Choose between thy silver – and thy flesh and blood!'

'Abraham and all the Fathers assist me,' cried Isaac, 'I cannot. I have not the means!'

'Very well; seize him and strip him, slaves,' said the knight, 'and let the fathers of his race assist him if they can.'

The henchmen plucked Isaac up and held him between them, awaiting the Baron's signal. The shaking prisoner eyed both them and Front-de-Boeuf in the hope of some sign of mercy, but the Baron's face exhibited only the same cold, sarcastic smile. Isaac looked at the now red-hot furnace over which he was to be stretched and seeing no hope, his resolution finally gave way.

'I will pay,' he said, 'the thousand pounds of silver. That is,' he added, after a moment's pause, 'I will pay it with the help of my brethren, for I must beg as a mendicant at the door of our synagogue ere I find such a sum. When and where must it be delivered?'

'Here,' replied Front-de-Boeuf, 'it must be delivered, weighed and counted upon this dungeon floor. Nor will I part with thee until then.'

'And what is my surety,' said Isaac, 'that I shall be freed thereafter?'

'The word of a Norman noble.'

'I crave pardon, noble lord,' said Isaac, 'but why should I rely on the word of one who will not trust mine?'

'Wert thou now in thy treasure-chamber at York' said the knight, 'and I craving a loan of thy shekels, it would be *thine* to dictate the terms; but this is *my* treasure-chamber; here I have thee and my terms I will not repeat.' Isaac groaned deeply.

'Grant me, then,' he said, 'my own liberty and that of my companions. They aided me, thus bringing a share of my evil upon them. Also, they may contribute to my ransom...'

'Yonder Saxon churls?' said Front-de-Boeuf, 'their ransom will be upon terms different. Mind only thine own concerns I warn thee, Jew.'

'Let my daughter Rebecca go forth to York with your safe conduct. As soon as man and horse can return, the ransom shall be counted on this floor.'

'She is thy *daughter*!' said Front-de-Boeuf, 'I would I had known this. I reckoned her thy concubine; I gave her so to Brian de Bois Guilbert.'

The yell which Isaac raised at this made the very vault to ring, so astounding the two Saracens that they let go their hold. Isaac availed himself of his freedom to throw himself to the ground before Front-de-Boeuf.

'Take all that you have asked,' said he, 'Sir Knight, reduce me to beggary, but spare my daughter. Spare the honour of a helpless maiden, the image of my dead Rachael.'

'Be it so,' said Front-de-Boeuf; 'but it aids us not. My word is passed to my Templar comrade in arms and I would not break it for ten Jews – and Jewesses to boot!'

'Templars!' exclaimed Isaac, wringing his hands in agony; 'when did Templars bring aught but dishonour to women! Villain, I will pay thee nothing; not one silver *penny* unless my daughter is delivered to me in safety!'

'Art thou out of thy senses?' roared the Norman.

'I care not!' shouted the now desperate Isaac. 'No silver will I give thee unless I pour it molten down thy throat! Not a silver penny, Nazarene! Take my life – and see that Jews know how to die!'

'We shall *indeed* see that,' said Front-de-Boeuf; 'Slaves! Strip him. Chain him to the bars!'

The Saracens tore Isaac's upper garment from him and were proceeding to disrobe him when the sound of a bugle from outside the castle, penetrated the dungeon. Loud voices were then heard calling for Sir Reginald Front-de-Boeuf. Unwillingly, the Baron signalled the slaves to desist and hurriedly quitted the dungeon with them. He left Isaac of York to thank Jehovah for his own deliverance – and to lament his daughter's fate.

chapter twenty-three

Nay, if the gentle spirit of moving words
Can no way change you to a milder form,
I'll woo you, like a soldier, at arms' end,
And love you 'gainst the nature of love.
Shakespeare: *Two Gentlemen of Verona*

The apartment into which the Lady Rowena was shown was fitted up with some rude attempts at ornament and magnificence, a mark of respect not offered to the other prisoners. However, the wife of Front-de-Boeuf, whose room it had been, was long dead and neglect had overtaken the few ornaments which had adorned it. Tapestry hung from the walls in several places, faded from the sun, or tattered and decayed by age. Desolate indeed was the apartment judged fit for the Saxon heiress and here she was left to contemplate her fate. There had been a council of Front-de-Boeuf, De Bracy and the Templar at which, after a long and heated debate, they had settled the fate of their prisoners. It was about the hour of noon when De Bracy, by whom the expedition had been planned, appeared to press his suit for Rowena.

The interval had not entirely been devoted to the council, for De Bracy had found time to decorate his person with the foppery of the times. The green cassock and vizard[1] were now flung aside. His long, luxuriant hair was trained to flow in tresses down his richly furred cloak. His beard was closely shaved, his doublet reached to the knee and the girdle which secured it and supported his ponderous sword was embroidered and embossed with gold. The points of his shoes were turned up and twisted like the horns of a ram. Such was the dress of a gallant of the period, the effect being aided by the handsome person and demeanour of De Bracy, whose manners shared the grace of a courtier with the frankness of a soldier.

He saluted Rowena by doffing his velvet bonnet with which he gently motioned the lady to a seat. As she remained standing, the knight ungloved his right hand and motioned to conduct her there. Rowena dismissed the proffered compliment, saying,

'If I be in the presence of my gaoler, Sir Knight, it best becomes his prisoner to stand and learn her fate.'

'Rowena,' said De Bracy, 'you are in the presence of your captive, not your jailor. It is from your own fair eyes that De Bracy must receive the fate which you expect from him.'

'I know you not, Sir,' said the lady with the pride of offended rank. 'I know you not – and familiarity is no apology for violence.'

'To thyself, fair maid,' answered De Bracy in his former tone, 'may be ascribed whate'er I have done to the chosen queen of my heart.'

'I repeat, Sir Knight, that I know you not. But I do know that no man in chain and spurs ought to intrude upon an unprotected lady.'

'That I am unknown to you,' said De Bracy, 'is my misfortune. Yet let me hope that the name of De Bracy has been heard when minstrels have praised deeds in the lists or on the battlefield.'

'To minstrels, then, leave thy praises, Sir Knight,' replied Rowena. 'It is more suited to *their* mouths than yours. Now tell me, which of them shall sing the memorable conquest of *this* night? The capture of an old man and a few timid servants; a maiden transported to the castle of a robber?'

'You are unjust, Lady Rowena,' said the knight, biting his lip in confusion and dropping the affected gallantry. 'Free from passion yourself, can you not excuse that of another?'

'Sir Knight,' said Rowena, 'cease this language of common minstrels. It becomes not a knight.'

'Damsel,' said De Bracy, angered that his gallantry had produced only contempt, 'thou shalt be as proudly encountered. It is perhaps more thy humour to be wooed with longbow and bill, than with courtly language.'

'*Your* courtesy,' said Rowena, 'is a knight's girdle around the breast of a clown. Better to keep the dress and language of an outlaw, than veil your villainy in gentle language.'

'You counsel well, lady,' said the Norman, 'So, in the language of action, I tell thee that thou shalt only leave this castle as Maurice De Bracy's wife. I am not used to be thwarted, nor does a Norman noble need to justify conduct to a Saxon. Thou art a proud one, Rowena, and thereby the fitter to be my wife. How else to escape from a mean Grange where a Saxon's swine is his only wealth?'

---

1 Vizard: a mask or visor.

'Sir Knight,' replied Rowena, 'the Grange you condemn has been my shelter from infancy. Trust me, when I leave it, it shall be with someone who does not despise my family.'

'I guess your meaning, lady,' said De Bracy, 'Do not dream that Richard Coeur de Lion will return, far less that his minion Ivanhoe will ever take thee as a bride. Know, lady, that Ivanhoe is in my power and that I can reveal his presence in this castle to Front-de-Boeuf – whose jealousy will be rather more fatal than mine...'

'Wilfred – *here*?' said Rowena. De Bracy looked at her steadily.

'Wert ignorant of this?' said he; 'Wilfred of Ivanhoe travelled in the litter of the Jew. A strange conveyance for a Crusader whose aim was to reconquer the Holy Sepulchre!' and he laughed scornfully.

'And if he were here,' said Rowena, in a tone of indifference, though now suddenly trembling, 'in what is he the rival of Front-de-Boeuf?'

'Rowena,' said De Bracy, 'Front-de-Boeuf will eliminate any who opposes his claim to the barony of Ivanhoe. Smile on my suit, however, and he shall have nothing to fear from Front-de-Boeuf. Otherwise, prepare to mourn him, for he is in the hands of one without mercy.'

'Save him, for the love of Heaven!' cried Rowena, her firmness finally giving way.

'I can and I will,' said he, 'when Rowena consents to be the bride of De Bracy. Who shall dare to lay a hand upon the son of her guardian and her companion? But it is thy *love* that must buy his protection. Be mine and he is safe. Refuse me and Wilfred dies; with thee no nearer to freedom.'

'I cannot *believe*,' answered Rowena, 'a plan so wicked.'

'Keep thy disbelief,' said De Bracy, 'until time shall prove it. Thy lover lies wounded in this castle. He also lies betwixt Front–de-Boeuf and *land* – which is what Front-de-Boeuf loves more than either ambition or beauty. The blow of a poniard or the thrust of a javelin will silence Ivanhoe forever. Cedric also...'

'And Cedric also,' murmured Rowena, 'My guardian. I deserve evil for forgetting his fate.'

'Cedric's fate also depends upon thy decision,' said De Bracy, 'I now leave thee to come to it.'

Hitherto Rowena had sustained her part with undismayed courage. Accustomed to Cedric himself giving way before her, she had the self-confidence of constant deference. Her demeanour, however, now deserted her as her eyes opened to her danger and that of her lover and guardian. She quailed; casting her eyes around as if looking for aid, she raised her hands and burst into tears. De Bracy was not unmoved; he paced the apartment exhorting the terrified woman to compose herself, yet now hesitating over his own course of action. If I am moved by her distress, thought he, I lose her – and gain the ridicule of Prince John.

'And yet,' he said to himself, 'I cannot look on the agony in that face or those eyes in tears. Would that I had Front-de-Boeuf's hardness!' Amid these thoughts, De Bracy was interrupted by the same horn which was interrupting and alarming others in the castle.

chapter twenty-four

I'll woo her as the lion woos his bride.
John Home: *Douglas: A Tragedy.*

While these scenes passed in other parts of the castle, Rebecca was awaiting her fate in the remote turret to which she had been taken by two of her abductors. Thrust into the little cell, she found herself in the presence of an old Sibyl.[1] This person was murmuring a Saxon rhyme to herself, as if to beat time to the revolving dance of her spindle upon the floor. The old woman raised her head as Rebecca entered and scowled.

'Up and away, old house-cricket,' said one of the men, 'our noble master commands it. Leave this chamber to a fairer guest.'

'Ay,' she grumbled, 'so thus is service rewarded? Once, my bare word would have cast ye out of service; and now I must away at the command of such as *thou*?'

'Dame Urfried,' said the other man, 'up and away! Thou hast had thy day, old dame, but thy sun has long set. Come, amble off.'

'Ill omens dog ye both!' cried the ancient; 'and a kennel be your burying-place! May Zernebock[2] tear me limb from limb if I leave with hemp still on my distaff!'

'Answer then to our lord, house fiend,' said the man, and retired, leaving Rebecca with the old woman.

'What devil's deed have they in the wind?' said the ancient, casting a glance at Rebecca; 'But it is easy to guess; bright eyes and black locks. Ay, easy to guess why they sent you to this turret, where no shriek can be heard. Thou wilt have owls for neighbours, fair one, and their screams will be as much regarded as thine own. Outlandish, too,' she said, noticing the dress and turban of Rebecca. 'Of what country art thou? A Saracen? Egyptian?'

'Be not angry, good mother,' said Rebecca.

'Say no more,' replied Urfried, 'men know a fox by its train and a Jewess by her tongue.'

'For mercy's sake,' said Rebecca, 'tell me what to expect. Is it my life they seek?'

'Thy life, minion?' sneered the sibyl; 'what would taking thy life pleasure *them*? Trust me, thy *life* is in no peril. Such usage shalt thou have as befell me, a noble Saxon. Look at me. I was as young and twice as fair as thou. When Front-de-Boeuf's father and his Normans stormed this castle, my father and my seven brothers defended it; storey to storey they went and chamber to chamber. There was not a room, nor a step of the stair not slippery with their blood. They died, every man. Ere their bodies were cold I had become the plaything of the conqueror!'

'Is there no help? Are there no means of escape?' said Rebecca.

'Think not of it,' said Urfried. 'There is no escape except through the gates of death. Fare thee well! Hebrew or Gentile, thy fate would be the same. They are men without pity. My thread is spun out – but thy task is yet to begin.'

'Stay with me for Heaven's sake!' said Rebecca.

---

1 An aged prophetess.

2 An evil god of the Slavic peoples. Mistakenly believed by Scott to be Saxon.

'The presence of the Mother of God would be no protection,' answered the old woman. 'There she stands,' pointing to a rude image of the Virgin, 'see if *she* can avert the fate that awaits thee.' She left the room locking the door behind her and Rebecca heard her cursing as slowly she descended the turret-stair.

Rebecca now expected a fate similar to that of Rowena. Yet she had one advantage, being better prepared in strength of mind to encounter her danger. She had also acquired the firmness and presence of mind necessary for direct action.

Her first care was to inspect the apartment; but it afforded no hope either of escape or protection. It contained neither secret passage nor trap-door and the door had no inside bolt or bar. The single window opened on to a battlemented space surmounting the turret which gave Rebecca at first sight some hope. However, she soon found that, being an isolated bartizan, or balcony, it had no exit to any other part of the battlements. The bartizan was surrounded by a parapet with embrasures from which archers might flank the castle wall on that side.

The prisoner trembled, however, when a step was heard on the stair and the door of the turret-chamber slowly opened. A tall man dressed as one of the *banditti* slowly entered and shut the door behind him. His cap concealed the upper part of his face and he held his mantle in such a way as to muffle up the rest and thus he stood before the affrighted prisoner. A ruffian by his dress, he seemed initially at a loss to express his purpose. Rebecca anticipated it. She unclasped two bracelets which she proffered.

'Take these,' she said, 'and for God's sake be merciful to me and my aged father! These jewels are trifling to what he would give you for our freedom.'

'Flower of Palestine,' said the man, 'these diamonds are brilliant, but they cannot match you; and ever since I have taken to this trade, I have preferred beauty to wealth.'

'Do not deny yourself,' said Rebecca; 'take the ransom and have mercy! Gold will purchase your pleasure – to mistreat us would only bring remorse. My father's ransom will purchase freedom from outlawry.'

'Well spoken,' replied the outlaw in French, finding it difficult to converse in Saxon, 'but know, lily of Baca's vale,[1] that thy father is already in the hands of a powerful alchemist who will distil from him all he holds dear. Thy ransom must be paid by love and beauty; in no other coin will I accept it.'

'Thou art no outlaw!' said Rebecca in French. 'No outlaw would refuse such an offer; no outlaw in this land uses that dialect. Thou art Norman; cast off that mask!'

'And thou,' said Brian de Bois Guilbert, dropping the mantle from his face, 'art a rose of Sharon. I would rather hang thy neck and arms with the diamonds than deprive thee of them.'

'What do you want of me?' said Rebecca, 'We can have naught in common.'

'Indeed?' replied the Templar, laughing; 'wed a Jewess? *Despardieux!* Not if she were the Queen of Sheba! Were the King of France to offer me his daughter with Languedoc for a dowry, I could not wed her. It is against my vow to love any woman other than as a *paramour* – and as such will I love thee. I am a Templar; behold the cross of my Holy Order.'

'Thou darest appeal to it?' demanded Rebecca.

'And if I do so?' said the Templar.

---

1 The valley of Baca is in Lebanon and on the pilgrim route to Jerusalem. See Psalms 84:5–6.

'What *is* your belief,' said Rebecca, 'when you break your vows as knight and churchman?'

'Well preached!' answered the Templar. 'Marriage is indeed a crime on the part of a Templar, but whatever *other* folly I may practise will be absolved at the next Preceptory of our Order. Neither King Solomon, nor his father David had wider privileges than we soldiers of the Temple of Zion won by its defence. The protectors of Solomon's Temple claim license by the *example* of Solomon.'

'Using Scripture to justify assault is a crime,' said Rebecca.

The eyes of the Templar flashed at this reproof.

'Hearken, Rebecca,' he said, 'I have spoken mildly to thee till now, but hear now the language of thy master. Thou art my captive and subject to my will; I will take whatever be refused.'

'Stand back!' cried Rebecca.' Stand back and hear me! I will proclaim thy villainy, Templar, from one end of Europe to the other. Thy Order shall learn that thou hast sinned with a Jewess. Heretic! You will be *accursed* for dishonouring the Cross.'

'Thou art keen-witted,' replied the Templar, well aware of the truth of her charge, 'but a voice must be loud to be heard beyond the walls of *this* castle. Laments and screams die silently here. One thing only can save thee, Rebecca; submission.'

'Submit to my fate?' said Rebecca. 'Sacred Heaven! To what fate? Coward, I spit at thee. The God of Abraham opens one escape to his daughter – even from *this* hell!'

Still speaking, she threw open the latticed window leading to the bartizan and sprang through it on to the parapet. There was now nothing between her and the depths below. Unprepared for this, Bois Guilbert had no time to intercept her. As he made to advance, she exclaimed,

'Templar! One step nearer and I drop. My body will be on that courtyard before *you* touch it!'

The Templar hesitated, his resolution giving way to admiration.

'Come down!' he cried, 'I swear I will do thee no offence.'

'I trust thee not, Templar.'

'You do me an injustice,' exclaimed the Templar; 'I swear by the crest of my fathers that I will do thee no injury. If only for *thy* father's sake, come down! I will be Isaac's support – and in this castle he will need it...'

'I know it too well,' said Rebecca.

'Commandments I may have broken,' said Brian de Bois Guilbert, 'but my word, *never*.'

'Then I will trust thee,' said Rebecca, '*thus* far.' She descended from the verge of the battlement but remained close by one of the embrasures.

'Here,' she said, 'I take my stand. Take one step nearer and I trust my soul to God!'

As Rebecca spoke, her resolve and beauty combined to give her a dignity more than mortal; the realisation that she had her fate under command and could escape to death, gave a brilliant fire to her eye. Bois Guilbert, himself proud and high-spirited, had never beheld beauty so animated and so commanding.

'Let there be peace between us, Rebecca,' he said.

'Peace, then,' answered Rebecca, 'but with this space between.'

'Thou needst no longer fear me,' said Bois Guilbert.

'I fear thee not,' replied she. 'Thanks to him that reared this tower so high – and to the God of Israel; I fear thee not.'

The Templar said, 'Hear me, Rebecca. Never did knight take lance in hand with a heart more devoted to a lady than once did Brian de Bois Guilbert. She was the daughter of a Baron of the Landes de Bordeaux. And how was I rewarded? When I returned from Palestine I found her wedded to a Gascon squire! So now my manhood must know no home nor wife; my grave will be solitary and no child will bear the ancient name of Bois Guilbert. A Templar can possess neither lands nor goods; he lives, moves and breathes only at the will and pleasure of another.'

'Indeed,' said Rebecca coldly, 'and what could compensate for such sacrifice?'

'The prospect of ambition, Rebecca.'

'An evil recompense,' said she.

'Say not so,' answered the Templar, 'Ambition is a temptation which could disturb even the bliss of Heaven itself. He paused a moment, then added,

'Rebecca, she who would prefer death to dishonour must have a powerful soul. Mine thou must be; but with thy consent and on thine own terms. Thou must share my future with me. I am already one of the Chief Commanders of the Order and one day its Grand Master. I have long sought a kindred spirit to share it; and I have found such in thee.'

'Thou sayest this to one of *my* people?' answered Rebecca.

'Do not cite the difference in our creeds,' said the Templar. 'Our Founders forswore every human delight to die martyrs by hunger and scimitar defending a barren desert. Our Order soon adopted wider views and found a better purpose for our sacrifice. Our possessions in every kingdom of Europe, our military fame which brings to us the flower of chivalry, these are now dedicated to ends our pious founders little dreamed of! But I will not draw back the veil of our mysteries…' he paused, listening,

'That bugle requires my presence; I must go. What I threatened was necessary to reveal thy character; gold can be proved only by the applying the touchstone. Think on what I have said. Farewell!'

He descended the stair leaving Rebecca scarcely less terrified at the prospect of death than at the furious ambition of the man. When she re-entered the turret chamber, her first duty was to thank the God of Jacob – imploring protection for her and for her father. Another name glided into her petition; that of the wounded Ivanhoe whom fate had placed in the hands of his avowed enemies. Her heart checked her; but she had already breathed Ivanhoe's name and nothing could induce Rebecca to wish it recalled.

chapter twenty-five

A damn'd cramp piece of penmanship as ever I saw in my life!
Oliver Goldsmith: *She Stoops to Conquer*

When the Templar reached the hall of the castle, he found De Bracy already there. 'I see that your love-suit,' said De Bracy, 'has been disturbed like mine by this summons; I presume your *rendezvous* was more agreeable than mine.'

'You failed with the Saxon?' said the Templar.

'By the bones of à Becket,' answered De Bracy, 'Rowena must know that I cannot endure a woman's tears.'

'Away!' said the Templar; 'thou, a leader of a Free Company, regard a woman's tears? A few such sprinkled on a love torch makes the flame the brighter.'

'Gramercy,' replied De Bracy; 'she wept enough to extinguish a beacon.'

'And fiends occupy the bosom of the Jewess,' said the Templar. 'Not even Apollyon[1] himself could have inspired such pride. Now, where is Front-de-Boeuf? That horn is sounding urgently.'

'Negotiating with the Jew,' replied De Bracy, coolly; 'The howls of Isaac will have drowned the bugle. Parting with his treasure on Front-de-Boeuf's terms will sound louder than any horn.' They were then joined by Front-de-Boeuf, indeed disturbed in dealing with Isaac.

'Let us see the cause of this accursed clamour,' he snapped, 'Here is a letter sent in by a messenger under a truce flag; and in Saxon if I mistake not.'

He handed it to De Bracy. 'It may be magic spells for aught I know,' said the illiterate De Bracy.

'Give it here to me,' said the Templar.

'Let us profit by your *reverend* literacy, then,' said De Bracy; 'What says it?'

'It is...a formal *challenge*,' answered the Templar. 'By our Lady, if this be not a jest it is...extraordinary.'

'Jest?' said Front-de-Boeuf; 'Who dares jest with me? Read it.' The Templar read:

'I, Wamba, the son of Witless, Jester to the noble Cedric of Rotherwood and I, Gurth, the son of Beowulph, the swineherd...'

'Thou art *mad*,' interrupted Front-de-Boeuf.

'It is thus set down,' snapped the Templar. He went on:

'I, Gurth, the son of Beowulph, swineherd unto the said Cedric with the assistance of our confederates in this our feud, namely, the good Knight, called Le Noir Faineant, *and Robert Locksley, called* Cleave-the-Wand: to *you, Reginald Front de Boeuf, and your accomplices whomsoever:*

To wit, that whereas you have, without feud declared, wrongfully seized upon the person of our lord, the said Cedric; also the Lady Rowena of Hargottstandstede; also the noble Athelstane of Coningsburgh; also the Jew, Isaac of York, together with his daughter and certain horses and mules: which aforesaid persons, were all in peace and travelling as liege subjects upon the king's highway;

---

1 Apollyon: The demon king of the bottomless pit. *See* Revelation; 9:1–11.

Therefore we require and demand that the said persons be, within an hour, delivered to us unharmed in body and goods.

Failing which, we do pronounce that we hold ye as robbers and traitors, and will wage our bodies against ye in battle, siege, or otherwise to your destruction.

Signed by us upon the Eve of St Withold's day, the above being written down by a Clerk to God, our Lady and St Dunstan, of the Chapel of Copmanhurst.'

The knights looked at each other in silent amazement, utterly at a loss to know what this could portend. De Bracy was the first to break silence by an uncontrollable fit of laughter, wherein he was joined by the Templar. Front-de-Boeuf, however, seemed impatient of their mirth.

'I give you warning, Sirs,' he said, 'that you had better decide how to respond, rather than give way to merriment.'

'Front-de-Boeuf has clearly not recovered his nerve since his unhorsing,' said De Bracy to the Templar; 'He is cowed by a message from a jester – and a swineherd!'

'These fellows ,' rasped Front-de-Boeuf, 'would not dare act unless supported by strong force; and there are enough armed outlaws in this forest. I tied one to the horns of a wild stag which gored him to death in minutes – and had as many arrows shot at me as that target at Ashby. Here, fellow,' he added to one of his attendants, 'what force supports this challenge?'

'There are at least two hundred armed men in the woods,' answered a squire.

'So, here is a pretty matter!' said Front-de-Boeuf. 'This comes from granting you the use of the castle. You cannot manage your affair quietly; but bring this nest of hornets about my ears!'

'Hornets?' said De Bracy; 'Stingless drones.'

'Stingless?' snapped Front-de-Boeuf; 'fork-headed shafts a cloth-yard in length are sting enough.'

'For shame, Sir Knight!' said the Templar. 'Let us summon our people and sally forth at them.[1] One knight, aye one man-at-arms, is a match for twenty such peasants.'

'Enough,' said De Bracy; 'I should be ashamed to couch lance against them.'

'True,' growled Front-de-Boeuf; 'if they were Turks or Moors, Sir Templar; or craven French peasants, De Bracy; but these are English *yeomen*! Over these we have no advantage save our weapons and horses which are little use in the forest. Sally out, said thou? We have scarce men enough to defend the castle. The best of mine are at York – as is your entire band, De Bracy.'

'Could they attempt a storming?' said the Templar.

'No,' answered Front-de-Boeuf. 'They may have a daring leader, but without machines or scaling ladders the castle will defy them.'

'Send, then, to thy neighbours,' said the Templar. 'Entreat them to assemble their people and come to the rescue of three knights besieged in the castle of Front-de-Boeuf by a jester and a swineherd!'

'You jest, Sir Knight,' answered the baron; 'to whom should I send? Malvoisin is at York with his retainers and so are my other allies; and so should *I* have been, but for *your* infernal enterprise!'

---

1 Sally. A counter-attack by a besieged garrison. Castles often had a special gate, or sally-port, for this purpose.

'Then send to York and recall our people,' said De Bracy, 'they will flee my standard unfurled – and the sight of my Free Companions.'

'And who shall bear such a message?' said Front-de-Boeuf. 'They will beset every path and rip the errand out of his bosom.' He paused for a moment,

'Sir Templar, thou can write as well as read; return an answer to this challenge.'

'I would rather do it at the sword's point,' said Bois Guilbert; 'but be it as you will.' He wrote:

'*Sir Reginald Front-de-Boeuf, with his noble allies, receives no defiances at the hands of slaves, bondsmen, or fugitives. Touching the prisoners, we do in Christian charity require you to send one to receive their Confession, it being our intention to execute them afore noon. Wherefore we require you to send a Priest to reconcile them to God.*'

This was delivered to the squire, and by him to the waiting messenger who returned to a great oak some three arrow-flights from the castle. Here awaited the Black Knight and Locksley with their allies and the hermit. More than two hundred yeomen had already assembled, with others coming in.

Besides these troops, a less orderly force of Saxon inhabitants of the neighbouring townships and bondsmen from Cedric's extensive estates, had arrived to assist in his rescue. Few were armed with more than rustic weapons adapted for military purposes. Boar-spears, scythes, flails and the like were their chief arms, the Normans being cautious in permitting Saxons the use of sword and spear. To the leaders of this motley army the letter of the Templar was now delivered. The chaplain was desired to read it.

'By the crook of St Dunstan,' said he, 'I swear this French jargon is beyond me.'

'I must be clerk, then,' said the Black Knight. Taking the letter he read it over aloud in Saxon.

'*Execute* the noble Cedric?' exclaimed Wamba; 'by the rood, thou must be mistaken, Sir Knight.'

'Not I.'

'Then we must take the castle,' replied Gurth, 'if we must tear it down with our bare hands!'

'We have little *else* to tear it with,' replied Wamba.

'This is only a contrivance to gain time,' said Locksley; 'they dare not do this!'

'I wish,' said the Black Knight, 'there were one among us who could gain entry to the castle and see how things stand; but hold! They require a holy confessor; this hermit might exercise his vocation and bring us intelligence.'

'A plague on thee!' cried the hermit; 'I tell thee, Sir Slothful, that when I doff my Friar's frock, my priesthood and sanctity come off with it. In this green jerkin, I kill deer; I do not confess Christians.'

'Then,' said the Black Knight,' is there no-one here able to play father confessor?' All looked silently on each other.

'I see,' said Wamba, eventually, 'that the fool must risk his neck where wise men shrink. I wore russet before I wore motley. I was trained to be a Friar until a brain fever left me only wit enough to be a fool. In the hermit's frock, I could administer comfort to Cedric.'

'On with the frock, then,' said the knight, 'and bring us an account of the situation within. Their numbers must be few and they may indeed be taken by a bold attack.'

'And in the meantime,' said Locksley, 'we will watch the place so closely, that not even a fly shall leave it. My friend,' he continued, addressing Wamba, 'assure these tyrants that whatever violence they show to their prisoners, shall be repaid upon them.'

'*Pax vobiscum*,' said Wamba, now muffled in his religious disguise; and with the solemn deportment of a Friar, he departed.

chapter twenty-six

The hottest horse will oft be cool,
The dullest will show fire;
The friar will often play the fool,
The fool will play the friar.
Anon (prob. Scott): *Old Song*

The Jester, arrayed in the cowl and frock of a hermit and with a knotted cord twisted round his waist, stood before the castle of Front-de-Boeuf. The warder demanded his name and errand.

'*Pax vobiscum*,' answered the Jester, 'I am a brother of the Order of St Francis, come to do my office to certain prisoners within this castle.'

'Thou art a bold friar,' said the warder, 'Saving our drunken confessor, a cock of thy feather hath not crowed here these twenty years.'

'Tell mine errand to thy Lord,' answered the pretended friar. 'Trust me, it will find acceptance and all of you shall hear the cock crow.'

The warder left his turret and carried the intelligence that a holy Friar stood before the gate demanding admission. Wondering, he received his master's commands to admit the holy man. The self-confidence which had emboldened Wamba to undertake his mission, paled when he now found himself before the dreaded Front-de-Boeuf. He brought out his '*pax vobiscum*' with more anxiety and hesitation than hitherto. Front-de-Boeuf, however, accustomed to see menof all ranks tremble in his presence, found no cause for suspicion.

'Who and whence art thou, priest?' said he.

'*Pax vobiscum*,' reiterated the Jester, 'I am a poor servant of St Francis. I was travelling through this wilderness, as Scripture hath it, '*quidam viator incidit in latrones*', that is, I fell among thieves. They sent me unto this castle to do my office on two persons condemned by your honour.'

'Ay, right,' answered Front-de-Boeuf; 'and canst thou tell me, holy father, the number of those thieves and *banditti*?'

'Gallant sir,' answered the Jester, '*nomen illis legio*, their name is legion, for they are many.'

'Tell me their numbers in plain terms priest, or thy cloak and cord will not protect thee.'

'Alas!' said Wamba, '*cor meum eructavit*, that is to say, my heart was like to burst with fear, but I conceived they were at least five hundred.'

'What?' said the Templar, coming into the hall, 'the wasps muster so thick? It is time to stifle this mischievous brood.' Then taking Front-de-Boeuf aside; 'Knowest thou this priest?'

'He is from a distant convent,' said Front-de-Boeuf; 'I know him not.'

'Then trust him not with thy plans,' answered the Templar. 'Let him carry a written order to De Bracy's Free Companions to return to their master's aid. In the meantime, let him prepare the Saxon hogs for the slaughterhouse.'

'It shall be so,' said Front-de-Boeuf, directing a domestic to conduct the Friar to Cedric and Athelstane.

The impatience of Cedric had been fired rather than diminished by his confinement. He strode from one end of the hall to the other, talking mainly to himself and sometimes addressing Athelstane who passively awaited his fate, while digesting a liberal noonday meal. His captivity, he had concluded, would end in Heaven's good time.

'*Pax vobiscum*,' said the Jester, entering the apartment; 'the blessing of St Dunstan, St Dennis, St Duthoc and all other saints whatsoever, be upon ye.'

'Enter freely,' answered Cedric; 'thy purpose here?'

'To bid you prepare yourselves for death,' said the Jester.

'Impossible!' replied Cedric, starting. 'They dare not!'

'Alas!' said the Jester, 'to restrain them by any sense of humanity is futile. Reflect, noble Cedric and Athelstane, on crimes of the flesh you may have committed – for this day will ye answer to a higher Tribunal.'

'Athelstane,' said Cedric; 'we must rouse up to a last action. Better to die like men than live like slaves.'

'I am ready,' answered Athelstane.

'Wait yet a moment, good uncle,' said the Jester, reverting to his natural voice; 'look long – before you leap in the dark.'

'By my faith,' said Cedric, 'I know that voice!'

'It is that of your jester,' answered Wamba, throwing back his cowl. 'And had you taken this fool's advice, you would not have been here now. Take a fool's advice now and you will not be here long.'

'What mean'st thou?' demanded Cedric.

'Just this,' replied Wamba; 'take this frock and cord. March quietly out of the castle. Leave me your cloak and girdle.'

'Leave *thee* in my place?' said Cedric, astonished at the proposal; 'why, they would hang thee.'

'Let them do as they will,' said the jester.

'Wamba,' answered Cedric, 'I grant thy request, provided thou make the exchange with Lord Athelstane here. Let an old tree wither so that the hope of the forest be preserved. Save noble Athelstane, Wamba! It is the duty of all Saxons. Thou and I will die together while he rouses our countrymen to avenge us.'

'Not so, Cedric,' said Athelstane, 'I will not make an escape which a slave has designed for his master.'

'You are wise, sirs,' said the Jester, 'and I am but a fool; but it is the fool that shall decide this for ye. I am like John-a-Duck's mare that would let no man mount her but John-a-Duck. I came to save my master, and if he will not consent; *basta,* enough – I go away.'

'Go, Cedric,' said Athelstane. 'Your presence will encourage our friends to attempt a rescue. Remain here and you ruin us all.'

'Is there prospect of rescue?' said Cedric to the Jester.

'Indeed there is!' echoed Wamba. 'Fill my cloak and you don a general's cassock. Five hundred men are outside. Go, master; be kind to Gurth. Let my cockscomb hang in Rotherwood hall in memory that I was faithful...' The last word came out with an expression betwixt jest and earnest. Tears stood in Cedric's eyes.

'Thy memory shall be preserved,' he said, 'But I trust I shall find means to save you, Rowena and Athelstane.' The exchange of dress was then accomplished, when a sudden doubt struck Cedric.

'I know no language but my own,' he said, 'and a few words of Norman. How shall I pass for a reverend brother?'

'The spell lies in two words,' replied Wamba. '*Pax vobiscum* will answer all queries. If you go or come, bless or ban, *Pax vobiscum* carries you through like a charm.'

'*Pax vobiscum*,' said the master. 'I shall remember. Athelstane, I will save you or return to die with you. The Saxon blood royal shall not be spilt while mine flows. Farewell.'

Cedric sallied forth and it was not long ere he had occasion to test the force of the Jester's password. In a low-arched and dusky passage, by which he worked his way to the hall of the castle, he was interrupted by a female form.

'*Pax vobiscum!*' said Cedric, endeavouring to hurry past, when a soft voice replied,

'*Et vobis quaso, domine reverendissime, pro misericordia vestra*,' said Rebecca, permitted by Urfried to leave the turret for her services in tending Ivanhoe.

'I am somewhat deaf,' replied Cedric in good Saxon, immediately muttering to himself, 'A curse on the fool and his pax vobiscums, I have lost my javelin at first cast.'

'I pray you of dear love, reverend father,' she replied softly in Saxon, 'that you visit a wounded prisoner and do thy holy office.'

'Daughter,' answered Cedric, much embarrassed, 'my time here does not permit such duties. I must go forth; there is life or death upon my speed.'

'Father, I entreat you,' replied the suppliant, 'Do not leave this endangered man without succour.'

'May the Fiend leave me with Odin!' muttered Cedric impatiently. He would have proceeded in the same tone, but was interrupted by the harsh voice of Urfried from the turret.

'Is this how you reward my permission to leave thy cell, Jewess?'

'A Jewess?' cried Cedric, 'Let me *pass*, woman!'

'Come this way, father,' said the old hag, approaching, 'Thou'rt a stranger in this castle and cannot leave it without a guide. Come hither; I would speak with thee. Jewess, go back to the sick man's chamber; tend him till my return – and woe betide thee if ye quit it again!'

chapter twenty-seven

Fond wretch! and what canst thou relate,
But deeds of sorrow, shame, and sin?
Thy deeds are proved; thou know'st thy fate;
But come, thy tale; begin; begin!
George Crabbe; *Hall of Justice*

Urfried ushered Rebecca back to the apartment from which she had sallied. She then conducted an unwilling Cedric into a smaller room and locked the door.

'Thou art Saxon, father. Deny it not.'

Observing that Cedric hesitated, she continued,

'The sounds of my native language are sweet to mine ears. They are seldom heard save from wretches and serfs who drudge here. Thou art a Saxon, father – a Saxon.'

'Do not Saxon priests visit this castle, then?' replied Cedric.'

'They come not,' answered Urfried, 'For ten years this castle saw no priest save a debauched Norman who partook of the revels of Front-de-Boeuf; and he is long gone. But thou art a *Saxon* priest and I have a question for thee.'

'I am Saxon,' answered Cedric, 'but unworthy of the name of priest. Let me begone and I swear to send one more worthy to hear thy confession.'

'Stay yet a while,' said Urfried. 'This voice will soon be choked with the cold earth, but I would not descend into it like the beast I have lived. Wine must give me strength to speak my tale.' She poured a cup, and drank. 'It stupifies,' she said.

'I was not born a wretch, father,' she went on, 'I was free, honoured and beloved. I am now a miserable slave. I was the sport of Front de Boeuf's passion while I still had my beauty, and an object of their contempt now it has passed; a decrepit hag. I am the daughter of the Thane of Torquilstone.'

'*Thou*, daughter of Torquil Wolfganger?' said Cedric, astonished, 'the daughter of my father's comrade in arms?'

'Thy father's comrade?' echoed Urfried; 'then...Cedric must stand before me, for Hereward of Rotherwood had but one son. But if thou *art* Cedric, art also a priest?'

'It matters not,' said Cedric; 'Proceed.'

'There is,' said Urfried,' black guilt lying on my breast, that the fire hereafter cannot cleanse. These halls are stained with the blood of my father and brethren; my guilt is to have lived, the paramour of their murderer.'

'Woman,' exclaimed Cedric, 'the friends of thy father said requiem masses for his soul, his valiant sons and murdered Ulrica. You tell me now that while we honoured the dead, thou *lived* – lived in *union* with a murdering tyrant; with *him*!'

'But not in love! Hatred of Front-de-Boeuf and his kind governed my soul.'

'You hated him, and yet you lived on with him,' replied Cedric; 'Was there no poniard or knife – no bodkin? Had I *dreamed* that the daughter of Torquil lived with the murderer of her father, my sword had found thee!'

'Thou art then a true Saxon,' said Ulrica, 'but I also have had vengeance; I fomented their quarrels and turned drunken revelry into murder! I set the elder Front-de-Boeuf against young Reginald and he fell – by the hand of his own son!'

'Seek penance,' said Cedric. 'I cannot longer wait.'

'Stay a moment!' said Ulrica; 'If Front-de-Boeuf found you in this disguise, your life would be short.'

'Just so,' said Cedric; 'But I die a Saxon; detain me not!'

'Be it so,' said Ulrica, 'Forget that I am daughter of thy father's friend. Farewell! Thy scorn has burst the last tie to my people.'

'Ulrica,' said Cedric, softened by this appeal, 'Wilt thou despair with thine eyes now open?'

'Cedric, thy words have shown me the means of revenge. Whatever was Ulrica's life, her death will show her to be Torquil's daughter. Lead the attack! When a red flag waves from the donjon turret, scale the wall, for that flag means the Normans have trouble within...Begone. Follow thine own fate; and leave me to mine.' Cedric would have pressed her further, but there came the voice of Front-de-Boeuf.

'Where tarries that priest? I will make a martyr of him if he hatches treason!'

Ulrica vanished through a side door just before Front-de-Boeuf entered the apartment. Said he to Cedric,

'Thy penitents, father, have made a long shrift; hast prepared them for death?'

'I found them,' said Cedric, in halting French, 'expecting the worst. They knew into whose power they had fallen.'

'Friar,' replied Front-de-Boeuf, 'thy speech smacks of the Saxon tongue?'

'I was schooled in the convent of St Withold at Burton,' answered Cedric.

'Indeed?' said the Baron; 'St Withold's is an owlet's nest worth harrying.'

'God's will be done,' said Cedric, in a tremulous voice which Front-de-Boeuf imputed to fear.

'Do me one holy office,' said he, 'and thou shalt sleep safe in thy cell.'

'Speak your commands,' said Cedric.

'Follow me to the postern gate,' said the knight, striding ahead.

'Thou seest yon herd of Saxon swine surrounding Torquilstone? Tell them whatever can detain them there for a day. Meantime, take this scroll. Canst read?'

'Not a jot I,' answered Cedric, 'save on my breviary.'

'Then the fitter art thou for my purpose. Carry this scroll to the castle of Philip de Malvoisin. Say it is from me and the Templar, de Bois Guilbert, and that I pray him to send it to York with all speed. Tell him to fear not, for he shall find us sound behind our battlements. I say to thee again, Priest, keep the knaves where they are until our friends can bring up their lances. My vengeance is awake and will be gorged.'

'Your commands shall be obeyed,' said Cedric, 'Not a Saxon shall stir from before these walls.'

Front-de-Boeuf had led the way to a postern from which they crossed the moat on a single plank and reached a small barbican, or exterior defence. This communicated with the open fields by a fortified sally-port.

'Begone, then. Do mine errand and return for as much Malvoisie wine as would drench thy whole convent.'

'Assuredly we shall meet again,' grimly answered Cedric.

'Something in hand meantime,' continued the Norman; and thrust into Cedric's hand a gold Byzant, adding, 'Remember, priest; fail, and I will flay off thy cowl – and skin.'

'I give thee leave to do both,' answered Cedric, leaving the postern and striding over the field. Turning back towards the castle, he hurled the piece of gold towards the donor, exclaiming,

'Norman, may thy money perish with thee!'

Front-de-Boeuf heard the words imperfectly, but the action was suspicious.

'Archers!' he called to the warders on the outward battlements, 'fire an arrow through yon monk! No, stay,' he said, as they were stringing their bows, 'We must trust him since we have no better. He dares not betray me. Ho! Giles gaoler, bring Cedric of Rotherwood before me with that churl of Coningsburgh, Athelstane. Their very *names* reek of pigmeat. Bring wine also, to wash away the taste and put it in the armoury with the prisoners.'

Later, entering that Gothic apartment, hung with spoils of his own and his father's exploits, he found wine on the massive oaken table and his two Saxon captives guarded by four of his men-at-arms. Front-de-Boeuf took a long draught of wine. Wamba drew his cap down over his face.

'Gallants of England,' said Front-de-Boeuf, 'how relish ye Torquilstone? Are ye yet aware what your *surquedy* and *outrecuidance*[1] merit, for scoffing at the hospitality of royal John? By God and St Denis, if ye pay not the ransom, I will hang ye up by the feet from the bars of these windows, till the hoody crows make skeletons of ye!

Speak out, Saxons, what bid ye for your lives? How say you of Rotherwood?'

'Not a *doit* I,'[2] answered Wamba 'and as for hanging up by the feet, my brain has been topsy-turvy ever since the biggin[3] was first bound around my head. Turning me upside down may restore it again!'

'Saint *Genevieve*!' cried Front-de-Boeuf, 'what have we got here?' Striking Cedric's cap from the head of the Jester he revealed the silver neck collar – the fatal badge of servitude.

'Giles; Clement!' exclaimed the furious Norman, 'what have we here?'

'I think I can tell you,' said De Bracy, entering the apartment. 'This man is Cedric's clown.'

'I shall settle them *both!*' raged Front-de-Boeuf; 'They shall hang on the same gallows, unless his master and this Coningsburgh pay well for their lives. They must also carry off the swarms besieging the castle. Go,' said he to his attendants, 'fetch me the real Cedric hither. You mistook a fool for a Saxon franklin.'

'Ay,' said Wamba,' but you will find there are more fools than franklins among us.'

'What means he?' said Front-de-Boeuf, looking towards his men who said, falteringly, that if this man were not Cedric, they knew not what had become of him.

'Saints of *Heaven*,' exclaimed De Bracy, 'he must have escaped in the monk's dress!'

'Fiends of hell!' roared Front-de-Boeuf, 'it was the boar of Rotherwood that I sent out – and with my own hands! Thou,' he said to Wamba, 'I will shave thy crown

---

1 *Surquedy* and *outrecuidance*: Norman French; insolence and presumption.

2 Doit: a small Dutch copper coin, i.e. a trifling sum.

3 Biggin: A close-fitting mediaeval cap worn by children.

for thee. I will tear the scalp from thy head and pitch thee from the battlements. Thy trade is jester is it; well canst jest *now*?'

'The red cap *you* propose,' said Wamba evenly, 'will make a Cardinal of a simple monk.'

'De Bracy,' said Front-de-Boeuf, 'you stand there listening to a fool's jargon while destruction gapes! We are outnumbered and without contact with our friends; we must expect an assault!'

'To the battlements then,' said De Bracy; 'Call the Templar; let him fight as well for his life as he has done for his Order. And to the walls thyself. Here, Saxon,' he continued, addressing Athelstane, and handing a cup to him, 'rinse thy throat with liquor and say what thou wilt give for thy liberty.'

'Dismiss me with my companions,' answered Athelstane, 'and I will pay ransom of one thousand Marks.'

'And wilt thou withdraw the scum outside?' said Front-de-Boeuf.

'In so far as I can,'said Athelstane, 'I will.'

'We are agreed then,' said Front-de-Boeuf. 'Thou and they are to be set at freedom. Peace it is to be on both sides, for payment of a one thousand. It is a trifling ransom, Saxon; and mark you, it extends not to the Jew Isaac.'

'Nor to his daughter,' said the Templar, who had now joined them.

'Neither of them,' said Front-de-Boeuf, 'belong to this Saxon's company.'

'Deal with the unbelievers as ye wish,' replied Athelstane.

'And neither does the ransom include the Lady Rowena,' said De Bracy.

'Neither,' snarled Front-de-Boeuf, 'does our treaty refer to this Jester, of whom I will make an example...'

'The Lady Rowena,' interrupted Athelstane, 'is my affianced bride. I will not part with her.'

'Thy affianced bride? The Lady Rowena affianced to the likes of thee?' said De Bracy, 'Saxon, thou'rt dreaming.'

'My lineage, Norman,' replied Athelstane, 'is more ancient than that of a beggarly Frenchman. Kings were *my* ancestors.'

'De Bracy,' said Front-de-Boeuf, well pleased with this rebuff to his companion, 'the Saxon hath hit thee fairly.'

'I care not,' said De Bracy, rejoining to Athelstane 'thy glibness will not win freedom for the Lady Rowena.'

They were then interrupted by Giles, a servant, who announced that a monk was demanding admittance at the postern gate.

'In the name of Benedict,' said Front-de-Boeuf, 'have we a real monk this time, or another impostor? Search him! If ye have a second fraud palmed upon you, I will have hot coals in your eye sockets.'

'My lord,' said Giles, 'this be a real one. Your squire Jocelyn knows him as brother Ambrose, a monk of Jorvaulx.'

'Admit him,' said Front-de-Boeuf; 'he likely brings us news from his Prior. The Devil surely keeps holiday that priests are strolling through the country. Remove these prisoners. Saxon, think on what thou hast heard.'

'I claim,' said Athelstane, 'an honourable captivity with treatment as becomes my rank and as one in treaty for ransom. Moreover I hold you, Front de Boeuf, bound to answer to me in combat for my detention. There lies my glove!'

'I answer not to a challenge from a prisoner,' said Front-de-Boeuf; 'and neither shalt thou, De Bracy. Giles,' he continued, 'hang the franklin's glove upon yonder antlers until he is a free man. Should he demand it, he will have to face me!'

The Saxon prisoners were accordingly removed, as in came the monk Ambrose in great perturbation.

'This is the real *Deus vobiscum*,' said Wamba.

'Holy Mother,' said the monk to the assembled knights, 'am I safe and in Christian keeping?'

'Safe thou art,' replied De Bracy; 'with Baron Reginald Front-de-Boeuf and the Knight Templar de Bois Guilbert.'

'Ye are allies of our reverend father in God, Aymer, Prior of Jorvaulx,' said the monk, 'Ye owe him aid by knightly faith. Know that murderous caitiffs, casting aside the fear of God and his Church, and not regarding the bull of the Holy See, *'Si quis, suadende Diabolo'*...'[1]

'Priest!' snapped the Templar, 'all this we know. Just *tell* us if thy master the Prior is a prisoner and if so, to whom?'

'Surely,' said Ambrose, 'he is in the hands of men of Belial, infesters of these woods.'

'Instead of rendering *us* any assistance,' said Front-de-Boeuf, turning to his companions, 'the Prior of Jorvaulx requests aid at *our* hands. Speak up, priest. What does thy master expect?'

'So please you,' said Ambrose, 'the men of Belial rifled his mails, stripped him of two hundred gold marks and are demanding a large ransom; the reverend father prays you to rescue him, either by paying the ransom, or by force of arms.'

'The foul *Fiend* quell the Prior!' shouted Front-de-Boeuf; 'A Norman baron is to unbuckle his purse for a churchman whose moneybags are *ten* times as weighty as ours? And how, pray, are we to free him, cooped up as we are by *ten* times our number and expecting assault?'

'I was about to tell you,' cried the terrified monk, 'that they are raising a bank against thy castle walls.'

'To the battlements!' said De Bracy, 'let us mark what these knaves do.' So saying, he opened a latticed window which led to a projecting bartizan and called back,

'Saint Denis, the monk be right! They bring forward *mantelets* and *pavisses*,[2] and their archers are mustering on the skirts of the wood.'

Reginald Front-de-Boeuf also looked out and immediately snatched his bugle. He winded a long and loud blast, commanding his men to their posts on the walls.

'De Bracy, take the eastern side, where the walls are lowest. Bois Guilbert, look thou to the western. I will take the barbican. But do not confine yourselves to any one

---

1 A famous decree of Pope Innocent II in 1131, enacting that anyone maliciously laying hands on a cleric or monk incurred, *ipso facto,* anathema.

2 Mantelets were defences formed of planks, under cover of which assailants advanced to the attack. Pavisses were a species of large shields covering the whole person, employed on the same occasions. *Scott.*

post! We must this day be everywhere, wherever the attack is hottest. Our numbers are few, but we are only dealing with rustics.'

'But, noble knights,' exclaimed Father Ambrose, amidst the bustle and confusion of the preparations for defence, 'will none of ye hear the message of the reverend Aymer of Jorvaulx? Hear me, noble Sir Reginald!'

'Go patter thy petitions to Heaven,' snapped the Norman, 'we have no time to listen. Anselm, see that the boiling pitch and oil are ready to pour and see that the cross-bowmen have bolts aplenty. Hoist my banner with the old Bull's Head; let the knaves see with whom they have to deal!'

'Noble sir,' continued the monk, still trying to draw attention, 'let me discharge my Superior's errand.'

'*Away* with this prating dotard!' shouted Front-de Boeuf, 'lock him up in the chapel.'

In the meantime the Templar had been watching the doings of the besiegers with a more professional eye than Front-de-Boeuf or his companion.

'By my faith,' he said, 'these men approach with more than a touch of discipline. See ye how they use every cover to avoid our crossbow fire? I see neither banner nor pennon among them and yet... I wager that they are led by a veteran of the wars.'

'I see him!' said De Bracy, 'I see a knight's crest and the gleam of armour. See yon tall man in the black mail marshalling the farther troop of the yeomen. I think him the Black Knight who overthrew thee at Ashby, Front-de-Boeuf!'

'So much the better', said Front-de-Boeuf grimly, 'if he comes to give me revenge. The hilding[1] fellow dared not stay and claim the tourney prize. Right glad am I!'

The enemy's immediate approach cut off all farther discourse as each knight headed to his post at the head of his troops. There, and with calm determination, they awaited the assault.

chapter twenty-eight

This wandering race, sever'd from other men,
Boast yet their intercourse with human arts;
The seas, the woods, the deserts, which they haunt,
Find them acquainted with their secret treasures:
Anon. (prob. Scott): *The Jew*

When Ivanhoe collapsed after the lists at Ashby, Rebecca immediately prevailed on her father to have the young knight transported from the lists to a Jewish house in the outskirts of the town.

'Holy Abraham!' he exclaimed, 'he is a good youth, and my heart bleeds to see his blood stain his rich *hacqueton*[2] and his corselet of such goodly price. But to carry him into our house; by our Law, only in commerce may we deal with a Gentile.'

---

1 Contemptible

2 A shirt-like garment used as padding below armour. Hacquetons were made of buckram and stuffed with cotton.

'Father,' replied Rebecca, 'We may not mix with them in social congress, but a wounded Gentile is the Jew's brother.'

'Would that I knew what Rabbi Ben-Tudela would say on it,' replied Isaac, 'nevertheless he must not bleed to death; let Seth and Reuben bear him to Ashby.'

'Nay, place him in my litter,' said Rebecca, 'I will take one of the palfreys.'

'That would expose thee to the gaze of those dogs of Ishmael,' exclaimed Isaac, glancing towards the crowd of knights and squires. 'Beard of Aaron! What if the youth perishes? If he dies in our custody shall we not be held guilty?'

'He will *not* die, father,' said Rebecca, 'unless we abandon him; when we would be answerable to God.'

'Nay,' said Isaac, releasing his hold, 'it grieveth me to see his blood. Miriam of Manassas has made thee skilful in the art of healing. Do as thy mind moveth thee.'

The fears of Isaac, however, were not ill-founded. The benevolence of his daughter exposed her, on her return to Ashby, to the gaze of Brian de Bois Guilbert. The Templar twice passed and repassed them on the road, casting ardent eyes on the beautiful Jewess.

Rebecca had Ivanhoe transported to their temporary home and then proceeded to examine and bind up his wounds. Jews, male and female, possessed and practised medical science in all its branches, Jewish physicians being much sought after for their medical arts which they took care to conceal from Christians. Rebecca, with her powerful intellect, had acquired her knowledge under Miriam, daughter of one of their most celebrated Rabbis. Miriam was now dead, a fallen sacrifice to the fanaticism of the times, but her skill survived in her pupil. Rebecca was hence universally respected by her people, even her father frequently deferring to her opinion.

Ivanhoe reached the house of Isaac's friends still unconscious from loss of blood. Rebecca examined the wound, dressed it, applied her balsam to it and told her father that if fever could be averted, he would live. Indeed the next day he might safely travel with them to York. Isaac looked blankly at this, since his charity would willingly have ended there at Ashby, leaving the wounded Christian in the house. Against this, however, Rebecca raised two arguments: on no account would she put her balsam into the hands of another physician, even one of their own tribe. Furthermore, Ivanhoe was an intimate favourite of Richard Coeur-de-Lion. Were that monarch to return, Isaac, who had supplied his rebellious brother John with finance, would need a powerful protector.

'Sooth, Rebecca,' said Isaac, giving way, 'Better for me to fall into the hands of a lion of Idumea,[1] than those of the Lionheart, if he hears of my dealings with John. The youth shall journey with us unto York and our house shall be his until he is healed. And if the Lionheart returns, as is now rumoured, Wilfred of Ivanhoe may be a defence. If he doth not return, Wilfred may nonetheless repay us when he gains treasure by the sword.'

It was not until evening was nearly closed that Ivanhoe regained consciousness. He was unable for some time to recall his fall in the lists. A sense of wounds and injury was mingled with the recollection of blows dealt and received; of steeds rushing;

---

1 Idumea is the biblical land of Edom, a region south of the Dead Sea. Edom means 'red' in Hebrew and probably derives from the region's red sandstone.

of overthrowing and being overthrown and of shouts, the clashing of arms and the tumult of a fight.

To his surprise, he found himself in a room magnificently furnished with cushions instead of chairs. It was so Oriental that he began to wonder if he was back to Palestine. This impression was reinforced when a female form, dressed as in the Levant, glided through the door, followed by a swarthy servant.

As the wounded knight was about to address this apparition, she imposed silence with a finger to her lips. Her attendant proceeded to uncover Ivanhoe's side as she satisfied herself that the bandaging was in place and the wound healing. Rebecca's directions to her servant were given in Hebrew, the old domestic obeying without reply. Ivanhoe allowed them to dress his wounds in silence and it was not until his physician was about to retire, that he spoke.

'Madam,' he began in the Arabic learned on his Eastern travels, 'I pray you, gentle maiden, of your courtesy,' But here he was interrupted by Rebecca, her face dimpling for an instant with a smile.

'I am of England, Sir Knight and speak the English tongue.'

'Damsel,' again began Ivanhoe and again Rebecca interrupted him.

'Sir Knight,' she said, 'you should know that your handmaiden is the Jewess daughter of Isaac of York in whose household you are tended.' The knight gazed on the lustrous eyes, shaded and mellowed by the fringe of long silken eyelashes as she told him of the necessity of moving on to Isaac's house at York until his health was restored. Ivanhoe expressed unwillingness to further trouble his benefactors, asking if there was not some Saxon franklin in Ashby who would shelter him? At the Saxon convent at Burton he was sure to find sanctuary with his kinsman Waltheof, Abbot of St Witholds.

'Unless you dismiss your physician,' said Rebecca, with a melancholy smile, 'you cannot change your lodging. Our nation can heal wounds with secrets handed down from the days of Solomon. Some of these have already been applied to you; no Christian doctor could enable you to bear your armour within a month.'

'And how soon wilt *thou* enable me to bear it?' said Ivanhoe.

'Within eight days.'

'By Our Lady,' said Wilfred, 'this is no time for a knight to be bedridden. Keep thy promise and I will repay thee with my casque full of crowns.'

'I will keep my promise,' said Rebecca, 'armour thou shalt bear on the eighth day; but grant me one thing.'

'If it be in my power.'

'Believe henceforward,' answered Rebecca, 'that a Jew may do service to a Christian, desiring only the blessing of He who made both Jew and Gentile.'

'It were a sin to doubt it,' replied Ivanhoe, 'and now, kind physician, what of Cedric and his household? What of the lady...,' he stopped, unwilling to speak Rowena's name, 'who was Queen of the Tournament?'

'Selected by you, Sir Knight – and a judgment admired,' replied Rebecca. The blood loss of Ivanhoe did not prevent a flush from crossing his cheek.

'It was less of her I would speak,' said he, 'than of Prince John; and my faithful squire. Why does he not attend me?'

'Let me entreat you to keep silence,' answered Rebecca, 'Prince John is gone in all haste to York with the nobles, knights and churchmen of his party. Men say he plans to assume his brother's crown.'

'Not without its defence!' cried Ivanhoe, raising himself upon the couch.

'That you *may* be able to do,' said Rebecca touching his shoulder, 'but now, observe my directions and remain quiet.

'Maiden,' said Ivanhoe, 'what of Cedric and his household?'

'His steward was here a brief while since,' said Rebecca, 'panting with haste, to ask my father for certain monies. I learned from him that Cedric and Lord Athelstane of Coningsburgh had left Prince John's lodging for home in high displeasure.'

'Did any lady attend them to the banquet?' said Wilfred.

'The Lady Rowena,' said Rebecca, 'did not attend the Prince's feast. The steward reported that she is now on her way back to Rotherwood with her guardian Cedric. And touching your squire, Gurth...'

'Ha!' exclaimed the knight, 'thou knowest the name? But of course it was but yesterday he received a hundred zecchins from thee.'

'Speak not of that,' said Rebecca, blushing deeply, 'how easy it is for the tongue to betray what the heart would conceal.'

'That sum,' mused Ivanhoe, gravely, 'my honour is concerned in the repaying of it.'

'As indeed thou wilt,' said Rebecca, 'when eight days have passed.'

'Be it so, kind maiden,' said Ivanhoe, 'it was ungrateful to dispute thy commands. But tell me the fate of Gurth – and I have done with questions.'

'I grieve to tell, 'answered Rebecca, 'that he is arrested by Cedric.' Observing Wilfred's concern, she added, 'But Oswald the steward said that Cedric would pardon him as a faithful serf. His error was committed out of the love he bears to Cedric's son. Moreover, Oswald said that should Cedric's ire continue, he and the Jester Wamba would aid Gurth to escape.'

'Would to God they do so!' said Ivanhoe, 'I seem destined to bring ruin on whoever shows kindness to me. My king, whose brother seeks to grasp his crown; my regard brings down trouble on Rowena – and now my father may slay Gurth for his service to me! I am ill-fated. Be wise and let me go ere misfortune track thee also.'

'Nay,' said Rebecca, 'heaven has sent thee a friend and a physician. Be of good courage; take the medicine which I shall send thee by Reuben and rest before the morrow's journey. Adieu.' The sedative secured the patient a sound sleep. In the morning she found him free of fever and fit to travel in the same horse-litter which had brought him from the lists.

Isaac, like the rich traveller in Juvenal,[1] always had a fear of robbery. Conscious that he was fair game both for marauding Norman noble and Saxon outlaw, Isaac journeyed at a great rate with short halts. He thus bypassed Cedric and Athelstane who had had several hours start on him, but were delayed by their feasting at the convent of Saint Withold. Yet such was the effect of Miriam's balsam and the strength of Ivanhoe's constitution that he sustained the journey.

---

1 Decimus Iunius Iuvenalis, anglicised to Juvenal. (*fl.* late 1st Century AD) In his tenth satire, *The Vanity of Human Wishes* he writes that the rich traveller trembles at the shadow of a reed shaking in the moonlight, while the empty-handed itinerant will sing in the robber's face.

Isaac's haste, however, had produced more than just good speed. The rapidity with which he insisted on travelling raised a dispute between him and his guards.

These men were Saxons hoping to feed off the wealthy Jew and, displeased both by the rapidity of progress and by the quantity of ale allowed them at each meal, they deserted. This left Isaac, his daughter and her wounded patient to be found by Cedric; only to fall, as already described, into the hands of De Bracy and his confederates. At first, little notice was taken of the horse-litter which might have remained behind, but for the curiosity of De Bracy. He peered into it, hoping that it might contain Rowena, the object of his enterprise. His astonishment was thus considerable when he discovered that the litter contained a wounded man who, believing the ambushing 'outlaws' to be Saxons, revealed himself to be Sir Wilfred of Ivanhoe.

The chivalry which never quite abandoned De Bracy, prevented him from doing the defenceless knight any injury. It equally stopped him from betraying Ivanhoe's identity to Front-de-Boeuf, who would have instantly put to silence his rival for the Ivanhoe estate. On the other hand, to liberate Rowena's lover was beyond De Bracy's generosity. A middle course was adopted: he ordered two of his own squires to remain with the litter and to permit no one to approach it. If questioned, they were to say that it was transporting one of Cedric's comrades wounded in the ambush. On arriving at Torquilstone, while the Templar and Front de Boeuf pursued their own schemes with Isaac and Rebecca, De Bracy's squires conveyed Ivanhoe, *incognito,* to a remote apartment. This was their explanation to Front-de-Boeuf when he demanded why they did not man the battlements upon the alarm.

'A wounded companion!' he replied in wrath. 'No wonder that churls and yeomen lay siege to castles; no wonder clowns and swineherds send defiances to nobles, since men-at-arms and Free Companions are turned nurses! The castle is about to be assailed. To the battlements, ye loitering villains!' he cried, raising his stentorian voice, 'to the battlements, or this truncheon will splinter your bones!' The men sulkily replied that their master De Bracy had commanded them to tend the dying man.

'The *dying* man, knaves?' rejoined the Baron; 'I promise thee we shall *all* be dying men unless we stand to arms!'

'Now, comrades,' cried Front de Boeuf to his assembled troops, 'here are arblasts, with windlaces and quarrells.[1] To the barbican with you – and see you drive each bolt through a Saxon brain!' He also sent for Urfried.

'Here, fiend of a Saxon witch. Go tend this bedridden fellow if he must be tended. Begone.'

Thus was the care of Ivanhoe transferred to Ulrica. Her mind, however, was turning on new hope of vengeance with the likely storming of the castle. She was thus content to leave to Rebecca the care of the wounded knight.

---

1 The arblast was the crossbow; the windlace the machine used in bending that weapon, and the quarrell, so called from its square or diamond-shaped head, was the bolt adapted to it. *Scott.*

chapter twenty-nine

Ascend the watch-tower yonder, valiant soldier,
Look on the field, and say how goes the battle.
Friedrich Von Schiller: *Maid of Orleans*

Finding herself once more by the side of Ivanhoe, Rebecca had a keen sensation of pleasure at a time when danger was all around. As she felt his pulse, there was a softness in her touch. It trembled. Ivanhoe said,

'Is that you, gentle maiden?' which recalled her to herself. She asked him how he was.

'Better,' he said, 'dear Rebecca, to thy skill.'

'He calls me *dear* Rebecca,' she murmured to herself.

'My mind,' continued Ivanhoe, 'is worse than my body. I am a prisoner and, if I judge that hoarse voice aright, I am in the castle of Front-de-Boeuf. How will this end; how can I protect Rowena and my father?'

'He names not us Jews,' thought Rebecca. She told Ivanhoe that Bois Guilbert and the Baron Front-de-Boeuf were commanders within the castle. It was beleaguered, but by whom she knew not. She added that there was a priest about who might have more information.

'A Christian priest?' said the knight joyfully; 'fetch him Rebecca. Say that a sick man desires his counsel. I must attempt something; but not till I know how matters stand without.'

As we have seen, Rebecca's attempt to bring Cedric to the wounded knight's chamber was defeated by Ulrica's interception of the supposed monk. Rebecca returned to tell Ivanhoe this, but they had little time to reflect on it, as the bustle and clamour of defensive preparations now increased. The heavy step of men-at-arms traversing the battlements resounded through the winding passages and stairs leading to the various bartizans and points of defence. The voices of the knights were heard directing the defence, their commands often drowned by the clash of armour. Ivanhoe was impatient at his inactivity and in ardent desire to mix in the coming affray.

'If I could drag myself to that window,' said Ivanhoe, 'I might see how this game is like to go.'

'Fret not,' answered Rebecca, 'the sounds are ceased.'

'A dead pause,' said Wilfred; 'means that the men are now all at their posts on the walls. The storm will soon burst; could I but see from that window!'

'I will stand there and describe what passes,' said Rebecca, seeing his anxiety.

'You must *not*!' exclaimed Ivanhoe; 'each aperture will be soon a target for the archers; an arrow shaft…'

'… shall be welcome,' murmured Rebecca, as with a firm pace she ascended the three steps leading up to the window.

'Rebecca!' exclaimed Ivanhoe, 'This is no woman's pastime; at least take that old shield and show little of yourself.'

Placing a large buckler against the lower part of the window, Rebecca could now witness the preparations for the storming. Indeed her position was ideal, being on an angle of the main building. She could not only see what passed outwith the castle, but could also view the outwork, likely the first object of assault.

The outwork was an exterior fortification of no great height or strength, intended simply to protect the postern-gate through which Cedric had been dismissed by Front-de-Boeuf. The castle moat divided this barbican from the rest of the fortress, so that were it taken, its link to the main castle could be broken by pulling up the temporary bridge. In the outwork was a sally-port opposite to the castle's postern gate, the whole being surrounded by a strong palisade. From the large number of men defending this position, Rebecca saw that the besieged were concerned for its safety, while from the massing of assailants opposite, it was clearly selected as a point of attack. Rebecca described all this to Ivanhoe, adding;

'The skirts of the wood seem lined with archers, although only a few are advanced from under its shadow.'

'Under what banner?' demanded Ivanhoe.

'No ensign of war that I can see.'

'Singular,' muttered the knight, 'to advance to a storming without pennon or banner displayed... their leaders?'

'A knight in black armour is the most obvious,' said Rebecca; 'armed from head to heel, he seems to be directing all around him.'

'What device is on his shield?' asked Ivanhoe.

'Something resembling a bar of iron with a blue padlock on a black shield.'

'A fetterlock and shacklebolt *azure,*' mused Ivanhoe; 'I know not who bears this device. Is there a motto?'

'I can scarce see the device itself, but when the sun glances on his shield, it shows as I tell you.'

'Are there other leaders?' exclaimed Ivanhoe.

'None that I can see,' said Rebecca; 'Ah, they prepare to advance. God protect us; what a sight! Those in front bear huge shields and defences made of planks; others bend their bows as they come on. They raise their bows now; God of Moses!'

Her description was here interrupted by a blast of a shrill bugle, the signal for assault, answered by a flourish of Norman trumpets from the battlements. These, mingled with the hollow clang of kettle–drums, defiantly answered the challenge of the besiegers. The battle-cries of both parties augmented the din, the assailants crying 'Saint George for England!' and the Normans answering with '*En avant De Bracy!; Beau-seant! Beau-seant! Front-de-Boeuf a la rescousse!*'

The efforts of the assailants were met by an equally vigorous defence. The yeoman archers with their longbows saw to it that no defender escaped their cloth-yard arrows. Thick and sharp as hail against each embrasure and opening in the parapets, the shafts also flashed into every window where a defender might be stationed, several of the garrison being thus slain and wounded.

Confident in the proof of their armour and in the cover of their battlements, Front-de-Boeuf and his allies were obstinate in defence. They replied with crossbows, longbows, slings and other missiles – and as the assailants were poorly protected, did considerably more damage than they received. The whizzing of shafts and missiles on both sides was interrupted by cries when either side inflicted or sustained some notable loss.

'And I must lie here like a bedridden monk,' raged Ivanhoe, 'Look out again, Rebecca, but beware of archers beneath. Do they still advance?'

With patient courage, Rebecca again took sheltered post at the lattice.

'I see nothing but clouds of arrows. They fly so thick that they hide the bowmen.'

'This cannot last,' said Ivanhoe; 'Unless they carry the castle by force, their archery will avail little against stone walls and bulwarks. Look for the Knight of the Fetterlock, Rebecca.'

'I see him now,' said Rebecca, 'He leads a body of men close under the outer barrier of the barbican.[1] They are pulling down the piles and palisades; they hew down the barriers with axes; his black plume floats over the throng like a raven. They have made a breach! They rush in – and are thrust back! Front-de-Boeuf heads the defenders. I see his giant form above the press. They throng again to the breach and the pass is fought over, hand to hand. God of Jacob, it is like two fierce tides!'

She turned her head from the lattice, unable to endure the sight.

'Look out again, Rebecca,' said Ivanhoe, mistaking the cause of her retreat; 'the archery must have ceased if they are at it hand to hand. There will be less danger now.'

Rebecca again looked out and immediately exclaimed,

'Front-de-Boeuf and the Black Knight fight hand to hand in the breach. There are roars from their followers watching the combat. He is *down*!'

'*Who* is down?' cried Ivanhoe.

'The Black Knight,' answered Rebecca, faintly; 'but no; he is back on foot again and fights on. His sword is broken; he snatches an axe from a yeoman; he gives Front-de-Boeuf blow on blow. The giant totters; he *falls*!'

'Front-de-Boeuf?' exclaimed Ivanhoe.

'*Front-de-Boeuf* ! His men rush to the rescue, headed by the Templar; they are dragging him back within the walls.'

'The assailants have won the barriers?' said Ivanhoe.

'They have – they *have*!' exclaimed Rebecca 'they press the besieged hard now upon the outer wall; some plant ladders, some are climbing upon the shoulders of each other. Down go stones and tree trunks upon their heads; as fast as they carry the wounded to the rear, fresh men take their place!'

'Who yields?' said Ivanhoe.

'The ladders are hurled down,' replied Rebecca, shuddering; 'soldiers lie under them; crushed. The besieged have the better of it.'

'St George strike for us!' exclaimed the knight; 'do the yeomen retreat?'

'No!' exclaimed Rebecca, 'The Black Knight approaches the postern with his axe; you can hear his thundering blows above the din. Stones and beams are hurled down at him!'

'Saint John of Acre,' said Ivanhoe, raising himself joyfully on his couch, 'there is but one man in all England that might do such a deed…'

---

1 Castles had, beyond the outer walls, a fortification composed of palisades, called barriers, which were often the scene of severe skirmishes, as these had to be carried before the walls themselves could be approached. *Scott*

'The postern gate shakes,' continued Rebecca; 'it crashes – it is splintered by his blows – they rush in – the outwork is *won*! Oh God...they are hurling the defenders from the battlements – throwing them down into the moat. O spare those who surrender!'

'The bridge; the bridge to the castle, have they won that?' demanded Ivanhoe.

'No,' replied Rebecca, 'The Templar has destroyed the plank on which they crossed. A few of the defenders escaped with him into the castle; the shrieks and cries are from those left outside.'

'What now, Rebecca?'

'It is over for a while,' she answered; 'our friends are reinforcing the outwork they have taken; it gives them shelter.'

'Our friends,' said Wilfred, 'will not abandon the enterprise. No! I will put my faith in the Knight. Singular,' he again muttered to himself, 'if there are two who can do such a deed... A fetterlock and a shacklebolt on a field sable; what does that *mean*? Rebecca, is there naught else to mark the Black Knight?'

'Nothing,' said the Jewess; 'all about him is black as a raven's wing, but I would know him again among a thousand. There is more than mere strength there; fearful, magnificent...'

'Rebecca,' said Ivanhoe, 'I would endure ten years' captivity to fight by that knight's side!'

'And what is chivalry,' said the fair Jewess, 'but a sacrifice to a vain demon, a passing through the fire to Moloch?'

'Thou art not Christian, Rebecca. Chivalry is the nurse of pure affection; the stay of the oppressed, the curb of the tyrant's power.'

'I am sprung,' said Rebecca, 'from a race whose courage was famous; but the sound of the trumpet wakes Judah no longer. But well spoken, Sir Knight. Until our God raises a second Gideon or Maccabeus for his people, it ill becomes a Jewish girl to speak of war.' She looked towards the couch of the wounded knight.

'He sleeps,' she said. 'Is it a crime to look upon him, mayhap for the last time? I will rend this folly from my heart, though it bleed as I tear it away!' Wrapping herself closely in her veil, she sat down at a distance from the couch of Ivanhoe, her back towards him. Thus she sought to fortify her mind against the evil without, but also against the emotions within...

chapter thirty

Approach the chamber, look upon his bed.
His is the passing of no peaceful ghost...
Anon (prob. Scott): *Old Play*

During the pause in the fighting which followed the besiegers' initial success, they regrouped to pursue their advantage while the garrison strengthened their defences. The Templar and De Bracy held a brief council.

'Where is Front-de-Boeuf?' said De Bracy who had led the defence on the other side. 'Men say he is slain.'

'He lives,' said the Templar, coolly, 'he lives as yet; but had he worn ten plates of iron, he would have gone down before yonder axe. In a few hours Front-de-Boeuf will be with his fathers.'

'And an addition to the kingdom of Satan,' said De Bracy, 'This comes of reviling saints and ordering holy images to be flung down on the heads of these *rascaille.*'

'Thou fool,' said the Templar,' thy superstition is on a level with Front-de-Boeuf's lack of faith.'

'*Benedicite*, Templar,' replied De Bracy, 'Rule your tongue when my name is upon it. Mother of Heaven, I am a better Christian man than thou – or thy holy Order of the Temple.'

'I care not,' said the Templar, 'let us make good the castle. How fought these villain yeomen on thy side?'

'Like fiends incarnate,' said De Bracy. 'They swarmed up to the walls, headed by that knave who took the prize at the archery; I knew him by his horn and baldric. Had I not been in proof armour, he would have brought me down like a buck. His shafts hit every rivet on my armour and rapped my ribs. Without Spanish mail I was finished.'

'But you held your post?' said the Templar, 'We lost the outwork here.'

'A dangerous loss,' said De Bracy. 'The knaves now have cover to assault the castle and break in upon us. Our numbers are too few for the defence of every point. Front-de-Boeuf is dying. How think you, Sir Brian? Better to make a virtue of necessity and settle with these rogues by releasing our prisoners?'

'Deliver up our prisoners!' exclaimed the Templar, 'and be ridiculed as men who can abduct travellers by night, yet cannot defend a strong castle against outlaws, swineherds and *jesters;* the very refuse of mankind? For shame, De Bracy! This castle shall bury me ere I make a settlement.'

'To the walls, then,' said De Bracy, carelessly. 'No man breathed who held life lighter than I do. But there is no shame in wishing I had forty of my Free Companions here.'

'Wish as thou wilt,' said the Templar, 'but let us make a defence with the soldiers who survive here.'

'So much the better,' said De Bracy, 'let us up and be doing. Live or die, thou shalt see Maurice De Bracy as a gentleman of lineage.'

'To the walls,' answered the Templar.

The Normans readily agreed that the point of greatest danger was that opposite to the outwork possessed by the assailants. The castle was divided from that barbican by the moat and it was thus impossible for the besiegers to assail the postern-door opposite the outwork without crossing the water. The Templar and De Bracy agreed that the besiegers would try to draw the defenders' forces to this point by a formidable assault, whereupon they would attack elsewhere.

It was decided that De Bracy would command the defence of the postern, while the Templar should keep with him a score of men as a reserve to reinforce any other threatened point. The loss of the barbican also meant that despite the superior height of the castle walls, the besieged could not see the operations of the enemy as clearly as before.

Meanwhile, the lord of the castle lay upon a bed of bodily pain and mental agony. He was not one of those who sought to atone for their crimes by donations to the Church with the hope of forgiveness. Front-de-Boeuf preferred denial of the medicine, to paying the expense of the physician. However, the moment had now arrived for the savage Baron when earth and all her treasures were gliding away before his eyes. He became appalled as he gazed forward into the darkness of futurity.

'Where be these dog-priests now?' growled the Baron. 'Where be all those unshod Carmelites? Old Front-de-Boeuf founded their convent of St Anne. Where are the greedy hounds now? Swilling ale, I'll warrant, or playing their tricks at the bedside of some miserly churl. Me, the heir of their founder; me whom their Foundation binds them to pray for. Ungrateful *villains*! Tell the Templar to come. He is a priest; but no, I might as well confess myself to the Devil. Bois Guilbert cares neither for heaven nor hell!'

'Reginald Front-de-Boeuf!' cried a shrill voice close by his bedside. The shaken nerves of Front-de-Boeuf heard this as the voice of one of the demons believed to haunt the beds of dying men to distract them from thinking on eternity.

'Who is there?'

'I am thine evil angel, Reginald Front-de-Boeuf,' replied the voice.

'Then let me see, if thou'rt a fiend,' replied the dying knight.

'Think on thy sins, Reginald Front-de-Boeuf,' said the unearthly voice, 'on rebellion and murder! Who stirred the evil John to war against his royal father – *and* against his brother?'

'Fiend or devil,' cried Front-de-Boeuf, 'Not I alone stirred John to rebellion. We were fifty knights and barons; must I answer for fifty?'

'In *peace* thou shalt not die,' repeated the voice. 'Even in death shalt thou think on the blood on these floors! Think of thy father's death in a banquet-room flooded with his blood and shed by the hand of a son!'

'Ah!' answered the Baron, after a long pause, 'if thou knowest *that*, thou art that Saxon witch Ulrica!'

'Ay, Reginald,' answered she, 'Ulrica, daughter of murdered Torquil and sister of his slaughtered sons!'

'Ho! Giles, Clement!' shouted Front-de-Boeuf, 'Saint Maur and Stephen! Seize this witch. Hurl her from the battlements. She has betrayed us to the Saxon!'

'Call on them again, valiant Baron,' said Ulrica with a grisly smile, 'Summon thy vassals. But thou shalt have neither answer nor aid. Listen.' The din of recommenced assault and defence now rang loud from the battlements.

'*Saxons*, Reginald! The scorned Saxon assails thy walls. Thou shall die no soldier's death, but suffocate like the fox in a fired den. Smell the smoke in this chamber? Remember the magazine of fuel beneath!'

Woman!' he exclaimed with fury, 'thou hast not set fire to it? By heaven, thou *hast*; the castle is aflame!'

'And flame rises fast,' said Ulrica. 'Farewell, Front-de-Boeuf! May Zernebock and the fiendish gods of Saxony attend you!'

Front-de-Boeuf heard the clash of the ponderous keys as she locked and double-locked the door behind her. In agony he shouted again to his serfs;

'Stephen, Saint Maur! Clement and Giles! I *burn* here! *Au secours* Bois Guilbert, De Bracy...'

chapter thirty-one

Once more unto the breach, dear friends, once more,
Or, close the wall up with our English dead.
And you, good yeomen, whose limbs were made in England,
show us here the mettle of your pasture...
Shakespeare: *King Henry V*

Cedric reported Ulrica's promise of help to the Black Knight and Locksley who were encouraged to find they had an ally within. They and Cedric agreed that a storm must be attempted as the only means of liberating Front-de-Boeuf's prisoners.

'The royal blood of Alfred is in peril,' said Cedric.

'And a noble lady,' said the Black Knight, 'now, Locksley, shall Cedric lead the assault?'

'Not I,' returned Cedric; 'I have never studied how to take those Norman abodes.'

'Since it stands thus,' said Locksley, 'I will direct the archery.'

'Well said, yeoman,' answered the Black Knight; 'I will lead the attack on the walls.' The duties thus distributed, they commenced the first assault already described.

When the barbican was carried, the Black Knight ordered Locksley to maintain a strict watch lest the garrison sally out to recover the lost outwork. Both were keen to prevent this, conscious that their untrained and poorly-armed volunteers would be up against Norman veterans.

The knight employed the interval in having constructed a floating bridge, in fact a long raft, to cross the defended moat. This took some time, which the leaders minded the less as it gave Ulrica more time to create a diversion. The raft completed, the Black Knight addressed his troops:

'It avails not waiting any longer, friends. The sun is setting and I may not tarry another day. Besides, cavalry will be upon us from York unless we speedily accomplish our purpose. Locksley, send a volley of arrows at the opposite side of the castle and move forward as if to the assault. You others, stand by me and be ready to thrust the raft over the moat when the postern gate is thrown open. Follow me across and aid me to burst open yon sally-port in the main castle wall. Those of you who like not this duty, or are ill-armed for it, man the top of the outwork. Bowstrings to your ears men, and hit whoever tries to man the rampart. Noble Cedric, wilt command those which remain?'

'No!' said the Saxon. 'Lead I cannot, but I will be with the foremost. This quarrel is mine.'

'Saxon,' said the knight. 'Thou hast neither hauberk, nor corselet – only that light helmet and shield.'

'The better!' answered Cedric; 'I shall be the lighter to climb these walls. Sir Knight, thou shalt this day see the bare breast of a Saxon as bold as any steel corselet on a Norman.'

'In the name of God, then,' ordered the knight, 'fling open the gate and launch the floating bridge!'

The portal leading from the inner-wall of the barbican to the moat, and facing the sally-port in the main wall of the castle, was now opened. The temporary bridge was thrust into the water between castle and outwork, forming a slippery and precarious passage for two men abreast to cross the moat. Aware of the advantage of surprise, the Black Knight closely followed by Cedric, threw himself on to the bridge and crossed to the opposite side. Here he began to thunder with his axe upon the gate of the castle, protected from the shot and stones of the defenders by the ruins of the drawbridge. This the Templar had demolished in his retreat from the barbican, leaving the counterpoise still attached to the upper part of the portal. The followers of the Black Knight had no such shelter; two being instantly shot with crossbow bolts, while two more fell into the moat; the others retreated back into the barbican.

The situation of Cedric and of the Black Knight was now dangerous and would have been more so but for the archers in the barbican, who showered arrows upon those manning the battlements. This afforded some respite to their two chiefs but their situation was perilous and becoming more so.

'Shame on ye all!' cried De Bracy to the soldiers around him, 'Call yourselves crossbowmen and these two yet under our walls? Heave over the coping stones; get pickaxes and levers and send down with that great pinnacle,' he said, pointing to a heavy stone carving which projected from the parapet.

At this moment the besiegers caught sight of Ulrica's signal, a red flag was being waved from the angle of the tower. Locksley saw it first as he was hasting to the outwork.

'Saint George!' he cried, 'Saint George for England! To the charge! The castle is ours, we have friends within. See yonder? It is the signal; one more push and the place is ours!' He drew his bow and sent a shaft through the chest of one of the men-at-arms obeying De Bracy's order to loosen a section of battlement to drop upon Cedric and the Black Knight. Another soldier caught the crowbar from the dying man and was loosening the pinnacle when an arrow went through his head-piece and he also dropped into the moat. The other men-at-arms cowered down; no armour seemed proof against this tremendous archer.

'Do not give ground!' cried De Bracy; '*Mountjoye, Saint Denis*! Give *me* that lever!' Snatching it up, he attacked the loosening pinnacle, heavy enough to destroy the remnant of the drawbridge sheltering the two assailants and sink their crude float of planks. All could now see the danger and the boldest, even the stout Friar himself, avoided setting foot on the raft. Three times Locksley fired on De Bracy and thrice his arrow rebounded from the knight's proof armour.

'Curse on that Spanish steelcoat!' cried Locksley. 'Comrades! Cedric! Come back; let the ruin fall!' His warning went unheard amidst the din of the Black Knight's axe blows upon the postern. Gurth then sprang forward onto the planked bridge to warn Cedric or to share his fate. But his warning would have come too late. The massive pinnacle was already tottering and De Bracy, heaving at his task, would have sent it over, had not the voice of the Templar sounded suddenly in his ear:

'All is lost, De Bracy; the castle burns.'

'No!'

'It is all alight on the western side.' Delivered with his usual stern coolness, Bois Guilbert's hideous news astonished his comrade.

'Saints of Paradise!' cried De Bracy;

'Listen to me,' said the Templar, 'throw open the postern-gate; there are only two men on that float. Fling them into the moat and push across for the barbican. I will charge from the main gate and attack the barbican on the outside. Regain that and we can defend ourselves until we are relieved, or at least till they grant us fair quarter.'

'Very well,' said De Bracy. 'Templar, thou wilt not fail me?'

'Hand and glove, I will not!' said Bois Guilbert. 'Now haste, in the name of God!'

Drawing his men together, De Bracy raced down to the postern-gate which he threw open. But scarcely was this done than the tremendous strength of the Black Knight forced his way inward, despite De Bracy and his men, two of whom fell and the rest retreated despite their leader.

'Dogs!' shouted De Bracy, 'will ye let *two* men win our only way for safety?'

It is the *Devil*!' cried a man-at-arms, retreating from the blows of their black antagonist.

'And if he *is* the devil,' shouted De Bracy, 'would you flee into the mouth of Hell? The castle burns *behind* us. Villains! Let me go *forward*; I will deal with him myself.'

Well did De Bracy live up to his fame. The vaulted passage to which the postern gave entrance rang with furious blows as these two redoubtable champions fought now hand to hand; De Bracy with his sword, the Black Knight with his great axe. At length the Norman received a blow which, though parried by his shield, fell on his helmet crest and he crashed to the paved floor.

'Yield!' cried the Black Champion, stooping over him and holding against the bars of his helmet the fatal *poniard* , the dagger of mercy with which knights dispatched a fallen enemy. 'Yield thee, Maurice De Bracy, rescue or no rescue, or thou'rt a dead man.'

'I will not yield,' replied De Bracy faintly, 'to an unknown. Be it never said that a De Bracy yielded to a nameless churl.' The Black Knight leaned forward whispered something into his ear. De Bracy stared at him, then said, in a tone of deep and sullen submission,

'I yield, rescue or no rescue.'

'Go to the barbican,' said the victor, 'and await my orders.'

'Yet first let me tell you,' said De Bracy, 'that Wilfred of Ivanhoe is here, wounded and a prisoner. Without help he will burn with the castle.'

'Wilfred of Ivanhoe a prisoner! Forfeit is the life of every man in this castle if a hair of his head be singed. Show me!'

'Climb yon winding stair,' said De Bracy wearily, 'It leads to his apartment.'

'Get thee to the barbican and await my orders. I trust thee not.' De Bracy arose from the ground, took off his helmet in token of submission and slowly went to the barbican, surrendering his sword to Locksley on the way.

During this combat and as soon as the postern opened, Cedric and a body of men including the Friar had pushed across the bridge. They drove back the followers of De Bracy, of whom the greater part fled towards the courtyard. As the fire grew, signs of it soon became apparent in the chamber holding Ivanhoe and Rebecca. Awakened by the noise of the battle and at his urgent request, she was again at the window to describe the attack. Now, however, the volume of smoke rolling into the apartment and cries for water showed this new danger.

'The castle burns!' she cried.'

'Fly! Save thy life,' was Ivanhoe's response.

'I will not,' answered Rebecca; 'we will be saved or perish together. Great God, what will be the fate of my father?' At this moment the door of the apartment flew open to reveal the ghastly figure of the Templar, gilded armour broken and bloody, his plume partly shorn away and partly burned from his casque.

'I have found thee,' said he to Rebecca; 'and I will share weal or woe with thee. There is but one path to safety; up instantly and follow!'[1]

'Go alone,' answered Rebecca, 'I will not follow thee. Save my father – and this knight!'

'A knight,' answered the Templar, 'must meet his fate whenever it comes; and who cares how a Jew meets his?'

'Savage!' cried Rebecca, 'I would rather die than go!'

'Thou shalt not choose!' So saying, he seized her and bore her out of the room, heedless of the threats which Ivanhoe thundered after him. It was to no avail, they were gone. Shortly thereafter the Black Knight burst into the apartment,

'I had not found thee, Wilfred,' said he, 'but for hearing thy shouts.'

'Think not of me,' said Wilfred, 'Save the Lady Rowena and look for Cedric!'

'In their turn,' answered he, 'thine is first.' Raising Ivanhoe, he bore him off with as much ease as the Templar had carried off Rebecca and rushed him to the postern. Leaving Ivanhoe with the yeomen, he returned to the castle to find the other prisoners.

One turret was now in flames which flashed out from the windows and shot-holes. But in other parts the great thickness of the walls and the vaulted roofs of the apartments resisted the progress of the fire. There the rage of men still triumphed, while the fire held mastery elsewhere. The besiegers pursued the garrison from chamber to chamber, satiating their vengeance on the men of Front-de-Boeuf. Most resisted to the uttermost; few asked quarter; none received it. The air filled with the clash of arms as the floors became slippery with the blood of screaming and expiring men.

Through this scene of confusion rushed Cedric in quest of Rowena, Gurth following him closely. The Saxon reached his ward's apartment just as she abandoned all hope of safety. A crucifix clasped to her, she lay in expectation of death. Cedric had Gurth conduct her back to the barbican, now cleared of the enemy and not yet closed by fire. To the old hall went Cedric, now in quest of Athelstane.

---

1 The author has some idea that this passage is imitated from the appearance of Philidaspes, before the divine Mandane, when the city of Babylon is on fire and he proposes to carry her from the flames. *Scott*

In that hall, when the noise of the conflict was at the hottest, the Jester began to shout, at the top of his lungs,

'Saint George and the Dragon! Saint George for England! The castle is won!' and he banged together pieces of rusty armour scattered around the hall. Guards stationed in the outer room and already in a state of alarm, took real fright. Leaving the door open behind them, they rushed to warn the Templar that foemen had penetrated the old hall. Meantime the prisoners escaped into the ante-room and from thence into the court of the castle, now the final scene of contest. Here they found the Templar on horseback with several of the garrison who had joined their leader to take their last chance of safety. The drawbridge had been lowered but the passage to it was under attack from archers. These now thronging the entrance to prevent the escape of any of the garrison and secure booty before the castle should burn down. A party of besiegers who had entered by the postern now poured into the courtyard and attacked the remnant of the defenders who were now assaulted on two fronts.

Animated by despair and following the example of their leader, the remaining castle soldiers fought on desperately, succeeding more than once in driving back the assailants. Rebecca, thrown on horseback before one of the Templar's mounted Saracen slaves, was in the midst of the group with Bois Guilbert, frantically protecting her. Ignoring his own defence, he held in front of her his triangular shield. Then, shouting his war-cry, he dashed forward, striking down the most forward of the assailants. Athelstane then saw that it was a female form that the Templar protected. Thinking it was Rowena, he shouted,

'He is mine!'

'Watch what you do!' cried Wamba; 'Yonder is not Rowena; see her dark locks – and you are without armour!' But with Athelstane now roused to fury, it was the work of a moment for him to snatch up a mace from its dying owner and rush at the Templar's band, levelling men as he went. He was soon within yards of Bois Guilbert.

'Turn, Templar!'

'Dog!' cried the Templar, 'I will teach thee.' Half-wheeling his steed, he made a *demi-courbette* towards the Saxon and rising in the stirrups to take full advantage of the descent of the horse, he brought down a fearful blow upon the head of Athelstane. The Saxon raised his mace to parry, but the Templar's weapon shattered the tough, plaited handle of the mace as if it were a twig. The blow smashed down on Athelstane's head and levelled him with the earth.

'*Beau-seant!*' cried Bois Guilbert; 'Follow me!' He then pushed on across the drawbridge, scattering the archers, followed by his Saracens and some mounted men-at-arms and also followed by shafts sent after him. He galloped round to the barbican.

'De Bracy, *De Bracy*!' he shouted, 'art there?'

'I am here,' called De Bracy, 'but I am prisoner.'

'Can I rescue thee?'

'No, I have rendered me. Save thyself. There are hawks abroad. Put seas betwixt you and England; I dare not say more!'

Those of the garrison who had not gotten to horse, fought on after the flight of the Templar, though now in despair of mercy. They had also hope of escape as the conflagration now spread rapidly throughout the castle. Ulrica, who had kindled it, now appeared on a turret like one of the ancient Furies, yelling a pagan war-song of the scalds of Saxony. Her long and dishevelled grey hair flew back from her uncovered head; the delight of vengeance shone in her eyes with the fire of insanity as she brandished the distaff in her hand like one of the Fatal Sisters.[1]

The towering flames had now surmounted every obstruction, and rose to the evening skies like a huge burning beacon, seen far and wide across the adjacent country. Tower after tower crashed down, their blazing roof and rafters driving the combatants from the courtyard. The few defenders still alive scattered into the neighbouring woods while the victors gazed upon the flames, their ranks and weapons glancing dusky red. The manic figure of Ulrica was long visible on her turret, tossing her arms in wild exultation over the inferno she had raised. The whole turret finally gave way with a terrific crash, silencing the watchers who for several minutes stirred only to make the sign the Cross. The voice of Locksley was then heard,

'Shout, yeomen! The den of tyrants is *no more*!

chapter thirty-two

Trust me, each State must have its policies:
Kingdoms have edicts, cities have their charters;
Even the wild outlaw in his forest-walk,
Keeps yet some touch of civil discipline;
Anon (prob. Scott): *Old Play*

Daylight dawned upon the glades of the oak forest. Assembled around the Trysting-tree in the Harthill-walk, the outlaws had spent the night resting after the siege: some with wine, some with slumber, many with hearing and recounting the events of the day and anticipating the plunder now at the disposal of their Chief.

The spoils were indeed great. Much had been consumed by fire, but a great deal of plate, armour and splendid clothing had been secured by the outlaw fighters. The laws of their society being strict, no one ventured to claim any part of the booty, now brought into one common mass at the disposal of their leader.

The place of rendezvous was an aged oak at the centre of a woodland amphitheatre within half a mile of the now razed Torquilstone. Here Locksley, his followers around him, assumed his throne; a seat of turf erected under the twisted branches of the tree. He assigned a seat at his right hand to the Black Knight and a place upon his left to Cedric.

'Pardon my freedom, noble sirs,' he said, 'but in these glades I am the monarch. They are my kingdom and my wild subjects here would little respect my power were I to yield place to any mortal man. Now, sirs, who hath seen our chaplain? Where is our curtal Friar?[2] A Christian Mass best begins a busy morning.'

---

1 The three Fates of classical mythology: Clotho, Lachesis and Atropos.

2 From Fr. *Court*, short; i.e. wearing a shortened or 'tucked-up' frock, thus permitting extra-clerical activities – such as armed combat.

No one had seen the Clerk of Copmanhurst.

'Gods forbode!' said the alarmed chief, 'I trust the priest is only detained by the wine-pot. Who saw him since the castle was taken?'

'I marked him,' said the Miller, 'at the door of a cellar. He was swearing by each Saint he would taste Front-de-Boeuf's Gascon wine.'

'Those very saints *forfend*,' said the Captain, 'lest he drank too deep and perished as the castle fell. Away, Miller! Take men with you to that place. Throw moat water on the scorched ruin. I will move them stone by stone ere I lose my Friar.'

Men hastening to this duty when a division of spoil was imminent showed how the outlaw troop cared for their spiritual father.

'Meanwhile, let us proceed,' said Locksley; 'for when our deed is sounded abroad, De Bracy, Malvoisin and other allies of Front-de-Boeuf will move against us. For our safety we will retreat from hence. Noble Cedric,' he said, turning to the Saxon, 'the spoil is divided into two portions; choose what best suits thee to recompense thy people who were with us.'

'Yeoman,' said Cedric, 'my heart is heavy, for Athelstane of Coningsburgh is no more; the last sprout of the sainted Confessor! Hopes perished with him which can never now return. My people wait to transport his remains to the Lady Rowena at Rotherwood. I should have already left but I waited, not for booty, but to render thanks to thee and thine for my life and honour.'

'Nay,' said Locksley, 'we did but half the work at most. Take of the spoil what may reward your neighbours and followers.'

'I am rich enough to reward them.'

'And some,' said Wamba, 'have rewarded themselves; they do not leave empty-handed.'

'They are welcome,' said Locksley; 'our laws bind none but ourselves.'

'But thou, my poor fool,' said Cedric, turning round to his Jester, 'how shall I reward thee, who feared not death in place of me?'

'Uncle,' said the Jester, 'if you would please me, pardon my friend Gurth. He stole a week from your service to bestow it on your son.'

'*Pardon* him?' exclaimed Cedric; 'I will both pardon and reward him! Kneel, Gurth.'

'*Theow* and *Esne*[1] art thou no longer,' said Cedric, touching him. '*Folkfree* and *Sacless*[2] art thou in town, forest and field. A hide of land I give to thee in my steads of Walbrugham forever. God's malison on his head who this gainsays!'

Gurth sprang to his feet.

'Bring a smith and a file,' he cried, 'to do away the collar from the neck of a free man! Master, doubled is my strength by your gift!'

'Never think I envy thee, Gurth,' said Wamba. 'The serf sits safe by the hall fire when the freeman must to the battlefield. And what saith Oldhelm of Malmsbury? "*Better a fool at a feast, than a wise man at a fray.*"'

The tramp of horses was now heard and the Lady Rowena appeared. She was surrounded by several riders and a strong party of footmen, who shook their pikes and clashed their brown-bills. She was mounted on a dark chestnut palfrey, only a

---

1 A serf and bondsman. *Scott*

2 A lawful freeman. *Scott.*

degree of paleness showing her recent suffering. She knew that Ivanhoe was safe, and that Athelstane was dead. The former assurance gave delight, while the latter set her free from the only matter on which she had differed from her guardian.

As Rowena turned her steed towards Locksley's seat, he and his followers rose to receive her by a general instinct of courtesy. The blood rose to her cheeks as she bent low to express her obligations to Locksley and her other deliverers.

'God bless you, brave men,' she said, 'Our Lady also bless you and requite you! If the Normans drive ye from these walks, Rowena has forests of her own where ye may range at full freedom and never a Ranger.'

'Our thanks, gentle lady,' said Locksley; 'To have saved you rewards itself.'

Bowing once more from her palfrey, Rowena turned to depart. Pausing while Cedric was also taking his leave, she found herself unexpectedly close to the prisoner De Bracy who stood under a tree. Rowena hoped that she might pass him unobserved, but he looked up and saw her, as a deep flush suffused his handsome countenance. He stood a moment, irresolute; then, stepping forward, he took her palfrey by the rein.

'Will the Lady Rowena deign to cast an eye on a captive knight?'

'Sir Knight,' answered Rowena, 'with you, dishonour lies not in failure, but in success.'

'Conquest, lady, should *soften* the heart,' answered De Bracy; 'let me but know that the Lady Rowena forgives an ill-fated passion. She shall soon learn that De Bracy knows how to serve her in better ways.'

'I forgive you, Sir Knight,' said Rowena, 'as a *Christian*.'

'And *that* means,' said Wamba aside, 'that she does not forgive him at all!'

'But I can never forgive the misery your madness has caused,' continued Rowena.

'Unloose the lady's rein,' said Cedric, coming up. 'Be assured, Maurice De Bracy, thou shalt *smart* for thy share in this foul deed.' Cedric had also expressed his particular gratitude to the Black Knight and earnestly entreated him to accompany him to Rotherwood.

'I know,' he said, 'that Knights Errant carry their fortunes on the point of the lance and care not for land or goods; but war is a fickle mistress. Thou hast earned a home in the halls of Rotherwood, noble knight. Cedric has wealth and all is at his deliverer's command. Come to Rotherwood not as a guest, but as a son or brother.'

'Cedric has already made me rich,' said the knight. 'He has taught me Saxon virtue. To Rotherwood will I come soon, but matters of moment detain me from your halls. But when I come, I will ask such a favour as will put even thy generosity to the test.'

'Granted ere spoken,' said Cedric, striking his hand into the gauntleted palm of the Black Knight.

'Give not thy promise so lightly,' said the Knight of the Fetterlock. 'Meanwhile, *adieu*.'

'I have still to say,' called out Cedric in Saxon to the company, 'that during the funeral rites of the noble Athelstane, I shall be at the halls of his castle of Coningsburgh. They will be open to all.'

'Ay, ay,' said Wamba, who had resumed attendance on his master. 'Rare feeding there will be; and a pity that the noble Athelstane cannot banquet at his own funeral. He sups in Paradise.'

'Silence! Move on,' said Cedric, his anger at this untimely jest checked by Wamba's recent services. Rowena waved a graceful *adieu* to the Black Knight while the Saxon bade God speed him. Off they moved through a wide glade of the forest.

They had scarce departed when a procession emerged from the greenwood, swept slowly through the sylvan amphitheatre and took the same direction as Rowena and her escort. It was the priests of a neighbouring monastery who, in expectation of an ample donation, or *soul-scat* from Cedric, surrounded the wagon in which lay the body of Athelstane. Again the outlaws arose and paid to death the same homage which they had so lately rendered to beauty, the slow chant and mournful step of the priests bringing back memories of their fallen comrades. But such recollections are short among those who live dangerously and the outlaws were soon busy in the distribution of their spoil.

'Sir Knight,' said Locksley to the Black Champion, 'without your mighty arm, our enterprise must have failed. Will it please you to take from the mass of spoil whatever may best serve you?'

'Accepted,' said the knight, 'I ask to dispose of Sir Maurice De Bracy at my own pleasure.'

'He is thine,' said Locksley, 'and just as well for him, for otherwise he had hung from the highest bough of this oak with those of his Free-Companions we hold. He is thy prisoner.' The Knight rose and went over to him.

'De Bracy,' said the knight, 'thou art free. Depart. But beware of the future, lest worse befall thee. Maurice De Bracy; I say, *beware*!'

De Bracy bowed low and in silence and was about to withdraw. The yeomen saw this and burst into shouts of execration and derision. The knight took one of the horses of Front-de-Boeuf, vaulted into the saddle and galloped off through the wood.

When the bustle had settled, the chief Outlaw took from his neck the horn and baldric from the archery contest at Ashby.

'Noble knight,' he said, 'if you disdain not the bugle of an English yeoman, I pray you keep this as a memorial. If ye chance to be attacked in any forest betwixt Trent and Tees, wind three motes[1] upon the horn thus, *Wa-sa-hoa* and ye shall find helpers and rescue.' He then raised the bugle, and twice more winded the distress call.

'Gramercy,' said the knight; 'Better help than thine and thy rangers would I never find.' And in his turn he winded the call.

'Well blown and clearly,' said the yeoman; 'Comrades, mark these three notes. It is the call of the Knight of the Fetterlock. Hasten to serve him at need.'

Locksley now proceeded to the distribution of the spoil. The *tithe*, a tenth part of the whole, was set apart for the Church. A portion was assigned to the widows and children of the fallen, or to be expended in Masses for the souls of those with no surviving family. The rest was divided amongst the outlaws according to rank and merit. The Black Knight was not a little surprised to find that such men were so equitably governed; all he observed adding to his opinion of their leader. When each had taken his share of the booty, the Church's portion remained unclaimed.

'I wish,' said the leader, 'we could hear tidings of our Chaplain. He was never

---

1 The notes upon the bugle were anciently called *mots* [Fr.'Words'] and are distinguished in the old treatises on hunting, not by musical characters, but by written words. *Scott.*

absent when meat was to be blessed or spoil to be divided and it is his duty to take the Church's tithe. Also, I have a holy Prior and brother of his a prisoner; fain would I have the Friar here to help me deal with him.'

'I am right sorry for his fate,' said the Knight of the Fetterlock, 'for I stand indebted to him for his hospitality and a merry night in his cell.'

But even as he spoke, loud shouts among the yeomen announced an arrival. The stentorian voice of the Friar himself was then heard, long before they saw his burly person.

'Make room, my merry men!' he exclaimed. 'Room for your godly Father and his prisoner. I come, noble leader, like an eagle with prey!' Making his way through the ring and amid the laughter of all, he appeared in majestic triumph. In one hand was his huge partisan and in the other a halter, one end of which was fastened to the neck of Isaac of York. The priest shouted,

'Where is Allan-a-Dale, to chronicle me in a ballad? By Saint Hermangild, the jingler is always absent when there is need of a song to valour!'

'Priest,' said the Captain, 'In the name of Saint Nicholas, whom hast thou there?'

'A captive to my sword, noble Captain,' replied the Clerk of Copmanhurst. 'Or rather to my bow and halberd; I have redeemed him by my divinity from a *worse* captivity. Speak, Jew. Have I not ransomed thee from Satan? Have I not taught thee the *credo*, the *pater* and *Ave Maria?* Did I not spend the whole night in the expounding of mysteries to thee?'

'For the love of God!' ejaculated Isaac of York, 'will no one free me from this madman... I mean this *holy* man?'

'How's this, Jew?' said The Friar, menacingly; 'dost thou recant? Isaac, repeat the words after me. *Ave Maria...!*'

'Nay, we will have no profanation, mad Priest,' said Locksley; 'let us hear how you came by this prisoner.'

'By Saint Dunstan,' said The Friar; 'I found him where I sought for better ware! I stepped into the cellars to see what might be rescued there. I had had one runlet of sack when I saw a strong door. Aha! thought I, the choicest wine of all must be in this secret crypt – and the key in the door... In therefore I went, and found nothing besides rusted chains and this Jew. I was proceeding to lead my captive forth when; crash! Down topples the masonry of an outer tower and blocks the passage. I gave up hope, but unwilling to leave this world in company with a Jew, I took up my spiritual weapons for his *conversion*!'

'We can bear witness to this,' said Gilbert; 'when we had cleared away the ruin and found the dungeon stair, we found the runlet of sack half empty, the Jew half dead, and the Friar more than half *exhausted* – as he terms it...'

'Ye lie!' retorted the offended Friar; 'It was you and your companions that drank up the sack. But the Jew is converted. He understands all I have told him, very nearly, if not altogether, as well as myself!'

'Isaac of York,' said the Captain, 'can this be true?'

'May I find mercy,' said the Jew; 'I know not one word which this reverend prelate spake to me all this fearful night.'

'Thou liest, Isaac,' said The Friar; 'Thou promised to give all thy substance to our holy Order.'

'So help me The Promise, fair sirs,' said Isaac, even more alarmed than before; 'no such sounds crossed my lips! I am an aged, beggar'd man and now *childless*, I fear. Have mercy on me. Let me go!'

'Nay,' said The Friar, 'if thou retract vows to Holy Church, thou must do penance.' He raised his halberd, but the Black Knight stopped him.

'By Saint Thomas,' said The Friar; 'I will teach thee, Sir Lazy, to mind thine own matters, *maugre* thine iron casing there!'

'Be not wroth with me,' said the knight. 'Thou knowest I am thy sworn comrade.'

'I know no such thing,' answered The Friar; 'and I call thee a meddling coxcomb!'

'Peace, all!' said the Captain. 'Isaac, think of thy ransom; think of an offer. Meanwhile I shall examine a prisoner of a different cast; a jolly monk riding to visit his lady friend, to judge by his horse-gear and dress.

Between two yeomen, Prior Aymer of Jorvaulx was brought before the woodland throne of the outlaw chief.

chapter thirty-three

Cominius: *Flower of warriors,*
How is't with Titus Lartius?

Marcius: *As with a man busied about decrees,*
Condemning some to death and some to exile,
Ransoming him or pitying, threatening the other.
Shakespeare: *Coriolanus.*

The captive Abbot's features and manner exhibited deranged foppery, offended pride and sheer bodily terror.

'Now, my masters,' said he, with a voice blending all three emotions. 'What order is this among ye? Be ye Turks or Christians, that manhandle a churchman? Release my brethren, tell down an hundred crowns for Masses at the high altar of Jorvaulx – and mayhap you shall hear little more of this madness.'

'Holy Father,' said the chief Outlaw, 'it grieves me to think that you have had such usage from my followers.'

'Usage!' echoed the priest, encouraged by the mild tone, 'it were usage unfit for a *hound* – much less the Prior of a holy community. Here is a profane and drunken minstrel called Allan-a-Dale who has threatened me with assault, nay with death itself, unless I pay four hundred crowns of ransom. He has already robbed me of gold chains, gymmal rings, my pouncer-box and silver crisping-tongs.'

'It is impossible that Allan-a-Dale can have thus treated a man of your reverend bearing,' replied the Captain.

'It is true as the gospel,' said the Prior. 'He swore he would hang me up on the highest tree in the greenwood!'

'Did he so? Then, reverend father, I think you had better comply, for Allan-a-Dale is a man to abide by his pledged word.

'You jest with me!' said the astounded Prior.

'I am as grave as a father confessor.' replied the Outlaw.' You must pay a ransom, Sir Prior, or your convent will know you no more.'

'Are ye *Christians*,' said the Prior, 'to use this language to a churchman?'

'Christians! Ay, marry, we are indeed and we have divinity among us to boot,' answered the Outlaw. 'Let our buxom chaplain stand forth and expound the texts which concern this matter.'

Friar Tuck, half drunk, had cast a Friar's frock over his green cassock and now summoned together whatever scraps of learning he had acquired by rote in former days.

'Holy father,' said he, *Deus faciat salvam benignitatem vestram* – you are welcome to the greenwood.'

'What mummery is this?' said the Prior.

'Sir Prior, *facite vobis amicos de Mammone iniquitatis* – make yourselves friends of the Mammon of unrighteousness, for no other friendship will help you.'

'Here is a good thought,' said a lieutenant of the gang aside to the Captain, 'that the Prior should name the Jew's ransom – and the Jew name the Prior's?'

'Good!' said the Captain; 'Jew, step forth. Look at this Prior of the rich Abbey of Jorvaulx and tell us at what ransom we should charge him? Thou knowest the income of his convent, I warrant.'

'Assuredly,' said Isaac. 'I have trafficked with the good fathers; bought from them wheat, barley and also much wool. It is a rich abbey. They live upon the fat and drink sweet wines, these good fathers of Jorvaulx.'

'Hound of a Jew!' exclaimed the Prior; 'No one knows better than thy own cursed self that our holy house of God is in debt for the finishing of our chancel.'

'All this helps nothing,' said the leader. 'Isaac, pronounce what he may pay.'

'Six hundred crowns.' said Isaac.

'Six hundred crowns,' said the leader, gravely; 'I am content.'

'Ye are *mad*,' said the Prior, 'it will be necessary that I go to Jorvaulx myself; ye may retain my two priests.'

'That would be a blind trust,' said the Outlaw. 'We will retain *thee*, Prior, and send *them* to fetch thy ransom.'

'Or, if so please you,' said Isaac, seeking favour with the outlaws, 'I can send to York for the six hundred crowns, if the most reverend Prior will grant me a quittance.'

'He shall grant it thee, Isaac,' said the Captain; 'thou shalt pay the redemption money for Prior Aymer – as well as for thyself!'

'For myself? Ah, sirs,' said Isaac, 'I am a broken and impoverished man.'

'The Prior shall judge of that matter,' replied the Captain. 'How say you, Father Aymer? Can the Jew afford a ransom?'

'Can he *afford* a ransom?' spluttered the Prior, 'His house at York is full of gold and silver.'

'Hold, father,' said the Jew, 'remember that I force my monies upon no one. But when churchman or layman come knocking at Isaac's door, they borrow with words. It is then '*Friend* Isaac, will you pleasure us in this matter,' or '*Kind* Isaac, show yourself a friend in this need!' But when the day comes for settlement, I hear but *Damned* Jew, and the curse of Egypt on your tribe!'

'Prior,' said the Captain, 'the Jew though hath spoken well. Name his ransom as he named thine.'

'None but a *latro famosus*,' said the Prior, 'would place a Christian prelate and an unbaptized Jew upon the same bench. But since ye require me to put a price upon this caitiff; not a penny under a thousand crowns.'

'A sentence!' exclaimed the chief Outlaw.

'God of my fathers help me!' said the Jew, 'Will ye thus treat an impoverished creature? I am from this day childless; will ye deprive me also of livelihood?'

'Was thy daughter dark-haired?' said one of the outlaws; 'wore she a veil broidered with silver?'

'She did, she *did*!' said the old man, trembling with eagerness.

'It *was* she, then,' said the yeoman, 'who was carried off by the Templar when he broke through us. I drew my bow at him, but feared to hit her.'

'Oh God!' cried the Jew, 'I would to God thou had pierced her! Better the tomb of her fathers than the bed of that savage Templar. *Ichabod! Ichabod!*'[1]

'Friends,' said the Chief, looking round, 'this old man's grief touches me. Deal straightly with us, Isaac. Will a thousand crown ransom leave thee penniless?' Isaac, worldly goods now contending with parental affection, stammered that there might be some, *small* surplus...

'Well,' said the Outlaw, 'we will not deal with thee too hardly, for without treasure thou will never redeem thy child from Bois Guilbert. We will take thee at the same ransom as Prior Aymer, or rather at 100 crowns less. Thus we avoid rating a Jew merchant as high as a Christian prelate and leave thee six hundred crowns to negotiate thy daughter's ransom. Templars love the glitter of silver shekels as much as the sparkle of black eyes. Make them chink in the ear of Bois Guilbert.'

'Prior Aymer,' went on the Captain, 'come aside with me. Men say you love wine, a lady's smile and a purse of gold. But I have never heard thee to be a cruel man. Now, here is Isaac willing to give thee a hundred marks of silver, if thy intercession with the Templar brings freedom for his daughter.'

'What surety am I to have for this?' said the Prior.

'When Isaac returns successful, through your mediation,' said the Outlaw, 'I swear by St Hubert I will see that he pays thee the money in good silver.'

'Well then, Jew,' said Aymer, 'let me have thy writing-tablets.'

The Prior sat down and composed an epistle to Brian de Bois Guilbert. He carefully sealed up the tablets and delivered them to Isaac, saying,

'This will be thy safe-conduct to the Preceptory of Templestowe. Remember, it is more likely to accomplish the delivery of thy daughter if well backed with lucre.

Trust me, Bois Guilbert does naught for naught.'

---

1 Hebrew *l-kavod* (אִיכָבוֹד) without honour.' *See* 1 Samuel 4:21, where Eli's daughter-in-law names her child Ichabod, saying, 'The glory is departed from Israel.'

'Well, Prior,' said the Outlaw, 'I will detain thee no longer here than to give the Jew a release for the six hundred crowns at which thy ransom is fixed!'

The Prior, this time with bad grace, wrote a release, discharging Isaac of York of six hundred crowns, advanced to him in his need for acquittal of his ransom.

'And now,' said Prior Aymer, 'having satisfied you for my ransom, I pray you restore my mules and palfreys and the reverend brethren attending upon me; also of the gymmal rings, jewels and vestures.

'Your brethren, Sir Prior,' said Locksley, 'shall have their freedom, as will your horses and mules. But concerning rings, jewels, chains and the like, we would not subject a holy man like yourself to temptation by the wearing of such baubles.'

'I will take care of that, reverend Prior,' said the Hermit of Copmanhurst; 'for I will wear them myself.'

'Thou art a *hedge-priest*!'[1] shouted the Prior in great wrath, '*excommunico te!*'

'Thou art *thyself* more like a thief and a heretic,' said the friar, equally indignant. '*Ossa ejus perfringam*, I will break his bones, as the Vulgate hath it.'

'Hola!' cried the Captain, 'reverend brethren using such language! Prior, provoke the Friar no further. Hermit, let the reverend and ransomed father depart in peace.' The yeomen separated the incensed priests who continued to vituperate each other in bad Latin. The Prior, aware that he was squabbling with a *hedge-priest*, rode off with considerably less pomp than he had exhibited on arrival.

It remained that the Jew should produce some security for the ransom which he was to pay on the Prior's account, as well as his own. Accordingly, he issued a mandate sealed with his signet to a brother of his tribe at York, requiring him to pay to the bearer the sum of one thousand crowns – and to deliver the merchandises specified.

'My brother Sheva,' he said, 'hath the key of my warehouses.'

'Be liberal, Isaac. Spare not thy purse for thy daughter's safety. Believe me, any gold thou shalt not commit to her cause will give thee as much agony as if it were poured molten down thy throat.' Isaac acquiesced with a groan and set out on his journey, accompanied by two tall foresters as guides. The Black Knight, who had been watching with no small interest, now also took his leave.

'Sir Knight,' said the outlaw, 'we have each our secrets. You are welcome to form a judgment of me as I will of you. Since I do not ask admittance into your mystery, be not offended if I preserve my own.'

'I crave pardon,' said the knight. 'Your reproof is just. Fare thee well!'

Thus, they parted.

1 A priest, but without a parish, or any link to an established Order of monks.

chapter thirty-four

King John*: I'll tell thee what, my friend,*
He is a very serpent in my way;
And wheresoe'er this foot of mine doth tread,
He lies before me – dost thou understand?
Shakespeare: *King John*

There was brave feasting in the Castle of York, to which Prince John had invited those nobles, prelates and leaders with whose assistance he hoped to acquire the throne. His able and political agent Waldemar Fitzurse was quietly at work to bring them to the pitch of courage necessary to declare their support. They were being delayed, however, by the absence of several of the confederacy: the daring, brutal courage of Front-de-Boeuf; the buoyant and bold bearing of De Bracy; the martial experience and valour of Brian de Bois Guilbert were important to their success. While secretly cursing their unexplained absence, neither John nor his adviser dared move without them. Isaac the Jew also seemed to have vanished; and with him the financial subsidy contracted by Prince John.

It was on the morning after the fall of Torquilstone that a confused report began to spread abroad in the city of York that De Bracy and Bois Guilbert, together with their confederate Front-de-Boeuf, had been captured or slain.Waldemar brought the rumour to Prince John, adding that he feared its truth. He told the Prince that they had set out to ambuscade the Saxon Cedric and his attendants. At any other time John would have seen their plan as a good jest; but as it now interfered with his own plans, he erupted, shouting of broken laws; the infringement of public order and of private property.

'The marauders!' he raged, 'Were I monarch, I would hang them over their own castles.'

'To become monarch of England,' said Fitzurse coolly, 'your Grace must not only endure such marauders, but also protect them, despite your laudable zeal for the Law. As your Grace is aware, it would be dangerous to move without Front-de-Boeuf, De Bracy, and the Templar; and we have gone too far to retreat.' Prince John struck his forehead with impatience.

'The villains,' he said, 'the base, treacherous *villains*, to desert me at this pitch!'

'Nay, rather the feather-headed madmen,' said Waldemar, 'toying with follies when great business is in hand.'

'What is to be done?' said the Prince.

'I have ordered Winkelbrand, De Bracy's lieutenant, to have his trumpets sound "to horse" and set out for to the castle of Front-de-Boeuf, to see what yet may be done for our friends.'

At that moment a figure was given admittance to the Prince's presence. Both he and Fitzurse stared and the latter said,

'Whom have we here, by the Rood? De Bracy himself – and in strange guise...'

It was indeed De Bracy. His armour bore all the marks of the recent fray, being defaced and bloodstained. He himself was covered with clay and dust from crest to spur. He placed his helmet on the table and stood a moment as if to collect himself.

'De Bracy,' said Prince John, 'what means this? Speak! Are the Saxons in rebellion?'

'Speak indeed,' said Fitzurse. 'Where are the Templar and Front-de-Boeuf?'

'The Templar is fled,' said De Bracy. 'Font-de-Boeuf has a red grave among the embers of his castle. I alone am escaped to tell you.'

'This is cold news,' said Fitzurse.

'There is worse yet,' answered De Bracy; and, approaching Prince John, he uttered in a low and emphatic tone;

'Richard is in England: I have seen and spoken with him.'

Prince John paled and caught the back of an oaken bench.

'Thou *ravest*, De Bracy,' said Fitzurse, 'it *cannot* be.'

'It is truth itself,' said De Bracy. 'I was his prisoner, and spoke with him.'

'With Richard Plantagenet, sayest thou?' continued Fitzurse.

'With Richard Plantagenet,' replied De Bracy, '*Coeur-de-Lion*; Richard of England.'

'Thou wert his *prisoner*?' said Waldemar; 'is he at the head of an army?'

'No. Only a few outlaw yeomen were around him; and to these his identity is unknown. He joined them only to assist at the storming of Torquilstone. I offered Richard the services of my Free Lances and he refused them. I will march them to Kingston-upon-Hull, and take ship for Flanders. In these times, a soldier will always find employment. Waldemar, wilt lay politics aside and share whatever God sends?'

'I am too old, Maurice;' answered Fitzurse, 'I will take sanctuary in the Church of Saint Peter here at York; the Archbishop is my sworn brother.'

Prince John had gradually become attentive to what was passing.

'Hell and fiends,' he said to himself, 'I am deserted.' He broke in on their conversation.

'My good lords, methought ye bold and ready-witted men; yet ye throw away wealth and all that our noble game promised; and at the very moment it might be won!'

'Your Highness,' said De Bracy, 'as soon as Richard's return is noised about he will be at the head of an army. All is over with us. I counsel you, my Lord, fly to France or take the protection of the Queen Mother.'

'I seek no safety for myself,' said Prince John, haughtily. 'I could secure *that* by a word to Richard. De Bracy and Fitzurse, I should not delight to see thy heads blackening on Clifford's gate yonder. The wily Archbishop will not save thee, Waldemar, when delivering you would make his peace with King Richard. And De Bracy, recall that Robert Estoteville lies betwixt thee and Hull with strength enough to drive all thy Free Lances into the Humber. Essex is also gathering troops. If we had reason to fear these levies *before* Richard's return, is there is any doubt now where their leaders will turn?' Fitzurse and De Bracy looked at each other in dismay.

'There is but one road to safety,' continued the Prince, 'the object of our terror, Richard, journeys alone. He must be met...'

'Not by me,' said De Bracy immediately; 'I was his prisoner, and he took me to mercy. I may not harm a feather on his crest.'

'Who spoke of harming him?' said Prince John, with a hardened laugh.' A prison were better; and whether in England or Austria, what matters it? Things will then be as they were when we began our enterprise, hoping that Richard would remain captive in Europe.'

'Ay,' said Waldemar, 'but your royal father Henry sat more firmly in his seat than your Grace can. I say the best prison is that which is made by the sexton; there is no dungeon like a church-vault!'

'Prison or tomb,' said De Bracy, 'I wash my hands of this.'

'Peace, Sir Knight,' said Waldemar; 'And you, my good lord, forgive the scruples of De Bracy; I trust I may soon remove them.'

'That is beyond even *your* eloquence, Fitzurse,' replied the knight.

'Sir Maurice,' rejoined the wily politician, 'shy not like a scared steed. Only a day ago it was thy dearest wish to have met him hand to hand in battle.'

'Ay,' said De Bracy, 'but that was indeed hand to hand! Thou never heard me speak of assaulting him alone and in a forest.'

'De Bracy, we are requiring an action of thee as Captain of the Free Companions who are hired for Prince John's service. Thou art apprised of our enemy, but you balk, though thy Patron's fortunes are at stake!'

'I tell you,' said De Bracy, sullenly, 'that he gave me my life. True, he dismissed me and refused my homage, so I owe him no allegiance. But I will not lift my hand against him.'

'It needs not be thou, De Bracy. Send Louis Winkelbrand and a score of thy lances.'

'I will abide by you as becomes a knight,' said De Bracy, 'but a highway ambuscade such as this, *no*!'

'I will take on this enterprise,' said Fitzurse, 'De Bracy, I trust to thee to keep up the spirits of the doubters and to guard Prince John. If you receive such news as I hope to send you, our enterprise will no longer be in doubt.'

'Page,' he said, 'to my lodgings, and tell my armourer to be there in readiness; and bid Stephen Wetheral, Broad Thoresby and Spyinghow, come to me instantly. Let the scout Hugh Bardon attend me also. Adieu, my Prince, till better times.'

He left the apartment.

'He goes to make my brother prisoner,' said Prince John to De Bracy, 'I trust he will observe our orders, and use our dear Richard's person with due respect.' De Bracy only answered by a smile.

'By the light of Our Lady's brow,' said Prince John, 'our orders to him were *most* precise – though it may be you heard them not as we stood together in the oriel. Most clear and positive was our charge that Richard's safety should be cared for. Woe to Waldemar if he transgress it!'

'I had better pass to his lodgings,' said De Bracy, 'and make him fully aware of your Grace's pleasure. Since it escaped my ear, it may not have reached his.'

'Nay, nay,' said Prince John, impatiently, 'I promise thee he heard me. Besides, I have further occupation for thee, Maurice. Hither; let me lean on thy shoulder.'

They walked a turn through the hall in this familiar posture, and Prince John, with an air of the most confidential intimacy, said,

'What thinkest thou of Waldemar Fitzurse, my De Bracy? He expects to be our

Chancellor. Surely we will pause ere we give so high an office to one who so readily undertakes this enterprise against Richard. The arrest of my unfortunate brother forms no good title to the high office of Chancellor but thy courage establishes thee to the truncheon of High Marshal. Think on this, De Bracy, and begone to thy charge.'

'Fickle tyrant!' muttered De Bracy, as he left the presence of the Prince, 'But High Marshal of England! Now that,' he said, extending his arm as if to grasp the baton, and assuming a firmer stride, 'that is indeed a prize *worth* playing for!'

De Bracy had no sooner left the apartment than Prince John summoned his master-scout.

'Bardon,' said the prince, 'what did Waldemar desire of thee?'

'Two resolute men, well acquainted with these northern wilds and skillful in tracking the tread of man and horse.'

'And thou hast fitted him?'

'One is from Hexham,' answered the spymaster, 'the other is of Sherwood. He knows each glade and dingle betwixt here and Richmond.'

''Tis well,' said the Prince. 'Waldemar goes with them?'

'He does.'

'With what attendance?' asked John, carelessly.

'Broad Thoresby goes with him and Wetheral, called Stephen Steelheart; and three northern men-at-arms of Ralph Middleton's gang of Spyinghow.'

''Tis well,' said Prince John; then added, after a moment's pause, 'Bardon, it is vital that thou keep a strict but secret watch on Maurice De Bracy. Let us know of his motions from time to time; with whom he converses and what are his plans. Fail not in this, as thou wilt be answerable.'

Bardon bowed, and retired.

'If Maurice betrays me,' said Prince John, 'if he betrays me, as I now fear... I will have his head.'

chapter thirty-five

Arouse the tiger of Hyrcanian deserts,
Strive with the half-starved lion for his prey;
Lesser the risk, than rouse the slumbering fire
Of wild Fanaticism.
Anon. (prob. Scott)

Isaac of York, mounted upon an outlaw mule and with two yeomen as guards and guides, headed for Templestowe to negotiate for his daughter's release. The Templars' Preceptory was a full day's journey from Torquilstone but Isaac had hoped to reach it before nightfall. He dismissed his guides with a piece of silver at the verge of the forest and pressed on with such speed as his weariness permitted. His strength, however, failed him when he came to a small market town some four miles short of the Temple-Court. Here there lived a Rabbi eminent as a physician and well known to Isaac. Nathan Ben Israel welcomed his suffering countryman.

'To Templestowe?' said his host with surprise

'And why not to Templestowe?' answered Isaac, 'I grant thee, Nathan, that it is an abomination; yet business sometimes carries us among bloodthirsty Nazarenes.'

'I know it well,' said Nathan; 'but Lucas Beauma*noir* the Grand Master is himself at Templestowe.'

'Beaumanoir is well known to me,' said Isaac; 'a man zealous unto death for their Nazarene law; a fierce killer of Saracens but also a cruel tyrant to the Jew.'

'True,' said Nathan. 'Other Templars may be seduced by pleasure, or bribed by gold; but *Beaumanoir*! He is of a different stamp. What he desires is a crown of martyrdom. O God of Jacob! – speedily *send* it unto him, and unto them all!'

'Nevertheless,' said Isaac, 'I must to Templestowe.'

He then explained to Nathan the cause of his journey. The Rabbi listened with interest, saying,

'Ah, thy daughter! Alas for the beauty of Zion.'

'Thus it stands,' said Isaac, 'I may not tarry. Perhaps the presence of Beaumanoir may turn Bois Guilbert from evil and deliver Rebecca to me.'

'Go thou,' said Nathan Ben Israel, 'and be wise, for wisdom availed Daniel in the lions' den. Keep away from the presence of the Grand Master and speak with Bois Guilbert in private.'

About an hour's riding brought Isaac before the Preceptory of Templestowe which was strong, well fortified and set amidst fair meadows and pastures. Two black-clad halberdiers guarded the drawbridge. Others, in the same livery, glided to and fro upon the walls, spectres more than soldiers. A knight was now and then seen crossing the court in his long white cloak, head down on his breast, arms folded. They passed each other, if they chanced to meet, with a slow, solemn and mute greeting, the stern ascetic rigour of Templar discipline seemingly revived at Templestowe under the eye of Lucas Beaumanoir. Isaac paused at the gate to consider how he might best seek entrance, well aware that his race would be the object of hate while his wealth might expose him to extortion.

Meantime, Lucas Beaumanoir was walking in the Preceptory's garden, well within its exterior defences. With him was a brother of his Order who had come with him from Palestine. The Grand Master was a man advanced in age, as testified by his grey beard and the shaggy eyebrows. These, however, overhung eyes whose fire was unquenched by the passing years. A formidable warrior, his severe features retained a soldier's expression, while as an ascetic they were marked with the spiritual pride of the devotee. Yet within these traits there was something striking and noble, arising from the exercise of supreme authority over high-born knights, themselves united by the Rule of the Order.

In his hand he bore the *abacus*, or staff of office, on which was engraved the cross of the Order, inscribed within an heraldic *orle*. His companion wore the same dress in all respects, only his deference showing that there was no other equality between them. The Preceptor, for such was his rank, walked just sufficiently behind the Grand Master so that Beaumanoir could speak to him without turning his head.

'Conrade,' said the Grand Master, 'dear companion of my battles, I confide my sorrows to thee alone. I tell thee that since I came to this kingdom, not *one* object in England pleasured mine eye, save the tombs of our brethren in our Temple Church yonder. O valiant Robert de Ros; William de Mareschal! I would rather fight a one thousand pagans than witness the decay of our Holy Order.'

'It is but true,' answered Conrade Mountfitchet; 'it is only *too* true; the irregularities of our brethren here are grosser even than those in France.'

Beaumanoir said, 'We should wear no vain ornament, no crest on helmet, no gold upon stirrup or bridle. Yet, who is pranked out more proudly than the Templars of England? They are forbidden to take one bird by means of another, to shoot beasts with bow or *arblast*,[1] or to follow the horn. But *now*, in hunting and hawking, who so active as Templars? They are forbidden to read and to hear only holy recitations. But lo! Their ears are at the command of idle minstrels. Simplicity of diet is prescribed, but behold their tables; groaning! Their drink was to be water, but now men boast of being able to 'drink like a Templar'! This very garden would better suit the harem of an infidel Emir than the plot of Christian monks. We were forbidden to receive women. The Rule saith that female society seduces from the path to paradise. We are prohibited from offering, even to our sisters and our mothers, the kiss of affection. I am shamed to speak – I shame even to *think* of the corruptions which flood upon us. The brethren *wallow*, Conrade, in foul and shameful luxury. Soldiers of the Cross who should shun the glance of a woman like the eye of a basilisk[2] live in open sin; and not only with females of their own race, but with daughters of the accursed heathen, and the yet more accursed *Jews*! But I will apply the Rule. I *will* purify the fabric of the Temple!'

'Yet consider, reverend father,' said Mountfitchet, 'these stains are engrained by time and use. Let thy reformation be cautious, as well as just.'

'No, Mountfitchet,' answered the old man, 'it must be sharp and *sudden*! If we do not, mark my words, the Order of the Temple will be no more known among the nations.'

'May God avert!' said the Preceptor.

'Amen.'

At this moment a squire entered the garden. He was clothed in the threadbare vestments of aspirants for the holy Order, cast-off garments of the Knights. Bowing before the Grand Master, he stood silent.

'Speak,' said the Grand Master.

'A Jew stands without the gate, noble and reverend father.' said the Squire. 'He prays to speak with Brother de Bois Guilbert.' The Grand Master turned to his companion.

'What must we know of Bois Guilbert?'

'Reports speak of him as brave and valiant,' said Conrade.

'Indeed,' said the Grand Master. 'But Brother Brian came into our Order a moody

---

1 Crossbow.

2 From the Greek βασιλίσκος *basilískos*, or 'little king.' A legendary reptile. Styled the king of serpents, it was said to be able to cause death with a single glance.

and disappointed man and since then, he hath become an agitator, a *murmurer* and a *machinator*. Lead the Jew to our presence.'

With a bow the squire departed and in a few minutes returned with Isaac of York.

No naked slave, ushered into the presence of some mighty prince, could approach with more reverence and fear than that of the Jew before the Grand Master. When he had approached within three yards, Beaumanoir made a halt sign with his staff. Isaac kneeled; then, rising, he stood before the Templars, hands folded on his bosom and head bowed on breast.

'Damian, retire,' said the Grand Master. 'Have a guard ready to await our call and suffer no one to enter the garden until we shall leave it.' The squire withdrew.

'Jew,' continued the old man, 'mark me. Be brief in thy answers to questions. If thy tongue doubles with me, I will have it torn from thy misbelieving jaws. Now, what is thy business with our brother Brian de Bois Guilbert?'

Isaac was seized with uncertainty; to tell his tale would scandalize the Order; yet unless told, what hope of achieving his daughter's deliverance? Beaumanoir saw his mortal apprehension.

'Fear not,' he said, 'for thy wretched person. Thy business with de Bois Guilbert?'

'I am the bearer of a letter to him,' stammered Isaac, 'so please your reverence, from Prior Aymer of the Abbey of Jorvaulx.'

'Are not that these evil times, Conrade?' said the Master. 'A Cistercian Prior sends a letter to a soldier of the Temple and can find no more fitting messenger than this. Give me the letter.' With trembling hands, Isaac approached, hand extended.

'Back, dog!' said the Grand Master; 'I only touch unbelievers with the sword.

Conrade, take the letter and give it here.' Beaumanoir inspected the outside carefully and then proceeded to undo the packthread securing its folds.

'Reverend father,' said Conrade, interposing, though with deference, 'wilt thou break the seal?'

'And will I not?' said Beaumanoir, with a frown. 'Is it not written in the Rule's 42 Chapter, *De Lectione Literarum*[1] that a Templar shall not receive any letter without reading it in the Grand Master's presence?' He then perused the letter with an expression of growing surprise and horror. He read it over again more slowly; then, holding it out to Conrade with one hand and striking it with the other, he exclaimed,

'Read it aloud, Conrade.'

Mountfitchet read:

'Aymer, by divine grace, Prior of the Cistercian house of Saint Mary's of Jorvaulx, to Sir Brian de Bois Guilbert, Knight of the holy Order of the Temple, wisheth health and the bounties of Bacchus and my Lady Venus.

Dear Brother, we are captive in the hands of lawless and godless men who have put us to ransom. We have also learned of Front-de-Boeuf's death but that thou hast escaped with a Jewish sorceress. We rejoice in thy safety; nevertheless, we pray thee to be on thy guard with this Witch of Endor; for your Grand Master cometh from Normandy to punish misdoings.

Her father, Isaac of York, prays you to ransom her and will pay you as much as

---

1 Concerning the reading of letters.

will secure fifty damsels upon safer terms; damsels whereof I trust to have my part when we next convene as brethren of the wine-cup.

For, saith the text, 'Vinum laetificat cor hominis'[1]

'Till which meeting we wish you farewell.

Given, from this den of thieves, about the hour of Matins,

Aymer, Pr. S. M. Jorvolciencis.'

'What sayest thou to this, Conrade?' said the Grand Master. 'No wonder that we retreat before the infidel when we have such churchmen as this Aymer. And what means this 'Witch of Endor?' Mountfitchet explained that Rebecca must be the person described.

'There is more to this than thou dost guess, Conrade.' Turning to Isaac, he said, 'Thy daughter, then, is a prisoner of Brian de Bois Guilbert?'

'Ay, reverend sir,' stammered Isaac, 'and whatsoever ransom a poor man may pay for her deliverance...'

'Silence!' snapped the Grand Master, 'Thy daughter hath practised the art of healing?'

'Ay, gracious sir,' answered Isaac with more confidence; 'knight and yeoman bless the gift which Heaven hath assigned to her.'

'Thy daughter works cures, I doubt not,' he said to Isaac, 'by words and sighs, *periapts*[2] and other cabalistic mysteries.'

'Nay,' answered Isaac, 'chiefly by a balsam of marvellous virtue.'

'Whence had she that secret?' said Beaumanoir.

'It was delivered to her...' answered Isaac, reluctantly, '...by one Miriam, a sage matron of our tribe.'

'False Jew!' snarled the Grand Master; 'that witch Miriam was abominated throughout Christendom.' The Grand Master crossed himself; 'She was burnt at the stake and her ashes scattered to the four winds. I will teach this Rebecca to throw spells over the Soldiers of the Temple! Damian, spurn this Jew from the gate and shoot him dead if he resists. We will deal with his daughter.'

Isaac, all his entreaties and offers ignored, was hurried away out and expelled from the Preceptory gates. He could do no better than return to the house of the Rabbi and await his daughter's fate. Having feared for her honour; he now trembled for her life. Meanwhile, the Grand Master grimly ordered the Preceptor of Templestowe into his presence.

chapter thirty-six

Say not my art is fraud; all live by seeming.
The beggar begs with it, and the gay courtier
Gains land and title, rank and rule, by seeming
In church, or camp, or state; so wags the world.
Anon (prob. Scott): *Old Play.*

Albert Malvoisin, the Preceptor of Templestowe, was brother to Philip Malvoisin. He was also, like that baron, in close league with Brian de Bois Guilbert, but

1 Wine gladdens the heart of Man.

2 A charm worn as protection against mischief and disease; an amulet.

unlike him, Malvoisin knew how to draw a veil of hypocrisy over his vices and ambition. Had the arrival of the Grand Master been foreseen, he would have seen nothing at Templestowe to suggest any loss of discipline. Albert Malvoisin had listened with apparent respect and contrition to the rebukes of his Superior. He had dealt with the areas censured, spreading a mask of ascetic devotion over an Order actually devoted to license and pleasure. Indeed, Lucas Beaumanoir had begun to develop a high opinion of the Preceptor's morality.

However, these favourable sentiments were shaken by the intelligence that Malvoisin had received within their religious house, a Jewish captive and the alleged *paramour* of a brother of the Order. Thus when Albert appeared before him, he was regarded sternly.

'Sir Preceptor, is there, within this mansion of the holy Order of the Temple,' said the Grand Master severely, 'a Jewish woman, brought by a Brother – and with thy connivance?' Albert Malvoisin demurred. Rebecca of York had been confined in a remote and secret part of the building and every precaution taken to conceal her presence. In Beaumanoir's question he saw ruin to Bois Guilbert and himself.

'Why are you mute?' demanded the Grand Master.

'Surely, reverend father,' answered the Preceptor, 'I have not risen to this office in the Order while ignorant of its prohibitions.'

'How comes it then, that thou hast suffered a brother to bring a *paramour*, and the said *paramour* a Jewish sorceress, into this holy place to its stain and pollution?'

'A Jewish *sorceress*?' echoed Malvoisin. 'Angels guard us!'

'Ay, brother, a *Jewish* sorceress!' said the Grand Master, sternly. 'Do you deny that this Rebecca, daughter of that usurer Isaac of York and pupil of that witch Miriam, is now lodged within this very Preceptory?'

'Your wisdom, reverend father,' answered the Preceptor, 'hath rolled away the darkness from my understanding. Much did I wonder that so good a knight as Brian de Bois Guilbert was so besotted by this female. I received her into this house merely to place a bar betwixt their growing intimacy.'

'Nothing, then, has yet occurred betwixt them in breach of his vow?' demanded the Grand Master.

'What? Under *this* roof?' said the Preceptor, crossing himself. 'St Magdalene and the 10,000 virgins forbid! But since you reveal her to be a sorceress, perchance *that* may account for his enamoured folly.'

'It doth, it *doth*!' said Beaumanoir. 'See, brother Conrade, the peril of looking upon woman to gratify the lust of the eye. It may be that our brother Bois Guilbert deserves more pity than chastisement. Our admonitions may yet turn him from his folly.'

'It were a deep pity,' said Mountfitchet, 'to lose one of the Order's best lances when our Holy Community most requires the aid of its sons. Three hundred Saracens hath Brian de Bois Guilbert slain with his own hand.'

'With the Saints' aid,' said the Grand Master, 'He shall burst the bonds of this Delilah, as Sampson burst the cords with which the Philistines bound him. Concerning this foul witch who hath flung her enchantments over a brother of the Holy Temple, assuredly she shall die.'

'But the laws of England…' said the Preceptor, delighted that the Grand Master's resentment had been diverted from himself and Bois Guilbert. It had, however, taken another dangerous direction.

'The laws of England,' interrupted Beaumanoir, 'permit and enjoin each judge to execute justice within his own jurisdiction. Any Baron may arrest, try and condemn a witch found within his own domain. And shall that power be denied to the Grand Master of the Temple within a Preceptory of his Order? No! We will judge; and condemn. Prepare the Castle-hall for a trial.'

Albert Malvoisin bowed and retired; not indeed to prepare the hall, but to warn Bois Guilbert how matters were likely to terminate. It was not long ere he found him, foaming with indignation at another repulse from the Jewess.

'The unthinking,' he said, 'the *ungrateful*! To scorn the man who saved her life at the risk of his own! My shield was for *her* protection; and now the self-willed bitch upbraids me for *not* leaving her to perish!'

'The devil,' said the Preceptor, 'I think has possessed. How oft have I preached caution to you, and continence? By the Mass, I think old Beaumanoir is right; she hath indeed cast a spell over you.'

'Lucas Beaumanoir!' said Bois Guilbert reproachfully. 'Has the old dotard learned that Rebecca is here?'

'How could I help it?' said the Preceptor, 'But you are safe if you renounce the witch. She is a sorceress – and must suffer as such.'

'She shall *not*, by Heaven!' said Bois Guilbert.

'By Heaven, she must – and *will*!' said Malvoisin. 'Neither you nor anyone else can save her. Beaumanoir is determined that the death of the Jewess will be a sin-offering, sufficient to atone for *all* the amorous indulgences of the Knights Templars.'

'I have it.' said Bois Guilbert. 'Albert my friend, connive at her escape. I will take her to some secure place of greater secrecy.'

'I cannot,' replied the Preceptor. 'Templestowe is filled with the attendants of the Grand Master and others devoted to him. Be guided by my counsel. Give up this wild-goose chase; fly your hawk at some other game or Beaumanoir will surely ruin thee over this Jewish sorceress. Give him his head in this matter; when the staff is in *thine* own grasp, caress the daughters of Judah – or burn them – as best suits thine own humour.'

'Malvoisin,' said Bois Guilbert, 'thou art a cold-blooded…'

'*Friend*,' said the Preceptor in haste, 'a cold-blooded *friend* – and thus fit to give thee advice. I tell thee once more; thou cannot save this Rebecca and may perish with her. But for the present, we part. We must not be seen to hold close conversation and I must order the Hall for his judgment-seat.'

'So soon?' said Bois Guilbert.

'Ay,' replied the Preceptor, 'a trial moves rapidly when the Judge has already fixed the sentence.' He had hardly given the necessary orders, when he was joined by Conrade Mountfitchet.

'It is surely a dream,' said Malvoisin, 'We have many Jewish physicians and we call them not warlocks though they work wondrous cures.'

'The Grand Master thinks otherwise, Albert' said Mountfitchet. 'I will be straight with thee; it were better that this woman die, than that Bois Guilbert be lost to the Order. Better she suffers alone than Bois Guilbert dies with her.'

'I have been working on him to abandon her,' said Malvoisin. 'But hold, are there truly grounds to condemn this Rebecca for *sorcery*? Might the Grand Master change his mind when he sees that the evidence is so weak?'

'They must be strengthened, Albert,' replied Mountfitchet.

'Ay,' said the Preceptor, 'but there is little time.'

'Malvoisin, they must be *found*!' said Conrade. 'And it will be of advantage to both the Order – and *thee*... This Templestowe is a poor Preceptory while that of Maison-Dieu in Kent is worth double. I have influence with our old Chief. Find those who can carry this matter through and be Preceptor of Maison-Dieu.'

'There are,' replied Malvoisin, 'two fellows among those who came with Bois Guilbert whom I know well. For a *zecchin* they would swear their own mother was a sorceress,' said the Preceptor.

'Away, then,' said Mountfitchet; 'at noon the trial proceeds. I have not seen our Senior so earnest since he condemned Hamet Alfagi to the stake for relapsing to Islam.'

The ponderous castle-bell had tolled noon when Rebecca heard trampling of feet on the stair leading to her place of confinement. The sound of several persons gave her relief, for she was more afraid of the solitary visits of Bois Guilbert, than of any other evil. The door of the chamber opened and Mountfitchet and the Preceptor Malvoisin entered, attended by four warders in black and bearing halberds.

'Daughter of the accursed,' said the Preceptor, 'follow us.'

'Where,' said Rebecca, 'and wherefore?'

'Woman,' answered Conrade, 'it is not for *thee* to question, but to obey. Nevertheless, thou art to be brought before the court of the Grand Master, there to answer for thine offences.'

'God of Abraham be praised!' said Rebecca, folding her hands devoutly. 'A judge is to me a protector. Most willingly I follow thee; permit me to veil my head.' They descended the stair with slow and solemn step, traversed a long gallery and, by a pair of folding doors placed at the end, entered the great hall in which the Grand Master had, for the time, established his court.

The lower part of this ample apartment was filled with squires and yeomen who made way, not without some difficulty, for Rebecca, the Preceptor and Mountfitchet. Followed by the guard of halberdiers, they then moved forward to the seat appointed for her. As she passed through the crowd, arms folded and head lowered, a scrap of paper was thrust into her hand. She received it unconsciously and held it without examining its contents. The assurance that perhaps she had a friend in that awful assembly gave her courage to look around and to note into whose presence she was being conducted. Thus, her gaze fell upon the scene.

chapter thirty-seven

Stern was the law, which at the winning wile
Of frank and harmless mirth forbade to smile;
But sterner still, when high the iron-rod
Of tyrant power she shook, and call'd that power of God.
Anon (prob. Scott): *The Middle Ages*

The Tribunal, erected for the trial of the unhappy Rebecca, occupied the *dais* at the upper end of the great hall. On an elevated seat, directly before the accused, sat the Grand Master of the Temple. He was in full and ample robes of flowing white, holding in his hand the staff bearing the symbol of the Order. At his feet was placed a table occupied by two scribes of the Order, who would produce a formal record of the proceedings. The black dresses, bare scalps and demure appearance of these clerics were in strong contrast to the warlike appearance of the knights resident in the Preceptory attending the Grand Master. The Preceptors, of whom there were four present, occupied seats lower and somewhat behind that of their Superior. The knights were placed on benches still lower, preserving the same distance from the Preceptors as these from the Grand Master. Behind them again and in their white dresses, stood the esquires of the Order.

The remaining lower part of the hall was filled by guards holding partizans and by those drawn by sheer curiosity to see a Grand Master confront a Jewish sorceress. The greater part of these were connected with the Order and were distinguished by their black dress. Peasants from the neighbouring countryside were present, for it was the pride of Beaumanoir to render as public as possible the justice which he administered. He gazed around the assembly, elated by the merit of what he was about to perform.

A psalm, which Beaumanoir sang with a deep mellow voice undimmed by age, commenced the proceedings. The solemn *Venite exultemus Domino,* sung by the Templars before battle, judged appropriate for the approaching engagement with the powers of darkness. The deep prolonged notes, raised by a hundred masculine voices arose to the vaulted roof of the hall and rolled on amongst its arches.

The *Venite* ended, the Grand Master glanced slowly around the circle, observing that the seat of one of the Preceptors was vacant. Brian de Bois Guilbert had left his place. He was now standing at the corner of one of the benches occupied by the Knights of the Temple, one hand extending his long mantle to hide his face, the other holding his sheathed sword with which he was slowly drawing lines upon the oaken floor.

'Unhappy man!' said the Grand Master aside to Mountfitchet with a glance of compassion. 'Conrade, see how this holy work distresses him; and how a woman aided by Satan can fell a valiant knight. He cannot look upon us and he cannot look upon her. Who knows how she makes his hand form these cabalistic lines. It may be that our lives and safety are thus aimed at, but we defy the foul enemy.'

The Grand Master addressed the assembly.

'Reverend and valiant men, Knights, Preceptors, and Companions of our Holy

Order, my Brethren and children! Be it known to you that this Baton commits to us full power to try and to judge all that affects the Order. We have therefore summoned to our presence a Jewish woman, by name Rebecca, daughter of Isaac of York. This is a woman infamous for sortileges[1] and for witcheries, whereby she hath besotted the brain of our brother Brian de Bois Guilbert, a Preceptor of the Order and a zealous champion of the Cross. His arm hath wrought many deeds of valour in the Holy land and purified Holy places with the blood of the infidel.

Our brother's sagacity and prudence have been no less in repute among his brethren than his valour. Such a man, honoured and honourable, then suddenly cast away regard for his character, his vows, his brethren and his prospects and associated to himself a Jewish damsel. He defends her person in preference to his own and brings her to one of our own Preceptories. What should we surmise except that the noble knight is possessed by some evil demon or under a wicked spell?'

He paused. A low murmur went through the assembly.

'Great indeed,' he continued, 'should be the punishment of a Knight Templar who willfully offends against the rules of his Order. But if Satan, by means of this damsel's beauty, has obtained dominion over the Knight, we would turn the full edge of our indignation upon the female instrument. Stand forth, therefore, and bear witness, ye who have witnessed these doings, that we may judge this infidel woman.'

Several witnesses were called to attest the risks to which Bois Guilbert had exposed himself in saving Rebecca of York from the blazing castle and his neglect of his personal defence. The Preceptor of Templestowe was then called to describe the manner in which Bois Guilbert and the Jewess had arrived at the Preceptory. The evidence of Malvoisin was skilfully guarded. He attempted to spare the feelings of Bois Guilbert, hinting that he was labouring under a temporary alienation of mind, appearing to be deeply enamoured of the woman with him. With sighs of penitence, the Preceptor avowed his own contrition for having admitted Rebecca and her lover. 'My defence,' he concluded, 'has been made in my confession to our most reverend father the Grand Master. He knows my motives were not evil, though my conduct may have been irregular. I submit to any penance he shall assign me.' With a look of the deepest submission, the sly Preceptor of Templestowe bowed to the ground before his Superior and resumed his seat.

'Brethren,' said the Grand Master, 'let us now examine something into the former life and conversation of this woman, specifically her use of magical charms and spells.'

Herman of Goodalricke was the fourth Preceptor present; the other three being Conrade, Malvoisin, and Bois Guilbert himself. An ancient warrior, his face marked with scars inflicted by a Moslem sabre, he had rank and consideration among the brethren. He arose and bowed to the Grand Master.

'I crave to know, most Reverend Father, from our valiant brother Brian de Bois Guilbert himself what he says to these accusations – and how he regards his intercourse with this Jewish maiden?'

'Brian de Bois Guilbert,' said the Grand Master, 'Reply.'

The Knight turned towards the Grand Master but remained silent.

'He is possessed by a dumb-devil,' said the Grand Master. 'Speak, I adjure thee.'

---

1 Sorceries. Also, the prediction of the future by divination.

Bois Guilbert suppressed his rising indignation, well aware that to express them would little avail him.

'Sir Brian de Bois Guilbert,' he answered, 'replies not, most Reverend Father, to such wild and vague charges. If his honour be impeached, he will defend it with this sword which has often been drawn for Christendom.'

'Well now,' pursued the Grand Master, 'since our Brother of Goodalricke's question has been imperfectly answered, we pursue our quest, brethren, to the bottom this mystery of iniquity. Let those who can bear witness to the life and speech of this Jewish woman, stand forth.' Immediately there was a bustle in the lower part of the hall. A poor peasant, Saxon by birth and who had been treated by Rebecca, was dragged forward to the bar. He was terrified at the penal consequences of having been cared for by a Jewess. Perfectly cured he certainly was not, for he supported himself on crutches to give evidence. He testified that two years since, when residing at York, he was afflicted with paralysis while working as a carpenter for Isaac the Jew. He had been unable to stir from his bed until a balsamic remedy applied by Rebecca's direction, had in some degree restored the use of his limbs. Moreover, he said, she had given him a pot of the ointment and furnished him with money to return to the house of his father.

'And may it please your Reverence,' said the man, 'I cannot think the damsel meant harm to me, though she hath the ill luck to be a Jewess; for even when I used her remedy, I said the Pater and the Creed and it never operated a whit less kindly...'

'Silence,' said the Grand Master, 'and begone! Brutes like thee should not be tinkering with hellish cures, nor giving your labour to the sons of mischief. I tell thee, the Fiend can *impose* diseases for the very purpose of removing them, in order to credit some diabolical cure. Hast thou the unguent spoken of?'

The peasant, fumbling in his bosom with a trembling hand, produced a small box, bearing Hebrew characters on the lid. To most of the audience this was sure proof of the Devil standing apothecary. Beaumanoir, crossing himself, took the box into his hand, and, learned in most of the Eastern tongues, read with ease the motto on the lid; *The Lion of the tribe of Judah hath conquered.*

'Such strange powers of Satan,' said he, 'which can convert Scripture into blasphemy and mingling poison with our food! Is there a physician here who can tell us the ingredients of this?' Two *mediciners* then appeared; one a monk, the other a barber. With true professional jealousy of a successful practitioner of their art, they insinuated that since the medicine was unknown to them, it must have come from an unlawful and magical pharmacopeia. Their testimony ended, the Saxon peasant asked humbly to have the salutary medicine returned to him. The Grand Master frowned severely at this.

'What is thy name, fellow?' said he to the cripple.

'Higg, the son of Snell,' said the peasant.

'Then Higg, son of Snell,' said the Grand Master, 'I tell thee it is better to be bed-ridden than to accept unbelievers' medicine. Better to despoil infidels of their treasure, than to accept gifts or do them service for wages. Go thou and do as I have said.'

Higg, the son of Snell, withdrew into the crowd and lingered until he should learn the fate of Rebecca, even at the risk of again encountering the Judge.

At this period of the trial, the Grand Master commanded Rebecca to unveil herself. Speaking for the first time, she replied, with dignity,

'It is not the habit of the daughters of Israel to uncover when alone in an assembly of strangers.' The sweet tones of her voice, and the softness of her reply, impressed the audience. Beaumanoir repeated his command. The guards were about to remove her veil when she stood up before the Grand Master and said,

'Nay, but for the love of your own daughters...Alas,' she said, recollecting herself, 'ye *have* no daughters! Yet for the love of your sisters and for female decency, let me not be thus manhandled in your presence.' She withdrew her veil, her beauty exciting a murmur of surprise among the knights. By silent glances they told each other that Brian's best defence lay in the power of her real charms, rather than of any imagined witchcraft. Higg, son of Snell, felt the effect of the countenance of his benefactress.

'Let me go out,' he cried to the warders at the hall door. 'Let me go forth! To look at her again will kill me, for I have had a share in murdering her.'

'Peace, poor man,' said Rebecca, who had heard his exclamation. 'There was no harm done by speaking the truth. I pray thee go – and save thyself.'

The two men-at-arms upon whom Albert Malvoisin had impressed the importance of their testimony, were now called forward. Hardened and inflexible villains as they were, the sight of the captive maiden and her beauty at first appeared to affect them until a powerful glance from the Preceptor restored their composure. They alleged that Rebecca was heard to mutter to herself in an unknown tongue which made the ears of the hearer tingle and his heart throb; that she spoke at times to herself and seemed to look upward for a reply; that her garments were unlike those of women of good repute and that she had rings with cabalistic devices.

There was further testimony which, however incredible, the assembly greedily swallowed. One of the soldiers had seen her work a cure upon a wounded man at the castle of Torquilstone. She made, he said, certain signs upon the wound and repeated certain mysterious words which, he blessed God, he understood not. Thereupon the iron head of a crossbow bolt disengaged itself from the wound which then closed; and the dying man was, within a quarter of an hour, assisting the witness in managing a mangonel.[1] It was difficult to dispute the accuracy of this witness when he drew from his pouch the very bolt-head which, said he, had been miraculously extracted from the wound.

His comrade had been a witness of the scene betwixt Rebecca and Bois Guilbert, when she was upon the point of throwing herself from the tower. Not to be outdone by his companion, this witness stated that he had seen Rebecca perch herself upon the parapet of the turret and there take the form of a swan. In this guise she had then flown three times round the castle of Torquilstone before settling again on the turret and assuming human form.

The Grand Master, having collected the evidence, now demanded of Rebecca in a solemn tone what she had to say before pronouncement of the sentence of condemnation.

'To invoke your pity,' said the lovely Jewess, her voice tremulous with emotion, 'would be useless, as I should hold it mean. To plead the impossibility of the many things which these men, whom may Heaven pardon, have spoken against me would avail me little, since you clearly believe them. Still less would it help me to explain

---

1 A military machine similar to the Roman *ballista*, used to hurl stones at an enemy.

that my dress, language, and manners are simply those of my people. Nor will I even vindicate myself at the expense of my oppressor Bois Guilbert, who stands there listening to these fictions making him, the tyrant, a victim! May God be the judge between him and me. I would rather submit to ten deaths than listen to what Bois Guilbert, that man of Belial, has urged upon me: a woman friendless, defenceless and his prisoner. But of course he is of *your* own faith and his slightest affirmation would outweigh the most solemn protestations of a distressed Jewess. Brian de Bois Guilbert, to thyself I appeal. Are not these accusations false and monstrous?'

There was a pause; all eyes turned to Brian de Bois Guilbert. He was silent.

'Speak,' she said, 'If thou art a man. If thou art a Christian, speak! I adjure thee by the tomb and the bones of thy father. Say, are these things *true*?'

'Answer her, brother,' said the Grand Master. Bois Guilbert seemed agitated by contending passions which convulsed his features and it was with a constrained voice that he at last replied, looking at Rebecca,

'The scroll – the *scroll*!'

'Aha,' said Beaumanoir, 'this is testimony! The victim of her witcheries can only name a scroll, a spell from which is doubtless the cause of his silence.'

The murmuring which ran through the assembly at the strange reply of Bois Guilbert, gave Rebecca time to examine and then crumple the scroll unobserved. Glancing at the slip of parchment in her hand, she found written in Arabic, *Demand a Champion*! The Grand Master spoke.

'Rebecca, daughter of Isaac, thou canst derive no help from the evidence of this Knight for whom Satan is yet too powerful. Have ye aught else to say?'

'There is yet one chance of life left to me,' said Rebecca, 'My existence has been miserable of late, but I will not cast away life, the gift of God, while he affords me the means of defending it. I deny these charges! I maintain my innocence and I declare the falsehood of this accusation. I claim the privilege of trial by combat, and will appear through a Champion!'

'And who, Jewess,' replied the Grand Master, 'will lay lance in rest for a sorceress?'

'*God* will raise me up a Champion,' said Rebecca. 'It is enough that I demand trial by combat. There lies my *gage*.' So saying, and to the astonishment and admiration of the knights, she took her embroidered glove from her hand and flung it down before the Grand Master.

chapter thirty-eight

...There, I throw my gage,
To prove it on thee to the extremest point
Of martial breathing: seize it, if thou darest.
Shakespeare: *Richard II*

Even Lucas Beaumanoir himself was now affected by Rebecca. He was not essentially a cruel man; but by nature cold and with a high sense of duty. His heart had been gradually hardened by his ascetic life and the supreme power which he enjoyed in eradicating heresy. His features relaxed their usual severity as he gazed upon the beautiful woman before him, alone and defending herself with such spirit and courage. He crossed himself twice, doubting whence arose this softening of a usually steely heart. At length he spoke.

'Damsel,' he said, 'if the pity I feel for thee arises from any of thine evil arts, great is thy guilt. But I rather judge it the kinder feelings of nature which grieves that so goodly a form should be a vessel of perdition. Repent, my daughter. Confess thy witchcraft and turn from thine evil faith. This do and live; for what has the Law of Moses done for thee, that thou should'st die for it?'

'It was the law of my fathers,' said Rebecca, 'delivered in thunder and storm upon Mount Sinai. If ye be Christian, ye believe this.'

'Let our chaplain,' said Beaumanoir, 'stand forth, and tell this obstinate infidel...'

'Forgive the interruption,' said Rebecca meekly. 'I am a maiden unskilled in debate on my religion. But I *can* die for it, if it be God's will! Give me your answer to my demand of a champion.'

'Give me her glove,' said Beaumanoir, looking over the flimsy texture and slender fingers. 'This is a slight and frail gage for a purpose so deadly! Rebecca, this light glove of thine is to one of our heavy gauntlets, as is thy cause compared to that of the Temple.'

'Then cast my *innocence* into the scale,' cried Rebecca, 'and that silken glove shall outweigh thy glove of iron!'

'You persist in refusal to confess; and in this challenge?'

'I do so persist.'

'So be it then, in the name of Heaven,' said the Grand Master; 'and may God show the right!'

'Amen!' replied the Preceptors around him; and the word went echoing round the whole assembly.

'Brethren,' said Beaumanoir, 'you are aware that we might well have refused this woman the benefit of trial by combat. But, though a Jewess and an unbeliever, she is also a stranger and defenceless. Moreover, we are knights and soldiers as well as men of religion. Rebecca, daughter of Isaac of York stands accused of sorcery practised on the person of a knight of our Order. She hath challenged combat in proof of her innocence. To whom, reverend brethren, should we deliver her gage of battle, thus naming him our champion on the field?'

'To Brian de Bois Guilbert!' said the Preceptor of Goodalricke. 'He best knows how the truth stands in this matter.'

'But,' said the Grand Master, 'what if our brother Brian be yet under the influence of a charm or a spell?'

'Reverend father,' answered the Preceptor of Goodalricke, 'no spell can affect a champion who comes forward to fight for the judgment of God.'

'Thou sayest right, brother,' said the Grand Master. 'Albert Malvoisin, give this gage of battle to Brian de Bois Guilbert.

We charge thee, brother,' he continued, now addressing him, 'that thou do thy battle manfully. And do thou, Rebecca of York, attend to this; we assign thee three days from the present, to present a champion.'

'That is but brief space,' answered Rebecca.

'We may not extend it,' answered the Grand Master; 'the combat must be in our own presence – and weighty causes call us on the fourth day from hence.'

'God's will be done,' said Rebecca; 'I put my trust in Him, to whom an instant is as effectual to save, as is a whole age...'

'Spoken well, damsel,' said the Grand Master. 'It remains only to name a fitting place of combat; and if required, of execution. Where is the Preceptor of this house?'

Albert Malvoisin, still holding Rebecca's glove in his hand, was speaking to Bois Guilbert very earnestly, but in a low voice.

'Malvoisin?' said the Grand Master, 'will he not receive the gage?'

'He will. He doth, most Reverend Father,' said Malvoisin, slipping the glove under his own mantle. 'And as for the place of combat, I hold the fittest to be the lists of Saint George here at the Preceptory.'

'It is well.' said the Grand Master, 'Rebecca of York, in those lists shalt thou produce thy champion. If thou fail to do so, or if thy champion fall in combat by the judgment of God, thou shalt then die as a sorceress. Let our judgment be recorded.'

Rebecca did not speak, but looked up to heaven. Folding her hands, she remained for a minute without change of attitude. She then said that she must be permitted free communication with her friends for the purpose of making her condition known and procuring a champion to fight on her behalf.

'It is just,' said the Grand Master. 'Choose a messenger and he shall have free communication with thee in thy prison-chamber.'

'Is there anyone,' cried Rebecca, 'who for love of a goodly cause, or for ample hire, will do the errand of a distressed woman?'

All were silent. None thought it safe to avow any interest in the presence of the Grand Master, even with the prospect of reward. Rebecca stood for a few moments in the greatest anxiety and then exclaimed,

'Is it really thus? Am I to lose my small chance of safety for want of an act of charity?' Higg, the son of Snell, then spoke.

'I am a maimed man, but that I can move at all was owing to thee. I will do the errand as well as a cripple can.'

'God,' said Rebecca, 'is the disposer of all. Go. Seek out Isaac of York. Let him have this scroll. Life and death are in thy haste. Farewell!'

The peasant took the scroll, which contained lines in Hebrew. Many of the crowd would have dissuaded him from touching a document so suspicious, but Higg was resolute. She had saved his body, he said, and he was confident she did not mean to imperil his soul.

But as it chanced, he did not have to go so far as York. Within a mile from the Preceptory gates he met with two riders who he saw to be Jews by their dress and large yellow caps. On approaching, he found one to be his old employer, Isaac of York, the other Rabbi Ben Samuel. Both had approached as near to the Preceptory as they dared on hearing that the Grand Master had summoned a chapter for the trial of a sorceress.

'How now brother Higg, son of Snell,' said the Rabbi.

Higg offered the scroll to Isaac who glanced at it, and uttered a groan.

'Brother,' said the Rabbi, 'I trust the child of thy house yet liveth?'

'She liveth,' answered Isaac; 'but she is as Belshazzar within the den of the lions. She is captive of men of Belial. Rebecca, daughter of Rachel, the shadow of death hath encompassed thee.'

'Read the scroll again,' said the Rabbi.

'You read it, brother,' answered Isaac, 'mine eyes are with tears.'

The physician read, in Hebrew:

'To Isaac, the son of Adonikam, peace and the blessing of the Promise be unto thee!

My father, can a Warrior be found to do battle for my cause, according to the custom of the Nazarenes, at Templestowe on the third day from this time? But if this may not be, mourn for me, for I am doomed to die for the crime of witchcraft.

One Nazarene warrior, Wilfred son of Cedric whom the Gentiles call Ivanhoe, might bear arms in my behalf. Say unto him, that whether Rebecca live or die, she is innocent.

My father, if it be God's will that thou shalt lose thy daughter, do not tarry in this land. Betake thyself to Cordoba and live with thy brother in safety under the throne of Boabdil the Saracen.[1] *Far less cruel are the Moors than the Nazarenes of England.'*

'Take courage, Isaac,' said the Rabbi, 'Seek out this Wilfred, son of Cedric; mayhap he will help thee. This man hath favour in the eyes of *Coeur-de-Lion* and constant now is the rumour that he hath returned. His signet on a letter may command these men of blood to desist.'

'I will seek him out,' said Isaac. 'He hath compassion. But if he cannot yet bear armour, what other Christian will do battle for Zion?'

'Nay,' said the Rabbi, 'gold buys Nazarene valour, even as it buys thy own safety. Be of good courage; find this Wilfred of Ivanhoe. I will also search at York where many warriors are assembled; I may find one who will do battle for thy daughter. Gold is their god. Farewell.'

They embraced and departed on their different roads. Higg remained for some time looking after them.

'Jews!' said he; 'They might have flung me a *mancus* or two!'

chapter thirty-nine

O maid, unrelenting and cold as thou art,
My bosom is proud as thine own.
Anna Seward: *Song*

In the twilight of the day of her trial, a low knock was heard at the door of Rebecca's prison-chamber. The inmate was engaged in the Hebrew evening prayer and hymn required by her religion:

---

1 *Abu Abdullah* (c.1460–c.1533) the Spanish rendering of his name being Boabdil: the 22nd and last Nasrid ruler of Granada in Moorish Spain. Rebecca had indeed powers of prophecy…

Our harps we left by Babel's streams,
The tyrant's jest, the Gentile's scorn
No censer round our altar beams,
And mute our timbrel, trump, and horn.
A contrite heart and humble thought,
Are mine accepted sacrifice.

When Rebecca's devotional hymn had died away to silence, the low knock at the door was again renewed and Sir Brian de Bois Guilbert entered the apartment. Alarmed at the sight of the root cause of her misfortune, Rebecca drew back into the farthest corner of the apartment. Her attitude was not of defiance but of resolution.

'You have no reason to fear me, Rebecca,' said the Templar; 'Or, you have at least *now* no reason to fear me.'

'I fear you not, Sir Knight.'

'You have no cause,' repeated Bois Guilbert, gravely; 'Within your call are guards over whom I have no power. They may conduct you to death, Rebecca, but would not permit you to be insulted.'

'Heaven be praised!' she said. 'Death is the least of my fears in this den of evil.'

'Peace, said the Templar.' Such discourse avails little now. Thou art condemned to die for what these diabolical bigots call thy crime.'

'And to whom do I owe this?' demanded Rebecca; 'Surely only to you whose brutal reasons dragged me here.'

'A truce, Rebecca,' said the Templar. 'I have my own cause of grief; do not add to it.'

'What *is* thy purpose, then?' she said. 'Speak briefly, or leave. The step between life and eternity is short and I have but a short time to prepare for it. You sat as a judge, knowing me to be innocent! You concurred in my condemnation and if I understood aright, *you* will appear in arms to assert my guilt!'

'Your words are bitter, Rebecca,' said Bois Guilbert, pacing the apartment. 'But I came not to bandy reproaches. That scroll which warned thee to demand a champion came from me!'

'A brief respite from death,' said Rebecca.

'Madam,' said Bois Guilbert, 'this was *not* all that I purposed. Had it not been for the interference of Beaumanoir and that fool Goodalricke, I myself would have appeared in the lists as thy champion. Thy innocence would then be avowed and I would have looked to thee for the reward of my victory.'

'Sir Knight,' said Rebecca, 'this is idle bragging. *You* received my glove. My champion, if I find one, must encounter *your* lance in the lists; yet *you* assume the air of friend and protector!'

'If I appear not in the lists,' said Bois Guilbert, 'I lose fame, rank, the esteem of my brethren and the hope of succeeding Beaumanoir. Such is certain unless I appear in arms against thy cause. Accursed be Goodalricke who baited this trap for me!'

'More rant,' answered Rebecca. 'Thou hast made thy choice between shedding the blood of an innocent woman, or of endangering thine own earthly hopes. Thy choice is made.'

'No, Rebecca,' said the knight, in a softer tone, and drawing nearer towards her; 'my choice is *not* made. Nay, it is *thine* to make the choice. If I appear in the lists and conquer then thou, Champion or no Champion, die at the stake. There lives no knight who is the match for me, save Richard *Coeur-de-Lion* and his minion of Ivanhoe and Richard lies in a foreign prison. If I appear, you die; even should thy charms induce some hot-headed youth to fight in thy defence.'

'And why repeat this so often?' said Rebecca.

'Thou must learn,' replied the Templar; 'to look at thy fate from every side.'

'Well, then, turn the tapestry,' said she, 'and let me see the other side.'

'If I appear,' said Bois Guilbert, 'in the lists, you die a slow and cruel death. But if I appear *not*, then I lose fame, honour and the prospect of such as scarcely Emperors attain – and *yet*, Rebecca,' he said, kneeling at her feet, 'all this will I sacrifice if thou wilt say, Bois Guilbert, I receive thee for my lover.'

'Think not of such foolishness, Sir Knight,' answered Rebecca. 'Hear me! Hasten to the Regent, the Queen Mother and to Prince John. They cannot allow these proceedings of your Grand Master. Thus, you shall give me protection without either sacrifice, or the pretext of requiring any reward from me.'

'I deal not with these people,' said the Templar, holding the train of her robe.'

'Be a man,' said Rebecca, afraid to provoke the wild knight, yet equally determined never to endure his passion. 'Be a Christian! Show that mercy which your sect claims and save me from this dreadful death.'

'No!' said the Templar, springing up. 'If I renounce fame and future ambition, I renounce it for thy sake and we will escape together. Listen to me, Rebecca,' he said, again softening his tone; 'England, even Europe, is not the world. We will go to Palestine; Conrade, Marquis of Montserrat, is my friend there. I will forge new paths to greatness,' he continued, again striding about the room; 'Thou shalt be a queen, Rebecca! On Mount Carmel shall we pitch the throne which my valour will gain for you!'

'A dream,' said Rebecca; 'an empty vision of the night. Go to the throne of *England*! Richard will listen.'

'Never, Rebecca!' said the Templar, fiercely. 'If I renounce my Order, for thee alone will I renounce it. Stoop my crest to Richard; ask a boon of *him*? Never, Rebecca, *never!*'

'God be gracious to me,' said Rebecca.

'Rebecca,' said the Templar; 'thou *wilt* yield to me!'

'Bois Guilbert,' answered the Jewess, 'I tell thee that not in thy fiercest battles hast thou displayed more courage than that shown by a woman called upon to suffer. I am fearful of danger and pain – yet when we enter the lists, thou to fight and I to suffer, my courage shall mount higher than thine. Farewell; I will waste no more words on thee; I seek the Comforter who hears the cry of those who seek him.'

'We part thus, then?' said the Templar. 'Would to Heaven we had never met!'

'There are noble things which cross thy mind,' said Rebecca, 'but it is as a garden without the gardener; and the weeds have choked any blossom.'

'Do thou forgive me, Rebecca?'

'As freely as ever a victim forgave her executioner…'

'Farewell, then,' said the Templar.

The Preceptor Albert awaited the return of Bois Guilbert impatiently in an adjacent chamber.

'Thou tarried long,' he said; 'What if the Grand Master or his spy Conrade had come hither? What ails thee, brother? Thy brow is as black as night.'

'Ay,' answered the Templar, 'as well as the wretch who is doomed to die within an hour. I am half resolved to go to the Grand Master and abjure the Order to his face.'

'Thou art mad!' answered Malvoisin; 'Beaumanoir will simply name another from the Order to execute his judgment and the Jewess will assuredly perish.'

'False! I will *myself* take arms in her behalf,' answered the Templar, 'And should I do so, Malvoisin, thou knowest not one of the Order who will keep his saddle before *my* lance.'

'Go to Lucas Beaumanoir,' said the wily adviser, 'and say thou hast renounced thy vow of obedience – then see how long he will leave thee in personal freedom. The words shall scarce have left thy lips, when thou wilt be an hundred feet underground, in the dungeon of the Preceptory, to await trial as a *recreant* knight. Thou must to the lists, Brian, or thou art a lost and dishonoured man.'

'Then I will break out and fly,' said Bois Guilbert, 'No blood of this creature shall be spilled by my sanction.'

'But thou *canst* not fly,' said the Preceptor; 'thy ravings have excited suspicion. Thou wilt not be permitted to leave the Preceptory. Try it! Command the drawbridge to be lowered and then mark the answer. Think on it. Where shall thy companions in arms hide their heads when Brian de Bois Guilbert, the best lance of the Templars, is proclaimed *recreant*? What grief at the Court of France! With what joy will Richard hear that the knight that darkened his renown, has lost fame and honour for a Jewish girl!'

'Malvoisin,' said the knight, 'I thank thee. Come what may, *recreant* shall never be added to the name of Bois Guilbert. Would to God that Richard or any of his minions of England would appear in these lists! But they will be empty; no-one will couch a lance for that woman.'

'The better for thee,' said the Preceptor, 'if no Champion appears. It is not then by *thy* means that this unlucky damsel dies, the Grand Master then has the blame.'

'True,' said Bois Guilbert. 'If no Champion appears, I am but a part of the pageant, sitting on horseback in the lists but having no part in what is to follow.'

'None whatever.' said Malvoisin.

'Well, I will resume my resolution,' said the Templar. 'She has despised me, repulsed me and reviled me. Why should I lose, for her sake, whatever estimation I have in the opinion of others? Malvoisin, I *will* appear in the lists.'

He left the apartment hastily as he uttered these words. The Preceptor followed to watch and confirm him in his resolution, since Malvoisin himself had a strong personal interest in Bois Guilbert's reputation. He expected much advantage from the Templar's being one day at the head of the Order, not to mention the hope of preferment from Mountfitchet, on condition that he forward the condemnation of Rebecca.

It required all Malvoisin's art to keep Bois Guilbert steady. He was obliged to watch the Templar to prevent his resuming the idea of flight and to intercept any communication with the Grand Master, lest they come to an open rupture. He also repeated the argument that by appearing as the Order's champion, Bois Guilbert, without affecting the fate of Rebecca, would follow the only course to avoid degradation and disgrace.

chapter forty

Shadows avaunt! Richard's himself again.
Shakespeare: *Richard III*

When the Black Knight left the trysting-tree of the outlaw, he headed straight to the Priory of St. Botolph; whither the wounded Ivanhoe had been removed by the faithful Gurth and Wamba when the castle was taken. After a long discussion, messengers were dispatched by the Prior in several directions, and on the succeeding morning the Black Knight was ready to set out with Wamba as guide.

'We will meet at Coningsburgh,' said he to Ivanhoe, 'the castle of the late Athelstane, where Cedric holds the funeral feast for his noble cousin; I will see your Saxon kindred together, Sir Wilfred, and become better acquainted with them. Meet me there and it shall be my task to reconcile thee to thy father.' So saying, he took an affectionate farewell of Ivanhoe.

'Rest this day; for thou wilt scarcely have strength to travel on the morrow. I need no guide but Wamba here, who can play priest or fool, according to my humour.'

'Sir Knight,' said Ivanhoe, 'since it is your pleasure to be known as such, I fear you have a talkative and troublesome fool as guide.'

'Fare thee well, Wilfred,' said the knight, 'travel not till the morrow at earliest.'

So saying, the King extended his hand to Ivanhoe, who pressed it to his lips. He took leave of the Prior, mounted his horse and departed with Wamba. Ivanhoe requested to see the Prior who came in haste, anxiously enquiring after his health.

'It is better,' he said, 'than my fondest hope could have anticipated. Either my wound was slighter than I supposed, or this balsam hath wrought a wonderful cure upon it. I feel already as if I could bear my arms and armour.'

'Now, the saints forbid,' said the Prior, 'that the son of Cedric should leave ere his wounds were healed!'

'Nor would I leave, venerable father,' said Ivanhoe, 'did I not feel able for the journey and compelled to make it.'

'But why so sudden a departure?'

'Holy father,' said the Knight, 'have you never felt an approaching evil?'

'But, wounded as thou art,' said the Prior, crossing himself, 'why follow the Black Knight? You could not aid him, were he attacked.'

'Prior,' said Ivanhoe, 'I am strong enough for any who might challenge me. But I may also aid him by other means. Saxons love not the Norman race; who knows what may happen if he comes among them when their hearts are roused by the death of Athelstane and their heads heated by the carousal? Thus I would ask of thee the use of a palfrey of softer pace than my *destrier*.'[1]

'Then you shall have Malkin, my ambling jennet.'

'I pray you,' said Ivanhoe, 'get her ready and bid Gurth attend me with my arms. Now, farewell!' Ivanhoe now descended the stairs, mounted the jennet, and followed the track of the Black Knight into the forest, as the Prior stood at the convent's gate, looking after him.

Meanwhile, the Black Knight and his guide were pacing through the recesses of the forest, their dialogue forming a whimsical mixture of song and jest. The Knight, tall, broad-shouldered and strong of person, was mounted on his mighty black charger. The visor of his helmet was raised, the lower part, or beaver, being closed so that his features were partly concealed. The Jester wore his usual fantastic habit, but his late adventures had led him to carry, instead of his wooden sword, a good cutting falchion[2] with a shield to match it. He had shown himself a skilful master of both during the storming of Torquilstone. On horseback, he was perpetually swung backwards and forwards, now on the horse's ears, now on its rump. At this point of their journey, the pair of them were engaged in singing a *virelai*:[3]

Let the birds to the rise of the mist, carol shrill,
Let the hunter blow his loud horn on the hill,
Softer sounds, softer pleasures, in slumber I prove,—
But think not I dream of thee, Tybalt, my love.

'A dainty song,' said Wamba, when they had finished their carol, 'and, I swear by my bauble, a pretty moral!' The Jester next struck up a comic ditty, to which the Knight, catching the tune, replied in the like manner.

There came three merry men from south, west, and north,
Ever more sing the Roundelay;
To win the Widow of Wycombe forth,
And where was a widow who'd say them nay?

'We must be cautious yet,' said Wamba, coming up to the Knight's side, 'there be men far more dangerous to travellers than Locksley's outlaws.'

'And who may they be?' said the Knight.

'Why, sir, Malvoisin's men-at-arms,' said Wamba, 'and now reinforced with escaped soldiers from Torquilstone. Should we meet with a band of them, we will have to pay for our feats of arms. Sir Knight, what would you do if we met two of them?'

'Pin the villains to the earth with my lance!'

'What if there were four of them?'

'The same!'

'What if they were six,' continued Wamba, 'and we barely two; would you sound Locksley's horn?'

'What, sound for aid?' exclaimed the Knight, 'against such *rascaille*?'[4]

---

1 War horse.

2 A Falchion, from Lat. *Falx*, the sickle, was a single-edged sword favoured by some knights who had been on Crusade. This sword was similar to the Saracen heavy scimitar.

3 A form of medieval French verse. It is one of the three *formes fixes*,(i.e. of fixed format) the others being the *ballade* and the *rondeau*.

4 A mediaeval and plural form of rascals.

'Then,' said Wamba, 'I pray you for that horn .'

The Knight undid the clasp of the baldric and handed it to his companion who hung the bugle round his own neck.

'Content you, Sir Knight, it is in safe keeping. When Valour and Folly travel, Folly should bear the horn, because she can blow the best.'

'Keep the horn,' said the Knight. They proceeded on their way.

'Sir Knight!' said Wamba suddenly, 'There are men in yonder brake!'

'What makes thee say so?' said his companion urgently.

'A commotion amongst the leaves; were they honest men, they would have kept the path...'

'By my faith,' said the Knight, closing his visor, 'I think thou art right!' And just in good time did he close it, as three arrows flew from the suspected spot against his head, one of which would have hit, had it not been deflected by the steel visor. The other two were averted by the shield around his neck.

'Thanks, armourers,' grunted the Knight, 'Wamba, close with them!' and he rode straight into the thicket. There he was met by six or seven men-at-arms who charged him, lances levelled. Three of the weapons struck him but splintered as against a tower of steel. The Black Knight's eyes flashed through the aperture of his visor. He rose in his stirrups, crying,

'What means this, my masters?'

The men made no other reply than by drawing their swords and crying, 'Die, *tyrant*!'

'Saint Edward! *Ha*! Saint George!' cried the Black Knight, striking down a man; 'have we traitors here?' His opponents, determined as they were, recoiled from an arm which carried death in every blow and it seemed as if his sheer strength would gain the combat, even against such odds. Then, a knight in blue armour spurred forward and taking aim with his lance not at the rider but at his steed, wounded the noble animal mortally.

'A *felon* stroke!' exclaimed the Black Knight, as the horse crashed to earth, his rider with him. At that moment Wamba winded the bugle. The blast of sound made the assailants hesitate, allowing Wamba to rush in to assist the Black Knight to rise.

'Cowards!' cried he of the blue armour who led the assailants, 'Ye flee from a Jester's horn?'

Animated by his words, they attacked the Black Knight anew, who now placed his back against an oak and defended himself with his sword. The felon knight took another lance, waited for a moment when his formidable antagonist was closely pressed, and then galloped against him to nail him against the tree with the lance. His purpose was foiled when Wamba, hovering on the edges of the fight, slashed with his sword and hamstrung his horse. Horse and man went down. The situation of the Black Knight continued precarious, pressed as he was by several men and beginning to be fatigued by his violent defence. Suddenly, a gray-goose arrow shaft stretched one of his assailants on the earth as a band of yeomen broke into the glade. Headed by Locksley and the Friar, they rapidly disposed of the attackers, all of whom soon lay slain or mortally wounded.

The exhausted Black Knight thanked his deliverers, saying,

'Wamba, I must discover who were these. Open the visor of yon Blue Knight.'

The Jester approached the leader of the assassins, still entangled under his wounded steed.

'Come, *valiant* sir,' said Wamba, 'I must be your armourer and equerry. I have dismounted you, and now I will *unhelm* you.' So saying, and with no gentle hand, he undid the helmet of the Blue Knight.

'Waldemar Fitzurse!' he said, astonished.

'Richard,' said the captive knight, looking up, 'see now to what revenge can lead.'

'Revenge?' answered the Black Knight; 'I never wronged thee; on me there is *naught* to revenge.'

'My daughter, Richard, whose alliance thou did scorn.'

'Thy *daughter*?' replied the Black Knight; 'a proper cause of enmity; and followed up to a bloody outcome? Stand back, all. I will speak to him alone. Now, Fitzurse, who sent thee on this traitorous path.'

'Thy father's son,' answered Waldemar, 'who avenges thy disobedience to thy father.'

Richard's eyes sparkled with indignation as he pressed his hand against his brow and remained an instant gazing on the humbled Baron, whose pride now contended with shame.

'Thou dost not ask thy life, Waldemar?' said the King.

'For him in the lion's clutch,' answered Fitzurse, 'it is time wasted.'

'Take it then, unasked,' said Richard; 'The lion preys not on prostrate carcasses. Take thy life, but with this condition; in three days thou shalt leave England. Go hide thine infamy in thy Normandy castle and never mention the name of John of Anjou as connected with thy felony. If thou art found on English ground after the days allotted thee, it is death. Breathe aught that taints the honour of my house and by Saint George I will hang thee out to feed the ravens from thine own castle. Give this creature a steed, Locksley, and let him depart.'

'I will not argue,' answered the yeoman, 'But I would fain send a shaft into the skulking villain and spare him a long journey.'

'Thou hast an English heart, Locksley,' said the Black Knight, 'and well art thou bound to obey. For I am Richard of England.'

At these words, pronounced in a tone suited to the rank and character of *Coeur-de-Lion*, the astonished yeomen sank to their knees asking pardon.

'Arise, my friends,' said Richard, looking on them with his habitual good-humour, his features now retaining nothing of the late conflict save the flush of exertion.

'Arise,' he said again. 'Any misdemeanours are atoned by the loyal services you rendered before the walls of Torquilstone and by the rescue this day of your Sovereign. Arise, my liegemen, and be good subjects in future. And thou, brave Locksley...'

'Call me no longer Locksley, my Liege, but by the name which I fear may have reached even your ears. I am Robin Hood, of Sherwood Forest.'[1]

---

1 From the ballads of Robin Hood, we learn that this celebrated outlaw sometimes assumed the name of Locksley from the village where he was born, but where situated we are not distinctly told. *Scott.*

'King of Outlaws, and Prince of good fellows!' said the King, 'the name that has been borne as far as Palestine. Be assured that no deed done in our absence shall be held against thee.'

'True says the proverb,' said Wamba, 'When the cat is away, the mice will play...'

'What, Wamba, still here?' said Richard; 'I have been so long since hearing thy voice, I thought thou had flown.'

'I – take *flight*?' said Wamba; 'When do you ever find Folly separated from Valour? There lies the trophy of my sword, that good grey gelding, whom I heartily wish upon his legs again, provided his master lay hamstrung in his place! It is true I gave a little ground at first, for a motley jacket[1] does not blunt lance-heads like a steel doublet.'

'And to good purpose, honest Wamba,' replied the King. 'Thy good service shall not be forgotten.'

'*Confiteor! Confiteor!*'[2] exclaimed a voice near the King's side 'My Latin will carry me no farther. I confess my treason and pray leave to have absolution before execution!'

Richard looked around and beheld the jovial Friar on his knees and telling his rosary. His quarter-staff, in action during the skirmish, lay beside him. His countenance was gathered to express the most profound contrition, his eyes being turned up and the corners of his mouth drawn down. Yet this affectation of penitence was belied by a ludicrous smirk on his huge features.

'Why art cast down, mad Priest?' said Richard; 'Art afraid thy Bishop should learn how thou do serve Our Lady and Saint Dunstan? Tush, man, fear not. Richard betrays no secrets that pass over the flagon.'

'Nay, most gracious sovereign,' answered Friar Tuck, 'it is not the crosier I fear, but the *sceptre*. Alas! That my sacrilegious fist should ever have landed upon the ear of the Lord's anointed!'

'Aha!' said Richard, 'is that it? In truth I had forgotten the buffet, though after it mine ear sang for a day. I will be judged by the good men around if it was not as well repaid!

'Good my Liege,' said The Friar, 'I pray you to leave me as you found me; as the poor Clerk of Saint Dunstan's cell in Copmanhurst, to whom any small donation will be most acceptable.'

'I understand,' said the King; 'The Holy Clerk shall have a grant of vert and venison in my woods of Warncliffe. Mark you, only three bucks every season.'

'Your Grace may be assured,' said The Friar, 'that, with the grace of Saint Dunstan, I shall find a way of multiplying thy most bounteous gift.'

'I nothing doubt it,' said the King. 'And as venison is dry food, our cellarer shall deliver to thee a butt of sack, a runlet of Malvoisie,[3] and three hogsheads of ale, yearly. Come to court and become acquainted with my butler!' The Friar bowed profoundly and fell back to the rear.

---

1 The multi-coloured jacket of the Jester.

2 Lat. I confess!

3 A cask of Madeira wine. A dangerous drink; in 1478, George, Duke of Clarence, brother of Edward IV, drowned in a butt of it. *See*; *Richard III*; I. 4.

chapter forty-one

All hail to the lordlings of high degree,
Who live not more happy, though greater than we!
Our pastimes to see, under every green tree,
In all the gay woodland, right welcome be ye.
Andrew MacDonald: *Love and Loyalty.*

Wilfred of Ivanhoe arrived in the glade on the Prior of Botolph's jennet, attended by Gurth on the Knight's own warhorse. Astonished, he discovered his royal master blood-bespattered and surrounded by bodies from the battle. Nor was he less surprised to see Richard surrounded by so many outlaws of the forest, a perilous retinue for a prince. He hesitated, unsure whether to address the King as such, or as the Black Knight-errant; Richard saw his embarrassment.

'Wilfred,' he said, 'fear not. Address Richard Plantagenet as himself. Thou seest him in the company of true English hearts. Treason hath been with us, Ivanhoe, but now that we think on it, thou art disobedient. Were not our orders to repose at Saint Botolph's till thy wound be healed?'

'It *is* healed, Sire,' said Ivanhoe. 'It is not now of consequence. But why, my Prince, expose your life as if it were that of a mere knight-errant?'

'Richard Plantagenet,' said the King,' desires no more fame than his good lance and sword may acquire him.'

'But your kingdom, my Liege,' said Ivanhoe, 'is threatened with civil war. Your subjects would be menaced with every species of evil, were they deprived of their Sovereign.'

'My kingdom and my subjects?' answered Richard, impatiently; 'I tell thee, Sir Wilfred, the best of them are most willing to repay my follies in kind. When Richard's return is announced, he shall be at the head of such a force as shall subdue any treason without unsheathing a sword. But Estoteville and Bohun will not be strong enough to move on York for a day yet. I must have news of Salisbury from the south; of Beauchamp in Warwickshire and of Multon and Percy in the north. The Chancellor must secure London. Too sudden an appearance would subject me to dangers too great for my own lance and sword.'

Wilfred bowed, well aware how vain it was to contend with his master's wild spirit of chivalry. The young knight sighed and held his peace. Richard turned to Robin Hood.

'Now, king of outlaws,' he said, 'have you no refreshment to offer to your brother sovereign?

'In troth,' replied the Outlaw, 'for I scorn to lie to your Grace, our larder is chiefly supplied with…' He stopped, embarrassed.

'With *venison*, I suppose?' said Richard; 'Better food there can be none; and truly, if the King will not remain at home to slay his own game, he should not bawl too loud if he finds it killed to his hand.'

'If your Grace, then,' said Locksley, 'will honour one of our *rendezvous* with your presence, the venison shall not be lacking; and a stoup of ale withal.'

In the lion-hearted King, the brilliant but useless character of a knight of romance was in great measure realised and revived. The personal glory which he acquired by his own deeds of arms was far more dear to him than government. He was gay,[1] good-humoured and fond of manhood in every rank of life.

Beneath a huge oak-tree the sylvan repast was hastily prepared for the King by men outlawed to his government, but who now formed his court and guard. As the flagon went round, the rough foresters soon lost their awe for Majesty. The common sense of Robin Hood demanded that that the scene should be closed ere anything should disturb its harmony. He had also observed Ivanhoe's anxiety.

'We are honoured,' he said to Ivanhoe, 'by the presence of our gallant Sovereign; yet I would not that he dallied.'

'Well and wisely spoken,' said Wilfred; 'They who jest with Majesty even in its gayest mood, are toying with the Lion.'

'You have touched the very cause of my fear,' said the Outlaw; 'my men are rough by practice and nature. It is time this revel was broken off.'

'It is you must manage it,' said Ivanhoe; 'for each hint I give only induces him to prolong it.' Said Robin;

'Here, Scathlock, get thee behind yonder thicket and wind me a *Norman* blast on thy bugle!' Scathlock obeyed and shortly the revellers were startled by the sound of a horn.

'It is the bugle of *Malvoisin*,' cried the Miller, starting to his feet, and seizing his bow. The Friar dropped his flagon and grasped his quarter-staff. Wamba stopped in the mid-jest and took up his sword and target. All stood to their weapons. Richard called for his helmet and while Gurth was armouring him, he laid strict injunctions on Ivanhoe not to engage in any skirmish.

In the meantime, Robin Hood had sent off several of his followers in different directions, as if to *reconnoitre* the enemy; and when he saw the company effectually broken up, he approached Richard who was now completely armed. Kneeling down, he craved pardon.

'For what, good yeoman?' said Richard.

'The bugle you have heard was none of Malvoisin's, but blown by my direction to break off the banquet, lest it intrude upon matters of dearer import.'

'The king of Sherwood,' said Richard, 'grudges his venison and his wine-flask to the King of England? Thou art right, however. Let us to horse and away; Wilfred has been impatient this last hour to be on to Coningsburgh.'

The King extended his hand to Robin Hood and assured him of his future favour.[2]

Having set off, attended by Ivanhoe, Gurth and Wamba, Richard arrived without further interruption within sight of Coningsburgh Castle while the sun was yet on the horizon.

There were few more beautiful or striking scenes in England, than those presented

---

1 Thought by historians to be true in both the ancient and modern senses of the word.

2 Richard's good intentions towards the Outlaw were to be frustrated by the King's untimely death; and the Charter of the Forest was extorted from the unwilling hands of King John when he succeeded his heroic brother. *Scott*.

by the vicinity of this ancient Saxon fortress. The gentle river Don swept through an amphitheatre in which farmlands richly blended with woodland. On a hill, ascending from the river and well defended by walls and ditches, rose the ancient fortress which, as its Saxon name implies,[1] had been a royal residence of kings of England before the Conquest.

As *Coeur-de-Lion* and his retinue approached, a huge black banner was floating from the top of the tower, announcing that the obsequies of its late owner were still in train. It bore no emblem of the deceased's birth or quality, the heraldry of the Normans being unknown to the Saxons. Above the gate, however, was another banner on which the rudely painted figure of a white horse, the symbol of Hengist and his Saxon warriors, indicated the nation and rank of the deceased.

All around the castle was a scene of busy commotion. Saxon funeral banquets were times of profuse hospitality, of which everyone with the most distant connection with the deceased were invited to partake. The wealth and consequence of the deceased Athelstane required this custom to be observed to the fullest extent.

Numerous parties were ascending and descending the hill on which the castle stood; and when the King and his attendants entered the open, unguarded gates of the external barrier, the scene was not easily reconciled with the cause of the assemblage.

In one place cooks were toiling to roast huge oxen and fat sheep; in another, hogsheads of ale had been broached to be drained freely by all comers of every description who were devouring the food and liquor. Here the Saxon serf was drowning his half-year's thirst and hunger in one day of gluttony and drunkenness; there the more pampered burgess and guild-brother was eating his meat with gusto. A few of the poorer Norman gentry were also to be seen, distinguished by their shaven chins and short cloaks. They kept together, looking with scorn on the whole occasion, while availing themselves of the good cheer liberally supplied.

Mendicants there were of course by the score, together with strolling soldiers returned, allegedly, from Palestine. Pedlers were displaying their wares, travelling mechanics were enquiring after employment beside wandering palmers and hedge priests. Saxon minstrels and Welsh bards were muttering prayers and extracting mistuned dirges from their harps: one set forth the praises of Athelstane in a doleful panegyric; another, in a Saxon genealogical poem, rehearsed the harsh names of his noble ancestry. Jesters and jugglers were present, nor did the occasion render the exercise of their profession indecorous or improper. Indeed the ideas of the Saxons on these occasions were as natural as they were simplistic. If sorrow was thirsty, there was drink; if hungry, there was food; if it saddened the heart, here were the means of mirth or at least of amusement. Every now and then, however, as if suddenly recollecting the cause which had brought them together, the men groaned in unison, while the females raised their voices and shrieked their woe.

Such was the scene in the castle-yard at Coningsburgh as Richard and his followers entered. The seneschal, or steward, did not deign to take notice of the groups of inferior guests entering and withdrawing, unless necessary to preserve order. Nevertheless he was struck by the appearance of the Monarch and Ivanhoe, especially as he found the features of the latter familiar. Besides, the approach of two knights was a rare event

[1] From Anglo-Saxon *Cyningesburh*; the King's burgh.

at a Saxon solemnity and could be regarded as an honour to the deceased and his family. In his sable dress and holding his white wand of office, the seneschal made way through the guests and conducted Richard and Ivanhoe to the entrance of the tower. Gurth and Wamba, having found acquaintances in the court-yard, intruded no farther.

chapter forty-two

I found them winding of Marcello's corpse.
And there was such a solemn melody,
'Twixt doleful songs, tears, and sad elegies,—
Such as old grand dames, watching the dead,
Are wont to outwear the night with.
John Webster: *The White Devil*

The entrance to the great tower of Coningsburgh Castle reflected the rude simplicity of the times in which it was erected. A flight of steps, so steep and narrow as to be almost precipitous, led up to a low portal in the south side of the tower, by which access was gained to a small stair. This lay within the thickness of the main wall of the tower, which led up to the third story of the building. The two lower, being dungeons or vaults, received neither air nor light, save by a square hole in the third story. By this difficult and complicated entrance, King Richard, followed by Ivanhoe, was ushered into the round apartment which occupied the whole of the third storey. Wilfred, during the ascent, muffled his face in his mantle, so as not to present himself to his father until the King's signal.

Assembled in this apartment and around a large oaken table were a dozen representatives of distinguished Saxon families in the adjacent counties. All were elderly men; for the younger generation, to the great displeasure of their seniors, had like Ivanhoe broken down many of the barriers separating Norman from Saxon. The downcast looks of these venerable men and their silence was a strong contrast to the levity of the revellers outside. Their grey locks, long full beards, antique tunics and loose black mantles suited the rude apartment in which they were seated. They gave the appearance of a band of ancient worshippers of Odin, recalled to life to mourn the loss of their national glory.

Cedric, though seated in equal rank among his countrymen, seemed by common consent to act as Chief of the assembly. Upon the entrance of Richard, known to him only as the Knight of the Fetterlock, he arose gravely, and gave him welcome by the ordinary salutation, *Wæs þu hæl*, raising at the same time a goblet to his head. The King, no stranger to the customs of his English subjects, returned the appropriate greeting of *Drinc hæl!* and partook of a cup from the sewer.[1] The same courtesy was offered to Ivanhoe who pledged his father in silence, giving only an inclination of his head, lest his voice be recognised.

The introductory ceremony performed, Cedric arose. Extending his hand to

---

1 Not from a drain, but from Anglo-Norman *asseour*, a servant seating guests at table.

Richard, he conducted him into a small and very simple chapel excavated out of one of the external buttresses. As there was no opening, save for a narrow loop-hole, the place would have been dark but for two *flambeaux,* or torches, whose red and smoky light showed an arched roof, naked walls and a rude altar with a crucifix of stone.

Before this altar lay a bier, on each side of which kneeled three priests who told their beads and muttered their prayers with the greatest external signs of devotion. For their services, a splendid *soul-scat*[1] had been paid to the convent of Saint Edmund's by the mother of the deceased. That the donation might be fully deserved, the entire convent brethren, saving their lame Sacristan, had transferred themselves to Coningsburgh. There, while six of their number were constantly performing divine rites at the bier of Athelstane, the others partook of the refreshments and amusements going on at the castle. In maintaining this pious watch and ward, the good monks were particularly careful not to interrupt their hymns for an instant, lest Zernebock, the ancient Saxon Apollyon, or Devil, should lay his clutches on the departed Athelstane. Nor might any unhallowed layman touch the pall which, being that used at the funeral of Saint Edmund,[2] would be desecrated if profanely handled.

If in truth these attentions could be of any use to the deceased, he had some right to expect them at the hands of the brethren of Saint Edmund's. Besides the hundred *mancuses*[3] of gold paid as his soul-ransom, the mother of Athelstane had announced her intention of endowing that foundation with the better part of the lands of the deceased, in return for perpetual prayers for his soul and that of her departed husband.

Richard and Wilfred followed the Saxon Cedric into the apartment of death where their guide pointed with solemn air to the untimely bier of Athelstane. They then followed his example in devoutly crossing themselves and muttering a brief prayer for the weal of his departed soul. This done, Cedric again motioned them to follow him as he glided over the stone floor with a noiseless tread. After ascending a few steps, he opened with caution the door of a small oratory which adjoined the chapel. It was about eight feet square and hollowed, like the chapel itself, out of the thickness of the wall. The loop-hole which enlightened it facing west, the setting sun found its way into its dark recess, revealing a dignified female whose countenance retained the remains of majestic beauty. Her long mourning robes and her flowing wimple[4] of black cypress, enhanced the whiteness of her skin and the beauty of her fair hair, which time had neither thinned nor mingled with silver. Her countenance expressed deep sorrow and resignation. On the stone table before her stood a crucifix of ivory, beside which was laid an illuminated missal, its boards adorned with clasps of gold.

'Noble Edith,' said Cedric, after having stood a moment silent, to give Richard and Wilfred time to look upon the lady of the mansion, 'these are worthy strangers, come to take a part in thy sorrows. And this, in especial, is the valiant Knight who fought so bravely for the deliverance of him whom we this day mourn.'

'His bravery has my thanks,' returned the lady; 'although it was the will of Heaven that it should be displayed in vain. I thank, too, his courtesy and that of his

---

1 Money paid to clergy for saying prayers for the souls of the dead.

2 King of East Anglia, killed in 869AD by heathen Danes; hence a Christian martyr.

3 An Anglo-Saxon gold coin equivalent to thirty silver pence.

4 A linen or silk garment worn by women to enclose the head and face.

companion, who now behold the widow of Adeling and mother of Athelstane, in her lamentation. Kind kinsman, I entrust them to your care and hospitality.'

The guests bowed deeply to the mourning parent and withdrew. Another winding stair conducted them up to an apartment on the storey immediately above. From this room came a low and melancholy song. When they entered, they found themselves in the presence of about twenty matrons and maidens of distinguished Saxon lineage. Four maidens, with Rowena leading, raised a hymn for the soul of the deceased:

Dust unto dust, to this all must;
The tenant hath resign'd
The faded form, to waste and worm -
Corruption claims her kind.

While this dirge was being sung in a low, melancholy tone by the choristers, the other women were divided into two bands: one was embroidering a large silken pall to cover the bier of Athelstane; the others busied themselves in selecting garlands for the same purpose from baskets of flowers.

The behaviour of the younger maidens was decorous, if not marking deep affliction; a whisper or a smile calling forth a rebuke from the matrons. Here and there was a damsel more interested in how her mourning-robe became her, than in the dark ceremony for which they prepared. The sudden appearance of the two strange knights occasioned much looking up, peeping and whispering, Rowena alone paying her greeting to her deliverer with a graceful courtesy. Her demeanour was serious, thoughts of Ivanhoe claiming as great a share in her thoughts as the death of her kinsman. To Cedric, however, not notably clear-sighted on such occasions, the sorrow of his ward seemed so deep that he whispered;

'She was the affianced bride of the noble Athelstane...'

Cedric then conducted them to a small room for the exclusive use of honourable guests. He assured them of every attention and was about to withdraw, when the Black Knight took his hand.

'I remind you, noble Thane,' he said, 'that when we last parted, you promised to grant me a boon for the service I had the fortune to render you.'

'It is granted ere named,' said Cedric; 'Yet, at this sad moment...'

'Of that also,' said the King, 'I have bethought me, but my time is brief. It seems to me fitting that, when closing the grave over noble Athelstane, we should deposit therein certain prejudices and opinions.'

'Sir Knight of the Fetterlock,' said Cedric, colouring and interrupting the King in his turn, 'I trust that your boon regards yourself and no other. In anything concerning the honour of my house, it is scarce fitting that a stranger should mingle.'

'Nor do I wish to mingle,' said the King, mildly, 'unless you admit that I have an interest. As yet you have known me only as the Black Knight of the Fetterlock. Know me now as Richard Plantagenet, King of England.'

'Richard of Anjou!' exclaimed Cedric, stepping backward with the utmost astonishment.

'No, Richard of *England*, whose deepest interest and whose deepest wish is to see her sons united with each other. Now, worthy Thane, hast thou no bended knee for the King?'

'To Norman blood,' said Cedric, 'it hath never bended.'

'Reserve thine homage then,' said the Monarch, 'until I shall prove my right by my equal protection of Norman and English.'

'Prince,' answered Cedric, 'I have ever done justice to thy bravery and thy worth. Nor am I ignorant of thy descent from Matilda, niece to Edgar Atheling and daughter of Malcolm of Scotland.'

'I will not dispute my title with thee, Thane,' said Richard, calmly; 'but consider; where thou wilt find another to be put into the scale against it.'

'And hast thou travelled hither, Prince, to tell me so?' said Cedric. 'To upbraid me with the ruin of my people, ere the grave closes o'er the last of Saxon royalty?' His countenance darkened as he spoke. 'It was boldly; it was *rashly* done!'

'Not so!' replied the King; 'it was done in the frank confidence which one brave man may repose in another.'

'Well said, for King thou art and wilt be, despite my opposition.'

'And now,' said the King, 'I require of thee, as a man of thy word, on pain of being held faithless and man-sworn and *nidering*,[1] to forgive and receive into thy paternal affection this good knight; who is Wilfred of Ivanhoe.'

'And this is – *Wilfred* ?' said Cedric, pointing to his son.

'Father,' said Ivanhoe, prostrating himself at Cedric's feet, 'forgive me.'

'Thou hast it, my son,' said Cedric, raising him up. 'The son of Hereward knows how to keep his word. But let me see thee use the dress of thy English ancestry; the son of Cedric, must show himself of English ancestry... Thou art about to speak,' he added, sternly, 'and I can guess the topic. Hear me. The Lady Rowena must complete two years' mourning for her betrothed. All our Saxon ancestors would disown us were we to consider a union for her ere the grave closed over him, The ghost of Athelstane himself would stand before us to forbid such dishonour to his memory.'

It seemed as if Cedric's words had raised a spectre. Scarce had he uttered them ere the door flew open and, arrayed in the garments of the grave, Athelstane stood before them. Pale and haggard he seemed indeed, as one arisen from the dead! Cedric started back to the wall of the apartment; leaned against it and gazed on the figure of his friend, eyes fixed and open mouthed. Ivanhoe crossed himself, repeating prayers in Saxon or Latin as they occurred to his memory, while Richard alternately said,

'*Benedicite*', and swore, '*Mort de ma vie*!' In the meantime, cries were heard from below stairs, shouts of

'Secure them, the treacherous monks!' and 'Down to the dungeon!' or 'Pitch them from the battlements!'

'In the name of God!' said Cedric, addressing the spectre of his departed friend, 'If thou art mortal, speak! Living or dead, Athelstane, *speak!*'

'I will,' said the spectre, 'when I have collected breath. Alive, said thou? I am as alive as one can be, fed on bread and water for three days. Yes, bread and *water*! By Heaven and all the Saints in it, food hath not passed my weasand[2] for three livelong days, and it is only by God's providence that I am here to tell of it.'

'Athelstane,' said the Black Knight, 'I myself saw you struck down by the Templar at the storm of Torquilstone. I thought your skull cloven to the teeth.'

---

[1] Infamous.

[2] Gullet.

'You thought amiss, Sir Knight,' said Athelstane; 'My teeth are in good order. No thanks to the Templar though; his sword struck me flatlings,[1] averted by the handle of my good mace. Down I went, senseless but alive. Others of both sides were felled and slaughtered above me, so that I never recovered my senses until I found myself in a coffin – an open one, by good fortune – before the altar of Saint Edmund's church. I awakened, groaned and would have risen. The Sacristan and Abbot came running in terror and were no way pleased to find alive the man whose *heirs* they supposed themselves to be. They gave me wine but it must have been drugged, for I slept even more deeply than before. I then found my arms and feet tied when I awoke in a place utterly dark – the *oubliette*,[2] I suppose, of their accursed convent. From the smell I guess it to be used for burials. I had strange thoughts of what had befallen me, when the door of my dungeon creaked and two villainous monks entered. They would have persuaded me I was in Purgatory but I knew the voice of the Abbot. Saint *Jeremy*...!'

'Patience, noble Athelstane,' said the King, 'take breath.'

'A barley loaf and a pitcher of water; *that* they gave me, the niggardly traitors,' raged Athelstane. 'My father and I myself had enriched them. The foul ungrateful *vipers*! Barley bread and *ditch* water to such a patron as I; I will smoke them out of their nest!'

'But, in the name of Our Lady, Athelstane,' said Cedric, grasping the hand of his friend, 'thy escape; did they relent?'

'Relent?' echoed Athelstane. 'Do rocks melt with the sun? I would have been there still, had not their procession here summoned the swarm out of their hive. And they *knew* how and where I was buried alive. At length down weaved the Sacristan, reeking of wine he was, and left the door ajar. The staple holding my chains was more rusted than the villain Abbot had supposed...'

'Take breath, Athelstane,' interposed Richard.

Edith had now followed the living corpse to the strangers' apartment, attended by as many of the guests as could squeeze into the small room. Others, crowding the staircase, caught up an error-strewn version of the story, transmitting it yet more inaccurately to those beneath. Athelstane continued:

'Freed from the staple, I dragged myself up the stairs as well as might a man loaded with shackles and weak with fasting. After much groping about, the sound of music led me to an apartment where the Sacristan was holding a Devil's Mass with a huge beetle-browed monk who looked like a thief. I burst in on them. The sight of my grave-clothes and the clanking of my chains, made them think me a ghost; I knocked down the Sacristan but his pot-companion fetched me a blow with a huge quarter-staff.'

'This *must* be our Friar Tuck,' said Richard, looking at Ivanhoe.

'Fortunately,' said Athelstane. 'he missed the aim and when I closed with him, he took to his heels and ran for it while I freed my feet with the sexton's fetter-key. I thought of beating out the knave's brains with the bunch of keys, but left him with a brace of hearty kicks. In the stable I found my best palfrey set apart for the use of

1 With the flat of the blade rather than the edge.

2 A form of dungeon, accessible only from a hatch in a high ceiling.

the holy Abbot. And hither I came with all speed the beast could manage, every mother's son taking me for a spectre and fleeing, especially as I had the corpse-hood over my face. I only gained my own castle by being mistaken for a juggler and only disclosed myself to my mother ere I came for you, noble friend.'

'And you found me,' said Cedric, 'I tell thee, tomorrow will be an auspicious day for the Saxon race.'

'I am intent,' said Athelstane, 'on punishing that villain Abbot. He shall hang from Coningsburgh Castle in his cope and stole; and if the stairs are too narrow for his fat carcass, I will have him craned up.'

'My son,' said Edith, 'consider his sacred office.'

'Consider my three days' *fast*,' replied Athelstane; 'I will have their blood, every one of them. Front-de-Boeuf was burnt alive for a lesser matter; mark you, he kept a good table for his prisoners... only there was too much garlic in his last dish of pottage. But these hypocritical, ungrateful *slaves*, so often the *self-invited* flatterers at my board, who gave me neither pottage nor garlic; they *die*, by the soul of Hengist!'

'For shame, Athelstane,' said Cedric; 'forget such wretches in the career which lies open before thee. Tell this Richard of Anjou, that *coeur de lion* as he is, he shall not hold the throne of Alfred while a descendant of the Holy Confessor lives.'

'How?' said Athelstane, 'is *this* King Richard?'

'The Plantagenet himself,' said Cedric.

'Then, by my faith!' said Athelstane; 'I here tender him my allegiance, heart and hand.'

'My son,' cried Edith, 'think!'

'*And* think on England!' cried Cedric.

'Mother and friend,' said Athelstane, 'a truce to your upbraiding. I rose from the tomb a wiser man. I tell you, I will rule in my own domains – but nowhere else. And my *first* act of dominion shall be to hang that Abbot!'

'And Rowena,' said Cedric, 'I trust you will not desert her?'

'Father Cedric,' said Athelstane, 'be reasonable. The Lady Rowena cares not for me. She loves the little finger of Wilfred better than me – and there she stands to avow it. Cousin Wilfred of Ivanhoe; in thy favour I abjure Rowena. Hey! by Saint Dunstan, our cousin Wilfred is vanished – yet I saw him stand there even now.'

All looked round for Ivanhoe, but he was indeed gone. It was then discovered that a Jew had arrived seeking conference with him; after which he had urgently called for Gurth and his armour and had left the castle.

'Fair cousin...' said Athelstane, turning to Rowena, only to find that, embarrassed by her situation, she had also escaped from the apartment.

'Women,' quoth Athelstane, 'are surely the least to be trusted of all animals, monks and abbots excepted. These cursed grave-clothes have surely a spell on them; every one *flies* from me. To you I turn, noble King Richard, with the vows of allegiance which...' But the King was gone also. It was learned that in the courtyard, he had summoned the Jew who had spoken with Ivanhoe and, after a short discourse, had cried '*To horse!*' mounted a fast steed, compelled the Jew to mount another and had set off at speed.

'By God!' said Athelstane, 'Zernebock hath possessed himself of my castle in my absence. I return in grave-clothes, restored from the very *sepulchre*, and every one I speak to vanishes.

Come, my friends – such as are left. Follow me to the banqueting hall lest any more of us disappear! It is yet loaded as becomes a Saxon noble. Come, tarry not. Who knows, the Devil may fly off next with our supper!'

chapter forty-three

Be Mowbray's sins so heavy in his bosom,
That they may break his foaming courser's back,
And throw the rider headlong in the lists,
A caitiff recreant!
Shakespeare: *Richard II*

At the Castle, or Preceptory, of Templestowe the bloody die was about to be cast for the life or death of Rebecca. It was a scene of bustle, the whole vicinity pouring forth its inhabitants as if for a rural feast. A considerable multitude now attended the procession, while still greater numbers already surrounded the tiltyard, a piece of level ground adjoining the Preceptory. It occupied the brow of a gentle eminence and was carefully palisaded. Templars welcomed spectators to witness their skill in chivalry and hence the tiltyard was supplied with galleries and benches. A throne was erected for the Grand Master at the eastern end, surrounded with seats for the Preceptors and Knights of the Order. Over these floated the *Le Beau-seant*, the sacred standard of the Templars.

At the opposite end of the lists was a pile of faggots arranged around a stake deeply fixed in the ground. A space was left for the victim to enter the fatal circle and be chained to the stake by fetters, which hung ready. Beside this deadly apparatus stood four black slaves, their African features fearful to the multitude gazing at them. These men shifted and placed the ready fuel, ignoring the crowds.

'Have you not heard, Father Dennet,' said one rustic to another, 'that the devil has carried away the Thane Athelstane of Coningsburgh?'

'Ay, but he brought him back again, by the blessing of God and Saint Dunstan.'

'How's that?' said a brisk young fellow, in a green cassock embroidered with gold. He bore upon his back the harp which betrayed his vocation. This minstrel seemed of no common rank. Besides his braided doublet, around his neck was a silver chain from which hung the *wrest*, or key, with which he tuned his harp. On his right arm was a silver plate, which, instead of bearing the badge of the Baron to whose family he belonged, had only *Sherwood* engraved upon it.

'How mean you by that?' said the minstrel again to the peasants; 'I came to seek one subject for my rhymes and, by our Lady, I find two.'

'It is well avowed,' said the elder peasant, 'that after Athelstane of Coningsburgh had been dead four *weeks*...'

'Impossible,' said the Minstrel; 'I saw him alive at the Passage of Arms at Ashby.'

'Dead, however, he was,' said the younger peasant; 'for I heard the Monks of Saint Edmund's singing the Death Hymn for him. And there was a rich death-meal at the Castle of Coningsburgh'

'Ay, dead was Athelstane,' said the old man, shaking his head, 'and the more pity it was, for the old Saxon blood...'

'But, your story, my masters; your *story*,' said the minstrel impatiently.

'Ay, tell us the story,' said a burly Friar, who now stood beside them, leaning on a pole that was between a pilgrim's staff and a quarter-staff and probably both.

'Your story,' said the Friar; 'we have but short time to spare.'

'If it please your reverence,' said Dennet, 'a drunken priest came to visit the Sacristan at Saint Edmund's...'

'It does *not* please my reverence,' answered the churchman, 'either that there be a drunken priest, or if there were, that a layman should so speak of him. Be mannerly, my friend; the holy man was perhaps wrapped in meditation which makes the head dizzy.'

'Well, then,' answered Father Dennet, 'a holy *brother* came to visit the Sacristan at Saint Edmund's. This visitor was a hedge-priest who kills deer and loves the sound of a pint-pot better than the sacring-bell. He be a good fellow who will flourish a quarter-staff and draw a bow with any man in Yorkshire.'

'But the story; the *story*, my friend,' again said the Minstrel.

'Why, the tale is but this; Athelstane of Coningsburgh was buried at Saint Edmund's.'

'That's a lie; and a great one,' said the Friar, 'for I saw him borne to his own Castle of Coningsburgh!'

'Right, then, tell the story *yourself*, my masters,' said Dennet, sulkily and it was with difficulty that he could be prevailed on to renew his tale;

'These two *sober* friars,' said he at length, 'had been drinking good ale and wine for the best part for a summer's day. They were then aroused by a deep groan and a clanking of chains and the figure of the deceased Athelstane entered their apartment, saying, *'Ye evil shep-herds...!*''

'False!' said the friar, hastily; 'he never spoke a word.'

So ho, Friar Tuck,' said the Minstrel, drawing him apart from the rustics; 'we have started a new hare!'

'Allan-a-Dale, I *tell* thee,' said the Hermit, 'I saw Athelstane of Coningsburgh.

He had his shroud on and smelled of the sepulchre. A butt of sack will not wash it out of my memory.'

'By Saint Hubert,' said the Minstrel, 'this is a wondrous tale, and fit to be set to a tune.'

'Laugh, if ye must,' said Friar Tuck; 'but if ye catch me singing on such a theme, may the devil carry me off! No, I instantly formed the purpose of attending some good work, such as the burning of a witch or some other godly service – and therefore am I here.'

As they conversed, the heavy bell of the Church of Saint Michael of Templestowe cut short their argument. One by one the sullen sounds fell on the ear, leaving only sufficient space for each to die away, before the air was refilled by another iron knell. These sounds, the signal of the approaching ceremony, chilled the assembled multitude whose eyes were now turned to the Preceptory, expecting the approach of the Grand Master, his champion and the criminal.

At length the drawbridge fell, the gates opened and a Knight bearing the great standard of the Order sallied from the castle followed by the Knights Preceptors, two by two, with the Grand Master coming last on a stately horse. Behind him came Brian de Bois Guilbert, armed *cap-a-pie*[1] in bright armour, his lance, shield and sword borne by two esquires behind him. His face, though partly hidden by the long plume of his barrel-cap, bore a strange mixed expression in which pride seemed to contend with irresolution. He looked ghastly pale, as if he had not slept for nights, yet reined his pawing war-horse with his habitual ease and grace. His general appearance was commanding; but men read something in his dark features and withdrew their eyes.

On either side rode Conrade de Mountfitchet and Albert de Malvoisin, acting as godfathers to the Champion. They were in their robes of peace, the white dress of the Order. Behind them followed other Companions of the Temple with a long train of esquires and pages clad in the black of aspirants. After these came a guard of warders on foot, in the same sable livery, amidst whom was seen the pale form of Rebecca, moving with a slow but undismayed step. She was stripped of all her ornaments, lest there be among them the amulet with which Satan was known to deprive his victims of the power of confession even under torture. A coarse white dress had been substituted for her Oriental garments; yet there was such an exquisite mixture of courage and resignation in her look that the most hardened regretted that fate had converted such a creature into a slave of the Devil.

This slow procession moved up the gentle eminence, on the summit of which was the tiltyard. Entering the lists, they marched once around them in a circle from right to left and made a halt. There was then a momentary bustle as the Grand Master and all his attendants, excepting the champion and his godfathers, dismounted.

Rebecca was conducted to the black chair near the stake and faggot pile. On her first glance at the terrible sight she was seen to shudder and shut her eyes. She seemed to be praying, for her lips moved though no speech was heard. She opened her eyes, looking fixedly on the pile as if to familiarize her mind with the object and then slowly turned her head away.

Meanwhile, the Grand Master had assumed his seat. When the chivalry of his order was placed around and behind him, each in his due rank, a loud and long flourish of the trumpets announced that the Court were seated for judgment. Malvoisin, godfather of the champion, then stepped forward and laid the glove of the Jewess and pledge of battle, at the feet of the Grand Master.

'Valorous and reverend Father,' said he, 'here stands the good Knight, Brian de Bois Guilbert, Knight Preceptor of the Order of the Temple. He, accepting the pledge of battle now at your reverence's feet, is bound to do his *devoir* in combat this day. He will maintain that this Jewish maiden, by name Rebecca, hath justly deserved the sentence passed upon her by this most Holy Order of the Temple of Zion,

---

1 Head to foot.

condemning her to die as a sorceress. Here, I say, he standeth such battle to do, if such be your pleasure.'

'Hath he made oath,' said the Grand Master, 'that his quarrel is just and honourable? Bring forward the Crucifix and the *Te igitur.*'

'Sir, and reverend father,' answered Malvoisin 'our brother here present hath already sworn the truth of his accusation to the good Knight Conrade de Mountfitchet. He ought not to be sworn again, given that his adversary is an unbeliever and may take no oath.'

This explanation was satisfactory, to Malvoisin's great relief. For that wily knight had foreseen the impossibility of prevailing upon Brian de Bois Guilbert to take such an oath before the assembly. The Grand Master now commanded the Herald to stand forth and do his *devoir*. The trumpets again flourished, and a Herald proclaimed:

'*Oyez, oyez!* Here standeth Sir Brian de Bois Guilbert, prepared to do battle with any knight who will sustain the combat allotted to the Jewess Rebecca of York. This being to try, by Champion, in respect of lawful *essoine*[1] of her body. To such Champion the reverend Grand Master allows a fair field and a fair combat.'

The trumpets again sounded. There was a dead pause.

'No Champion appears for the appellant,' said the Grand Master. 'Go, Herald, and ask whether she expects anyone to do battle for her in her cause.' The Herald went towards the chair in which Rebecca was seated. Bois Guilbert, suddenly turning his horse's head, rode to the side of Rebecca's chair as quickly as the Herald, ignoring cautions on either side from Malvoisin and Mountfitchet.

'Is this regular, and according to the law of combat?' asked Malvoisin, looking from Bois Guilbert to the Grand Master.

'It is.' answered Beaumanoir; 'In this appeal to the judgment of God we may not prohibit parties from having a communication with each other which may bring forth the truth.'

The Herald spoke to Rebecca:

'Damsel, the Grand Master inquires if there is a Champion to do battle this day in thy behalf, or if thou yieldeth as one justly condemned?'

'Say to the Grand Master,' replied Rebecca, 'that I maintain my innocence and am unjustly condemned. Say to him that I demand such delay as he will permit, to see if God will raise me up a deliverer; and when such space is passed away, may His holy will be done!'

The Herald retired to carry this answer to the Grand Master.

'God forbid,' said Lucas Beaumanoir, 'that Jew or Pagan should accuse us of injustice! Until the shadows be cast from the west to the eastward will we await a Champion. When the day is so far passed, let her prepare for death.'

Rebecca bowed her head submissively, folded her arms and looking up towards heaven, seeming to expect from above, the aid which she could not promise herself from man. During this awful pause, the voice of Bois Guilbert broke upon her ear; it was but a whisper, yet it startled her more than the summons of the herald.

'Rebecca,' said the Templar, 'hear me!'

---

1 'Essoine' signifies excuse. Here it relates to the appellant's privilege of appearing through her Champion, her own person being excused on account of her sex. *Scott.*

'I have no portion in thee; cruel man,'

'Mount behind me! In one short hour the pursuit will be far behind.'

'Hear me, tempter,' said Rebecca, '*begone!* Not in extremity can thou move me one hair's-breadth, surrounded as I am by foes. I hold thee my worst and most deadly enemy. Get thee *gone*, in the name of God!' Albert Malvoisin, alarmed at the duration of their conference, now advanced to interrupt it.

'Hath she acknowledged her guilt?' he demanded of Bois Guilbert; 'or is she resolute in its denial?'

'She is resolute.' said Bois Guilbert.

'Then,' said Malvoisin, 'noble brother, resume thy place. The shadows are moving on the circle of the dial.

'This waiting has good reason,' said Friar Tuck, 'seeing she is a Jewess. And yet it is hard that so young and beautiful a creature should perish without one blow being struck in her behalf!'

The knights, instigated by Malvoisin, whispered to each other that it was time; the pledge of Rebecca was forfeit.

At that instant a knight, urging his horse to speed, appeared on the plain and advanced towards the lists. A hundred voices exclaimed,

'A Champion! A *Champion*!'

The multitude cheered as the knight rode into the tiltyard. A second glance, however, served to destroy any hope excited by his timely arrival. His horse, urged for many miles to its utmost speed, appeared to reel from fatigue while the rider, however undauntedly he presented himself in the lists, seemed scarce able to support himself in the saddle.

To the summons of the herald, who demanded his rank, name, and purpose, the stranger knight answered readily and boldly.

'I am a good knight and noble, come to sustain with lance and sword the just and lawful quarrel of this damsel, Rebecca, daughter of Isaac of York. I assert the sentence pronounced against her to be false and I name Sir Brian de Bois Guilbert a traitor, a murderer, and a liar. This will I prove upon this field with my body against his, by the aid of God and our Lady.'

'The stranger must first show,' said Malvoisin, 'that he is a good knight, and of honourable lineage. The Temple does not send her knights against nameless men.'

'My name, Malvoisin,' said the Knight, raising his helmet, 'is Wilfred of Ivanhoe.'

'I will not fight thee,' said the Templar immediately, in a changed and hollow voice, 'Get thy wounds healed, purvey a better horse and mayhap I will later scourge this bravado out of thee.'

'Templar,' said Ivanhoe, 'hast forgotten falling twice before this lance? Remember the lists at Acre; remember the fight at Ashby. I will proclaim thee, Templar, a coward in every court in Europe and in every Preceptory of thine own Order, unless thou do battle *forthwith!*'

Bois Guilbert turned towards Rebecca and then exclaimed, looking fiercely at Ivanhoe, 'Dog of a Saxon! Take lance and prepare for death.'

'Does the Grand Master allow me the combat?' said Ivanhoe.

'I may not deny what thou hast challenged,' said the Grand Master, 'provided she accepts thee as her Champion.'

'Thus as I am and not otherwise.' said Ivanhoe; 'It is the judgment of God, to whose keeping I commend myself.' He rode up to the fatal chair.

'Rebecca,' said he, 'do thou accept of me as thy Champion?'

'I do,' she said, 'I do accept thee as the Champion whom Heaven hath sent me. But, thy wounds are unhealed! Do not meet that man; why perish also…?' But Ivanhoe was already at his post, visor closed and his lance couched. Bois Guilbert did the same, his esquire noting as he clasped his visor shut that his face, which had been ashy pale, was now flushed.

The herald, seeing each champion in his place, uplifted his voice and repeated thrice;

'*Faites vos devoirs, preux chevaliers*!'[1] After the third cry he withdrew to one side of the lists and again proclaimed that none, on peril of death, should dare to disturb this field of combat. The Grand Master, who held Rebecca's glove, the gage of battle, now threw it into the lists and pronounced the fatal words of signal, '*Laissez aller!*'

The trumpets sounded and the knights charged straight at each other in full career. As all had expected, the wearied horse of Ivanhoe – and its no less exhausted rider – went down before the well-aimed lance and vigorous steed of the Templar. This outcome of the combat all had foreseen; but although the spear of Ivanhoe only hit the shield of Bois Guilbert, he reeled in his saddle, lost his stirrups and crashed down in the lists.

Ivanhoe, extricating himself from his fallen horse, was soon on foot, his sword drawn. His antagonist, however, did not rise. Wilfred, placing his foot on his breast and the sword's point to his throat, commanded him to yield or die on the spot. Bois Guilbert returned no answer.

'Slay him not, Sir Knight,' cried the Grand Master, 'he is unshriven and unabsolved. Kill not body *and* soul![2] We concede him vanquished.'

He descended into the lists and commanded the unhelming of the conquered champion. His eyes were found to be closed – the dark red flush still on his brow. As they looked on him in astonishment, the eyes opened – but they were fixed and glazed. The flush passed from his brow, giving way to the pallid hue of death. Unscathed by the lance, he had died a victim to the violence of his own contending passions.

'This is indeed the judgment of God,' said the Grand Master, looking upwards; '*Fiat voluntas tua!*'[3]

chapter forty-four

So! now 'tis ended, like an old wife's story.
John Webster: *The White Devil.*

---

1 'Do your duty, gallant knights!'

2 The teaching of the Catholic Church was that the soul of a person dying *unshriven* (unconfessed) and *unabsolved* (unforgiven) might not enter Paradise.

3 Thy will be done.

When the first moments of surprise were over, Wilfred of Ivanhoe demanded of the Grand Master, as judge of the field, if he had done his duty in the combat.

'Manfully and rightfully,' said the Grand Master. 'I pronounce the maiden innocent and free. The arms of the deceased are at the will of the victor.'

'I will not despoil him of his weapons,' said the Knight of Ivanhoe, 'nor condemn his corpse to shame. He fought in the past for Christendom and it was God's arm that struck him down. But let his funeral be private, as is fitting for a man dead in an unjust quarrel. And for the maiden...'

Here he was interrupted by a clattering of horses' feet, advancing in such numbers and so rapidly as to shake the ground before them. The Black Knight galloped into the lists. He was followed by a numerous band of knights in full armour and men-at-arms.

'I see I am too late,' Said Richard, looking around him; 'I had marked Bois Guilbert for mine own property. Ivanhoe, was this wise of thee?'

'Heaven,' answered Ivanhoe, 'took this man. He was not to die as you designed.'

'Peace, then, be with him.' said Richard, looking steadfastly on the corpse. 'He died in his steel harness. But we must waste no time; Bohun, do thine office!'

A Knight stepped forward from the King's attendants and laying his hand on the shoulder of Albert de Malvoisin, said,

'I arrest thee of High Treason.' The Grand Master had hitherto stood astonished at the appearance of so many warriors. He now spoke.

'Who dares arrest a Knight of the Temple of Zion within the girth of his own Preceptory and in the presence of his Grand Master?'

'I make the arrest,' replied the Knight. 'I, Henry de Bohun, Earl of Essex and Lord High Constable of England.'

'And he arrests Malvoisin,' said the King, raising his visor, 'by the order of Richard Plantagenet, here present. Conrade Mountfitchet, it is as well for thee that thou art no subject of mine. But as for thee, Malvoisin, thou diest with thy brother Philip, ere the world be a week older.'

'I will resist this,' said the Grand Master to Malvoisin.

'No, Templar,' said the King; 'Look up. Behold where the Royal Standard of England floats over thy towers instead of thy Temple banner! Be wise Beaumanoir, and make no opposition; for thy hand is in the lion's mouth...'

'I will appeal to Rome,' said the Grand Master, 'for usurpation of the immunities of our Order.'

'Be it so,' said the King; 'but for thine own sake, tax me not with usurpation now. Dissolve thy Chapter and depart with thy followers to another Preceptory – if thou canst *find* one which has not been the scene of treason against the King of England. Or, if thou wilt, remain to behold our justice.'

'To be a guest where I should command?' said Beaumanoir, '*Never!* Chaplains, raise the Psalm, *Quare fremuerunt Gentes.*[1] Knights, squires and followers of the Holy Temple, prepare to follow the banner of *Beau-seant*!'

The Grand Master spoke with a dignity which matched that of England's king. He inspired courage in his dismayed followers who gathered around him with dark

---

1 Why are the Nations in an uproar.

brows of defiance and looks of the hostility that they dared not articulate. They drew together in a dark line of lances from which the white cloaks of the knights were visible among the dusky garments of their retainers, like the lighter-coloured edges of a black cloud.

The Earl of Essex, beholding the pause in their assembled force, dashed the rowels into his charger's sides and galloped backwards and forwards to array his followers in confrontation to a band so formidable. Richard alone, as if enjoying the danger his presence had provoked, rode slowly along the front of the Templars, calling aloud,

'What, sirs! Among so many gallant knights, will none dare splinter a spear with Richard?'

'The Brethren of the Temple,' said the Grand Master, riding forward to the head of their body, 'do not fight in idle and profane quarrels. Not with thee, Richard of England, shall a Templar cross lance. The Pope shall judge our quarrel. If unassailed, we depart assailing no one. To thine honour we refer the armour and goods of the Order which we leave behind us – and on thy conscience we lay the offence thou hast this day given to *Christendom*!'

With these words, and without awaiting a reply, the Grand Master gave the signal of departure. Their trumpets sounded the wild Oriental march, always the signal for a Templar advance. They changed their array from a line to a column of march, moving off as slowly as their horses could step, as if to show it was the Grand Master, rather than fear of any superior force, which was compelling them to withdraw.

'By Our Lady's brow!' said the King. 'It is the pity that these Templars are not as trustworthy as they are valiant.' The multitude, like a cur which waits to bark till the object of its challenge has turned his back, raised a feeble shout as the rear of the squadron left the ground.

During the tumult which attended the retreat of the Templars, Rebecca saw and heard nothing. She was locked in the arms of her aged father, giddy from the rapid change of circumstances around her.

'Let us go,' he said, 'my recovered treasure. Let us throw ourselves at the feet of the good Ivanhoe.'

'Not so,' said Rebecca, 'O no – *no*! At this moment I dare not speak to him, for I would say more... No, father, let us leave this evil place.'

'But, my daughter,' said Isaac, 'to leave him who held his life as nothing so he might redeem thy captivity...'

'It is most devoutly acknowledged,' said Rebecca; 'It shall be still more so, but not now! For the sake of thy beloved Rachel, father, grant my request – not *now*!'

'True, my wise Rebecca; let us hence. Money Richard will lack, for he has just returned from a prison. He has pretext for exacting it, should he need any, from my simple traffic with his brother John. Away!' Hurrying his daughter along, he conducted her safely from the lists and on to the house of the Rabbi Nathan.

Since the fair Jewess, whose fortunes had formed the principal interest of the day had now departed unobserved, the attention of the populace now transferred to the Black Knight. They now filled the air with;

'Long life to the Lion's Heart! '

'Despite all this lip-loyalty,' said Ivanhoe to the Earl of Essex, 'it was well that the King took the precaution to bring thee with him.' The Earl smiled and shook his head.

'My gallant Ivanhoe,' said Essex, 'I was drawing towards York, having heard that Prince John was also making for there, when I met the King. Like a knight-errant he was galloping hither to assist, in his own person, in this adventure of the Templar and the Jewess. I accompanied him with my band, almost *maugre*[1] his consent.'

'And what news from York?' said Ivanhoe; 'will the rebels await us there?'

'No more than December's snow will abide July's sun,' said the Earl; 'they disperse; and who should come posting with the news, but John himself!'

'The traitor – the insolent *traitor*!' said Ivanhoe; 'did not Richard order him into confinement?'

'Oh, he received him,' answered Essex, 'as if they had met after a hunting party. Then, pointing to me and our men-at-arms, he said: "brother, I have angry men with me. Thou wert best to go to our mother. Carry to her my duteous affection and abide with her until men's minds are pacified."'

'And this was *all* he said?' enquired Ivanhoe; 'he invites treason by such clemency.'

'Aye,' replied the Earl, 'like the man who invites death by entering combat with a wound unhealed...'

'I forgive thee the jest, my Lord,' said Ivanhoe; 'but, remember, I hazarded only my own life; Richard hazarded his kingdom.'

'Those,' replied Essex, 'who are careless of their own welfare, are seldom attentive to that of others. However, let us haste to the castle, for Richard meditates punishing some of the subordinates of the conspiracy, though he has pardoned their Principal...'

---

1 In spite of: Mod. Fr. *malgré*.

Epilogue

There now remained only two obstacles to the desire of Ivanhoe and Rowena to marry: Cedric's obstinacy and his dislike of the Norman dynasty. The former feeling gradually gave way before the endearments of his ward and the pride which he could not but feel in the fame of his son. Besides, he was not insensible to the honour of allying his own line to that of Alfred.

The nuptials were celebrated in the noble Minster of York, the King himself attending. From the countenance which he afforded on this and other occasions to the distressed and hitherto degraded Saxons, he gave them a more certain prospect of attaining their just rights than they could reasonably hope from the precarious fortunes of a civil war.

Gurth, gallantly appareled, attended as squire upon his young master whom he had served so faithfully. Likewise did Wamba, decorated with a new cap and set of silver bells. As sharers of Wilfred's dangers and adversity they remained, as they had a right to expect, the partakers of his subsequent career.

It was upon the second morning after this happy bridal, that the Lady Rowena was told by her handmaid Elgitha that a lady desired to speak with her without witnesses. Rowena wondered, hesitated, became curious and ended by commanding the lady to be admitted.

There then entered a noble figure, the long white veil in which she was shrouded shadowing rather than concealing the elegance of her person. Her demeanour was that of respect, without the least shade either of fear or desire for favour. Rowena arose and would have conducted her visitor to a seat. The stranger, however, looked at Elgitha and again intimated a wish to speak with the Lady Rowena alone. Elgitha had no sooner retired when, to the surprise of the Lady of Ivanhoe, her fair visitant kneeled, pressed her hands to her forehead and, bending her head, kissed the embroidered hem of her tunic.

'What means this, lady?' said the surprised bride.

'Because to you, Lady Ivanhoe,' said Rebecca, rising up and resuming her usual quiet dignity of manner, 'I may now pay the debt of gratitude which I owe to Wilfred of Ivanhoe. I am she for whom your husband hazarded his life at Templestowe.'

'Lady,' said Rowena, 'Wilfred that day only repaid your care of his wounds and help in his misfortunes. Is there aught in which he or I can yet serve thee?'

'Nothing,' said Rebecca, calmly, 'unless you will transmit to him my grateful farewell.'

'You leave England, then?' said Rowena.

'I leave it, lady. My father had a brother high in favour with Mohammed Boabdil, King of Grenada. Thither we go, secure of peace and protection.'

'But are you not well protected in England?' said Rowena. 'My husband has favour with the King who is just and generous.'

'Lady,' said Rebecca, 'I doubt it not. But the people of England are a fierce race, ever ready to plunge the sword into each other; such is no safe abode for the children of my people.

'But you, maiden,' said Rowena, '*you* surely can have nothing to fear, you who nursed Ivanhoe.'

'Thy speech is fair, lady,' said Rebecca, 'and thy purpose fairer. But it may not be. Farewell. Yet ere I go, indulge me one request. Pray raise thy bridal-veil and let me see the features of which fame speaks.'

Rowena raised it accordingly and blushed intensely; cheek to bosom suffused with crimson.

'Lady,' said Rebecca, 'thy countenance will dwell in my remembrance. I bless God that I leave my noble deliverer united with you...'

She stopped short, her eyes filling with tears. She hastily wiped them and answered to the anxious enquiries of Rowena,

'I am well, lady... but my heart swells when I think of Torquilstone and the lists of Templestowe. Farewell. One last duty remains. Accept this casket; and pray startle not at its contents.'

Rowena opened the small silver-chased casket and saw within a *carcanet*, or necklace with ear-jewels of diamond, obviously of immense value.

'It is impossible,' she said, 'I cannot accept such a gift.'

'Keep it, lady,' said Rebecca. 'Think ye that I prize these sparkling fragments above my liberty? Or that my father values them in comparison to the honour of his only child? Accept them, lady, I will *never* wear jewels again!'

'You are then unhappy?' said Rowena, struck with the manner in which Rebecca uttered the last words; 'Oh, remain with us! The counsel of holy men will wean you from your Law and I will be sister to you.'

'No, lady,' answered Rebecca, the calm melancholy returning to her soft voice. 'That may not be. I may not change the faith of my fathers like a garment. Unhappy I will not be. God, to whom I dedicate my future life, will be my comforter.'

'Have you a convent?' asked Rowena.

'No, lady, but among our people, since the time of Abraham, there have been women who have devoted their thoughts to Heaven and their actions to tending the sick and relieving the distressed. Among these will be Rebecca. Say this to thy lord, should he chance to enquire the fate of her whose life...' In these last words was an involuntary tremor and tenderness which betrayed more than she would willingly have expressed.

'Farewell,' she said. '*A Dieu je vous recommande*. May He who made Jew and Christian shower on you his choicest blessings.' So saying, she glided from the apartment leaving Rowena feeling as if a vision had passed before her. She later related this singular conference to her husband, on whom the impression would also be deep and lasting.

Ivanhoe distinguished himself in the service of Richard, and was graced with farther marks of the royal favour. He might have risen still higher, but for the premature death of the heroic Coeur-de-Lion, before the Castle of Chaluz, near Limoges. With the life of that generous but rash and romantic monarch, perished all the projects which his ambition and his generosity had formed; to whom may be applied, with a slight alteration, the famous lines of Samuel Johnson:

His fate was destined to a foreign strand,
A petty fortress and an humble hand;
He left a name at which the world grew pale,
To point a moral – or adorn a TALE...

Some other books published by **LUATH** PRESS

As Others See Us: Personal views on the life and works of Robert Burns

Portraits by Tricia Malley and Ross Gillespie

ISBN 978-1-906817-06-0 HBK £9.99
ISBN 978-1-906817-52-7 PBK £7.99

As Others See Us is a unique, innovative photographic project produced by award-winning photographers Tricia Malley and Ross Gillespie

The challenge here was to capture not only each individual sitter's character but also try to convey something of the essence of his or her favourite Burns poem in a single portrait. The work of Robert Burns can be quite abstract or highly visual... sometimes both. Inspiration came from being reminded of the works of Burns, being introduced to new pieces and seeing them through the eyes of the sitters.

As we discovered during the time spent on this project, Robert Burns is just as relevant, entertaining and inspiring today as he was 250 years ago.

TRICIA MALLEY & ROSS GILLESPIE

Blind Ossian's Fingal: Fragments and Controversy

Compiled by James Macpherson, Introduced and Edited by Allan Burnett and Linda Andersson Burnett

ISBN 978-1-906817-55-8 HBK £15

James Macpherson's 18th-century translations of the poetry of Ossian, a third-century Highland bard, were an instant success. These rediscovered Ossianic epics inspired the Romantic movement in Europe, but caused a political storm in Britain at the time and up to recently have been denounced as one of the greatest literary hoaxes of all time.

Editors Allan Burnett and Linda Andersson Burnett take a fresh look at the twists and turns of the Ossian story. This volume includes *Fragments of Ancient Poetry* and *Fingal* along with contemporary commentary.

They contain the purest and most animating principles and examples of true honour, courage and discipline, and all the heroic virtues that can possibly exist.

NAPOLEON

Details of these and other books published by Luath Press can be found at:
www.luath.co.uk

Luath Press Limited

committed to publishing well written books worth reading

LUATH PRESS takes its name from Robert Burns, whose little collie Luath (*Gael.*, swift or nimble) tripped up Jean Armour at a wedding and gave him the chance to speak to the woman who was to be his wife and the abiding love of his life. Burns called one of 'The Twa Dogs' Luath after Cuchullin's hunting dog in Ossian's *Fingal*. Luath Press was established in 1981 in the heart of Burns country, and is now based a few steps up the road from Burns' first lodgings on Edinburgh's Royal Mile.

Luath offers you distinctive writing with a hint of unexpected pleasures.

Most bookshops in the UK, the US, Canada, Australia, New Zealand and parts of Europe either carry our books in stock or can order them for you. To order direct from us, please send a £sterling cheque, postal order, international money order or your credit card details (number, address of cardholder and expiry date) to us at the address below. Please add post and packing as follows: UK – £1.00 per delivery address; overseas surface mail – £2.50 per delivery address; overseas airmail – £3.50 for the first book to each delivery address, plus £1.00 for each additional book by airmail to the same address. If your order is a gift, we will happily enclose your card or message at no extra charge.

ILLUSTRATION: IAN KELLAS

Luath Press Limited
543/2 Castlehill
The Royal Mile
Edinburgh EH1 2ND
Scotland

Telephone: 0131 225 4326 (24 hours)
Fax: 0131 225 4324
email: sales@luath.co.uk
Website: www.luath.co.uk